TRI

Living in Defiance

By Heather Blanton

Copyright 2009

Let go and let God!

My heartfelt thanks go to all the students at GRACE Christian School for your enthusiasm and support of this project; Salem Baptist Church for letting me hide in a classroom to write while my son attended pre-school; Mom, Dad, Dawn, June and Carl for your encouragement. And, of course, thank you, Whit, for believing I could step off into thin air.

This book is dedicated to my sister Susan, who chose life in more ways than one.

> "Your mistakes don't determine your destiny, God does."
> —Pastor Barton

Living in Defiance
Copyright © 2009
Heather Blanton
Trinity Publishing
1410 Hollands Chapel Rd
Apex NC 27523
Unless otherwise noted, Scripture quotations are from the King James Version of the Bible.

All rights reserved. No part of this publication may be reproduced, stored in a retrieval system, or transmitted in any form or by any means —electronic, mechanical, photocopying, recording, or otherwise—without the express written permission of the publisher and copyright owners.

Cover art fotolio.com; designed by Heather Blanton

Prologue

Charles McIntyre stared placidly at his cards and stifled a yawn. He had not expected young Isaac Whicker to present such an entertaining challenge. Their little game had started at noon and by four they were still playing, though in a nearly empty saloon now. This was the quiet before the usual Saturday night storm.

Absently noting the low rumble of thunder, McIntyre decided it was time to finish the game. He had to get things ready for this evening. Glancing across the table at his sallow-looking, gangly opponent, he could see the boy swaying and blinking as he fought against the effects of the whiskey. Hunched bleary-eyed over his cards, Whicker had fought surprisingly well to keep from losing his mercantile, but he never really stood a chance. McIntyre needed the store back and would have it back if he had to crush Isaac Whicker like a bug to get it.

Ironically, he realized, that wasn't the best way to start this new venture of making Defiance *respectable*, as the railroad gents had termed it. A lawless town would be a trackless town, they warned. Fine. Get a few legitimate businesses running, calm the town down, put a nice hotel where the mercantile is. *Then* the great American iron horse would come steaming into Defiance, bringing with it opportunity, success and wealth. Not to mention, carrying his gold away to the mint in Denver.

Oh, he knew he could simply bribe the right people, grease the wheels as it were, but he *preferred* to seek that as a last option. He even had the funds now to build his own railroad, if he desired, but McIntyre liked his money right where it was—in his own pockets. For the time being, he *preferred* to take the easy road.

Ending the game with more boredom than ceremony, he laid down his cards. A Royal Flush. He thought he heard Whicker's breath catch and looked up. The boy had turned impossibly pale and his blond hair looked suddenly dull and lifeless, like that of an eighty-year-old man. The tiniest speck of compassion attempted to make itself known to McIntyre, but he irritably flicked it away, like a greasy crumb on his silk vest.

Scratching his thin, black, and perfectly trimmed beard, he leaned back in his chair. "Unless you can beat that, I own the mercantile."

Whicker shook his head, and slowly placed his cards face-down on the table. "No," he whispered, "I don't reckon I can."

Satisfied that was an admission of surrender, McIntyre rose to his feet. This game was over and he was ready for a roll with the warm and delicious Rose catnapping in his bed. "You played a good game, Whicker," he drawled in a deceptively charming Georgia accent. "The best I've had in some time, but you were destined to lose. I'll give you forty-eight hours to clear out. As we agreed, the inventory and gold stake are mine. You may keep all of your personal effects, including the wagon and your horse."

That last was overly generous, but taking a man's horse was just plain mean and McIntyre did not consider himself that callous—although he was quite sure Rose would have something to say about it. That feisty Mexican wench held on to things with the death-grip of a mountain lion.

Whicker replied only with a lingering blank stare. McIntyre concluded that the boy was neither in a hurry to accept his fate nor to leave the saloon. Unwilling to be held up by the gloom in the air, he reached for the deed sitting forlornly in the middle of the table.

"Let yourself out, Whicker, and have a safe trip back to..." Missouri, was it? He waived his hand dismissively. "Wherever you're from." Then he added generously, "You're an enterprising young man. I'm sure you'll be able to start over again."

McIntyre was almost surprised at himself for offering the words of encouragement and raked his hand through his black, wavy hair as if that would clear these dark thoughts. He supposed it was that accursed Southern-upbringing which equated rudeness with horse-stealing. In the cold light of reality, though, Whicker was nothing to him but an obstacle. And now an obstacle removed.

Well, nearly. The boy still hadn't moved. Sighing, McIntyre tucked the deed into his breast pocket and headed upstairs to his room. He paused ever-so-briefly at the top of the stairs to again flick away that crumb of compassion. After all, it had been a truly fair game. McIntyre hadn't cheated. He hadn't forced the boy to drink, nor had he forced him to bet the store.

We make our own decisions and deal with the consequences, he preached mentally. *We choose our own paths. No one forces us to walk down them.*

Slapping the rail twice as if dismissing Whicker from his conscience, McIntyre strode across the hall to his room. Imagining a bath and Rose's decadent kisses, he turned the brass door knob and entered his room. From below, and barely above the soft thump of rain drops, he heard the boy mutter miserably, "Missouri. Hannibal, Missouri."

But the words were lost. McIntyre's eyes traveled over the delicate, naked back of the luscious tart waiting for him and, grinning lustfully, closed the door on Whicker.

~~~

Naomi knelt down and gently rested her hand on her husband's grave. The soil felt cool and damp. She sat, stunned by the feel of it, the finality of it.

Her beloved's *grave*.

The word sounded bitter and cold and tasted like acid in her mouth. She felt the pain of it burn through her body. "God, please help me," she whispered as tears fell, as agony clawed at her heart. "I don't want to hate you...I want to trust you, but this is more than I can bear."

A sob escaped her as she thought of her loving John, wrapped in a death shroud and buried so far below in this Rocky Mountain dirt. Standing beside her, her two sisters stroked her head tenderly. Their own grief at watching her suffer was written on their faces in flowing eyes and quivering chins. Time stopped for Naomi; there was only pain. She didn't know how long Rebecca and Hannah stayed, but eventually they nodded at each other and faded silently into the forest.

The Ponderosa pines seemed to lean in closer, standing guard over Naomi like mute sentinels.

She mourned in a dark world, lost between grief and fury...

Oh, God, how could you let this happen? How...

The grief winning for the moment, Naomi curled up beside her husband's grave and released a tidal wave of sobs. It began to rain and the drops, mingling with her tears, reminded her of a rainy April morning–the morning when the threads of her cozy, contented life had started unraveling...

Chapter 1

A storm blew in as Naomi was sweeping the kitchen floor. It darkened the normally bright and cheery two-story farmhouse and pounded like pebbles on the tin roof. Loud, it was still a pleasant sound that momentarily took her mind off her little sister sitting on the front porch. She could see Hannah outside, silhouetted against the gray rain, perched on the top step, away from the weather but close enough to reach out and touch it. Her shoulders were stooped from the weight of her predicament and Hannah hugged herself as if for comfort.

Naomi knew she should go sit with her and talk to her, but she just didn't know what to say. She didn't yet know how *she* felt about the situation. Hannah had made a grievous error in judgment and not only would she have to deal with her sin, but so would the baby she was now carrying.

Billy Page was the only member of the party involved who didn't give a fig about the "repercussions" of what had happened. He had simply left town.

Naomi's hands tightened around her broom handle. If only she could ring that boy's scrawny, dapper, bow-tied neck. But she couldn't and she hated that. No Page son would ever be made to face scandal or shame in Cary, North Carolina as long as their father ran the town. This whole situation was out of her hands and she hated that even more.

Abruptly, she shoved the broom up against the wall, daring it to fall, and marched out to the porch. Hannah did not look back to greet her and Naomi stood uncertain for a moment. The rain was a good one; it would soak the ground well for the planting they had just finished. There was no sound of thunder; only the good, solid cacophony of rain drops. She could just make out the distant hills and wondered if John would be working on the fence in the rain.

Accepting that such idle thoughts were not what had brought her out here, she settled in next to Hannah. Naomi admitted to herself that not only was she angry at Billy, she was more than a little mad at Hannah as well.

The girl had been raised better than this. Thank goodness Momma and Daddy didn't have to deal with the shame. It would have broken their hearts.

And where is Rebecca? she wondered irritably as she re-rolled her white sleeves up to her elbows. *She* was much better at the hugs and gentle conversations; Naomi was only good at shooting off her mouth.

Fidgeting with the end of her blonde braid, she revisited the moment Hannah had broken the news. Her little sister had come over with her eyes all red and puffy from crying, saying that she had something important to tell her. Uncomfortable with situations requiring a gentle, sentimental touch, Naomi had practically begged Hannah to wait on Rebecca. After several minutes of frustrating chitchat, though, the news had burst out of her little sister.

The announcement had hit Naomi like a slap across the face. For once in her life, she took a moment to think before she spoke, only the thoughts were jumbled and confused. Sitting down in a kitchen chair before she fell down, she had bit her fiery tongue and asked Hannah to wait for her on the porch. Looking deflated, Hannah complied.

Angry with herself for being so useless in these circumstances, Naomi tried to think what Rebecca would do. Of course she knew the answer. Hannah needed comforting, not scolding, and as bad as Naomi was at that sort of thing, she was going to have to try. Her little sister looked so pitiful, sitting there toying absently with a ribbon on her dress. The picture softened Naomi's heart...some. Before she could offer any kind words, Hannah spoke.

"Do you hate me?" Her voice was weak voice and choked with tears. Naomi's tough demeanor suddenly crumbled, taking the anger with it, and she hugged her sister tightly.

"No, no," she whispered earnestly. "And don't you ever think that. Ever."

"He said he wanted to marry me. He said he loved me. I would never have done it otherwise."

Naomi rolled her eyes and thought of shooting the boy. Everyone had warned Hannah, but she had fallen head-over-heels for him and that was that. The truly sad part was that Naomi knew this fifteen-year-old angel with the golden hair and innocent blue eyes would most likely love Billy Page all the days of her life. She had been blessed with a heart the size of a mountain valley, but her wisdom had been blinded by the flashy smile of a banker's son. Frank Page had no doubt insisted that his son skedaddle out of town and had probably bought him the train ticket.

"He could kiss me, Naomi, and just purely take my breath away," the girl recounted blissfully, forlornly. It was a humbling moment for Naomi. With a physical jolt, she remembered turning sixteen herself at a barn dance on a sultry August night ten years ago...her first intimate kiss with John. The way he had taken *her* breath away; the way the warmth of him, the smell of him, had clouded her thoughts and made her heart pound so hard in her chest it almost hurt. Perhaps, had her husband not been a gentleman and a Christian, she might have found herself grappling with this exact issue. Even now, seven years into their marriage, he could send lightning shooting through her body when he touched her.

"You had a moment of weakness, Hannah. It could've happened to any of us...But you said he wants to marry you. He'll come back and the baby will have a name—"

Hannah pulled away from her. "That was before. Afterwards, when we found out, he never mentioned it again..." she trailed off, weeping and wailing into her hands. "I've shamed my Lord, my family, Momma and Daddy..."

"Shh, hush now." Naomi pulled her back into the hug. "You've sinned, Hannah. There's no denying that, but you've asked the Lord to forgive you and he has...now you must forgive yourself and deal with this." Oh, that was so much easier said than done, Naomi knew from experience. And the town...well, it would not be so quick to forgive either. "As far as the rest of us, what's done is done. We'll all have to live with it. But we forgive you, Hannah. *We* forgive you."

We want to turn you over our knee for being so foolish, but we do forgive you, Naomi thought wearily.

Hannah laid her head in Naomi's lap and wept quietly. Naomi stroked her sister's head, covered in gleaming, golden waves of silky hair. Her heart aching for her, she thought about those stray and injured animals Hannah was always saving. She had constantly nursed the sick and the lost; maybe that was what she had seen in Billy. Maybe Hannah had that affliction most women contend with: thinking they can change a man. Naomi was grateful everyday God had sent her a true soul mate. Her marriage to John was as easygoing as floating down a lazy river. They had always fit together just perfectly, as if they truly were one.

Something made her look up and she was relieved to see Rebecca hurrying along the road, a drenched shawl held high over her head. As their oldest sister approached, Naomi saw alarm skittering across her face. Rebecca dropped the shawl and sprinted the last fifty feet.

"What is it?" she huffed out of breath, running up to them. "Hannah, honey, are you all right?"

Hannah sat up and breathed a deep sigh. "I'm going to have a baby."

Stunned, Rebecca stumbled back down one step, putting her in the rain again. She stood there for a moment, blinking away water that traveled obediently down her black curls and disappeared into her drenched, blue gingham dress. The shock of the news suddenly, cruelly, added years to her face, deepening the crow's feet around her eyes, and pulling the corners of her mouth down.

Wiping away the rain from her forehead, Rebecca also took a seat on the steps and stared out at the weather. "Where is Billy?" she deadpanned.

"Greensboro. His note said he went to get a job and that he'd be back for me." Hannah sounded uneasy with the explanation. Naomi thought the story was ridiculous.

"So, he has offered to marry you?" Rebecca asked in the same, controlled tone of voice.

"Before, yes, but after we found out, well, it didn't exactly come up. He didn't offer and I guess I was too proud to ask."

Naomi respected Hannah's attempt at pride but didn't think this was necessarily the time for it. The baby needed a father and they all needed to make an effort at restoring Hannah to some form of respectability. Without a father, without a husband, this situation was the small town version of a Biblical catastrophe. But the story that he had gone to Greensboro bordered on the absurd. If Naomi knew anything about Billy and his daddy Frank Page, Billy was somewhere north of the Mason-Dixon Line and still running.

Smoothing her ruffled, yellow skirt over her knees, Hannah asked a decidedly unladylike question. "Is it a sin that I enjoyed it?"

Perhaps it was just the need to release a little tension, but both Rebecca and Naomi let out a little snigger, which transformed into full-blown, contagious laughter. Momentarily, all three were laughing wildly, almost hysterically; laughing only the way sisters can. Naomi knew they had better enjoy it; spells of side-splitting, crazy hee-hawing like this would most likely be few and far between in the coming days.

After the laughter started fading, Naomi realized the serious question needed a serious answer. "No, I don't think the enjoyment was a sin," she told Hannah, muffling one last giggle. "The question now is, are you sorry or would you lie with him again?"

Hannah only had to think for a second. "No. I still love him and I'd still marry him, but things were different after we...It changed the way he looked at me...and the way I looked at myself." She cast her eyes down to her hands in her lap. "We only, you know, were together one time. It didn't make me feel free or unfettered like he said it would. It didn't make me feel closer to him. It just made me feel…" She seemed to struggle for the right words to define the change. Finally, she settled on, "Naked. I felt like I wanted to cover my shame and hide it from God. Oh, why was I so stupid?" In frustration, she covered her head with her arms, as if fending off blows.

Rebecca and Naomi nodded in approval of the answer. A lesson learned. Hannah would not make the same mistake again.

Rebecca tossed a philosophical wave to the air. "You're only human, Hannah, and you made a mistake. If sin wasn't pleasurable, then none of us would ever fall and need forgiveness. The fact is, though, sin can be downright intoxicating, stripping us of our reason, especially when our hearts are involved."

"Especially," Naomi agreed.

"Especially," Hannah echoed.

"Come on you two," Naomi prodded, getting to her feet. "Rebecca, you need some dry clothes and we need to get dinner started. John will be home soon. I assume you two are staying."

~~~

Hours later, standing again on the front porch, Naomi watched her sisters disappear down the road in the fading twilight. Leaning on a post, she listened to a choir of crickets serenade the rising moon, but couldn't find comfort in their voices. As nightfall settled on her, so did a sense of foreboding. Head bowed, she went back inside to be with John and hide in his strength.

He had accepted the news with a troubled brow but hadn't reprimanded or demeaned Hannah. Instead, characteristic of her beloved, he had listened and pondered, asking questions gently, but had kept his opinions to himself. He promised Hannah he would speak with Page Sr. and tried to assure her everything would be fine. The assurance did not carry his normal solid sound of conviction, or so Naomi thought.

She found him staring into the cold grate of an empty fireplace, lost in thought. Weary to the bone, fighting this unexpected sense of unease, Naomi plopped down on the settee next to him and waited. She knew the look. He was reasoning out the pluses and minuses of the situation.

Stretching, he slipped a muscular arm around Naomi and pinned her with breath-stopping hazel eyes. She had the urge to run her hands through his tousled blonde hair, or trace a finger along his wide, stubbly jaw, but the serious look on his face held her in check. She had waited for him through a war, then the failing health of his father. They had delayed the wedding yet again when Naomi's parents had perished in a flu outbreak. Now, as she studied John's face, tanned and weathered by hours behind a plow, her heart melted. Oh, how the wait had been worth it. She had married her best friend and soul mate.

"I guess this is bad." Compassion drenched his voice. "Everything is going to change for her. She'll even have to stop teaching Sunday school most likely." Naomi hadn't thought of that. Hannah loved her children and they adored her. Stepping down would break her heart.

John reached over and tugged on her braid, but he was looking into the future. "And can you see her going to the harvest festival in October with her condition showing?"

Naomi *could* see it. The cold stares. The clustered groups of whispering women. Awkward glances at the ceiling as Hannah waddled by. Naomi squeezed her eyes shut, already angry over what lay ahead.

"John, I won't be able to stand the way people are going to treat her. Hannah's going to handle it better than I will. I'll be in jail for smacking somebody."

He chuckled and hugged her close. She pulled away just enough to look at him with her brow creased. "I wasn't trying to be funny,"

He stroked her cheek and apologized. "Sorry. I was just thinking about 'never give up, never back down.'" Naomi's shoulders sagged. She wasn't necessarily proud of that assessment of her personality. She had often prayed that God would soften her quick tongue and quicker temper and give her the wisdom to let Him lead rather than trying to fix every situation on her own. Her mouth, her temper and her will had caused her no end of trouble…or apologies.

That was from God, at least: the ability to apologize. In her first years as a Christian, "I'm sorry" didn't exactly roll off her tongue, but God had been patient. Now she prayed he would teach her to back down a little rather than dive into quarrels with willful abandon. Perhaps just being able to listen to Hannah today and not scold her had been a first step.

Offering a contented laugh, John wrapped Naomi in a big, warm hug. She melted into his broad chest and let his scent invade her mind. "Your grit is one of the things I love about you, woman. I can't think of a man I would trust by my side more than you. You're a little hot-headed, but I think I'll keep ya."

His charming joke didn't soften her self-appraisal. Sometimes Naomi questioned why she couldn't be more gentle and kind like Hannah or mature and focused like Rebecca. Her life would be easier.

John kissed the top of her head then tugged on her braid again, forcing her to look up at him. He brushed her lips gently, reassuringly. "You're a work in progress. Give God time to finish it and quit second-guessing him."

He punctuated the sentence with a firm, slow kiss. The heat of it cascaded over Naomi's body and she wrapped her arms around him to draw him in closer. In a movement as smooth and supple as a panther's, he slid her delicate frame to the floor, slowly peppering her with hungry kisses from her mouth to her throat and back again. She felt her heart beating frantically. How could he still do this to her after all these years?

But she loved the way she felt in his big arms: small, delicate, feminine. Not the scrappy little wolverine that had to fight everyone's battles. In John's arms, she could just be…a woman. She ran her hands down his broad back and enjoyed the feel of the sinewy muscles moving underneath his flannel shirt. Deftly he kissed her then grinned mischievously as he moved down her and tugged her top button free with his teeth. He came back for another long, deep kiss, then, still wearing that grin, moved back to her buttons. Amazingly, another one slipped through its loop. Clearly pleased with his skill, he slid down towards another button.

Feeling almost faint from the fire they were igniting, Naomi cupped his face in her hands and made him look at her. Chest heaving, she whispered, "Our room." Grinning devilishly, he swept her into his arms and headed toward the stairs, all the while kissing her like there was no tomorrow.

Chapter 2

As it turned out, there were no more tomorrows.

Naomi blinked and came back to her grief here at their campfire in the wilderness. Despair and uncertainty held a stranglehold on the sisters' spirits. She could hear it in the sound of forks scraping listlessly against dinner pans. Her own plate of food rested on her lap, cold and untouched. The melancholy hoot of a nearby owl echoed her heartache.

Oh, their hopes had been so high, their expectations for a new life so shining. Eager to leave Cary and the scandal behind, they had drawn closer together than ever as a family, sold the farms and headed west. Rebecca had made up her mind to seek a new future, seven years after the death of her own husband and daughter. Even Hannah had found the courage to look forward and leave Billy in the past. They had been so certain God's hand was pointing them to the Golden West.

And now John was dead. He would never see California. He was not here to lead them out of this untamed darkness. Naomi's next step was as clear as mud.

She thought again of his arms around her, his warmth, his laughter, the way he always called her "Woman" in a joking, affectionate way, as if he were a rogue pirate commanding his wench. The memory made her smile.

With him she could have borne anything. Without him, the weight of a butterfly could send her to her knees, wailing in anguish and shaking her fist at heaven.

And make no mistake, she *was* angry. She was angry because God could have quite easily worked things differently. John didn't *need* to be in a better place. She needed him here, now. She couldn't even imagine going on without him. Aching to her very core, but trying to hold back tears, she set her plate on the ground and cradled her head in her hands.

After an awkward silence, Rebecca broke the quiet with a gentle voice and a hard declaration. "We have to make some decisions, Naomi. It's been three days. We can't stay here treading water forever."

Feeling disconnected and unsure of herself, Naomi hesitantly met her sister's gaze. Rebecca's eyes and hair were even darker in the firelight. She looked different now to Naomi. More confident and self-assured, more vibrant than her thirty-eight years had previously allowed.

"I know we have to do something, Rebecca." Naomi straightened up, facing her pain. "But I can't seem to think. One minute I'm grieving and the next I'm just numb." She purposely left out mentioning any other emotions.

Rebecca nodded. "I know, I know. I've been there, remember? But we can't afford to think about ourselves now, Naomi. There's the baby."

Hannah's baby. The reminder cut through Naomi's gloom like a knife. She looked over at her now sixteen-year-old sister who was staring blankly at her plate. One single act of youthful foolishness had resulted in such unimaginable consequences for them all. Naomi wasn't angry with her, though. She didn't have the energy.

"Hannah and I have been praying…" She shared a careful glance with her little sister. "We feel that we should keep going west."

"West?" Naomi was stunned. "West to where? All the way to California? Just the three of us with no man for protection? How far do you think three women alone would get?"

Hannah set her plate beside her on the log she was using as a seat and leveled an almost defiant gaze on Naomi. "We feel that if we keep moving, He'll reveal His plans to us. We just have to trust Him."

An angry rebuke rose to Naomi's lips and escaped before she could stop it. "Trust Him? We've trusted Him this far and look where we're sitting." She enunciated carefully in case her sisters didn't grasp the gravity of the situation. "In the middle of no-where. We're fifteen hundred miles from home and a thousand miles from California. We can't go forward and we can't go back."

Rebecca and Hannah pursed their lips in an obvious attempt to keep from commenting on Naomi's resentment. But their stares hammered her with guilt. Trust Him? How could she when He made no sense? The pointlessness of John's death plagued her, drowning her in doubt, grief and anger.

Naomi sighed heavily. "I'm sorry. I'm in the wilderness right now, in more ways than one." After the briefest hesitation, Rebecca and Hannah joined their sister and put their arms around her. Naomi hated to cry; she had always thought tears accomplished absolutely nothing. Even when Rebecca's husband and daughter had died in the fire she had cried little, reasoning that her grief would only add to Rebecca's pain. Now, however, it was pretty obvious that sometimes tears simply would not be stopped.

"How do I go on without him?" she wept miserably.

Rebecca let her sister cry for a moment then began to pray softly. "Heavenly Father, please help Naomi know that You weep with her over the loss of her husband. And help her to know that You will give her something beautiful from these ashes if she will just wait for You and trust in You. Your word says you know the plans you have for us; plans to prosper us and not harm us; plans to give us hope and a future. Father, here we are in this wilderness. You are a lamp unto our feet and a light unto our path. Help us to see, Lord, help us to hear Your voice—"

"Hellooo there at the fire!" a man's voice called from the dark woods.

Chapter 3

The male voice hailing from the darkness startled the sisters to their feet. With panicked gasps, they stampeded to the wagon in a noisy clattering of tin dinner dishes and grunts as they tripped over and bumped into one another. Naomi withdrew rifles from the back with a soldier's precision and passed them to her sisters. She grabbed one for herself and they all pointed the guns in the direction of the voice.

"Who are you?" Naomi called, drying her eyes. "What do you want?"

"Just an old bear skinner passin' through." The voice drew closer and the sisters saw branches move on the edge of their campsite. "Thought I might share a meal if ye've anything extry." Pause. "I'd settle for a cup of coffee to warm my bones."

The girls held their ground and their guns more firmly. "Are you alone?" Naomi asked with suspicion.

Another pause. "The Lord is with me; I'm never alone."

Startled to find a Christian here and now, Naomi slowly lowered her gun, more out of confusion than trust and her sisters followed suit. "All right. Come into the light."

A barrel-chested, elderly gentleman dressed in leather clothes like those of an Indian stepped into their firelight. His hands, the size of bear paws, were raised in a gesture of surrender, though he wore a revolver stuck in his belt and a rifle slung over his shoulder, along with a bed roll and sack. He grinned hugely, the light revealing a few lone teeth hiding in a wooly, gray beard. The girls waited and eventually Naomi lowered her gun completely. Hannah carefully collected the weapons from her sisters so they could tend to the stranger.

Rebecca moved towards the pot hanging over the fire. "We've some beans with bacon. We'd be happy to share."

"Oh, it would be a de-light," the man replied, shrugging off the gear. He found a comfortable rock to sit on by the fire and reached his cold, warped hands toward the warmth. "I don't know what makes me happier: some food that ain't year-old hardtack or the fact that it's been cooked by a woman's hand." He winked mischievously at Rebecca and Naomi then nodded a friendly greeting as Hannah approached.

Rebecca handed the man a plate of steaming beans and Naomi passed him a cup of coffee. He took both eagerly. "It's been a month of Sundays since I had company with a meal."

He surveyed the little group and cocked his head to one side. "Speakin' of, ye'ins seem to have a noticeable lack of male company." The girls shot each other nervous glances. The old man nodded as if he understood the situation. "That grave I passed back yonder. That'd be yorn then?" He said it as more of a statement than a question. When no one answered, he nodded again. "It's all right, girls. I've not come to harm ye. I reckon it's about all I can do to get up off'n the ground in the mornin's."

Visibly relaxing, the girls took their previous seats as the stranger dove into his vittles. For a man missing most of his teeth, Naomi thought he ate with thoroughness and efficiency.

She allowed him time for a few bites then asked, "What brings you so far away from home? That's an Appalachian accent I hear, isn't it?"

He savored a sip of the fresh coffee and laughed heartily. "God is good, ladies! Why just yesterday I said, 'Lord, I am an undeservin' sinner who has obediently carried yer word to the Cheyenne and Arapahoe, to the cattle towns and even the minin' camps and for reasons unknown to me, ye've let me live through it all. I should be grateful enough for that, but if ye could see yer way to providin' me with just one fresh, hot cup of coffee, I surely would appreciate it.' And looky here," he held up the tin cup up for all to see. "Now that's a God who loves even me." And he took another sip.

Naomi, Rebecca and Hannah shared quizzical looks. Was he a spirit-filled Christian wallowing in the joy of the Lord or had he just been in the wilderness too long? Naomi wondered. Feeling strangely compelled to get answers, she pressed the question. "So, you are a preacher? Are you from Appalachia somewhere?"

"Tazewell, West Virginia, near Harper's Ferry." He puffed up his chest, evidently proud of home. "My Pappy was a preacher in the Blue Ridge Mountains. Almost heaven, it was, but like many a foolish youth, I couldn't see the beauty afore me. I left nigh on to forty years ago to make a stand with ol' Davy Crockett…but I didn't make it in time, leastwise not for that fight, but I joined up with Sam Houston. Killed my share of Mexicans, I guess," he trailed off with a hint of regret in his voice. "Man is a violent creature. I wonder to this day how He can love us so much."

When the sisters didn't respond, he continued. "I just wound up wanderin', fightin', drinkin'…generally wastin' the blessin's of my youth. But the Lord took pity on me and when a preacher came to see me in jail in Fort Kearney, well, for once I was smart enough to listen to the Shepherd's voice. He's been sendin' *me* to jails ever since."

The odds of this encounter were not lost on Naomi. Rebecca and Hannah had told her they had been praying and now here sat this haggard, old, grizzly bear of a man who preached the gospel. She was angry with God but not foolish enough to deny his intervention.

He cast a gentle look to Naomi. "How did yer man die?"

She stammered for a moment, stunned by the confidence behind his question. "He, he, a snake spooked his horse. He fell off and his head hit on a rock." Just like that, with the snap of God's fingers, and he was dead. The grief stabbed at her heart but she clenched her jaw to fight the pain. "How did you know the grave belonged to my husband?"

"Life etches itself on to our faces, child." As if for proof, he pinned Rebecca with a knowing gaze. "Yours says you've almost healed, but hers," he scoured the shadows in Naomi's face and nodded. "Hers is a fresh and bleeding wound.

"Have a care that ye don't give Satan a foothold," he warned. "Trust that God has a better plan for ye, child, than ye do yourself and let him bring His about. He's here. Even in this wilderness, He's here watchin' over ye."

Naomi didn't know what to say as she stared into his old gray eyes, dancing with firelight. Goosebumps rose on her skin.

"Who are you?" she managed in a weak whisper. Then, inexplicably added, "Can you tell us which way to go?"

He pursed his lips in thought and the gesture caused his beard to so completely overtake his face he looked for a moment as if he had no mouth at all. She would have laughed, except for what he said next. "I can tell ye in the morning. *Ye'll* know in the morning."

Chapter 4

In the dream, Naomi sat alone at the campfire waiting for her guest. She tended to the fish in the skillet and kept a watchful eye. Shortly, Jesus joined her. He sat down on the other side of the fire and offered her a tender smile.

"Naomi, do you trust me more than these?" She was surprised to see that Rebecca and Hannah had joined them, too, though they acted unaware of her or Jesus.

"Yes, Lord, you know I trust you."

"Then go where I send you." She put the fork down on the rock next to the fire and looked at him, puzzled by his statement. Again he asked, "Naomi, do you trust me?"

Her brow furrowed. "Yes, Lord, you know I trust you."

"Then go where I send you." She sat back and crossed her legs, puzzled, but sure there was more. Staring at her with dark, intent eyes, Jesus asked again, "Naomi, do you trust me?"

She sighed, frustrated with Him. "You know everything; you know my heart. So you should know that I trust you."

"Then go where I send you.

"There are those around you living in defiance. Take to them the Good News. Love them as I do." The last sounded almost like a plea.

"I will go where you send me, Lord." Her heart ached to ask one question of him, though. "But can't you please tell me why you took Jo—"

Jesus put a finger to his lips, cutting off the question. His countenance and voice were gentle when he replied, "You'll have your answer in time. I have children lost in darkness. Take to them the Light.

"And play the man one hand of cards."

Naomi opened her eyes and looked up at the bottom of the wagon. A gray light crept stealthily upon them and she knew it was time to get moving. She heard the comforting crackle of their fire and surmised their guest was awake as well. Slowly, gingerly, she climbed over her sleeping sisters and crawled out from underneath a home she now despised.

The stranger was nowhere in sight and his gear was gone. A lonely apprehension seized Naomi as she wandered over to the fire he had built for them. It was burning well, leading her to believe he hadn't been gone long.

As she moved to sit on a dead tree, she stopped short. A piece of crumpled butcher paper had been carefully smoothed out and pinned to the log with a bone-handled knife. Perplexed, she jerked the knife free and picked up the paper. Scratched in shaky, spidery pencil, she saw one word: Defiance.

"Defiance...?" She puzzled. "What...?"

But the Lord's words leaped to her mind: *There are those around you living in Defiance. Take to them the Good News. Love them as I do.*

She knew the name. She had seen the town on John's map and it was only a few miles due west.

She also knew, with a searing dread, that it was their destination.

Feeling sick and overwhelmed, she closed her eyes and went back to that dream which was now painfully vivid. She had told Him three times she would go where He sent her.

Not willingly, she admitted. *Forgive me, Lord. I go grudgingly, to say the least. With John beside me, I would have gone to Hell and back. I had my heart set on growing old with him. Where didn't matter. Now nothing matters.*

The truth be told, Lord, I don't like you very much right now.

The admission broke her heart as much as the loss of her husband. If she didn't have the relationship with God that she had always counted on, then she had nothing. Yet, getting past her anger at this sudden destruction of her dreams was proving nigh unto impossible. No John, no God, no peace. She cried over her loss *and* her smoldering resentment and begged Him to help her get past them both.

Her crying woke Hannah, who quietly arose and joined her at the campfire. Naomi was embarrassed to be caught weeping...again. Being this weak and vulnerable was new territory for Naomi. "I'm sorry." She sniffled and wiped her eyes. "One of these days I'll run out of all this water."

Hannah smiled and laid an arm around her big sister. "It's all right. I still do it occasionally." After a short silence, she added, "And I'm so sorry." Hannah's voice cracked. "All this is my fault."

Naomi drew in a deep breath. "John's death isn't your fault. He wanted to come west. He wanted to see his brother again. If it hadn't been a good, old-fashioned scandal, I believe he would have found another reason." Her attempt at humor fell flat. Chuckling miserably, Naomi patted her sister's hand and tried to find solid emotional ground. "What matters now is what we do next. I'd better get Rebecca up. I have something to tell you both." She cut a sideways look at Hannah. "I know where we're going."

Around the fire and over coffee, Naomi told the girls about her dream and the apparent confirmation from the stranger, conveniently leaving out the part about the cards. She had convinced herself it was merely dreamy foolishness.

And just in case her sisters weren't clear on what Naomi thought about all this, she explained bluntly, "I don't want to go to this town. I sure as heck don't want to go in as a missionary."

Almost immediately she could tell that Hannah was not having the same reaction.

A slow smile spread across her little sister's face and she rubbed her arms. "I have goosebumps." Hannah sounded awed by the fact. "Don't you see, Naomi?" Excitement oozed from the girl and her eyes sparkled. "This is what it's all been about. Our whole lives, God has been directing our paths to this very spot. We've been brought here for such a time as this.

"It gives me hope because I know that neither our mistakes nor our sacrifices have been in vain. We're not lost in the wilderness. We are exactly where He wants us."

Naomi's mouth fell open at Hannah's reaction, though she was more irritated than shocked by it. She wouldn't be surprised if the girl sprung to her feet and did cartwheels, her joy was so evident. She had been watching Hannah's faith grow ever since her confession to their congregation. The resulting firestorm over the scandal had been the ugliest thing Naomi had ever seen. Her little sister, though, had continued maturing by leaps and bounds, perhaps precisely because of the Hell unleashed by their fellow *Believers* that night.

Naomi wished she could say the same thing about her own faith, but without John she felt empty and, frankly, a little put upon by such exuberant faith.

Hannah set her coffee cup down and leaned forward. "I realized the second that Billy ran off that I had been looking to him for my happiness. I'd let him become an idol. Then that night at the church when it got so ugly..." she shivered at the memory. "I kept going back to what Pastor told us. Do you remember?"

Naomi and Rebecca shook their heads, but Hannah's face positively glowed with the fondness of his words. "I do, every word. I even wrote it in my diary. He said, 'You go before the congregation, tell them what's going on so that there's nothing left for the rumor mill. Tell them you've asked for forgiveness…then live like you've received it.'" Naomi remembered the statement well, thinking it had been the most eloquent thing she had ever heard. "That's when it started."

"What?" She and Rebecca chorused.

"The idea that the farther I distanced myself from Billy, the closer I would move to God. That night, I asked Him to help me move to a place where He was all I needed." Hannah bit her lip sheepishly and glanced up at the wilderness surrounding them. "I didn't mean it literally."

In consternation, Rebecca swiped her hand over her face. "Literally and figuratively, that's exactly where we are." She squeezed Naomi's hand. "I'm sorry it has cost you so much, but I agree with Hannah. We're where we're supposed to be."

"Is that supposed to make me feel better?" Naomi snapped, pulling her hand away. "We could be *exactly where we're supposed to be,*" she mocked, "with John sitting right here amongst us." She stood and threw her cup to the ground. Glaring at her sisters, she waved an accusing finger at them. "He's the God of the universe. He could've engineered this a million different ways that didn't require John's life."

Rebecca rose to her feet as well, a stern look on her face, like a mother about to correct a petulant child. "But He chose *this* path. John's life *was* required of him. I don't mean to sound cruel, Naomi, but maybe you should quit asking why and just accept it."

"Oh, like the way you accepted Ben and Gracie's deaths?" Naomi stabbed, not caring that she had hit her sister squarely in the heart and Rebecca's pained expression showed it. "You think I don't know you went and sat at their graves every day for seven years? I don't think *you* need to give *me* advice on how to handle grief!"

Hannah rose to her feet then, as if her action would douse the argument. Rebecca's face drained of color and Naomi saw the tears pooling. Her anger dissipated like smoke, replaced with a deep, stinging regret. She bit her lip, would have bit her own tongue off if she could have found the courage. "I'm sorry, Rebecca. That was uncalled for."

Naomi's repentance was sincere, but too late. Rebecca looked down at the ground and nodded. "Perhaps you're right." Naomi heard the tears in her voice. "I wallowed in my grief and wrapped it around me like chains. Chains that weighed me down, kept me from living. It was my penance for surviving the fire." She gazed up then, a surprising steel returning to her countenance. "But you've always been the strong one, Naomi. You won't let John's death suck the life out of you…especially knowing that we need you."

Gently, Rebecca placed her hand on Naomi's shoulder and squeezed it. "You've always risen to the challenge. I know you will this time."

Chapter 5

The sun hung past the middle of the sky when the sisters' wagon topped the hill and they took their first look at Defiance. The town squatted on the floor of a perfectly flat valley ringed on all sides by astonishingly steep, snow-capped mountains. Thick, green pines and a lesser number of hardwoods covered their lower elevations as a wide, bustling stream snaked its way through the middle of the valley. The vast majority of the town, including its commercial district, sat on the western side of the water.

A booming, bustling settlement, the girls could see people scurrying about like ants. Defiance sported one main street which followed a large bend in the river. The buildings that created the avenue on both sides were new and still held the freshly-cut golden hue that pine and cedar cling to for awhile. Several more buildings were under construction on the north end of the street.

Off to the left, the valley was dotted with two fairly large groupings of tents. One section of these looked to be businesses of some kind, saloons Naomi guessed, and the other was composed of much smaller tents, most likely dwellings, with smoking stove pipes. They peppered the valley floor in wild and lonely confusion. The ragtag condition of most of these structures convinced her they had been there the longest. The initial settlement for the town, no doubt. She also noted that the valley floor was nearly devoid of trees, harvested apparently for lumber and firewood.

As Naomi and her sisters looked down on Defiance, shots pierced the air and a small mob of men spilled out of one of the larger tent buildings off to their left. They converged in the street, closing into a tight circle, but the sisters could see frenzied movement at the center, arms raised and waving, pushing, shoving, fists swinging, accompanied by hooting and hollering and the worst sort of cursing. Naomi couldn't recall that she had ever heard such vile profanity. More shots were fired and instantly the crowd calmed, spread out and finally disbanded as men slipped away, some back into the tent.

Naomi, Rebecca and Hannah could then plainly see a man lying in the street, face down in the mud. He did not move and no one came to his aid. Naomi was dumbfounded. Rebecca's and Hannah's mouths hung open in shock. Surely these people didn't just leave their dead or dying in the streets...did they?

As if in answer to her question, two men burst out of the building from which the mob of men had spilled. They picked up the unconscious, or dead, man by his feet and shoulders, never checking his condition, and carried him at a lazy speed to a tent two doors down. They entered, then re-emerged only a second later, both wiping their hands. The task completed, they headed back to the first tent, a happy spring in their steps, re-entering as if they had merely taken out the trash. Almost immediately, an out-of-tune piano struck up a fast and furious chorus of "Yankee Doodle Dandy" of all things. Drunken laughter and bawdy verses of the song assailed the sisters' ears.

"Welcome to Defiance," Naomi whispered with revulsion.

Rebecca hooked her arm through Naomi's. The two had barely spoken since breakfast of the previous day. Now Rebecca's preaching seemed a trivial matter to Naomi as they stared down upon that grungy little town.

"We are surely strangers in a strange land," Rebecca quoted softly.

Hannah hooked an arm around Rebecca's free arm. Clinging to one another, her sisters leaned closer. Naomi did not fail to notice that they huddled slightly behind her. Naomi felt unsure of everything, even her usual willingness to scrap. Now was not the time for someone to lean on her. Where had their confidence and goosebumps of yesterday gone? Where was this strength that Rebecca had seen in Naomi?

"If there are...prostitutes," Hannah uttered the word with difficulty. "If there are, I mean, well, won't there be good midwives or even doctors here?"

Naomi's breath caught in her throat. The question showed what Hannah was keeping in the forefront of her mind. No matter what else happened, Naomi promised herself that she would wade through this grief somehow and take care of that baby...and her baby sister.

Naomi straightened up and clutched the reins tighter in her hand. The leather was slick now as her hands had started sweating with her first look at this shoddy, trashy little town. Irritated, she wiped them, one at a time, on her skirt. Sweaty hands made it difficult to hang on to the reins and she wondered if perhaps God was making a point.

In her heart, Naomi felt a kettle of emotions trying to boil. A new ingredient mixed in with the grief and anger, though. For the first time in her life, Naomi was truly afraid. There was so much on the line now. Their future, their safety, their finances, the life of a baby. She had never realized, not once, how incredibly easy their lives had been back in Cary until this very moment.

Was this how Daniel felt going into the lion's den, or Joseph as he was thrown into prison…or Jesus as he faced his final hours? None of them had exactly rushed with joyful abandon to their particular calling. She certainly didn't feel like rushing headlong into that town. The thought made her stomach squirm. Why was God making this all so hard?

The jingle of another wagon coming up the hill from town brought her back to the moment. A large black horse plodded along as it pulled a precariously loaded freight wagon, packed with the delicacy of a Carolina hurricane. Chairs, tables, chests, bed frames sat askew, lopsided and desperately close to slipping out of sagging ropes.

The man driving the wagon, however, caught Naomi's attention. He was a young, gangly, sandy-haired fellow, stooped over his reins as if the world was resting on his shoulders. His face showed much grief and heartache, especially evident in his gaunt cheeks and deeply carved scowl—that is, what she could see of it hidden under a sweat-stained derby. He looked haunted and his expression gave Naomi chills. She prayed that much hopelessness would never be reflected in her own eyes.

She debated speaking to him, as he would pass close enough by, but his eyes were set resolutely straight ahead on some far-away destination. He looked as if he would drive right by, never glancing at the sisters, but Naomi hailed him.

"Excuse us, sir." For an instant he did ignore her, but apparently civility got the better of him. He pulled his horses up and rested his left hand on the brake. He nodded curtly to the women, without looking at them.

Now that he was stopped, Naomi didn't quite know what to say.

"Is there a decent hotel in this town?" Rebecca jumped in, sounding hopeful, as she had been telling her sisters for days she had her sights set on a soft bed and a hot meal. This town might be mean, but after more than three months of sleeping outdoors, Rebecca had confessed to feeling rather mean herself.

The man sighed deeply, as if a simple response took all the strength he had left. "I reckon not. There *is* nothing decent in Defiance." He looked up at the girls and studied them. Despair clouded his face. "You don't belong here. This town destroys everyone who comes in. Every imaginable and unimaginable wickedness runs wild in Defiance." He turned his head away quickly at that as if the sisters might read something awful in his face.

And his face was an open book. He wore his shame like a mantle. Naomi knew there was compassion not only in her own eyes, but Rebecca and Hannah's as well. She couldn't imagine what he had delved into, but at least he was getting out; that meant there had to be hope for him.

She let her gaze wander back to the town and felt only loathing and anger for its residents. The attitude tweaked her conscience and made her think of Jonah. Like the prophet of old, she could not see where people who chose to live in the filth and mire of sin were worth redeeming. People make their choices. Yet, carrying a heart of stone had landed Jonah in the belly of a whale, she recalled with unease. She didn't care to follow that path, either.

Hannah couldn't stand it. The look on the man's face, the emptiness in his eyes, broke her heart. She knew that pain and wouldn't wish it on her worst enemy. She had to tell him that no matter where he had been, no matter what he had done, God was waiting to welcome the prodigal son home. He was eager to forgive him, wash off the stains of his sins and let him start anew. There was no reason he had to live with the shame he now wore like a heavy, winter coat.

She heard her sisters gasp as she climbed out of their wagon. Unheeding, Hannah walked around the mules and over to the stranger.

"Hannah, what are you doing?" Naomi fumed. "Get back in this wagon."

Instead, she gazed up at the man. Clueless as to what exactly she wanted to say, Hannah prayed, then offered the first thing that came to her. "As far as the east is from the west, so far has he removed your transgressions...."

The closest thing to pure awe Naomi had ever seen struck the man's face.

"You don't know..." he whispered, breaking off. Tears glistened in his eyes. "Just yesterday I cried out to a God I haven't talked to in years to save me from—" he swallowed and hung his head. "From the drinking that led to the women that led to the gambling." He looked up again, seeking Hannah's face. "I finally lost it all. With one hand Charles McIntyre took everything

I'd worked for these last two years. The loss stripped me of my mercantile, its inventory, a gold stake, all of it. I have nothing left but shame."

"You have your soul. What's it profit a man if he gains the world but loses that?" Hannah's voice pleaded with him to believe it. "Mr...?"

"Whicker. Isaac Whicker." He offered Hannah his hand and the two shook. "How did you know what I needed to hear?" Hannah couldn't help but notice he held on to her hand like a lifeline.

She gave him a half-smile. "I know that look...and I know the one who takes away my shame. Your shame." Without waiting for a reply, she brightened and added, "I'm Hannah and these are my sisters, Rebecca and Naomi."

She motioned towards the two slack-jawed women sitting in the wagon.

Looking as if a thousand-pound weight had been lifted off him, Whicker smiled broadly at them; his expression was a shocking contrast to the look in his eyes only moments ago.

Obviously, Hannah had told Whicker what God had wanted him to hear and he rushed to tell her what he planned to do with his freedom. "I'm going to shake the dust of Defiance from my feet. God heard my prayer and he sent you to tell me so. There's no other explanation.

"I'm going home to Missouri and tell my family about the angel in the wilderness. You're my miracle."

Hannah looked away embarrassed and Whicker laughed. "I almost wish I was staying now." The thought triggered another and his smile faded.

"I meant what I said about this town," he advised them all more firmly than before. "It will eat you alive. You don't belong here." When none of the women responded, he added, "There ain't no hotel in Defiance, but my store might be a place you could stay...only it's not mine anymore. It's all but empty by now, too. You'd have to go through McIntyre to see if he'd put you up there. It's that or the saloon. He owns everything and everyone in Defiance. You're not careful, he'll own you, too."

"Where can we find him?" Naomi asked sounding like a condemned man looking for the nearest firing squad.

"The first building you come to in town." He motioned over his shoulder. "The Iron Horse Saloon."

He looked down at Hannah again, his entire countenance transformed. Her heart soared. "Thank you. If I hadn't run into to you, I think I would have jumped off a cliff. I can't believe what He's done for me and I won't forget." He hesitated for a moment, as if he wanted to say more to Hannah but changed his mind. With apparent resolve, Whicker shook the reins and put Defiance behind him.

She waited for the jingle of his wagon to fade away then Hannah fairly exploded with elation. "Did you see that?" she asked, grabbing the handrail up to their seat. "Did you see the way he just let God wash it all away!? He restored that man's hope, He made him a new creation! It was beautiful!"

Rebecca nodded, her eyes glistening with tears. "I've never seen anything like that. God has his hand on you, Hannah." Her voice was laced with awe.

And apparently *against* me, Naomi thought bitterly, but pushed away the idea, if not the emotion.

She had seen the undeniable, miraculous transformation in Whicker and would have to be blind to miss Hannah's new spiritual fervor...or Rebecca's surprising willingness to accept things at face value. More and more Naomi was feeling like Doubting Thomas traveling with Peter and John. Trying to unscramble her thoughts and think past her own grief and insecurities, she realized there were steps to be taken before she let these two apostles fall upon the town like Old Testament prophets. What was that scripture about being wise like snakes and gentle like doves?

"We can't barge into that town with Hannah preaching from the front seat like a snake oil salesman." Her sarcasm came across sounding mean-spirited. Softening her tone, Naomi explained, "In case neither of you has given this any thought, right now we're more like lambs for the slaughter than spiritual warriors."

Rubbing her chin, she pondered their next step. "We should pray before we go down there. We need to move away, find a quiet camp site."

The idea was as much for making ready to enter Defiance as it was a chance for Naomi to deal with her grief. The thought of heading into that town without John beside her was excruciating and frightening. Not to mention, her anger at God made her feel unguarded and vulnerable. Her thoughts were in a mess and she needed to pray, to talk to Him, probably argue with Him, and sort things out. Without a second look at Defiance,

Naomi waited for Hannah to climb up, then quickly turned the wagon around.

Chapter 6

The next morning, Naomi and Rebecca bustled around the camp packing up, preparing to meet this unknown and totally unexpected future. Hannah had not yet finished her prayer time and Naomi had no desire to rush her.

This is it, she thought with dread as she shoved a skillet and tongs into the side compartment on the wagon. *Today's the day we tackle Defiance.* She tried not to wax sarcastic or sullen. She wanted to forget her fears, forget the grief, but she was clutching them with a dead man's grip. God was going to have to use a crowbar to pry open her fingers.

Hannah sauntered up from the creek and stopped in the center of their camp. She folded her hands demurely in the center of her tattered apron, accentuating her slightly round stomach. "I think I know what we're supposed to do when we get there." Rebecca, pouring a dousing stream of coffee on the fire, stopped and waited. Naomi straightened, folded her arms across her chest.

"We're supposed to get Mr. Whicker's building and open a hotel and a restaurant."

Naomi and Rebecca looked at each other, but not with surprise. It took a lot to surprise them these days.

Naomi tugged on her ear, considering the statement. "And how did you arrive at that conclusion, considering that we don't know anything about running either?"

Hannah shrugged. "We know how to cook and clean. But to answer your question, I dreamed about it. I dreamed we had church in the dining room on Sunday mornings and Bible study in the kitchen on Wednesday nights—"

"I'm sorry," Rebecca interrupted. "Did you say we should open a hotel or a *church*?"

Naomi tried to hide a smile.

"A hotel and a restaurant," Hannah repeated louder as if her sisters were deaf. "The church will come later."

"She sounds very sure of it, doesn't she?" Naomi observed, knowing better than to cast a judgment on Hannah's dream. She might be a lot of things, but a hypocrite wasn't one of them.

Rebecca nodded. "Very sure."

This time, Naomi shrugged. "Well, if we stay, we have to do something. She's right. We know how to cook and clean and make beds. And we've got a right fair amount of money from selling the farms. I suppose we could bounce the idea off this Mr. McIntyre, since he's the closest thing to a businessman around here."

"But if we spend all of our money here," Rebecca cautioned, "we won't have enough to get started in California."

With Naomi, dreams died hard, but she did feel sure that California and their future there had dissolved like sugar in hot tea. "We're not ever going to see California," she prophesied out of hopelessness. "At least not any time soon."

Naomi had hoped their entrance into Defiance might go unnoticed, that they would blend with all the traffic, but that wasn't the case. All three of the sisters wore their bonnets in an attempt to hide their faces, but obviously women in this town were as rare as dancing elephants and garnered as much attention as a troop of them. As Rebecca drove, the men populating the street stared brazenly, and several even whistled and made obscene suggestions. After seeing a man killed before their very eyes, though, this particular kind of welcome had no shock effect at all. In fact, Naomi had expected nothing less. She glanced at the faces, wondering if any of these men had been involved in the possible murder they had witnessed. A question which led her to belatedly ponder their own safety.

As they passed the crudely painted "Welcome to Defiance" sign, Naomi could have sworn she felt the shadow of a dark and ominous presence. Attributing the unease to her grief, she studied the swirling sea of men. They were young and middle-aged, mostly bearded, dirty and flashing a dangerous glint of the untamed in their eyes. She reached under the seat for John's revolver. Knowing it was there and loaded made her feel some better.

When they pulled up in front of the saloon, Rebecca and Hannah both turned to Naomi expectantly. For whatever reason, they felt she should be the one to meet Mr. McIntyre and had told her so that morning. They had prayed about the meeting and until this moment, Naomi had suffered with butterflies.

Now, looking up at the sloppily painted white building with its cherry red trim and matching bat wing doors, she was at ease. Peaceful in fact, but not happy. She couldn't help but recall the meeting with Billy's father Frank Page and how she and John had handled it together. This time, Naomi was alone but grudgingly accepted that she was also right where God wanted her.

She was glad at least *somebody* was happy.

"I think you two should get in the back of the wagon before you draw a crowd," she told her sisters quietly as the men walking by stared and slowed their pace. Her sisters nodded and scrambled out of sight. Naomi climbed down, focused on the red saloon doors and sucked in a breath.

Chapter 7

Inside the Iron Horse Saloon, McIntyre drummed his fingers on his desk. The letter did not bring him the news he wanted and he despised not getting what he wanted. He read that one particular line again: "while Defiance is in an excellent location to provide a hub for spur lines up from Animas Forks and Pinkerton Springs, the town's lack of civil organization or for that matter, civility, distresses us."

The same complaint...again.

So Defiance was a bit on the wild side. He looked out the window of his office. Wine, women and song. What more could any man really want?

Possibly a hotel that provided a bed without a female already in it, he admitted grudgingly. Or a restaurant that served real food, not "grub." A night without the eruption of gunfire. A duly elected mayor. A legally deputized sheriff. Law and order. Churches. Schools.

He sighed like a man accepting his fate. Defiance had to be civilized. Getting the mercantile back was a start. If he wanted the railroad to come in, he was going to have to get on with his plans —

He heard the front doors squeak and looked up. His office afforded a view of the entire length of the bar and he sat up attentively as a pretty little blonde entered and removed her bonnet. Hands clenched tensely at her waist, her eyes were glued to the painting over the bar.

Whoever she was, she had never seen anything like that and he smiled as she looked away. How long had it been since he had seen a woman blush? He couldn't honestly recall. He enjoyed gazing upon her for a moment, taking in the slim, curvaceous figure and that long, golden braid running down her back like Rapunzel's. She was tanned from the sun and her dress showed a fair amount of wear. Still, she was enjoyable to study and it wouldn't take much for his mind to wander...

She looked around the rest of the empty saloon and finally her eyes found him. He stood as she approached his office door. "Are you Mr. McIntyre?"

"I am," he agreed in his most charming Southern accent. He skirted his desk and met her in the entrance, momentarily struck by the contrast of ocean-green eyes in a beautiful, tanned face. High cheekbones, freckles and a slightly pug nose, she was a fresh-faced, wholesome change from the women currently populating Defiance. And he had picked up on her accent before she had spoken her second word.

"A fellow southerner." Extending his hand, he admitted, "Though I can't quite place the accent, Ms…"

"We're from North Carolina and it's *Mrs*. Naomi Miller."

He nodded, accepting her correction. "Mrs. Miller. To what do I owe this distinct pleasure?"

He held on to her hand much too long as he appraised her up and down. Naomi awkwardly pulled her hand away. He grinned at her obvious discomfort, enjoying the sport. He could tell she didn't like him already.

"I was wondering if we might talk a little business?"

"Why certainly." He didn't know why, but he motioned to one of the green-topped poker tables behind her instead of his office. "Please have a seat and I'll get us some refreshments. I have everything from whiskey to coffee."

"Coffee?"

He grinned again. "I'll just be a moment."

Going behind the bar, he caught sight of himself in the mirror and wondered if she admired his wavy, jet-black hair, brown eyes and painstakingly trimmed mustache and beard. Tall, slender and well-dressed, he was a far cry from the filthy young buck who had explored this valley. Or, for that matter, the green lieutenant who had spent five years covered in blood and guts for his beloved Confederacy. He would never live like that again he vowed as he poured the coffee. For further proof, he admired his clean hands and superbly manicured nails.

McIntyre re-joined Naomi, bearing a silver tray dotted with sugar and cream vessels, sterling silver spoons and two delicate coffee cups filled with steaming coffee. The saloon was a rather rough and gritty-looking affair reeking of cigar smoke and sour whiskey so this touch of elegance was, he hoped, a pleasant surprise for her. With fluid, confident movements, he set her coffee before her, poured in cream at her nod, and stirred in one spoonful of sugar.

She sipped the coffee and for a fleeting moment seemed to forget where she was and why she was there. He thought she looked tired, her brown calico dress had seen better days and her bonnet, resting on the table beside her, was faded and well-worn. He assumed she had been traveling for quite some time. It pleased him to offer her this little moment of rest, though he couldn't say why. Probably for the same reason he gave a stray dog a scrap—he still claimed a morsel of unjaded humanity.

"Mrs. Miller, please forgive me for asking," McIntyre began as he prepared his own cup, "but I am not used to doing business with a woman. Might I enquire about your husband?"

She swallowed the coffee and huffed a heavy breath before answering. "My husband. He was killed over a week ago on the trail."

McIntyre's brow furrowed deeply offering her sympathy, but he could barely hide his disappointment. Just another flower for the garden, he thought. And he had been hoping for something more interesting.

"I am very sorry to hear that. However, it happens rather frequently in the west, especially in mining towns. Women are left with so few options under such circumstances. You are a very beautiful woman, though, Mrs. Miller. I can promise you won't starve. And generally speaking, I believe my flowers are fairly satisfied with their working conditions. I pay a generous percentage and the rooms are large and comfortable. You also receive all your meals for free—"

Naomi threw up her hand. "Stop talking!" she commanded. Suddenly, Mcintyre felt a bit like a court jester failing to properly amuse the queen.

Hand still up, she acknowledged with firmness, "I can see where that would be an assumption someone in Defiance could make about a woman, but it was rude, nonetheless, and wrong. Very, very wrong."

Amused by her imperious reaction, but also honestly apologetic, he lowered his head. "I'm sorry." He could have easily added, "Your Highness," but bit it back. Leaning back in his chair and crossing his legs, he made no attempt to hide his confusion. "Obviously I misconstrued the reason for your coming here. My assumption was inexcusable."

Naomi's cheeks were positively glowing. "To say the least."

Hiding a smile behind his coffee cup, he gave her time to compose herself.

"My sisters and my husband and I were on our way to California to join his brother there. Since his death, we've had a rather astonishing change of plans." He could see she was warring with the final statement and waited patiently for her to frame it. "We feel strongly led to stop our journey here in Defiance."

"Led?" He didn't miss the use of the word. "Are you Mormon missionaries?"

His voice had sounded vaguely disdainful, though he hadn't exactly meant for it to. God had no time to waste on Defiance and McIntyre was happy to return the favor.

"Not missionaries, so to speak, and not Mormons. We are Christians and we feel that God wants us to settle here, at least for awhile. Believe me, this place wouldn't be my first choice, but we met Mr. Whicker as he was leaving town and we know his building is vacant. That's what I came to speak with you about."

Whicker's name got his attention and McIntyre's mind hit a full gallop. Intrigued, he listened carefully and watched her over the top of his cup.

"We were thinking of opening up a hotel and restaurant." She looked out the window at the heavy traffic on the street and the bustling boardwalk. "The town at first glance seems busy enough. Would that building accommodate such a venture?" she asked, hope evident in her voice. "Could the town use a nice place?"

Before she had finished speaking, McIntyre had started plotting. He couldn't ignore the fortuitousness of her question since opening a hotel was exactly the reason he had reclaimed Whicker's building. But that had still left him with the troublesome issue of finding respectable innkeepers. Looking at Mrs. Miller, he believed the answer had fallen into his lap. Then an entertaining idea struck him. Pardon the pun, he thought wryly, but, in defiance of God, he wanted to trust his fate to what he knew best—cards.

He sat up, set his coffee off to the side and began absently shuffling a deck that had been sitting on the table. "So what you're saying is that you believe God has sent you to Defiance? To open a business? And then what? Will you try to save the town? Convert us all to Jesus?" There was no malice in the questions, just bland curiosity.

Naomi tilted her head to one side and bestowed a haughty look on him. "Forgive *me*, Mr. McIntyre, but why is the town named Defiance?"

He allowed a well-practiced, but admittedly insincere, smile to creep across his face. "Have you ever heard the expression that it is better to rule in Hell than serve in Heaven?"

Her face softened and she nodded slowly. Had he seen a glint of compassion in her eyes? he wondered, uncomfortable with anyone's pity.

Nonetheless, he briefly shared his story. "In 1860, I came to the San Juan range with a group of fourteen other prospectors, led by Capt. Charles Baker. We broke up into three groups so we could better scout the valley, but in dividing, one group fell under attack by a superior force of Ute Indians. A mere youth of seventeen, I watched while men two and three times my age begged God for death as their skin was flayed from their bodies." Goosebumps rose on Naomi's skin. "God did not save them; God stood silent while those men suffered and died.

"And I saw similar atrocities repeatedly during the war, proving to me that the white man is every bit as savage as the red man. When the war was over, I came back to our campsite to find the gold I'd buried. Georgia was in ashes; Sherman had seen to that, so I decided to stay here." He shrugged, surprised that he had told her so much. "I suppose all of that was just a long-winded way of saying the name just seemed appropriate. Perhaps in my foolish youth I was shaking my fist at God and daring Him to set foot in my town."

Naomi bit her lip as she pondered his tale. "A sort of line in the sand, is it?" Shadows of pain flitted across her face. "I wish I had answers for why God does what he does, *allows* what he does, but I'm still working on that one myself."

"Oh, I don't mean to make it sound as if I'm angry or to be pitied, Mrs. Miller. I'm truly content." He placed cards on the table with skilled, easy movements as he talked. "Taking God out of the equation frees a man to find his own destiny, make his own way without worrying about divine *whimsy*. I've done quite well for myself. I've got all the comforts any man *really* wants... There."

Naomi looked down and saw that he had placed three cards in front of each of them; two eights stared up at her but the third card was face down. He was looking at a king and a five beside another card, also face down.

"This game is called Twenty-one," he explained. "The object is to get as close to twenty-one as possible without going over. Whoever is the closest, wins. If you win, Mrs. Miller, I will give you that building for your hotel. If you lose, I'll sell it to you.

"It was originally designed as a hotel. I built it knowing that the Brunot Treaty would be ratified and this corner of Colorado would explode with settlers." He chuckled. "I didn't count on my geologist finding a sixty-foot thick vein of quartz in my mine. Silver, gold and even a little copper." He shook his head, still unable to take in his growing fortune. "Silver took precedence over the innkeeping business. So perhaps, all along, my hotel has been waiting for you and your sisters to transform it into an oasis of gentility in this wilderness of decadence."

Naomi eyed him warily. Plainly, she was unimpressed with his flowery talk. "Why not just sell it to us? Why play a game of cards—" But as the question left her mouth, he saw her expression change, as if she was remembering something startling.

He waited, hoping she might explain, but her lips were pressed tightly together. When she didn't elaborate, he tapped his cards absently. "I was just wondering if God speaks my language," he answered in truth.

"So you want to hear from Him despite your defiance?"

Their eyes locked in an unspoken battle of wills over the answer to her question. McIntyre suspected it might be the first of many skirmishes with this little princess from the South. The thought amused him and he chuckled good naturedly at her assumption.

"That's not what I meant exactly but you can put it that way if you like. I make my living with cards. *They* speak to me."

"All right," she nodded. "I think you ducked the question, but all right. We only play one hand, though."

"Winner takes all." He liked her spirit. "You're feeling lucky today, are you?"

She speared him with a somber gaze. "There's no such thing as luck, Mr. McIntyre. Like it or not, there's only the hand of God."

Her words hung in the air, throwing him off track for a moment. He saw great emotion behind her eyes, but couldn't tell of what ilk. "Perhaps," he muttered.

He recovered quickly, shifting in his chair and changing the subject. "The upstairs is unfinished space, easily transformable into rooms or suites. Downstairs in the back is a kitchen Whicker also used as his living space. You should be able to get, say, ten to twelve tables in the dining area."

He was ready to play his hand and looked down at his cards. Still, he felt compelled to share one last bit of information. "I have to admit, the timing of your arrival is, well, strangely opportune as I was pondering this venture again. It's the very reason I helped Mr. Whicker leave our little community."

"Then why would you want *us* to get the hotel," she asked with a I-don't-trust-you- as-far-as-I-can-throw-you look on her face.

"It has come to my attention that Defiance could be passed up for some opportunities if the town doesn't become more *civilized*." He raised his hands in a gesture of surrender. "I must give up a portion of my kingdom to decency if I want the town to grow."

Naomi stared at McIntyre and he could see the wheels turning behind those stormy green eyes. She was questioning everything about him and this situation. Though he knew somehow, she would go through with his challenge.

"Maybe that's what this is all about, Mr. McIntyre," she suggested, sounding both wistful and melancholy. "Maybe, now and then, we all have to give up a portion of our kingdoms, the things *we* hold dearest, to find what it is God wants for us." The thought intrigued him and he decided he was looking forward to doing business with her Ladyship.

She shook her head and heaved a great sight. "This is absurd. I should look at the building first, haggle with you over price, discuss it with my sisters...but I think that would defeat the purpose of why I'm here." Inexplicably, he suspected the admission was more for her benefit than his.

"Price shouldn't be an issue since you're going to win," he joked, light-heartedly mocking her faith. Finishing off his coffee, he added "However, if you do lose, I want $3800 for the building. Any remaining merchandise inside it is mine, of course."

Naomi opened her mouth, to protest he assumed, but though better of whatever she started to say. Instead of negotiating, she began, "I wish I could tell you—" A million things? If they could sit and talk like two polite people from genteel Southern society, what would she tell him?

Naomi shook her head again. "Someday I might tell you the story of how we came to this moment, Mr. McIntyre, but for now just show your card." He liked the grit he heard in her voice, her determination to face things unflinchingly. Oh, yes, he was quite sure he was going to enjoy having her in Defiance. Pun intended.

Without hesitating he flipped his card. A red queen of hearts gazed placidly back at them. "Dealer busts; you win."

Drumming her fingers, she reached for the card, hesitated, then flipped over a five of spades. "Twenty-one," Naomi whispered.

A slow, sad smile spread across her face. She looked up at McIntyre, her eyes sparkling with what he assumed was an expected, and possibly unwanted, victory. "Keep your ears open, Mr. McIntyre. I think you'll be hearing from Him again."

Chapter 8

For a man who had just lost a card game and a building worth more than three thousand dollars, Naomi saw not a hint of disappointment in Mr. McIntyre's eyes. Quite the opposite. He looked as jovial as if he had *won* three thousand dollars.

She, on the other hand, was trying desperately to remain calm and collected, much less look happy. The fact that she had just played a hand of cards to determine her and her sisters' destiny was almost overwhelming. Using a strategy that could be called anything but gambling, God had delivered a soon-to-be hotel and restaurant into her hands. She was clear-headed enough, however, to suspect that the particular method of transfer had been more for Mr. McIntyre's benefit than hers.

As they stood and shook hands, she couldn't help but wonder what plans God had for him. Admittedly, she would enjoy watching the Almighty take this pompous peacock down a peg or two...if she had time to bother with him.

"Mrs. Miller, I do believe you are going to make Defiance a far more enchanting place in which to live." He covered her hand with his and looked deeply into her eyes. "I truly want to your hotel to be successful. I hope you won't mind if I'm intimately involved with the details."

She jerked her hand away and scowled at him. "I'm quite sure my sisters and I can manage without your assistance."

"Not in my town." The comment had sounded light-hearted enough, but the look in his dark eyes walked a tightrope between menacing and bewitching. It gave Naomi a chill. "But I'll try not to be too much of a nuisance."

Why did she have the feeling she had just made a deal with the devil? What wasn't he telling her?

"The building is the third one from the end of town, this side of the street. You'll find it right where the street bends. I originally was going to call it the Elbow Inn," he shrugged noncommittally, "but I'm sure you'll choose a more refined name. Ten minutes?"

"We'll be waiting." What else did they have to do?

The end of their conversation was interrupted by a commotion outside. Naomi heard Hannah squeal in fright and both she and Mr. McIntyre bolted for the door. Together, they exploded through the bat wings to find three, mud-encrusted miners playing catch with Hannah's bonnet. She and Rebecca sat, clinging to each other, in the wagon and shrilly demanding the return of the hat.

"Gentleman!" Mr. McIntyre's commanding voice stopped the horse play cold. "That will be enough."

A grotesquely fat man with jiggling jowls caught the last pass of the bonnet and pressed it innocently to his grimy chest, as if it belonged to him in the first place. Furious beyond description, Naomi stomped towards the man and shoved him with all the ferociousness she could muster in her small frame. "Get away from my sisters!"

The man's eyes widened in shock at the violence of the attack, then a huge grin split his face, revealing rotten, yellowed teeth swimming in tobacco juice. Naomi's stomach threatened to rebel, but her anger overcame it and she snatched the bonnet from his dirty, fat hands.

"Ain't she a feisty one," the man joked, spitting on the ground. "I'll be your first customer, angel."

Before she could respond, Mr. McIntyre stepped between them and put a hand on the fat man's chest. "Be about your business, Sam. These girls are none of your affair." Naomi didn't miss the lowered tone in his voice and the way he looked around the street. The commotion threatened to draw a crowd and apparently Mr. McIntyre did not want that to happen. "You and your boys come back tonight and I'll give you one on the house," he looked at the other two men, just as filthy as the first. "I mean a drink. Now, go on. I'm sure you've got some place to be. Doesn't your shift start soon?"

Grudgingly, the three ambled away muttering something about bobcats and she-devils. The slowing sea of on-lookers picked up speed again, convinced there was nothing else to watch. Still, eyes stayed trained on Hannah and Rebecca in the wagon till necks wouldn't twist anymore.

Fighting for calm, Naomi forced her heart to slow, but the anger did not want to surrender. "Are you all right, Hannah?"

Fair cheeks blazing red and blue-eyes as wide as half-dollars, Hannah nodded weakly. Tucking a wayward gold strand of hair behind her ear, she reached for her bonnet. "They didn't hurt us."

"But they scared us to death," Rebecca volunteered breathlessly.

"I'm very sorry, ladies," Mr. McIntyre apologized from behind Naomi. "Beautiful women are as rare as ballerinas in Defiance, especially ones who don't work for me."

Naomi spun on him. "Yes, I noticed you cleared that right up." She hoped her sarcasm was palpable she was so angry with him. "You said the hotel is ours. We don't work for you. We shook hands on it."

"We did," he agreed, as a smile fought for freedom at the edges of his mouth. "In this particular instance, I thought it the better part of valor to get them on their way rather than engage in an explanation of your virtue. For the moment, you were under my protection." Naomi had the urge to smack that arrogant grin right off his suave, handsome face, but balled her hands into fists instead.

"I assure you, I will clear up any misunderstandings forthwith," he promised, sounding more amused than contrite. "For now, why don't you ladies proceed to the hotel where we can conduct our business away from all these prying eyes? I'll be there shortly."

Her emotions in a dither, Naomi huffed her disapproval and climbed up into the wagon. Mr. McIntyre retreated inside. For a moment, the three girls sat in silence. Looking as if she wanted to hide under a rock, Rebecca hunched lower in the seat and clutched the reigns so tightly, her knuckles were white. Hannah brushed the mud off her bonnet and gingerly replaced it on her head. Naomi drummed her fingers on her knees and stared straight ahead. She swallowed, attempting to loosen the tension in her jaw. She could feel the stares peppering them from everywhere. From the street, from the sidewalk, as the men passed by on horseback and strolled past on the sidewalk.

Oh, God, she cried out, *what are you thinking?*

"We have to move, Rebecca," she heard herself order, surprised at the steadiness of her voice. She didn't feel steady. Not one bit. But she had to hold herself together, at least until she was alone.

Rebecca straightened and lifted the reins. "Which way?"

"It's the third building from the end." Naomi pointed ahead of them. "It's right there in the bend of the road."

Rebecca clucked her tongue and the mules obeyed. As the wagon rolled forward, Naomi fumed aloud over the citizens. "They've the manners of pirates here, and stare like they've never seen women before."

"It's not just the men," Rebecca countered, tugging on the reins to veer away from an on-coming wagon. "We saw three women watching us from upstairs at the saloon."

"I waved at one of them," Hannah's eyes were wide with the scandalous admission, "but she jerked away from the window like I'd fired a gun at her."

Naomi looked over at her little sister and feared what kind of company she would be keeping in this town. If Mr. McIntyre so much as *looked* at her sisters the wrong way...Naomi curled her fingers into fists so tight her nails gouged her palms.

What kind of a man was so devoid of a conscience that he could sell women into prostitution as easily as one would hire out a man to chop wood? It was appalling and she heartily disapproved of his very existence. To think that he was a form of protection for them right now was almost more than she could comprehend...

~~~

McIntyre stood far enough back from the saloon's windows so he could study the girls without being seen. He was pleased to discover that the other two sisters were just as handsome as Mrs. Miller. However, he considered their planned future a waste of good flesh. Two golden-haired beauties and a dark one would draw in the miners; they always liked fresh meat, he thought disgustedly. The variety in their ages was alluring as well.

Alas, they would have to remain unsoiled and he would put the word out. Women were nearly as valuable as gold and silver in the West, but these three would have to be off limits, at least to the general public. He, of course was a different story. But that could wait for awhile, too.

Pulling his watch out of his vest pocket, he chuckled when he thought of Mrs. Miller throwing up her hand to stop his offer of employment. No one had talked to him like that in years. *And* he had even seen her blush. He didn't know women still did that. Yet, she had jumped ol' Sam like a wolverine trying to protect its young. Delicate and genteel but, by God, sassy as a red pepper! Whistling a cheerful tune, McIntyre went back to his office to grab his hat and the keys for the newest residents of Defiance.

~~~

Hannah tried for one last glance up at the window where she had seen the girls but as they pulled away, the wagon's bonnet blocked it. She settled back down in her seat, scratching at her waist, and pondered Defiance. The town terrified her. Even so, she could see past the wanton lust, the drunkenness, the false bravado exhibited so perfectly in their "welcoming committee." Against her better judgment, she looked into the sea of faces and met the bold stares. Looking deeper, she saw emptiness, loneliness, hopelessness. Like their clothes, threadbare and worn, so were their souls.

How could she know that? How could she sense it so perfectly?

Even more amazing, Hannah actually wanted to stand on the wagon seat and announce to them all that God was here. Even in this cesspool of darkness, God was here and He loved them. A tiny voice tried to convince her that she wasn't worthy to share that message, but she knew better. God had forgiven her, He could forgive them. Hannah also knew, however, that once word was out about the baby, these people would probably be more vicious than her "friends" back home had been.

Home.

Her memories of Sunday afternoon picnics, summer nights sitting on the front porch with Momma and Daddy, even the sweeter remembrances of Billy, had been shoved to the background because of that one, humiliating night. The thought of home now conjured up, in exquisite detail, the shame of confessing her sin before her congregation and the resulting torrential rain of judgment.

"She's young; she made a mistake."

"Young and loose it sounds like!"

"She's clearly asked for forgiveness!"

Hannah squeezed her eyes shut as if that would silence the voices in her head.

"We can't turn her out! It wouldn't be right."

"We can't have her teaching our children in Sunday school. It wouldn't look right."

"This should've never happened in the first place."

"We can't be seen as condoning this situation."

At her lowest point, when she was raw and bleeding from the verbal lashing, God had reminded her that she was not alone nor was she forsaken. She was forgiven. That thought on its own had made it possible for her to walk out of church instead of crawl.

The wagon lurched; Rebecca gasped and Hannah's eyes flew open. A man leaped up on the step, pulling himself to within inches of Naomi. Filthy and smelling like sweat, rotten food and alcohol, her sister winced as this new troublemaker removed his shoddy little derby in a grand, sweeping gesture. With the slurred Irish accent of a proficient drunkard, he announced, "Ladies, I am Dermott Guibne. Allow me to welcome ye to Defiance."

Naomi recoiled at his breath and scowled menacingly. "We've had enough of this town's welcome. Now, get off our wagon."

The man's drunken countenance changed instantly, darkening to a more threatening expression. "Ye need to learn some manners, missy," he growled, reaching out and grabbing hold of Naomi's wrist.

"Not today and not from you!" Acting on instinct, Naomi slammed her boot into the middle of his breastbone and shoved with a force that astonished Hannah. The man went flying, landing flat on his back and knocking his head against a hitching post with an audible thud. The men nearby who had the chance to witness the encounter roared with laughter.

It had happened so fast Rebecca hadn't stopped the mules and the wagon was still moving forward. "Pick up the pace, sister," Naomi commanded, the color draining from her cheeks. Hannah could see the fear her older sister was trying to hide and was unnerved by it. Rebecca urged the mules into a fast trot, doing her best to navigate them around the traffic.

Holding her hand over her mouth in a what-have-I-done gesture, Naomi looked back at the man. "What if I killed him? No, wait…He's moving…I think…"

The distress in Naomi's voice and her rapid breathing released Hannah from her shock at the violence of the incident. She reached out and took her big sister's hand. "If you ever wonder for one second why we need you, Naomi…" Hannah shook her head. "Don't."

"Amen," Rebecca agreed. "They'll think twice before tangling with us again…with you again."

Hannah wondered if that kind of reputation would serve them well in this Sodom or simply invite more trouble.

McIntyre had stepped outside the saloon just in time to see Guibne come flying off the wagon and land in the dirt with a breath-stealing "OOF." The sisters' wagon rolled on and McIntyre honestly wondered if they could make the next fifty yards without any further incidents. Good God, at least he hoped so. He didn't have the men available to assign a security detail to the belles.

Laughing in spite of the potential trouble, he slipped his hat on and strode down to where the offensive little Irishman lay in the dirt. Covering the drunkard with his shadow, McIntyre nudged him with the toe of a perfectly polished deer skin boot.

Guibne looked up, rubbing the back of his head. "Mr. McIntyre, yer new flowers need a wee bit of trimmin', I'd say."

"They're not flowers and they're not for sale." He looked up at the crowd that was still watching the scene play out. "I won't take it too kindly if they're accosted." A few brows rose at the use of the unfamiliar word. McIntyre rolled his eyes. "I do forget the company that I'm keeping." As if speaking to a slow child, he clarified the comment. "Don't touch them. They're not for sale. Pass the word." The crowd was none too happy with the order and disbanded, grumbling at his high-handedness. He waved them off like gnats and went to find his marshal.

As the sisters rode the rest of the way down the street, they didn't speak of Mr. Guibne but Naomi looked over her shoulder several times. The crowd filled in around him pretty quickly and she wasn't able to catch sight of him. She was comforted some by the fact that he didn't leap to his feet declaring his desire for revenge, but she was sick over her brazen, thoughtless tussle with the man. What if he'd had a knife or a gun? Rebecca or Hannah could have gotten hurt. Would this Guibne hold a grudge? Had she humiliated him enough to make him seek retribution?

Dear Lord, what is the matter with the men in this town? she cried in anguish. As if she didn't have enough to deal with, now she was seriously considering wearing John's gun on her hip. She realized in her present state of mind that was akin to throwing a match on a powder keg, but no one was going to hurt her sisters.

No one…

Chapter 9

Naomi, Rebecca and Hannah rode another few feet in silence, though Naomi could tell by their wide eyes and pale faces that her sisters had plenty to say about the run-in with Guibne. Now was not the time. Get indoors, away from all these curious, lewd stares, then they'd—

The wagon pulled up in front of the store, soon to be hotel, their hotel. The building, lapped in golden pine siding, featured four large windows across the front of both floors, sizeable French doors at the entrance, and a large balcony on the second story. The slats in the rail were made of crooked, though skillfully-placed, peeled branches. Unfortunately, the windows and doors were trimmed in that gaudy red.

Rebecca and Hannah nodded and smiled in an apprehensive way. Naomi thought it would do, since she had no choice anyway. An interesting building, she decided. Still rustic but far more finished-looking than most of the other structures in Defiance. It defined the town's transition from mining camp to permanent settlement.

The sisters quietly climbed down, trying to draw as little attention as possible to themselves, and took up positions at the windows. Sheltering their eyes, they each peered into the darkness. Naomi could see empty shelves and, toward the back, a bare counter. An L-shaped set of open-tread stairs hugged the wall on the right, a stone fireplace was built into the left, and a room in the back, which Naomi assumed was Whicker's small apartment, took up most of the rest of the building. Not as wide as the building, though, it left room for a hallway that led to a back door.

Naomi pulled away from the window and watched the passing reflections in the glass. The traffic on this end of the street was noticeably thinner. Perhaps because the buildings off to the immediate left were still under construction. Suited her just fine; maybe this was the quiet part of town. The way her muscles were singing from all this adrenaline, she was eager for some peace. A little hammering and sawing was a pleasant respite from the cat calls and lewd comments.

She leaned her head on the glass again and stared into the store. "Mr. McIntyre guessed it would accommodate a dozen or so tables. I didn't ask how many rooms we could squeeze upstairs."

"So, we've got to renovate and run a hotel." Rebecca snapped her fingers. "Nothing to it."

"What do you think we ought to do first?" Naomi asked, ignoring the sarcasm. By focusing on anything other than their fellow citizens and her gaping heartache, maybe, just maybe, she could manage not to fall apart until later, in private. Out of the corner of her eye she noticed Hannah scratching at her waist, something she had been doing more and more of late.

Puzzled, and interested in observing, she turned and leaned her shoulder on the window. "Get the restaurant up and running first? Even that's going to take some renovation and we've got to get tables and groceries from somewhere…" Hannah was still peering into the building and still scratching. Naomi couldn't take it anymore. Her nerves crawling from stress, she wanted the annoying action stopped. "Hannah, what is the matter with you? Have you got fleas?"

He sister jerked up, embarrassed, and her hand went to her back. "No, I don't have fleas." Her indignation over the question was obvious in her squared shoulders and rigid back.

Abruptly, Rebecca walked over and spun Hannah around so she could see her back. Raising her shirtwaist revealed that two of the buttons on her little sister's skirt were undone and the skirt still looked to be pinching her waist.

Rebecca hung her head. "Oh, honey. Why didn't you tell us?" She offered both her sisters a resigned smile and tried to stifle a laugh. "Hannah here is bursting out of her clothes."

Hannah whirled away angrily. "It's not funny. It's driving me crazy!"

"Simmer down, simmer down," Naomi urged, fighting a grin. "We're going to have to dig to the bottom of the wagon for that box of pinafores and dresses from Ms. Dawn."

Hannah was not amused. "Well somebody better do something or I'm just going to start sporting around in my pantaloons."

The ridiculous and irrational threat brought a snort out of Rebecca. "Trust me, eventually those won't fit you either."

Hannah looked as if she would like to offer another sassy reply, but the sound of boots at the far end of the porch drew their attention. The sisters turned to see Mr. McIntyre approaching with another man, a tall, muscular red-headed gent wearing a badge.

As they stomped up the steps, Naomi thought she saw the slightest limp in Mr. McIntyre's step.

"Ladies," Mr. McIntyre greeted them, taking Hannah's hand first. "I apologize for my rudeness earlier in not doing introductions. I'm Charles McIntyre."

"Well, we were all a little pre-occupied at the time," Hannah forgave. "I'm Hannah Frink." Naomi thought her little sister looked dangerously impressed by Mr. McIntyre's good looks and fancy clothes. He touched the brim of his hat in greeting, but froze before moving on to Rebecca. "Frink. I've heard that name somewhere." He puzzled over it briefly. Raising an eyebrow, he promised Hannah, "It'll come to me. It's an unusual name."

He turned to Rebecca, reaching for her outstretched hand. She smiled coolly at him. "I'm Rebecca Castleberry." Naomi knew that voice: polite but reserved; Rebecca was evaluating this man before she formed an opinion one way or the other.

"A pleasure. This is our town marshal, Wade Hayes."

The young man, his freckled face framed by shoulder-length, shaggy red hair and a beige cowboy hat, winked boldly. "Ladies."

Should we swoon now? Naomi wondered. This town positively overflowed with swaggering, arrogant men. A thought that took her directly back to missing John...

Mr. McIntyre fished the key out of his pocket and shoved it in the front door. "Mrs. Miller, after you've had a chance to look around, if you would be so kind as to accompany me to the bank," he flung the door open and ushered the group inside, "we can sign the papers and conclude our business."

She slid past him without meeting his gaze. "That would be fine." The sooner she was done with Mr. McIntyre, the better.

Hands in his pockets, McIntyre watched the sisters stroll around the large, empty room. Attempting to take his mind off their feminine curves, he tried to guess what they might see in this empty room. Could they imagine dining room tables covered with red-check table cloths, politely chatting customers, the sound of klinking silverware? On the other side of the building, hugging the far right wall, L-shaped stairs wound their way up to the second floor. He could envision the hotel desk sitting right below the landing, a few red velvet chairs and a settee gathered to create a small lobby. At least that was how he imagined it in a few years. To get started, they would have to be satisfied with log benches and mismatched furniture gathered up from everyone in town who owed him money.

"Were you raised by wolves, Mr. McIntyre?" Naomi's haughty tone and impatient glare perplexed him, until he realized she was looking at his hat. Feeling for an instant like he'd been chastised by his mother, he snatched the Stetson off his head.

Huffing, Naomi went back to surveying the new real estate.

The group made their way back to the apartment, but McIntyre saw Naomi consider the marshal who had stayed by the front door, arms folded across his chest as if he was standing guard. He was impressed with her awareness of her surroundings, a skill he'd learned to appreciate during the war. The marshal *had* been ordered to keep an eye out for trouble as McIntyre wasn't completely convinced Guibne was through sulking over his humiliation. McIntyre suspected, though, that if the annoying little Irishman tangled with Naomi again, the outcome would be the same.

Naomi stepped into the small back room and McIntyre heard a sigh of disappointment. He joined her in the doorway and watched as she and her sisters assessed the dirty, dusty little room. Barely larger than a generous parlor, it had one small buck stove anchored against the back wall, a cot shoved up against the far wall, a few cabinets hung entirely too high and a dry sink situated underneath them. Pretty much nothing in it was usable for a commercial kitchen.

After the girls spent a few minutes inspecting the apartment, however, he decided it was time to spell out their next steps. Burning daylight was not something he ever did on purpose.

"My architect, Ian Donoghue, has the finished blueprints for the hotel. I'll send him over tomorrow. Feel free to make changes as you see fit."

Naomi crossed her arms and tapped her foot.

Ignoring the message her drumming fingers were screaming at him, McIntyre casually rocked on his heels and addressed her sisters. "All the carpenters in town work for me, of course."

"Of course," she echoed under her breath.

"So I'll round up a crew to get the renovations started in here. I'll have them build some tables for the dining room until we can get decent ones from Pueblo or Denver. We'll need to draw up a building plan and create a list of supplies for the restaurant."

He looked back at Naomi. "I don't have enough in my store to provide for that, but there is a freight wagon that comes up daily from Silverton and a larger one that comes from Gunnison. I'll get you the names of some reliable grocers, farmers, suppliers, etc."

He wandered over to the one dirty window in the room and looked out on the backyard. Whicker had added a small corral and a lean-to, but there was still a roomy hundred feet or so of grass that rolled down to the banks of the La Plata, a tributary to the Animas River. His leg was weary already and without thinking, dropped his hand down to rub his thigh as he pondered the yard. "Oh, yes, your mules and the horse. If you don't wish to sell straightaway, you can keep them back there for awhile. They're a little footsore but they will sell. Animals are always needed for running the freight wagons—"

Naomi raised her hand, stopping his rapid fire assault of details. "Mr. McIntyre, no one died and made you God. We're not completely helpless and we would like some say in our own plans."

He grinned, amused by her spunk. Turning to her, he brazenly assayed the golden hair, interesting curves, and small waist, then attempted to explain to her how things worked here in Defiance. "I'm the closest thing you've got in Defiance, your Highness, and I'm only trying to help. We'll get more done if you won't try to be such a royal pain in the a—"

"Mr. McIntyre," Naomi interrupted, stopping the profanity. Her cheeks glowing, he wondered if from anger or his appraising eye, she took a step towards him. "Sadly, it is apparent that your help is unavoidable…" She let the insult sink in, then continued, obviously irritated with him. "But we need a few days to…recover from our trip and gather our thoughts. Can you understand that? Sampson was my husband's horse. He loved that animal. I…" She looked for words. "I—we just can't make all these decisions right now." She folded her arms across her chest, sending a clear message. "We need some time."

He looked at the other two, saw the lost and bewildered look in their eyes, and lowered his head. "My most sincere apologies, ladies. I'm a man of action. I don't believe in wasting time or opportunities. However, I should learn to be more sensitive." His eyes swung back to Naomi and he softened his voice. "You've been through a lot…all of you."

Naomi nodded curtly. He assumed she believed his sincere contriteness.

He stepped outside the door, quickly noted that Wade was still stationed at the front entrance then addressed Naomi again. "We can go to my attorney's office whenever you're ready. I'll tell Wade to bring your wagon around back. There's a large stoop just off the back door there," he motioned towards the door at the back of the building. "I'll also send one of my men over to assist with your heavier items."

"That's not necessary," Naomi countered.

"Oh, but I insist. That would be the gentlemanly thing to do…and I don't often get to be one of those."

The fact that Mr. McIntyre didn't often get to act like a gentleman was no one's fault but his own and Naomi came close to telling him that, but bit it back. This man riled her almost more than the hooligans from the street. She hated the way he so easily brought her anger to the surface. Perhaps it was the simple fact that a good man like John was dead and buried and this arrogant scoundrel was still walking around commanding things in this corner of hell.

"If you'll give me a few moments with my sisters, I'll meet you out front." It wasn't a request.

"Very well." In parting, he turned to Hannah and Rebecca and promised firmly, "You needn't fear for your safety in Defiance. What happened with the men today won't happen again. I'll make it clear that you are not to be accosted in any way."

Naomi appreciated him bringing that up and hoped Mr. McIntyre could deliver on the promise. Still, she had the uneasy feeling that the fox was watching the hens.

When he was gone, Naomi fell against a wall, closed her eyes and took a deep breath. It maddened her that she felt she had to be on her guard around him, wary of him as if he were some predator. She was tired and didn't want any more challenges. A lump formed in her throat and she had to fight back tears of exhaustion and frustration. She was tired of crying, downright sick of it in fact, and would be darned if she'd do it right here and now.

Rebecca ambled over and touched the cold buck stove. "We are in so far over our heads."

"Gee, you think?" Naomi retorted, opening one eye to watch her sister.

"Mr. McIntyre seems like he knows what he's doing," Hannah offered, acting as the eternal optimist among them.

"That's what I'm afraid of," Naomi tossed back. She couldn't shake that warning from Mr. Whicker. *If you're not careful, he'll own you too.* The thought rankled her.

Rebecca shrugged in an easy way that reminded them things could be worse. "Well, we just have to let him help us until we've got everything up and running. It's not like we have much choice."

"I suppose, but I don't like it," Naomi huffed, moving away from the wall. "I don't trust him. He struts around like a rooster."

Hannah walked over and took Naomi's hand, then pulled her over to Rebecca. Taking Rebecca's hand, she smiled wearily at her sisters. "We have a roof over our heads, a place to sleep, and food to eat. Mr. McIntyre says we're safe now, too. Why don't we just be grateful for that and not look for trouble?"

Naomi grinned, finding a grain of humor she didn't know she had left. "Roosters fry up the same as hens." She winked at her sisters. "If he gives us too much trouble, we'll just wring his neck, and throw him in the pan."

The bold statement gave them a good laugh, but then Hannah tightened her grip. "Why don't we pray for him first?"

McIntyre stood in the entry way and lit a cheroot. As he pondered his plans and the next steps for his new tenants, he realized he should mention the offer of a bed. He had an exceptionally large one in storage on the second floor and they could certainly make use of it. The thought of telling these proper young ladies what he'd intended to do with the bed made him smile. He was willing to bet such carnal ideas had never entered their pretty little heads.

In spite of the erotic goals for the bed, he thought this was a worthwhile sacrifice. He wouldn't guess how many nights it had it been since these girls had slept in a real one. Feeling generous, he gave the marshal instructions for it as the lawman climbed up into the wagon. As he walked back to tell the sisters, the sound of Rebecca's voice lifted up in prayer stopped him short.

"…and Father, we just ask that you would give us courage as we face the unknown here in Defiance. Help us to rely on You and trust completely in Your plan. We pray especially that You would strengthen Naomi, Father. She has the difficult burden of dealing with grief on top of all the additional challenges of building a new life. But Your word promises us that You won't put more on us than we can bear and we all know how strong You've made her. Give her, give all of us, wisdom and discernment as we deal with each new situation..."

He turned away and walked back to the porch, lost in thought. Suddenly he was ten-years-old again, sweat trickled down his brow and his tie grieved him fiercely. He remembered a preacher, new to Charleston, who had droned on and on in the suffocating August heat about the savior's great sacrifice. Even then McIntyre had been disinclined to accept that Jesus could love the whole human race so much he would willingly die for it. But he also remembered his mother beside him on the pew, lost in prayer, seeking the will of a god who loved *her*.

He cleared his throat. *But apparently no one else*, he mused, thinking over the monstrous acts of violence he had witnessed with his own eyes. God, he had firmly decided years ago, was a crutch for compassionate and genteel women who would never see the things he had seen.

"You all right, boss," Wade asked from the wagon seat "You look sort of like you've seen a rotten carcass."

McIntyre waved at him with that practiced air of dismissiveness. "I'm fine. See to those things I asked you about." Wade nodded and snapped the reins.

Strangely disquieted by the prayer, McIntyre took a puff on the cheroot and wondered if maybe he had made a mistake in letting these women come to his town. The thought was short-lived. How much damage could three Bible-toting, fair-skinned, Southern belles do in a town this mean? They would be lucky to survive it. He would be lucky to keep them from being kidnapped by randy miners or renegade Utes.

Troubled, he rubbed his neck. Yes, indeed, he hadn't thought of that. Muttering a curse, he snuffed the barely smoked cheroot under his boot and decided he would make sure Wade kept an eye on the little angels until further notice.

Chapter 10

As the Conestoga disappeared around the corner, Naomi stepped outside. McIntyre thought she looked, well, refreshed, or at least more relaxed. That was good, considering what was coming. Maybe she wouldn't reach for a gun when she found out the details of this business deal.

"The marshal has taken your wagon around back. I've asked him to find Emilio to help unload the heavy items."

"Thank you," she replied, less haughtily than he expected.

He pointed across the street. "The bank is just over there."

"Well, I'm ready."

As they crossed the street together, McIntyre asked, "When is your sister's baby due?" The stumble and quick clench of her jaw was all he needed to know he was right. He assumed, therefore, he was right about the absent father as well.

"Baby? What baby?" He thought her voice sounded shrill and shaky.

"Come now, Mrs. Miller," he chided as they negotiated street traffic. "You should remember that I have several women in my employ. I notice things about a woman's figure that most men don't."

"What you don't know..." She turned to him as they reached the boardwalk and raked him with an icy stare that would have sent Jesse James running for cover. "Is that not everything in Defiance is your business."

He begged to differ, but didn't say so. He had acquired enough of this woman's animosity and still might have more coming once they were in the attorney's office. Acquiescing only for the moment, he ushered her further down the walk. "You need to learn the difference between friends and enemies, Your Highness. Perhaps the question was rather impertinent of me, but I was thinking of Hannah's wellbeing. Should she need the services of a doctor or midwife—"

"We don't need anything," Naomi spat without looking at him, her lips pulled tight into an angry little line.

He took the hint and changed the subject. "Speaking of health, the man you encountered on the street today—"

"*Which* man? The one who took Hannah's bonnet or the drunk who nearly climbed in the wagon with us?" McIntyre didn't miss the subtle accusatory tone in her voice, as if all the rude behavior in Defiance could be traced back to him.

"Yes, Guibne. He doesn't bring much to this town, but he does have a lot of friends. In a matter of hours it will be all over Defiance that you're not in my employ and neither are you working girls. If there are any further...incidents, I'll see to it that the marshal and his deputies camp on your doorstep."

Naomi looked up at McIntyre with those green eyes that for the first time weren't storming like an angry ocean. For the sweep of an instant, she unexpectedly lowered the veil of defensiveness and sighed, a deep, melancholy sound. "Last July we were harvesting corn, planning picnics, eating watermelon and fried chicken after church. And now..." She trailed off, pain showing itself in her furrowed brow and tense lips.

He wished for something helpful to say but words eluded him. It had been so long since he had been required to offer even the smallest amount of comfort to another human that he felt incapable of it. Anything he could think to say would only earn him a fierce slap across the face and he preferred to delay that as long as possible.

Feeling a tad off balance, he touched her on the elbow and pointed at the next entrance trying to move them past this awkward moment. Opening the door for her, she entered the bank and several men, employees and customers, acknowledged her with appreciative glances. In turn, they also offered greetings to McIntyre as he and Naomi walked toward the back of the bank. They climbed a set of steps that took them to a door labeled Davis Ferrell, Esq.

Naomi didn't speak as she and Mr. McIntyre climbed the stairs. She did inhale his scent of a musky cologne and apple-sweetened tobacco. Pleasing odors even if the man was less-than-likable. She felt completely foolish for having dropped her guard that way, revealing such personal thoughts to this pirate. She attributed her momentary weakness to simply being overwrought with grief...and irritation. It grated on her nerves that he had spotted Hannah's condition right off... which brought her back to the statement he had made about women in his employ. How could he act like running a brothel was as respectable as managing a mercantile? Disgusting. Whatever the case, she would work harder to keep her chin up and back squared in front of this rogue.

They reached the door and Mr. McIntyre knocked but did not wait for an answer as he opened it for Naomi. They stepped into a small office and found Mr. Ferrell at his desk. He looked up from his paperwork, removing the spectacles from his nose.

Remembering his manners belatedly, he leaped to his feet and reached for Naomi's hand. "Pardon my manners. Mrs. Miller, it's a pleasure to meet you. McIntyre," he acknowledged him with a nod and his clients took the two seats in front of his desk.

A skinny but dapper man wearing a plain, grey suite, he moved with swift, jerky motions. Naomi wondered if he was always like that or if Mr. McIntyre made him nervous. "I've just finished up the transfer of deed for the building." He slid a piece of paper over to Naomi and held out his pen. "If you'll write your full name here and here and sign here and here, that will do it."

Naomi took the pen but also took a moment to review the deed. Mr. McIntyre leaned in uncomfortably close to her ear and whispered, "Davis may look and act like Ichabod Crane, but he's quite a gifted attorney."

Frowning, she moved away from his breath ruffling her hair and perused the legal document in her hand. Naomi noticed almost immediately that there was no description of lot size or water rights, only information on the building. "I—I'm sorry," she sputtered puzzled. "This doesn't seem to be complete. Why is there no mention here of the lot size? And there is a well, isn't there?" she asked, eyeing both men.

"Lot size?" Mr. Ferrell repeated questioningly. "I'm not sure I follow. I was under the impression you were getting the building only." He looked at Mr. McIntyre. "You were in a hurry when you stopped by, but I thought I understood it was the building and not the land."

"Not the land?" Naomi repeated toward Mr. McIntyre, knowing there were daggers in her eyes.

"Let me explain," he said, crushing out his cigar in Ferrell's ash tray. "You see, you came and asked to buy the building. You made no mention of the lot. I assumed you didn't need it or want it. This is a common practice here in the west."

Naomi was dumbfounded; struck completely speechless, but only for a moment. The glowing ember of anger in her gut caught fire. Her voice dropped to a deceptive calm as she addressed the attorney. "So we own the building, but not the land on which it sits. Is that right?"

"Yes," Mr. Ferrell answered simply.

She cut her eyes over to Mr. McIntyre. "Why would anyone buy a building and not the land? And why didn't you tell me you were separating the two?" She was furious, but mostly with herself for being so stupid.

"Buying the building without the land keeps things affordable and allows land owners to collect rent. I don't want rent, however. Just think of us as partners in the hotel business."

Naomi jumped up so suddenly, she nearly flipped her chair over. Fuming, she stomped away from the men as far as the little office would allow, all of about six feet. Looking out the window, she couldn't have cared less about the low afternoon sun reaching to kiss the distant shimmering mountains. She could've kicked herself a hundred times for getting in this mess and now she would have to explain it to her sisters. How could she have been so stupid?!

Think, think, think, she told herself angrily, determined to hold back tears or die trying. *Protect yourself. Lord, help me...*

She spun back around. "You are a scoundrel, Mr. McIntyre, but I have learned my lesson about dealing with you. You do want to own everything in this town, don't you?" He dropped his eyes, but only for an instant.

"So this is what *I* want." Though speaking to Mr. Ferrell, she kept her eyes on Mr. McIntyre. "I want it in writing that Mr. McIntyre cannot in anyway restrict us from the well. Also, I want monthly payments that will buy the lot in the space of one year. I'll give you $50 for it."

Mr. McIntyre snorted at the offer, but sobered quickly under her burning gaze. He studied her hard but Naomi didn't wilt or blush under the scrutiny this time. If anything, she straightened up more defiantly.

"All right." He pulled another cheroot out of his pocket. "The lot is a good acre. I'll take one hundred dollars for it."

"Seventy-five," she countered out of pure desire not to be taken advantage of again.

"Split the difference," he offered, striking the match on his boot and lighting the smoke. "Eighty-seven fifty."

"And the water rights," she demanded.

"And the water rights."

This time they shook on the deal. Naomi couldn't help but notice how fine and smooth his hands were, not big and calloused like John's. Funny how hands could speak volumes about a man. She wondered when he had last done some actual physical labor or did he have a "man" for everything?

"It'll take me a few minutes to write that up," Mr. Ferrel reminded them, peering over his spectacles. He looked as if he hoped they might take their obvious differences outside.

"We'll wait," Naomi assured him, fiery resolution in her voice. Mr. Ferrell looked at Mr. McIntyre for the final answer.

He shrugged. "It's fine, Davis. I don't need to be anywhere until 6:30."

"All right then." The attorney sighed and pulled out a fresh sheet of parchment paper. Mr. McIntyre tapped his cheroot on the ashtray then took his smoke to the window.

Naomi settled back into her seat and stared into the top of Mr. Ferrell's head.

"Mrs. Miller, I believe you and your sisters have arrived at an exciting time in Defiance's life," he offered in a conciliatory tone. "Our little town is growing. More people are coming every day. Businesses are expanding. A sixty-foot thick vein of quartz runs underneath our feet. They'll be digging silver and gold out of the ground for another century."

She did not respond to his speech, but he kept going anyway. "We've already got two stages coming in every week. I'm courting the railroad as well. Yes, sir, in the not-too-distant future, Defiance could rival Denver. We have the common goal of seeing your hotel and restaurant succeed. I hope you believe that."

She cut him a disdainful glance. "You're not a complicated man, Mr. McIntyre. You will help us as long as it benefits you. I believe that."

"Then we understand each other."

"Oh, completely." She turned her eyes back to Ferrell and focused again on the top of his balding head.

McIntyre considered how she spoke down to him, as if he were an annoying flea, but once they were passed this paperwork, he was quite sure he could win her over. Granted, she was probably the kind of woman who could hold a grudge for a month of Sundays, but his magnetism, money and power were relentless persuaders. He had charmed feistier women onto their backs and this arrogant, self-righteous little Southern belle would be no different.

On the way back to the hotel, McIntyre made a few more polite attempts to settle their little misunderstanding, but Naomi was having none of it. A stubborn woman, he knew she saw this as an excuse to keep him at arm's length. He thought about reminding her of her Christian duty to forgive trespasses, but decided to stay away from that subject matter. Finally, at the door, he made one more attempt at putting them on some kind of speaking terms. In his experience with Naomi thus far, there was only one thing that got her talking...anger.

"Look, your Ladyship, there's no reason to be upset with me. This mix-up was not intentional. You assumed the land was part of the deal. I assumed you knew what you were doing."

"My name is not your Ladyship!" She snapped. "Or Princess. It's Naomi." She shook her head for correction. "I mean *Mrs. Miller* to you. And *you* were the one who knew exactly what you were doing. But that was the first and last time you will take advantage of us, Mr. McIntyre." Naomi pointed an accusing finger at him for emphasis as her eyes flashed like a storm over the Rockies. "You're a scoundrel and a snake. I won't make the mistake of trusting you again."

He couldn't help but grin. "Now you're getting it. That's the only way to do business in Defiance, much less with me."

Naomi looked stunned. Rolling her eyes and collecting her thoughts, she grabbed the doorknob and spoke without looking at him. "I see. Now, for the next few days at least, could you leave us alone to settle in?"

He understood the reasons for her request and decided to offer some mercy. He had other enterprises that certainly needed his attention as well. Needling this little princess wasn't making him any money, even if it was grand entertainment. Emilio and Ian could keep him apprised of things here.

"As you wish, Mrs. Miller." He tipped his hat and started off for the Iron Horse, but stopped abruptly. "Oh, by the way..." He waited for Naomi to look at him. "I've left you and your sisters a gift upstairs." He flashed his most winning, most rakish smile at her. "Perhaps you'll think of me when you use it."

Chapter 11

When Naomi entered the hotel, she heard a commotion upstairs; voices and what sounded like furniture scraping across the floor. She called out to her sisters and they answered excitedly.

"We're up here, Naomi!"

"Come see what Mr. McIntyre has given us."

Was this the gift he'd mentioned? Tired of the emotional rollercoaster he caused her, she trudged up the stairs and turned the corner of the rail to discover her sisters and a lanky, young Mexican boy assembling a massive pencil post bed. Lying next to it was a gigantic mattress, factory-made and apparently stuffed with something other than cotton rags or corn shucks.

He hoped she'd think of him every time she used it? The audacity, arrogance and lewdness of the comment shocked Naomi. Had the man no decency whatsoever to say such things to a widow? She was utterly appalled.

Eager to forget Mr. McIntyre, she looked around the vast, open space of the upstairs floor which was intermittently broken up by the sparse, unfinished skeletons of walls. The area was warm and dry, though, and would sport a real bed in a few minutes. It was enticing, Naomi admitted grudgingly. Maybe she would actually sleep tonight.

When Hannah looked up and saw Naomi, she dropped the bed rail she was holding and ran to her sister. "You must see this," she commanded joyfully, leading Naomi over to the mattress. "Lie down on it." She pulled Naomi down to the mattress and forced her to recline on it. "Isn't it wonderful?" Hannah flopped down beside her, giggling.

Naomi had to agree it was far more comfortable than the ground underneath a wagon and even beat their cloth tick mattress back home. She closed her eyes and tried to lose herself in the relatively soft bedding, the way it supported and comforted her. Then there was the image of Mr. McIntyre and she sat bolt upright.

She hadn't slept well in over a week and the stress of it was beginning to show. The nights were hideously long. She dreaded the darkness, the silence, the loneliness of them. Would this bed be a magic carpet to dream land? Would she sleep through the night without waking and reaching for John? Tempted, she lay back on the mattress and gave into the experience.

"Naomi, this is Emilio." Rebecca spoke from the other side of the almost complete bed, tightening a screw in the headboard. "Emilio, this is my sister Naomi."

Naomi and Hannah both sat up. Just a gawky teenager, not much younger than Hannah, he dipped his chin and grinned sheepishly. "Hola, senora."

"We just couldn't help ourselves," Rebecca rushed on. "When Emilio told us about the bed, we came right up and started putting it together. I can't wait to sleep in it."

Naomi stood up and pulled a folded piece of paper from her waistband. "I don't know if we own the bed, but we own this hotel." She walked over and set the deed on the dusty windowsill. She decided not to share the story of why they didn't own the land upon which the hotel sat. That could wait.

She turned back to Hannah. "Why don't you and I start unloading the wagon and let them finish here? But don't worry, Rebecca, we'll save the heavy stuff until y'all come down." Naomi looked at Emilio. "Thank you for your help. We appreciate it."

The boy bobbed his head like an excited bird. "De nada."

As Hannah and Naomi strolled down the stairs, Naomi was curious about the boy and how he had come to live in Defiance. "Does Emilio speak any English?"

"A fair amount from what I could tell." Hannah answered. "He seems to get by—"

A knock at the front door as they reached the landing stopped their progress. They could see the shadow of a man through the frosted glass of the French doors.

Hannah quirked an eyebrow, clearly concerned. "Our first guest?"

Not likely, Naomi thought, headed for the door. Wishing she had her gun on her hip, she opened the door to discover the marshal fanning himself with a book. He greeted her with a cocky tip of his hat. "Ma'm. Mr. McIntyre asked that I drop this by to you." He handed her a Montgomery Ward catalog.

Oh, Naomi gasped. She was as pleased to see it as Hannah, who squealed with delight and took it off her hands.

"Thank you, marshal," Naomi quipped, unable to hide a grin over her sister's enthusiasm. Some normalcy in this new life was comforting and

Hannah did love to shop, even if she couldn't buy. "I'm surprised. Are we able to get Montgomery Ward to ship here?"

"Ma'm, there's a sayin' in mining towns: if you've got money, men and mules, you've got the world. There's a saloon over in Eureka that sports a real chandelier, come all the way from London, England around the horn to San Francisco to here. Not one crystal was broke." He smiled as if remembering the grandeur of the light. "The saloon over in Animas Forks has an Italian sculpture of a naked lady—oh, I do apologize, ma'm."

"Thank you, Marshal. You've made your point." She appreciated the apology. Obviously it wouldn't have fazed Mr. McIntyre a bit to share such lewd information. "But why is it that all the finer items go to the saloons?"

The marshal shrugged. "I reckon 'cuz the saloon owners are the only folks plannin' on stayin'. Most folks are just passin' through, lookin' for that big strike."

Naomi chewed her lip, pondering the transient, filthy, ill-mannered population of Defiance. As if reading her mind, the marshal added, "Also, ma'm, I just wanted to remind you that if you've any errands to run, it would be best to get them done before dark. After that, you might be mistaken for..."

"I understand. We were going to try to make the general store before it closes. Do you know what time that would be?"

"Yes'm, six o'clock." He pulled a watch from his vest pocket and flipped the lid open. "It's right now 4:30."

"Thank you again, marshal," she told him, slowly closing the door.

Marshal Hayes tipped his hat, grinned broadly and departed.

~~~

Rose watched the hotel through the telescope in McIntyre's room. The spirits of her ancestors had told her these women would be trouble for her. Her heart had burned with jealousy as she had watched McIntyre let them in the building. Then he escorted the skinny, golden one to the bank. Rose would not stand for another woman near her man; her plans were too delicate to be upset. This town was hers; Mac was hers. The other girls in the garden knew their place. She would teach these *gringa* girls theirs.

In an attempt to keep McIntyre in his, Rose lit a candle and set it on his dresser. Reaching between her breasts and down in her corset, she pulled out a small leather pouch. Working it open, she tapped a tiny amount of the brown powder over the candle. It fizzed and sparkled, then released a heavy, sweet scent into the room.

Rose smiled, confident in her powers and her potions. The scent would relax McIntyre's mind and make her suggestions more enticing to him. Satisfied she had used the right amount, she returned the pouch to her hiding place. It was a powerful mixture of herbs and prayers. One pinch in the candle eased the mind and the muscles. But a slightly larger amount in a glass of whiskey made a man willing to disclose the value of his claim or even how much gold dust he had in his pockets.

The mood set, she reached into a small box of cosmetics she kept on his dresser. She touched up her lipstick, deepening the red of her lips, and sketched a heavy line of coal around her dark chocolate eyes. Surveying her image in the mirror, she untied her sheer white robe and pushed her corset higher to lift her generous bosom.

Turning from side to side, Rose admired her curvaceous lines in the mirror. She liked the way her dark skin glowed against the pink silk undergarments and her eyes flashed a dangerous, consuming fire. She didn't really need the powder, she knew, but the voices encouraged her to trust them for more and more of their knowledge. She was desperate to gain all the knowledge that she could.

Pleased with the image in the mirror, she pulled a jet black curl from behind her neck and draped it down her cleavage like an arrow pointing to naughty pleasures. Rose was hungry for more than knowledge tonight.

A soft tap at the door made her step away from the dresser and slide her robe seductively off one shoulder. She grimaced sourly when little Daisy peaked around the door. "I thought you were Mac," Rose explained with disappointment as the girl let herself in the room.

Daisy's eyes widened. "No, he's still downstairs talking with the man from the stagecoach. He sent me up here to get his mail."

Rose knew she scared the girl. She watched with cruel pleasure as Daisy nervously searched his desk for the letters. *Daisy* was the perfect flower name for this wisp of a girl. She was small, frail, pale and delicate just like a wild daisy. And from what the customers told her, Daisy had all the passion of a dried flower. Not like Rose. She liked the power her long, tall, buxomly body gave her over men. Even McIntyre was weak-kneed around her at times, with or without the powder. Consequently, she could pick and choose her customers; Daisy had to take whatever filthy, drunken miner came her way.

"Daisy," McIntyre called irritably from downstairs. "Hurry up, girl."

"Got them, Mr. McIntyre!" She ran out the door with the mail in her hand, without looking back at Rose.

Rose grinned, delighted with her power and stretched herself out on his sofa. After nearly two years here, things had become routine. He would be up in just a moment, a snifter of whisky in his hand. She would massage his shoulders, then they would move to the bed and make love, the only passion for her since anything after that would be work, then they would sleep for awhile. At least, *he* would sleep.

Rose would stay awake, whispering dark prayers over him, prayers passed down from Mayan mothers to their daughters for centuries. When she uttered the words of her ancestors, she could hear their voices, and they would tell her things. Show her things. Someday, Defiance, McIntyre and all he owned would be hers. The voices had told her so. They had also told her to rid Defiance of the gringas as quickly as possible.

McIntyre entered the room, glanced at Rose, then went to his desk and sat down. Her brow furrowed with uncertainty. She had seen something in his eyes just then she didn't like. Had it been boredom? Disappointment? Something else? Deciding to overcome it, she rose and glided over to him. As he studied the liquor inventory, she rubbed his shoulders, reaching deep into the muscles, opening his mind to the scent in the air.

"Tell me about the gringa women," she purred in a silky Latin accent. He was more tense than usual. "Do they upset you? Your muscles are like guitar strings."

He slapped his pencil down. "They do not upset me."

Afraid of losing the moment, she moved to a fresh set of muscles, kneading them, caressing them. Slowly, she felt the tension turn to liquid and drain away. He leaned back in his chair, inhaled deeply and let her work her magic.

"They are sisters," he murmured, enjoying the feel of her hands, something he had not initially welcomed and that had puzzled him. "The middle one, I think, she lost her husband back on the trail. The other two aren't married." He almost mentioned the pregnancy, but tonight he was not interested in giving Rose fuel for the gossip fire.

"Did you offer them jobs? I saw them here earlier."

"Women like that don't work in saloons." He rolled his head around, loosening the tense muscles. "Bible-toters we call them. They think *God* told them to settle here in Defiance, so I gave them Whicker's building. The town needs decent women."

"Decent," Rose scoffed. "They sound crazy. And any woman, desperate enough, would work here for you, my love," she whispered, snaking her hands across his chest. He almost argued with her, but instead decided to fall into the hunger her shameless hands evoked. Rose with her dark skin, dangerous eyes and unabashed passion was a wonderful diversion. She could always take his mind off everything else and drown him in his own desires.

Nearly always.

~~~

The day was fading quickly and Rebecca and Naomi were running out of time to make a trip to the mercantile. They insisted this would be the time for Hannah to get some rest while they ran the errand. Helping Hannah into the bed for a nap, Naomi pulled a quilt up to her little sister's chin. "You relax, sleep if you can, and when you wake up, we'll have dinner ready."

Hannah wiggled down into the covers, undid one more button on her skirt and exhaled in obvious pleasure. Compared to the hard ground, Naomi figured a feather mattress had to make Hannah feel as if she was floating. "This is wonderful," her sister confirmed in a dreamy voice. "Heavenly, in fact. When was the last time we slept in a bed?"

Naomi leaned on the post at the end of the highly prized piece of furniture and stared at the wall. "Four hundred miles back." Time stopped for Naomi as she allowed memories of John to flood in. "The hotel in Denver. That was the last time we had a real bath, ate off china instead of tin plates..." Made love with her husband...

When she looked down again at Hannah, her sister was sleeping serenely. Naomi envied the peaceful oblivion her sister had found.

Emilio had insisted on walking with Naomi and Rebecca to the general store, telling them that if they didn't need his help, he would go on home.

Secretly Naomi was glad for the escort, even though she figured the lanky teenager wouldn't exactly intimidate a determined miner. She was tired of fighting this town but she refused to let it bully her.

They kept their heads down, bonnets hiding their faces and hurried through the crowd. A few men called to them, some whistled, a handful even followed from a distance, but no one attempted to stop them. Naomi could hear the whispers, though, as if the men were debating the repercussions of approaching them.

"Naomi, we didn't finish unloading the wagon, but I'm afraid something's missing." Naomi didn't miss the trepidation in her sister's voice. "I didn't see the box with the pinafores, dresses, and baby clothes in it."

Naomi tugged on Rebecca's sleeve and motioned with her eyes over her shoulder to Emilio. The less he knew the better. "I thought you said you packed it."

"I said I'd tend to it, but it was too heavy. I asked Hannah to ask John to load it."

Good grief, Naomi fretted. Had they gone off and left every stitch of motherly clothes for Hannah? And all those baby items from Suzy?

She shook her head. "If we forgot that, we've got a problem on our hands. You know I can't sew very well."

Rebecca chuckled. "I can, little sister. It will be all right."

As they discussed their plans without mentioning Hannah's condition, Marshal Hayes materialized out of nowhere. With a cocky tip of his hat, he fell into step beside Naomi and Rebecca. "Afternoon, ladies. Allow me to escort you on your errand." He glanced back at Emilio. "I think you could do with a bit more size to your bodyguard."

Naomi cut her eyes at her sister and responded to the marshal's request with ingrained politeness. "Oh, that's not necessary, Marshal." Then she remembered where they were. "Is it?"

"There's talk of a rematch between you and Guibne, but this time in the Pit. Does that answer your question?"

"The Pit?"

"In a minin' town, men'll fight just about anything and pay to see it. Drunk enough, I could see'em cartin' you off to our little arena. Which is one of the reasons Mr. McIntyre asked me to keep an eye on you and your sisters. By and by, the men'll get used to you being here and come to understand you're not," he lowered his voice, "loose women."

By and by? And just how long would that be? Naomi wondered.

Her question was cut short by a blood-curdling scream from somewhere in front of them. Abruptly they were confronted by an unmoving wall of plaid and leather-covered backs. The men were watching something, but Naomi and Rebecca couldn't see a thing. Instinctively, Noami put out her hand to halt her sister. The outburst was instantly followed by another, yet this voice was different. Naomi quickly realized the screams had come from women, but they had been filled with rage not fear.

Chapter 12

"Fight!" A man yelled, and the cry galvanized the witnesses. As if the crowd was one body, it surged to the edge of the boardwalk, sandwiching Naomi and Rebecca between smelly, cheering men practically quivering with excitement.

The marshal muttered, "Uh, oh," and pressed his way through the spectators, emerging onto the front row. Through the shifting bodies, Rebecca caught a flash of red and blue silk and what looked like gyrating ostrich feathers. She heard several slaps accompanied by astonishingly skilled swearing, grunts and more screams of rage. She'd never heard women carry-on so and kept thinking it couldn't be what it sounded like.

Curious, she, Naomi and Emilio wiggled their way to the front as well and beheld an eye-gouging, hair-pulling, fingernail-breaking catfight that would have rivaled mountain lions battling to the death. Two women, both barely dressed, circled each other warily. Blue and pink silk dresses hung in shreds from their bodies, feathers poked wildly from disheveled brown and blond hair, blood dribbled from noses and mouths. Everyone within sight of this hellish battle was frozen to the spot. The women lunged at each other and a raucous cheer went up from the crowd as nails sank into flesh.

Trying to work her hands around the blonde's throat, the brunette, fire blazing in her eyes, called the girl an unholy name, and demanded her money. "That's my fifty dollars and I'll get it if I have to follow you all the way to Denver!"

The blonde responded by slapping the woman's face so hard Rebecca was sure the sound could be heard at the other end of town. The girl then made an attempt to run, but the brunette grabbed a handful of hair and pulled her right back into the fight.

Rebecca was appalled by the barbarous display and was sure the marshal would put an end to it any minute. However, when she glanced over at him, he was grinning and shadow-boxing with glee. Rebecca, furious and for once reacting faster than Naomi, reached over and grabbed his arm. "Why aren't you doing something? Stop this before someone gets hurt."

"Ah, that's just Diamond Lil and one of her girls. She don't usually hurt'em too bad. It'll be over in another minute."

Naomi blinked, as if she'd been hypnotized by the melodrama, and shoved the marshal toward the street. "Do something or we will."

He withstood the shove, holding his ground, but Naomi scowled and shoved again. "I doubt Mr. McIntyre would appreciate it if we became embroiled in that."

That was enough to plant doubt in the marshal's mind. Frowning his disapproval, he looked into the crowd. "Come on, Floyd." He plucked a short, pudgy man from the front lines. "Help me break this up." Floyd looked perplexed by the request, but shrugged and followed the marshal into the street.

The women were on the ground now, rolling about like entwined, murderous snakes. The marshal grabbed the brunette, apparently Diamond Lil, and pulled her, kicking and screaming, off the little blond. Floyd grabbed the girl on the ground and helped her to her feet. Scratched and bleeding, she stared defiantly at the wild cat in the marshal's arms.

"All right, Lil!" He pinned the woman's arms to her side and hugged her tightly, picking her up off the ground. She fought harder and screamed louder. He squeezed harder, to the point, Rebecca guessed, her breathing was constricted. That did the trick and the fight went out of the woman. A disappointed roar shot up from the crowd, but the men quickly started drifting away.

The marshal relaxed his grip ever so lightly. "Now, Lil, you and what's-her-name go on back to Tent Town. Keep your trouble over there. You know Mr. McIntyre doesn't like this kind of stuff spillin' out here in front of God and everybody."

The two women singed the air with their hateful stares, but after an instant, Lil shrugged herself loose from the marshal. "Fine, we'll take care of this like ladies." No one missed the dripping sarcasm, including the marshal.

"Floyd, see to it they get back to the Wolf's Head in one piece."

The man brightened and released his delicate hold on his prisoner. "Fine with me. I needed a drink anyway."

And just like that, things were back to what passed for normal in Defiance. Naomi looked at Rebecca and shook her head. "These people act like animals." She shot Emilio an accusing stare. "Is it like this all the time?"

Pulling his shoulders up sheepishly, he nodded. "Ees Defiance."

Leaping up on the boardwalk, the marshal rejoined them, wearing a pleased expression. "Happy, ladies?"

Rebecca's mouth dropped open. "No, Marshal, we're not. Do you have no respect whatsoever for the badge you're wearing?" Marshal Hayes' face fell. "You're not doing your job."

A righteous indignation surfaced in Rebecca's heart and she decided to let it square her shoulders. It had been a long time since she'd been passionate about anything.

Standing to her full, impressive height, Rebecca took a step closer to the marshal, coming almost eye-to-eye with him. "That star on your chest is not a piece of jewelry. If you have any honor at all, then you know it's a *responsibility*." Turmoil filled the marshal's eyes. He opened his mouth to speak then snapped it shut.

Rebecca nodded. "I see."

"No, you don't." A kind of regret softened the younger man's features. "I'm no Wyatt Earp. Defiance has doubled in size since I put this here badge on. There are eight saloons now and a mine that runs twenty-four hours a day. If I tried to settle this town down on my own, I'd be dead before the next shift change."

Rebecca understood the young man was trying to tell her he was not a hero, but he was in over his head. She sympathized with that feeling and lowered her chin, letting some of the steam out of her anger. Taking Naomi's hand, she pulled her wide-eyed sister away from the humbled marshal. "Let's finish our errands before the next show."

The sisters gave one last glance to the street and the retreating saloon girls, still eyeing each other warily, and separated by a cautious Floyd. Disgusted, Naomi shook her head. What in the world was the matter with these people? Was there some beacon that called all the worst elements of society into this valley? Or did Defiance itself corrupt its citizens? Momma would have used the word *trash* to describe folks like this. Well, they were up to their eyeballs in it.

Women fighting in the streets like rabid dogs. Men cheering it on as if it were a boxing match. She still couldn't believe it. With each passing minute she could feel her heart hardening toward the filthy, opportunistic, immoral citizenry. Still, it had been impressive to see Rebecca react to something.

Naomi couldn't remember the last time her older sister had given anybody a good tongue-lashing.

The marshal and Emilio in tow, the sisters marched across the street to a building labeled Boot and Co. General Store. Two frightfully rotund Indian women sat out front with baskets of colorful, fresh berries for sale. Naomi looked longingly at the blueberries as they passed by and knew they would have to purchase some.

Once in the store, she and Rebecca looked around and were quite impressed with the well-stocked inventory. To their delight, the general store, though little more than a large log cabin, carried an abundant supply of fresh fruits and vegetables, a plethora of canned goods, and a remarkable selection of hardware and smoked meats.

Pleased with the inventory, Naomi glanced at the marshal with raised eyebrows. "Money, men and mules?"

The marshal nodded. "Money, men and mules." Folding his arms over his chest, he smiled, looking pleased that he'd proven his point. "Defiance might be a rowdy hole-in-the wall, but we do like our supplies."

~~~

Hannah was still sleeping when the sisters returned. Anxious about disturbing her, Naomi suggested they cook dinner outside over a fire one last time. The marshal excused himself, citing important duties, and Emilio started to slink away as well, but the girls weren't about to let him go without showing their appreciation for his help.

"Emilio, you must eat dinner with us," Rebecca coaxed, taking a box of groceries from him and setting them on the kitchen floor. "We'd love to have you stay if you don't have a better offer."

Naomi could see clearly that the boy was waffling and pushed him over the edge. "We insist. If you wouldn't mind chopping a few pieces of firewood, I'll get some rocks to ring a pit."

"Ok," he acquiesced, bobbing his head. "Eef you're sure ees OK?"

The warm smiles of his hostesses pretty much answered that question. Rebecca stayed inside to put some things away and check on Hannah while Naomi and Emilio hunted around for the ax. Whicker had left a fairly impressive pile of unsplit logs, but Naomi knew just from Southern winters, it wouldn't be enough.

Once their new helper was on task, she appraised the backyard. Whicker had slapped up a small corral and a rickety lean-to, both of which she had initially categorized as an eyesore. Now she was grateful for them. The chickens, in cages tucked under the lean-to, squawked and clucked when they saw her, eager for some corn. Sampson and the mules trotted over to the fence, neighing expectantly for their evening meal. She let her eyes roam past them to settle on the wagon, sitting alone and unhitched. It plucked a string of sadness in her. Would they ever use it again?

Fighting a melancholy mood that threatened to drown her, she meandered down to the stream and watched the sun balance precariously for a moment on the ridge of the distant mountains before its final descent for the evening. The mountains glowed a radiant purple in the retreating light and the disappearing sun colored the snowy peaks a pale shade of orange. The peaceful landscape gave her spirit rest. In spite of everything that had brought them here, everything they'd seen, she couldn't help but feel these mountains somehow ministered to her soul. If only John could be sitting here with her now…

Looking for some solace in the picturesque view, she sat down on a log by the water's edge. Closing her eyes, she lost herself in the sound of the rippling stream and warmth of the fading sun.

"Naomi, I thought you were going to bring up some rocks to ring the fire." Rebecca dropped down on the log beside her. Naomi didn't respond to the ribbing and kept her eyes shut, unwilling to give up this moment of peace and the tenuous control on her emotions. She felt Rebecca settle in closer to her. They sat in silence for several long minutes, lost in their thoughts. Barely audible over the rippling stream, they could hear the steady whack of Emilio's ax.

After a brief respite from reality, Naomi spoke without opening her eyes. "I still can't believe…any of this." Rebecca didn't reply, but Naomi knew she was listening. "What in the world are we doing here of all places?" A rhetorical question, she didn't expect an answer and turned the conversation to something more shallow. "I asked Mr. McIntyre to leave us alone for a few days. He's so arrogant I can hardly abide him."

There was no passion in her voice, just fatigue. Naomi thought of him as yet another knot to untie in this new upside-down life of theirs, a life in which everything that mattered to Naomi had been stripped away. "He's got all kinds of plans for us, but he won't take advantage of us again."

"I would wager that," Rebecca agreed. "Mr. McIntyre most likely doesn't understand that once someone falls out of your good graces, it's nigh unto impossible to get back in." Then she added soberly, "Better we learned now than later."

Naomi agreed, seeing the value of that observation. "You're right. We have the upper hand now." Feeling resolved, she stood and brushed off her skirt. She noted the brown calico was just about at the end of its life and Rebecca's hem was in tatters. Truthfully, they all needed some new clothes. "We'd better get to cooking."

Night had descended by the time they were all sitting down to supper. Naomi had gone to the extra work of finding unsplit logs to drag up and set around the fire creating a cozy little patio of sorts. She couldn't believe after months of camping, that she still had a desire to experience these mountains by starlight. Cool and clear, summer nights in the Rockies suited her perfectly. She didn't care if she ever sweated through the suffocating humidity of the South again.

They ate hungrily, especially Emilio, and the girls couldn't help but notice.

Hannah swirled a biscuit around her plate as she studied him. "Emilio, do you have family in town?"

"Si," he nodded, popping a piece of ham in to his mouth. "My seester ees here too."

"Oh, that's nice. What does she do?"

He stopped chewing abruptly, then slowly shrugged and swallowed. "She work for Meester McIntyre, too."

They knew enough by his reaction not to follow that line of questioning, but Naomi couldn't help but wonder why he was so hungry. "Where do the two of you stay? Who cooks for you?"

"I have a cot in the back room at the Iron Horse and Rose has a nice room upstairs. She brings me food from Martha's Kitchen or sometimes leftovers when she cooks for Meester McIntyre."

Naomi had noticed Martha's Kitchen on their way in. It was a dirty, slapped-together, open-air "restaurant" just a few buildings up the street.

Men ate on long tables out in front of it while a woman walked around with a pot dropping unappetizing mush onto the customers' plates. No wonder the child was half-starved. And he slept in the back of a saloon. Pitiful.

Naomi watched shock and compassion over Emilio's situation travel across her sisters' faces. She knew they were losing their hearts. "I don't mean to pry, Emilio," Rebecca pressed, "but where are your parents?"

He rested his plate on his knobby knees and thought for a moment. "Banditos burn our farm and shoot my parents when I was five." He shrugged. "I don't remember Mama and Papa. The men who burned us out made us go with them. We lived with them for a long time. I don't know, maybe cinco—um, five or six years. Then one night, Rose and I leave." He greedily scraped up some rice and cleaned his plate, satisfaction evident in the shadows on his face. "We found Defiance, um, I theenk two years ago."

Rebecca pursed her lips thoughtfully for a second. "What is it that you do for Meester—er, I mean, *Mr.* McIntyre?" Naomi and Hannah grinned at the slip. The boy's thick accent was infectious and endearing.

"Whatever he saze. Today, he say, help the seesters. Do what they say."

Rebecca nodded. "Well, Emilio, we hope that he lets you come back tomorrow. You've truly been an invaluable help, but please know there is always room for you at our table whether you work or not. Will you come to supper again sometime?"

The boy turned shy and awkward. He looked down and scratched his knee through holey trousers. Naomi could see he was struggling with the invitation and the unexpected friendship behind it. She was rather surprised herself by her enjoyment of his company, but he was such a sweet, unassuming boy. And he had been a tremendous help. She thought he was as out of place in Defiance as the three of them.

"We hope you'll come back to our table lots of times," Hannah invited between bites. "It's good to have a friend in town."

Scratching nervously at his collar, Emilio rose to his feet. "Eef I say to Meester McIntyre that you need more help, this would be true, yes?"

"Oh, yes," the sisters chorused.

"You've been more help than we can tell you," Rebecca chirped, an earnest plea in her voice.

The boy nodded resolutely. "Then I tell Meester McIntyre that." Quickly, he turned, set his plate on his seat and disappeared into the darkness, apparently taking a back trail to the saloon.

The boy's abrupt departure puzzled the girls. Listening for his footsteps to fade, the three sat quietly around the fire, but the quiet stretched on. Staring up at the stars, Naomi assumed they were all speculating about the future. Or perhaps knowing that they had a warm bed to sleep in made it easier to dawdle outside beneath this stunning canopy.

She had an urge to talk about the day, the rude men, the fighting prostitutes, but decided not to bring up any of it. Naomi felt so emotionally fragile, that she worried any talk about their current circumstances might break down her defenses. She needed to be alone before she thought any more about that.

Eventually, as they sat there, they became aware of the rising volume of noise in the town. Naomi had assumed with darkness Defiance would settle down a bit; if anything, it was more rowdy. Listening to the fire pop and hiss, they could clearly hear a raucous, non-stop piano belting out half-recognizable tunes down at the Iron Horse Saloon, accompanied by drunken laughter, raised voices, and the shrill giggles of tipsy women. From the street, the jangle of wagons and clip-clop of horses were punctuated by yelling, cursing and the thud of fists on flesh. Sounds they had heard throughout the day, but now they seemed twice as loud and a hundred times more frightening.

Naomi imagined the presence of something evil swirling around them and questioned if she was losing her grip on reality. Was she so rattled by everything that she was becoming paranoid? Or was it wise concern for their safety?

Hannah looked off in the distance, fear showing in her eyes. "It's noisy isn't it? Will they do this all night long? Be so rowdy?"

Naomi poked the fire and watched the sparks swirl towards heaven. She suspected the party was just getting started. "I fear it will."

As if she needed something else to keep her awake. Re-living the accident, feeling John's crushed skull beneath her fingers, had been enough to destroy her sleep. Now she was worried about unwelcome visitors in the night. Should they post a guard?

"Rebecca, why don't the two of you head off to bed? I'm going to stay up awhile."

~~~

Emilio made his way back to the Iron Horse as inconspicuously as possible. He took the trail down by the stream but when he encountered an amorous couple, cut back up between the clothing store and leather repair shop. Hugging the storefronts and keeping his head down, he hoped to avoid any drunks who might think he would be an amusing diversion. In the last year, he had been beaten, thrown into a horse trough and hung upside down from the hay lift down at the livery.

And even after all that, he could still distinguish between good and bad gringos, not like Rose who lumped them all together. The sisters were very kind and he knew it came from their hearts. His sister Rose told him repeatedly all gringos were bad, except apparently for Mr. McIntyre.

Moving fast and sure like a little mouse, he shot through the bat wing doors of the saloon and snaked his way around crowded tables back to the storage room. The Iron Horse was a noisy, boisterous, smoke-filled heap of smelly humanity, but he had learned long ago how to shut it out and sleep like a baby. He went straight to his cot and slid underneath the thin, worn blanket. He knew Rose would eventually show up with some food, but he didn't want it and he didn't want to talk to her. If he was asleep, she would set the food on the shelf and leave it for him...maybe.

He turned his back to the door and searched for sleep, but his mind kept going back to the three sisters. They had been so kind to him, not treating him like a worthless Mexican at all. In the short time he had helped them, they had shown him kindness, spoken nicely to him, thanked him repeatedly for the smallest effort and even shared their food. They made him feel...welcome.

"Emilio," snapped Rose, bursting through the door. "Wake up you lazy rat." Irritably, she snatched the blanket off him and threw it on the floor. "Get up," she ordered again, setting the plate in her hand down on a barrel and lighting the small lamp on the wall. Unwillingly, Emilio sat up and looked at his sister. She was wearing a faded yellow gown cut so low he thought her breasts might fall out if she breathed wrong. Her hair was twisted up in an elegant style, but she looked cheap and worn. Every day, more and more, it looked to him like her beauty was fading away, leaving something dark and angry in its place.

She sat down on a stool across from his cot. "I told you to find me before you went to bed. Tell me about the gringas."

He ran his hands through his black hair, frustrated with his bossy sister. "I don't know. They seem very nice. What ees it you want to know?"

She sighed and looked around, probably for something to throw at him. "Idiota," she growled. "I want to know more. Where do they come from? Why are there no men with them? Why are they in the old general store?"

Emilio racked his brain, trying to put together the little s of conversation he had heard. His English wasn't as good as Rose's, but he caught the gist generally. "They come from some place called North Carolina but were on their way to California. The skinny one, Senora Naomi, her husband died on the trail. I don't think there are any men with them.

"They're going to turn the store into a cantina." No, what was the word? "Restaurant. A restaurant and a hotel. That's all I know. But they want me to help again mañana."

Rose fiddled with the little gold crucifix at her neck. Emilio thought she looked worried, but momentarily an evil expression slithered across her face.

She smiled, but it was more like a sneer. "Surely it wouldn't be too difficult to get them to continue on their way to California. They just need to understand how inhospitable Defiance can be."

Emilio didn't miss the promise of violence. Though he knew better, he argued, "You should leave them alone. They don't want any trouble."

Angrily, Rose grabbed her brother's jaw and shoved him down into his cot, her eyes burning with hate. Gouging her fingers into the soft flesh of his cheeks, she hissed, "Did I ask for your opinion? Tell me something like that again and I'll gut you like a pig."

Giving him one last, vicious squeeze, she stood up and straightened her gown. "Sleep tight." Chin in the air, Rose turned and opened the door into the light and smoke. As she closed it, Emilio heard her laugh throatily at some customers, as if he was the furthest thing from her mind.

He rose from the bed and snuffed out the light. Furious and frustrated, he peered through a crack in the door and watched her swish and sway through the crowd, choosing a few customers to pay her way for the evening. At fourteen, Emilio was a man and knew he could take his sister; he didn't have to live under her fist. But he also knew, if they ever fought, he would have to kill her, such was her blood lust. He had seen her fight before and knew this to be true. No, better to stick with his original plan: keep saving up then just slip away one night.

Chapter 13

Naomi sat by the fire for a long while, her mind mercifully blank as she stared into the flames and glowing, orange embers. She dared not think about the most recent events. Not yet, at least. Instead, she felt around, searching for a pleasant, harmless memory. From the darkness, Sampson neighed and snorted contentedly, pushing her in the right direction.

She saw John riding his favorite mount into the backyard and right up to where she had been beating a rug without mercy. He trotted up so close she could feel Sampson's breath on her neck, then slid down from the saddle and swept Naomi up into a spinning embrace.

He laughed foolishly, almost hysterically as he held her tightly. "I asked for a piano and God gave us a wagon!"

His laughter was contagious and Naomi couldn't help but join in, albeit with bemused confusion. When he smacked a big, wet, silly kiss on her, Naomi pushed away with as stern a look as she could muster and threw up a hand to stop him from grabbing her again. "Now, hold on a minute, John Robert Miller! What is going on here?"

Laughing with abandon, he pushed past the hand and pulled her into a firm embrace and spun her around again as if she weighed no more than an arm load of cornstalks. Struggling to bring his giggles under control, he looked her in the eye and reported gleefully, "If I had tried, I probably wouldn't have been able to find a long-haul wagon for sale within a hundred miles of here, and James Maynard has one right down the road.

"A freight wagon?" Naomi still did not see the reason for his euphoria.

"A Conestoga. The best wagon ever made for hauling a family, not just freight. I was worried it might take days if not weeks to modify our farm wagon and I don't think Page will give us that kind of time. This wagon eliminates all the delays. It's a sign, woman. A sign. I asked God to drop a piano on me so I'd know we were doing the right thing. We've made the right decision to sell out and go to California. I know it now, just as surely as I know my own name."

He hugged her hard again and this time she allowed herself to melt to him. His excitement was so child-like, it gave Naomi a great deal of pleasure to see him this happy. But it worried her, as well.

"John, have you been so unhappy here?"

"No, no." He held her tighter to emphasize his answer. "I've been truly content here with you, Naomi. If you said right now that you didn't want to go, for whatever reason, then that would be that. We'd try to stick it out here with Hannah."

"It's just that the West beckons to me. There's a tug I can't deny. If I can take my family with me, then I'll go. That's the *only* way I'll go."

He kissed the top of her head as she snuggled deeper into his chest. "Wither thou goest, my love," she whispered softly. "Wither thou goest."

She squeezed him again, then stepped back some so she could see his face to tell him about Kate Page dropping by for a visit. "We had a few folks stop by today. You'd be interested in the second one." He held on to her, obviously not willing to let her go quite yet. "Kate came for a visit."

Stunned, he dropped his arms from around her and moved away so he could take in the whole picture. "Kate Page? What in the world did she want?"

"Initially, she wanted us to talk Hannah into taking some money to leave town. She pretty much offered any amount it would take. She's afraid that if Hannah doesn't leave, it may be years before Frank let's Billy come home."

"She sounds desperate."

"She is and she's pitiful." Naomi shook her head. "She worships her children, especially Billy. I took pity on her and told her you were going to suggest a selling price for our farms to Frank. If he took it, then she would have Billy home in no time. I suggested she use her spousal influence to talk him into accepting our price."

"What'd she say?"

"She said if Frank didn't take the offer, she would, with her own money."

Brow furrowed, John went and sat down on the back steps. "Kate's desperation has me second guessing our plans. It seems cruel to take advantage of her pain. I wanted to take a bite out of Frank, not his innocent wife."

Naomi joined him on the steps. "You know, I asked her if she'd thought even once of helping Hannah if she stayed in town. This look crossed her face like I'd just asked her to eat a snail. I took that as a no."

"They won't always be so high-and-mighty. Something will happen to break them," John observed, sounding a little prophetic. "Something always does."

Naomi leaned back on one elbow and watched John think. His mind was racing, she could tell, but for the moment she allowed herself to concentrate on the sprigs of blonde hair poking out from beneath his hat, the dimpled chin, those broad, strong shoulders, and arms that were the size of small trees. He was big, he was strong and he was perfect. And she'd known all along he would go to Page with a reasonable price on the farm. Her heart swelled with pride.

She saw him smile and knew that he knew she was watching him.

"Like what you see," he asked huskily.

"Have I ever told you that you are perfect?" She had the desire to curl up in his lap like a contented housecat.

A shot of lightning coursed through her when he turned those lusty blue eyes in her direction. He slid up alongside her, resting on an elbow as well. Face to face with him, Naomi had to fight to keep from losing her concentration. He kissed her and she felt the inviting softness of his lips. It was like a drop of water to a parched man lost in the desert. He encircled her and pulled her on top of him, his mind now distracted with things closer to home.

Hypnotic eyes, filled with desire, lassoed her will as he spoke in a husky voice. "Do you know what I'd like to do right now?"

"Well, I sure hope it's chores," Hannah quipped sarcastically from behind them. "Otherwise, I'd better leave."

Naomi and John jumped up as if they'd been shot out of a cannon. Naomi was sure they had never moved so fast as they straightened and tucked their clothing and smoothed down loose hairs. Despite the awkwardness of the moment, Hannah laughed richly, obviously enjoying their embarrassment.

"That's not funny," Naomi scolded. She looked at John and realized her cheeks were probably as bright as his. "What are you doing, sneaking up on us like that?"

Hannah shoved her hands onto her hips. "I cleared my throat but neither one of you heard me. Honestly, ya'll need a fence if you're going to roll around in your backyard like that."

"We weren't rolling around," John argued, but the laugh escaped his lips before he could finish the sentence. Undeniably caught in the act, he chuckled with resignation. "Well, I believe my work here is done. I'll go take care of Sampson."

As he walked by Hannah, he tossed her a mischievous little wink and strode on to the barn, Sampson dutifully following behind.

Hannah pushed past her sister heading for the back door. "Good grief, Naomi, you two act like you got married yesterday."

Still watching her husband, Naomi sighed, a dreamy, contented sound. "He's wonderful isn't he? I don't know what I'd do without him."

"Probably more housework." Hannah's sarcastic suggestion was followed by the slam of the screen door.

Naomi laughed aloud at the memory, longing for the easygoing life they all once shared. The reality of her own observation though, offered so lightly then, hit her with the force of a sledgehammer.

I *don't* know what to do without him.

A cloudburst of self-pity unleashed itself on her. John was dead. Hannah was with child. They were trapped in this horrible town. Mr. McIntyre was the devil in fancy clothes and the citizens conducted themselves with the grace and manners of wolves. She was sick of it…sick of it all.

Naomi knew she should pray…knew she should try to square her shoulders and face up to things. Instead, she put her face in her hands and wept with all the fury of a bursting dam.

~~~

Because of the surprising morning chill outside, the sisters used the little buck stove in the apartment to whip up some eggs and country ham. As Rebecca and her sisters sat on the floor cross-legged, eating hungrily, if not lady-like, they discussed the whereabouts of their stationary. Letters needed to be one of their first priorities.

Rebecca watched Naomi listlessly twirl scrambled eggs around her plate as they discussed who they should write. Of course, the obvious choice for the first letter was Matthew, John's brother, but Naomi didn't offer his name. Rebecca knew Naomi would write the letter but it would have to be in her own good time. Wanting to do her part, she volunteered to pen a letter to Pastor and Ruby. Hannah wanted to write her friend Suzy.

As they tossed around possible locations for their paper and ink, a man's voice calling from out front interrupted their discussion.

"Hellooo in the house," a heavy Scottish brogue quearied. "Ladies, are ye decent or shall I come back?"

Rebecca, closest to the door, leaned out and looked the man over carefully. "Can we help you?"

He snatched a strange-looking cap off his head and crammed it into his hands, where he was already holding a long roll of paper. "Ian Donoghue. I'm the architect Mr. McIntyre told ye about."

He was a tall, older gentleman, nicely dressed, handsome, but with grayish, thinning hair on top and a thickening waist covered by a colorful argyle sweater. "I'll come back if now's no' a good time. It's just that McIntyre asked me to jump right on this."

"I guess now is all right." Rebecca glanced back at Hannah and Naomi to be sure. They agreed readily enough with subtle nods and Rebecca scrambled to her feet. Stepping out in the hall, still holding her plate, she motioned toward the kitchen. "We're just having some breakfast. Can I fix you something, Mr. Donoghue?"

He walked quickly back to where she was and took her hand. "Ye are..."

"Rebecca Castleberry." She ushered him into the little room where Hannah and Naomi were climbing to their feet to greet their guest. "These are my sisters Naomi Miller and Hannah Frink."

"No, no. This willna do." His unexpected response drew quizzical looks from the girls. "Emilio," he called over his shoulder. They heard the front door open and the boy came running. "I canna work without a table and chairs. Go to Mr. McIntyre and tell him that *exactly*."

"Si, senor!" The boy practically lunged for the front door.

Ian turned back to the girls and winked. "Tis a true pleasure to meet ye. Now, I've had my breakfast..." His eyes sought Rebecca. "I could, however, do with a wee bit more o' coffee."

She smiled brightly at him. "Coming right up." She hurried to the back wall, rummaged through a wooden box sitting next to the stove and came up triumphantly with another cup. As she poured the coffee, Rebecca noticed that Naomi seemed to be watching Mr. Donoghue intently.

"McIntyre tells me that ye ladies have come all the way from North Carolina—Thank You." He took the cup from Rebecca who couldn't help but linger just a moment, his eyes were so jovial and such a warm shade of brown. "I've only been in America three years and still dunna my geography. It's somewhere in the South, isn't it?"

Rebecca grinned. "Just above Georgia and South Carolina, if that helps. I've never met anyone from Scotland. Your accent reminds me of the clip-clop of horses on a brick street."

Something akin to astonished delight illuminated Ian's face. "Tha' is the most wonderful description I've ever heard o' my accent. Are ye a writer?"

Rebecca cleared her throat and fought the color rising to her cheeks.

"Dear sister Rebecca used to work at a newspaper." Naomi stepped up to her sister and hugged her tightly, a move that struck Rebecca as obviously over-protective. "She is the writer among us."

"How fortunate for ye." Mr. Donoghue's cup was poised at his lips, yet he hadn't taken his first sip. Instead, he seemed keenly interested in Rebecca.

Uncomfortable with his fascinated scrutiny and Naomi's showy embrace, Rebecca shoved her hands into her apron pockets and wiggled her feet around. "That's what it reminded me of."

Ian cleared his throat, apparently aware of her discomfort. "The difference between the right word and the almost right word is the difference between lightning and the lightning bug. Or so states Mr. Mark Twain. I would believe, Mrs. Castleberry, that *ye* could describe lightning bolts from God's throne."

Rebecca couldn't stop an awed gasp. "That was beautiful. Do you read much?"

"In Defiance there are three things to occupy a man. Two of them are immoral. Reading is not." The joke worked, evoking a chuckle from the sisters.

Handsome and clever, Rebecca observed. She was quite amused by him.

Naomi tightened her grip again on Rebecca's shoulders. "How did you come to be in America, Mr. Donoghue?"

He sipped his coffee and pondered the answer. "I married my childhood sweetheart, but she was destined to die young." He stared blankly into his coffee seeing…what? Rebecca wondered. The bonnie hills of Scotland?

Fields of Heather? "I left Sco'land when I was twenty-seven and have never been back."

Ian shook his head as if clearing away the painful memories. "I'm sorry, I've no desire to be maudlin. I've traveled the world and seen everything from Bangladesh to Bombay, from the Taj Mahal to Buckingham Palace. It's been a fine adventure." He punctuated the confession with a wink tossed to Rebecca. "I think she would be pleased."

His smile, though a little sad, felt like a fresh breeze blowing dust off Rebecca's heart. The sensation took her by surprise. "I'm sure she would."

His pain was certainly something she understood, yet it hadn't seemed to break his spirit, like it had hers. She wondered if there was something she could learn from Ian Donoghue about living an adventurous life.

To Rebecca's dismay, Naomi chose that moment to take her plate to the dry sink. "I'm so sorry about your wife." She set the dishes down with a disturbing clatter. "How did you wind up in Defiance? If I'm not being too nosy."

"I met Mac—Mr. McIntyre in Denver. We struck up a conversation in a pub. He is a man with big dreams and he wanted an architect who could envision something o' the American spirit in his town. Oddly, he thought I was the man for the job and I agreed. I like Defiance very much and I'll like it even more when it settles down a bit."

"No joshin'!" Hannah joined Naomi and slid her plate into the sink as well. "*Buffalo Gals* is stuck in my head. Is it that noisy every night? I feel like I didn't get any sleep and my back is killing me." Grimacing, she stretched her arms over her head and arched her back in a long cat stretch. Rebecca watched in horror as the gesture emphasized her quickly rounding stomach. She was positive Ian noticed, but he didn't let on. He sipped his coffee, quickly averting his eyes. Rebecca appreciated his discreetness.

"Well, Mac wants the town to become more respectable and he knows the price will be high. The saloons can't stay open all night and the jail needs to be used for something more than drunks and vagrants. There must be real law, no' just his law.

"The advantage there to ye ladies is that he truly wants the hotel to succeed. He'll see to it that ye get all the business you can handle. If we could just get him started on civilizing the rest of the town."

A banging, scraping noise at the front alerted them that their furniture had arrived. Ian excused himself and returned a moment later with two chairs, his blueprints and his hat shoved under his arms, followed by Emilio also carrying two chairs, and two men the girls had not seen before carrying a green, felt-topped gaming table.

The two strangers looked questioningly at the sisters, and Naomi pointed at the center of the room. "Right there's fine." Unceremoniously, the two dropped the table and left without waiting for any thanks.

"Meester McIntrye saze he's sorry for the gaming table, but eet was all he had."

"That'll do nicely." Ian dropped the chairs and rolled out the blueprints. "Ladies, here is your hotel."

"Uh, excuse me…" Emilio timidly raised a hand to flag someone's attention. All eyes on him, he cleared his throat. "Mr. McIntyre saze it is all right to help you today. Do you need anything moved or can I chop wood?"

Naomi looked at Rebecca as if for confirmation. "The wood," they both agreed.

Ian nodded. "Aye, ye can't have too much fire wood in Defiance."

The boy nodded obediently and slipped out of the room.

The sisters drew in closer to Ian at the table, hunching over the plans. He spent the next half hour discussing the fifteen possible rooms and the kitchen layout. Initially, the sisters had thought they wouldn't make any changes to the floor plan, but it was obvious they needed living accommodations, and they agreed it would be good to allow each sister to have her own room. A larger room was assigned to Hannah, without explanation, despite Ian's questioning gaze. All the rooms would have sizable windows with stunning views of the San Juan range. Ian agreed with the changes and made sketches on the prints as they talked.

They chatted awhile longer about the dining room for which he had some helpful suggestions for table placement but everyone was satisfied with the design. The kitchen needed expansion, larger counters, two cook stoves, a window through which to pass food to the dining room, more storage, and a pump inside the building for easy access to water.

Comfortable with their goals, Ian deftly rolled the plans in to a tight wand. "We're to get started on this right away and that means today. I dare say, ye are about to experience life in a beehive."

Eager for the excitement of the renovation to begin, Rebecca escorted Ian to the door. He chatted comfortably about creating a building plan and the time he would need to make their changes to the blueprints. It struck Rebecca that every time their eyes met, her heart sped up a little and she chided herself for being a foolish, old woman.

She opened the door for Ian and looked up at him as bright morning sunshine streamed into the room. "How long do you think it will be before we can open?"

Ian studied her for an instant before answering. Then he blinked. "Yes, uh, timing." He rubbed his neck as if he was playing mental catch-up. "I should think ye could be serving meals by September sometime. That depends, of course, on when orders are placed and when items arrive."

"My..." Rebecca nodded. "That soon. Less than two months."

Ian opened his mouth, held a questioning look in his eyes, then changed course. Stepping through the door, he slipped his balmoral bonnet back on his head and turned again to Rebecca. "I've enjoyed meeting ye and yer sisters immensely, Mrs. Castleberry."

She scrutinized the hat and noted the embroidered military insignia. "You were in the military?"

"Aye. The Royal Scots, an infantry regiment. I've kept a fondness for the bonnet."

"I hope we'll get the chance to chat about Scotland sometime." Rebecca nearly bit her tongue off, aghast at her boldness, but she couldn't stop herself. "I've always wanted to see it."

Ian's eyes widened just a bit, then he smiled warmly and the spirit of it glowed in his eyes. Rebecca felt her heart trip over itself. "I would like very much to tell ye about my home."

They held each other's gaze for a moment longer, then he nodded and headed down the walk. Closing the door slowly, Rebecca heard him whistling a lighthearted tune.

As she made her way back to the kitchen, head down, lost in thought, she wondered if she had imagined his lingering gazes and attentive conversation. Was it all in her head? She was so old, surely he couldn't—

"My, my, my." Startled by Naomi's voice, Rebecca looked up and saw her sisters standing in the kitchen's entrance watching her, arms folded across their chests. Faster than she could say bonnie highlands, Rebecca's cheeks flamed with heat under the scrutiny of their bemused stares.

Naomi nudged Hannah in the ribs. "I think Rebecca has developed a sudden interest in Scotland."

Hannah giggled. "Rebecca's got a boyfriend, Rebecca's got a boyfriend…" Grinning slyly, she slipped back into the kitchen.

Naomi shot her big sister a warning look, though a grin played around her lips. "He seems nice, but we'll have to find out some things about him." Rebecca couldn't discern her sister's tone, which left her wondering if she was teasing a little or a lot. Before she could ask, Naomi rolled around the doorpost and disappeared into the kitchen.

~~~

"Well, that's the last of it." Feeling flushed and a bit sweaty, Naomi dropped a box on the bed and looked around this warehouse space they called their bedroom. Like the kitchen, it was now peppered with piles of boxes. Hannah and Rebecca stood amongst a grouping of open trunks and topless boxes. Hands resting on their hips, their disappointment was clear. Naomi patted the container she had just deposited. "This is a box of John's shirts."

The mention of his name dropped a palpable awkwardness on the three. Desperate not to give in to the pain, Naomi forced herself to cheer up, for her sisters' sakes. "You said it yourself, Rebecca. We'll just have to sew her some clothes."

Hannah's face brightened. "I did find this…" She dug through a trunk and came up with an arm load of Carolina blue fabric. "I bought this just before Christmas because I wanted to make a few spring dresses out of it." For a moment, her face darkened, perhaps mourning the lost dreams of a future bright with innocence.

Rebecca reached over and brushed the fabric with a loving hand. "I'll make you something nice out of it. You'll be beautiful."

A look passed between the two that Naomi almost envied. Rebecca and Hannah had always shared a special relationship, especially since the death of Rebecca's daughter. Naomi knew she had no one to blame but herself. She'd never been very good at letting her sisters in. She'd always felt the need to *protect* them, like some kind of guard dog.

If she was their rock, then John had been hers. How she had come to give him every inch of her soul, she would never know. Only with him could she comfortably soften and show weakness. And now she was floundering, drowning in uncertainty and grief. Her anger over their current circumstances was a kind of anchor, steadying this swaying, rolling thing she called her life...or so she tried to believe.

Deciding to delve into that at a later time, Naomi looked around the room again. "I don't recall seeing the sewing kit."

Rebecca gasped and slapped her forehead with the palm of her hand. "Oh, no, it was with the pinafores and baby clothes. I thought I was being so smart putting it with them in case they needed altering."

Naomi crossed her arms, unhappy with their next step. "You know what that means then."

Hannah hugged her material close. "We have to go out...down the street..."

Rebecca grimaced. "To the mercantile. Dare we try the journey without the marshal?"

"Yes." Naomi straightened up, refusing to be intimidated by this town. "We can't expect him to be with us every second. It's ten o'clock in the morning. You heard the noise last night. Everyone in this town probably sleeps till noon." The steady sound of traffic and voices from the street below argued against that, but the volume was less than it would be later in the day. "I wanted to look at the buck stove any way. We're going to need some heat up here and that one lonesome fireplace isn't going to do the trick."

Chapter 14

Hannah walked behind Naomi and Rebecca, her eyes roaming all over the town. The street was far less crowded than it had been on their arrival. Still, she was astonished at the busy, but industrious, pace of Defiance this morning. Everyone was doing something in a hurry: driving a wagon at a no-nonsense clip, packing a team of mules with practiced efficiency, hammering, measuring and sawing with deliberation, or engaging in important, animated conversations. The air positively vibrated with the sounds of squeaking wagons, creaking leather, whinnying horses and boisterous male voices.

The folks who were up at this hour were hitting the day hard and fast. Almost everyone of them, though, took time to stare. Two painters above them on a scaffold watched the girls boldly and one let out a catcall. His partner tagged him forcefully in the gut and apparently lashed him with some stern words. Immediately they went back to slapping paint on the defenseless building.

"At least they seem..." Naomi chewed her lip. "More *reserved* today."

Naomi and Rebecca told Hannah on their first trip to the mercantile they had been stared at with much more brazenness, until the cat fight, of course. Today, the men were more surreptitious with their attentions. Though they deliberately grazed the girls with arms and elbows, and without so much as an "excuse me," the unbridled bravado of yesterday was gone. Had Mr. McIntyre been true to his word and made it clear they were three women not on the menu in Defiance? Hannah wondered.

As they strolled along, not exactly feeling safe she decided, but at least less threatened, she considered how this walk would be different once her stomach couldn't be hidden under a pinafore or shapeless dress. Reminding herself that she was right where God wanted her, for good or bad, Hannah looked ahead at the general store, two buildings up on the opposite side of the street.

Smiling, she read aloud the sign painted on the store's false front. "Boot & Company. Meat market, storage, groceries, liquors, cigars...Well, I guess that just about sums up the basic necessities, doesn't it."

Rebecca chuckled. "All the comforts of home."

Hannah followed her sisters as they abruptly crossed to the other side of the street.

Rebecca let Naomi pull ahead just a bit then looked over her shoulder at Hannah. "I don't think Naomi wanted to cross over from the saloon."

Before the words were out of her mouth, they heard a deep, silky feminine voice call out to them. "Welcome to Defiance, girls!"

Squinting in the bright morning light, the sisters looked across the street to the second floor windows of the saloon. Perched in the sills, enjoying their morning coffee, four women stared down at them. Wearing no more than camisoles, petticoats and rouge, they watched the sisters intently, like a pride of lions planning a hunt.

A negro girl shifted as if to see the sisters better, causing her camisole strap to slide down, exposing a scandalous amount of flesh. "How do you like our town so far?"

"Maybe we could get together sometime," the woman sharing the window with her called in a husky, Hispanic voice. "We haven't met for our monthly quilting bee yet."

That was met with rich laughter from the negro girl, and a red-headed girl sitting in the other window. However, the young woman sitting with the redhead did not laugh. Hannah recognized her as the frail, skinny blonde at whom she had waved the other day. She looked desperately uncomfortable with the whole situation.

Rebecca smacked Naomi on the arm. "Don't look at them. That's just begging for trouble."

"And Lord knows we don't want any more of that." Naomi's reply carried a steely, sarcastic edge to it that concerned Hannah. Her voice had sounded so cold and defiant.

Apparently desperate to avoid being part of a street spectacle, Rebecca shoved Hannah and Naomi into the store, to the parting tease of, "Let's have tea and crumpets tomorrow. We'll bring the crumpets!"

What is a *crumpet?* Rose wondered as she watched the dark-haired gringa quickly shut the door behind her sisters. She didn't really care enough to ask, but Iris told her anyway from her perch in the other window.

"I don't know exactly what a crumpet is, but I had an Englishman a few months back who said he loves'em and they shouldn't be eaten with anything but Darjeeling tea."

Lily, the negro girl, sitting in the same window with Rose, looked at her Latin co-worker and rolled her eyes. "I keep telling Iris to pay less attention to the customer's and just do her job, but she never listens…at least not to us."

"Well, I'm impressed that she could remember the word Darjeeling." Daisy's mousy opinion, offered from the other window, grated on Rose's nerves. The little wretch *always* had something nice to say, whether it was true or not.

Rose heard Iris smack something, probably her thigh, and explode with laughter as bawdy as her fiery red hair. "You are a daisy, Daisy. You always see the silver lining, unlike these other wenches." Iris leaned into the room so Rose could see her face.

Rose waved her away, bored with the discussion. She had watched the gringas go into the store and wondered if she should go get a look at them. Mac had told everyone to leave them alone…but there was no harm in just looking.

Chapter 15

A fairly heavy crowd of men in search of a liquid breakfast did not prevent McIntyre from seeing Emilio slip in. He wouldn't have paid him any attention except for the fact that the boy headed upstairs instead of to his own room. Puzzling only a little over Emilio's destination, he went back to adding figures and entries to his ledger, but with an uneasy tickle in the back of his mind. As if by some sixth sense, he looked up several minutes later to see Emilio come back down and quickly ease his way out the front door.

McIntyre drummed his fingers on the desk. Emilio did his best to avoid Rose. Her temper was like a loaded gun with a hair trigger and the boy was her favorite target. So why would he be seeking her out…?

When Rose, Lily, Iris and Daisy, mostly dressed, followed close on the boy's heels, he knew something was awry. He dropped his eyes to his ledger again, but listened to the girls whisper as they attempted to leave without drawing attention to themselves. A few of the men in the saloon greeted them; they hushed them up with stern whispers and slipped outside.

Curious now, McIntyre rose and went to his window. He moved the lace curtain aside and watched Rose and her cleavage-baring entourage march across the street and invade the mercantile. He frowned, wondering what he was missing. Probably nothing, he told himself, returning to his work. He didn't have time to babysit everyone in town. He picked up his pencil and started writing again.

Once in the store, the sisters were pleasantly relieved to find it empty of customers. Rebecca and Hannah wandered over to the sewing section and started perusing buttons and bolts of cloth. Naomi strode to the back of the store to appraise two stoves on display. The proprietor, an astonishingly tall, balding man, who compensated for the lost hair by sporting a huge beard, shoved a pencil into his black apron and hurried over to her. "Because of the crowd yesterday, I didn't get a chance to introduce myself." He stuck out his hand. "I'm Luke Boot. Mr. McIntyre told me to help you ladies get anything you might need."

"I'm Naomi Miller." She shook his hand and nodded towards her sisters, introducing them by name. The girls greeted him from the other side of the store then fell back to studying buttons and a book of patterns.

"I heard you're gonna need several stoves," he told her turning back to the display. "Are you going to put one in every room or just in the suites? One in every room is gonna be a big order."

She nodded. "Yes, but we haven't made that decision just yet. I'd like one for our sleeping quarters now, such as it is. As soon as I see the final blueprints from Mr. Donoghue, I will place an order. How long will they take to get here?"

"Well," he scratched his head, apparently figuring the ins and outs. "It usually takes about six weeks to get supplies in from San Francisco. Give or take."

She peeked at the tag hanging from the buck stove and gasped over the inflated price. Disgruntled, she stepped over to look at the cooking stove, a beautiful, modern appliance with double ovens, six burners, glossy red paint and white porcelain fixtures on it. It shined like a new penny and Naomi was impressed. "How much for both stoves?"

"Mr. McIntyre told me I was authorized to give you a twenty-five percent discount."

That made the bottom line a bit more palatable, but she promised herself she would make a point of discussing Defiance's cost of living with Mr. McIntyre. "Well, I don't seem to have much choice." She eyed Mr. Boot, her brow creased. "All right, I'd like to get them both—"

The front doors burst open and a suffocating cloud of cheap perfume heralded the arrival of the flowers. Everyone in the store watched the girls from the Iron Horse saunter in, devilish laughter on their lips. Naomi quickly appraised the brightly dressed, scantily clad, heavily made-up crew then threw a glance to her sisters. Rebecca and Hannah stood stock still as the inquisitive eyes of the four sirens scanned the store.

Naomi had not appreciated their comments from before, but was not going to let them interrupt her business now. As the soiled doves spread out through the mercantile like wolves circling their next meal, she finished with Boot. "As I was saying, I'd like to get both of these along with all the necessary piping and hardware. Do you install?"

Boot was clearly focused on the swell of new females in his store and all the colorful, daringly low-cut silk dresses. Naomi cleared her throat irritably. Boot blinked and apologized. "Sorry. Yes, ma'm, I've got two boys who can deliver them tomorrow and get'em set up for ya."

"That will be fine."

"Right this way," he motioned, moving toward the counter. "I'll get your total for'em." Naomi was amazed the man could function, so intent was he on gawking at his lascivious customers.

Naomi, in turn, felt their stares, especially the tall, hispanic one, as she trailed Boot toward the counter.

Rose and her followers had sprinkled themselves throughout the store, shopping and glancing at merchandise, but they were clearly watching Naomi and her sisters. As Boot tallied up and went to the shelves repeatedly to check for hardware, Naomi leaned her hip on the counter and crossed her arms. Trying to look like she wasn't interested in a fight, she casually surveyed the store.

A pale, willowy girl wandered the closest to Rebecca and Hannah and was fingering a bolt of lilac-and-daisy cotton that Rebecca and Naomi had noticed the day before.

Hannah's eyes brightened. "Isn't that pretty?" Startled, the girl looked up and backed away slightly as Hannah stepped closer. "I love tiny, little flowers like that. Wouldn't it look nice with these buttons?" She showed her the ivory buttons she had picked out. "They're a little big, but this store is obviously more focused on clothing the men in Defiance. The pattern book is nothing but men's shirts." She pinned the jittery girl with a polite but direct stare. "Do you sew?"

"N-No," the girl stammered, her eyes wide and searching the store over Hannah's shoulder. "At least, not in a long time." Her worried gaze found Rose and the Hispanic woman shot back an ugly, warning look. Naomi didn't miss the exchange and assumed Hannah hadn't either. Clearly, Rose didn't want this girl speaking to strangers.

One of the other soiled doves, in her early twenties with vibrant red hair and wearing a shocking purple dress, sauntered boldly over to where Rebecca was flipping through the pattern book. The girl leaned in to take a look, muscling Rebecca out of the way. More than willing to walk away from trouble, Rebecca took Hannah's arm. "Come on. Let's get these and go start some dresses." Naomi bit down, consciously trying to stay out of Rebecca's business as her sisters walked up to join her.

Approaching the counter, Hannah noticed the jars, dozens of them, filled with bright, colorful candy and her eyes sparkled with wonder. "Oh, Rebecca, look at that: licorice."

Rebecca's eyes roamed over the delectable diversions. "And peppermint sticks."

In spite of the eyes burning holes in the back of their heads, Naomi grinned. "I take it you two would like a little candy?" It had been months since they had even seen candy, much less tasted any. She looked up at Boot, who was grinning as well, albeit nervously.

Rose, in a green, silk dress, slithered up just then and draped herself over the confections like a shiny, emerald python. Naomi had seen one at the circus years ago and thought the woman's eyes sparkled with the same cold malice. "What about horehound drops?" There was an evil hiss to her voice. "They're my favorite."

The smiles melted off the sisters' faces. Naomi straightened up and rested one fist on her hip. She didn't attempt to hide her irritation. After everything she had been through, now she had to deal with this? A bunch of rouged-up, disrespectful harlots with hateful attitudes? Unbelievable…

For a fraction of a second, Naomi thought Rose seemed taken aback by her angry expression. She wondered if this dark wench was expecting to roll right over them. If she did, then she had another thing coming and Naomi hoped it showed in her face.

"I'm Rose." She motioned to the red-head. "That's Iris…and Lily," the negro girl nodded. "And the frail wildflower over there is Daisy. We make up what the gentlemen in this town call The Garden." Iris and Lily sniggered, apparently over the use of the word *gentlemen*. "And I would advise you not to look down your nose at me like that." Her voice held a venomous warning. "We're the ones who really run this town, not the men. Give us any trouble and we'll run you out."

Naomi immediately thought of hers and John's frustrating meeting with Frank Page just prior to leaving Cary. Shooting off her mouth then had only made her feel small and foolish. While the burden of her grief and anger were almost more than she could bear, if she lost her temper, that would only give this trollop what she had come looking for. A dozen responses rose to Naomi's lips, but she bit them all back. Her sisters' pleading eyes helped her find that self-control that was often so elusive. *Lord, help me control my temper.*

In reply to Rose, she said simply, "We don't want any trouble."

"No, I guess you don't." Rose straightened to her full, impressive height. "So you were heading to California, huh? Mr. McIntyre thinks you are crazy. He called you Bible-toters. You know this word, yes?"

The description caught Naomi off guard and she couldn't help but laugh, as did Hannah and Rebecca.

"You think it is funny?"

Despite the tension in the air, the laughter wouldn't leave Naomi's voice. "Yes, actually I do. I guess we are crazy little Bible-toters."

"He said your God told you to come here." Her eyes narrowed. "Do you know things too?"

Somehow, Naomi understood exactly what she was asking and the laughter died. There was a bottomless darkness in Rose's eyes that sent a chill up her spine. But Naomi also unexpectedly felt a power surge through her and the birth of a steely determination. In an admission that came grudgingly, Naomi told Rose, "I know that God's called us here and nobody other than God is going to run us out."

Fire flickered in Rose's eyes then she shut them as if thinking. Taken aback, Naomi thought for an instant the woman was about to swoon. When Rose opened them again, she gazed piercingly at Hannah, appraising her carefully, slowly, top to bottom, then her gaze returned abruptly to the girl's barely protruding abdomen. Hannah and Naomi exchanged puzzled looks.

"Well, look here at the gringa baby with a bun in the oven!" Every person in the store sucked in a shocked gasped. Hannah's face turned ash gray as Rose's blood-red lips curved into a sneer. "Where's the papa?"

"He walked out on her." Naomi knew she had offered the explanation too quickly.

Hannah swallowed and raised her chin. "I can speak for myself."

"Really?" Rose took a step closer. "Were you married?"

"Explain to me how that's any of your business," Naomi snarled, inching her way in front of Hannah.

Like a serpent, Rose struck out and grabbed Hannah's left hand. Bringing it to eye level for examination she cried triumphantly, "Ha! No ring, no *sign* of a ring!" With a sneer, she tossed Hannah's hand away as if she were discarding a piece of trash. "At least we're smart enough to get *paid* for lying on our backs."

A fury unlike anything Naomi had ever known exploded in her brain. Fed up with watching Hannah suffer, she opened her mouth to launch an attack on this prideful, black-hearted witch, but Rose spoke first with a scathing indictment.

"You are really something. Come waltzing in here with your oh-so-pious attitudes, acting so saintly." She drew her hands up in front of her in prayer. "Oh, don't touch us. We're so pure and chaste. We say our Hail Mary every morning." Sounding supremely confident, she stabbed Hannah with a vicious truth. "You're no different than us."

Jaws clenched and her brain burning with rage, Naomi shoved Hannah aside. Thoroughly intent on putting this foul-tempered, filthy-talking harlot in her place, Naomi opened her mouth to commence the fight.

"Why Rose, darlin'," Mr. McIntyre called loudly from the doorway. "There you are." He strolled in, casually lighting a cheroot as if nothing in the world was wrong. "There are customers over at the saloon asking after you. Go tend to them...." His words were calm and soft, but edged with a steel bite as he tossed his match aside. He stepped between Rose and Naomi, gently, but firmly, shouldering Naomi out of the way. Though Mr. McIntyre was barely taller than Rose, his absolute authority towered over her. He blew a cloud of smoke into the woman's face and watched her blink. "If I wasn't clear, I meant now."

Rose's gaze flicked quickly between him and Naomi, and Naomi saw the fear. With a searing last glance at the both of them, Rose whirled and stomped out of the store as if Mr. McIntyre's words were commandments from God Himself.

Mr. McIntyre stared at the floor, chewing on the smoldering cheroot and the situation. His slow, measured breathing told Naomi that things here were not to his liking. Not at all. "Don't cross swords with her, Mrs. Miller." He turned to face her and Naomi saw the concern, for who or what she wasn't sure. "You will not dissuade Rose with a belligerent voice or the heel of your boot. If you fight with her, you will be fighting for your life...and your sisters need you alive. I'm not always going to be just across the street to come to your rescue."

Arrogance and adrenaline pushed Naomi to argue with him. Rebecca quickly placed a restraining hand on her sister's shoulder and begged her with her eyes to let it go. "She'll be careful, Mr. McIntyre. We all will," Rebecca promised with a warning look for her sister.

Mr. McIntyre nodded and marched out the door.

Boot waited for the door to slam shut then whistled a relieved tune. "You may never know how much of a favor he just did for you, little lady." He sounded as if he had just seen a narrowly averted train wreck. "Rose is mean and she ain't afraid to draw blood. Lots of it."

Naomi didn't really hear. She was still staring out the door. Mr. McIntyre caught Rose on the front steps of the Iron Horse. With what looked like a fierce grip on her arm, he shoved her roughly through the bat wing doors in to the darkness of the saloon. Naomi was surprised at herself for wondering if he would hurt her. She didn't wish a beating on anybody, even that particular she-devil, but she was also hoping that Rose would let things pass. As Naomi had told her, they weren't looking for trouble...but obviously Rose was.

Slowly coming back to the moment, Naomi looked at Rebecca with raised eyebrows and an incredulous shake of her head. Jittery with anger and frustration, she turned toward Mr. Boot and looked at the ticket on the counter. "Is that the total?"

"Yes, ma'm. That includes the delivery and installation. I took twenty-five percent off that as well."

"Fine, thank you." She began digging in the little reticule hanging on her wrist to find a small roll of bills. Her hand and her mind wouldn't work together, however, as she kept counting through the bills over and over. Rebecca reached over to take the purse off her wrist.

"I'll count it out." Naomi let her slip the purse off and watched quietly as her sister paid Boot. Naomi could not believe the viciousness of the woman or, sadly, her own willingness to fight. There had almost been a cat-fight in this store that would have rivaled that sordid cat fight of yesterday. Naomi had to admit Mr. McIntyre's timely arrival probably had averted a disaster. Oh, why was everyone in this filthy town bent on bringing out the worst in her?

While Naomi and Rebecca handled paying for their items, Hannah took the opportunity to walk back to Daisy, who was now flanked by the redhead and Negro girl. All three were still wearing shocked expressions.

Sensing that Daisy was the one with the softest heart, Hannah was willing to be mocked by the other two for reaching out. "Why does she dislike us so? We couldn't possibly have done anything to her. We haven't been in town long enough to offend anybody."

Daisy straightened up to talk. The fear of Rose that Hannah had seen in her eyes a few minutes ago was gone.

"Rose is crazy. She doesn't take to strangers anyway and she's jealous of your sister."

"You're talking too much," Lily, the Negro girl on her right, warned.

Hannah ignored her, eager to pounce on a chance to make a friend and get some information. But because the comment was so shocking, she lowered her voice. "She's jealous of Naomi?! Good grief, why? It's not like she wants her job."

"She's afraid she wants her man."

"What?!" Hannah was certain she had not heard the answer correctly.

"Rose and Mr. McIntyre sort of have a relationship."

"My sister lost her husband less than a week ago. She's not looking at Mr. McIntyre, or anyone else, right now. And when she does, I doubt it will be someone like him."

Daisy shrugged. "She wants her to keep away from him. That's all I know. Rose doesn't always make sense. In fact, she rarely makes sense."

"But she's always looking for a fight," the red-haired girl Iris warned. "Don't let Daisy gentle the situation. Rose is a mean witch—literally. If McIntyre doesn't kill her, you need to watch your backs."

"Now you have said too much," Lily fumed, throwing warning looks at both Daisy and Iris. But then it seemed she couldn't keep from adding to the gossip. "McIntyre may be planning to give Rose a good flogging—or worse—but she'll come out of it just as vengeful as ever. We'd better get our rear ends back to the saloon or he'll come lookin' for us next."

Conceding it was time to go, they filed towards the door, but Daisy hung back. She casually ran her hand over a bolt of fabric and waited for the other two girls to leave before she spoke up. "Is it true, what Rose said about you expecting a baby?"

For some reason, Hannah desperately wanted to be friends with this girl. She believed they were close in age and might have some other things in common. Regardless, God had called them to this place to witness and she figured a truthful admission might tear down some barriers. Besides, it wasn't as if she would be able to hide the baby forever.

"Yes, it's all true. Rose was right when she said we're no different. We all make mistakes, even us holier-than-thou-Bible-toters." Daisy managed to give her a fractious smile for the attempt at brevity. As she took a step to leave, Hannah gently grabbed her arm, curious to know one thing. "But how did she know?"

Daisy squirmed uneasily, pulling her arm free. "She thinks she's a witch. I think it's mostly Mayan mumbo-jumbo and she just uses it to scare people, but sometimes, she does know things." With that, she abruptly dashed back to work.

Chapter 16

McIntyre practically hurled Rose into his office and angrily slammed the door behind them. Before she could even stand up straight, he was on her again, this time with his hand around her throat. Nearly cutting off her air, he shoved her up against the wall and spoke with his face so close to hers their noses touched.

"You seem to have forgotten your place in our arrangement, Rose. I am your employer and you are my employee." He tightened his grip and she clawed at his hand; he could feel her pulse pounding wildly. "None, and I do mean, NONE of my business deals are of any concern to you.

"You will not speak to those women, you will not look at them. You will cross to the other side of the street if you see them coming. You will not ask Emilio to spy on them and you will cease practicing your voo-doo hoo-doo nonsense in my saloon."

He allowed himself to calm a little and breathe slower, but he didn't loosen his grip. "After the incident with Blossom last fall, I thought you and I were clear on how things are. Apparently I was wrong, so I will clarify it one *last* time." He could feel her pulse slowing as the strangle hold took effect. Her face swelled and her eyes threatened to roll back in her head. "Cross me again on this and I will send you back to Mexico in a pine box."

He released her as quickly as he had grabbed her and Rose collapsed to the floor, gasping for air and coughing through, he was sure, a nearly crushed wind pipe. McIntyre straightened his clothes and brushed lint off his shoulders. "Now, get ready for work."

McIntyre calmly closed the door behind him, leaving Rose to compose herself. The saloon, settling between shift changes, was empty now except for his bartender drying glasses. He couldn't believe the fury the wench ignited in him. He had never manhandled a woman before in his life and now it had happened repeatedly with Rose. Their relationship was a despicable quagmire and he was done with it.

Disgusted with himself, he trudged to the bar. The sensual painting of Eve gazed down on the room and he took a moment to appreciate the serene, languid look in her eyes. Why couldn't all women be so quiet and willing? Unlike Rose.

Unlike Naomi Miller. Wouldn't the feisty little belle just love to know what he had named the portrait? That would probably curl her hair, he speculated with a smirk.

Brannagh, the fifty-ish Irish bouncer he had hired a while back from a tough saloon in San Francisco, nodded at his boss and retrieved a bottle from behind the counter. Old, maybe, McIntyre mused, but still tough as nails and built like an oak. There had been no fights in the Iron Horse since Brannagh had laid down the law. As far as saloons went in mining towns, this was one of the safer ones. He liked to think that hiring Brannagh had been one of his best investments. Apparently hiring Rose was one of the worst.

The burly Irishman poured his boss a short shot and set it before him. "Rose givin' ye trouble...again?"

McIntyre fingered the drink. "Let's just say you've done a far better job, Brannagh, at controlling the drunken patrons in here than I've done handling one crazy, Mexican harlot."

"Ah, ye're flowers aren't so bad. I've seen worse. Why, I broke up a catfight one time in Frisco. Worse injuries I ever got. Said I'd never do it again. I got knifed, clawed and kicked in places that still hurt. Men fight like men. Women fight like unchained demons."

McIntyre chuckled and nodded in agreement, but he was struck by the truth behind the statement. He had never laid a hand on any of his girls until he'd hired Rose. Her desire for blood and violence seemed to infect those around her with a dark malaise, including himself. The realization was disquieting.

Before her arrival, he had never made a habit of running crooked games, watering his whiskey, advancing pay to his mine employees at exorbitant rates or encouraging the miners to bet their claims. Before, he had considered himself a mostly respectable man with slightly fluid business ethics. Now, he was more driven and ethics had become a nuisance. When had that happened?

Was he using Rose as an excuse? Surely years of selling whiskey and women, gambling, and associating with questionable persons couldn't have affected him on a basic level. He could hear his mother's sweet, lilting voice reminding him over and over that bad company corrupted good manners.

His eyes traveled over to his closed office door and he pondered the woman on the other side. He could argue that his lack of self-control added more fuel to an already out-of-control fire. Rose seemed to gain strength from these ugly encounters; they hardened her resolve to...what?

Therein lies the crux of the matter, he told himself. Rose has a plan to make herself the queen of Defiance.

Over my dead body, he thought as he pushed the shot of whiskey away.

~~~

Daisy hid behind the curtain in her room and watched the sisters leave the mercantile. She liked the youngest one; she had talked to her in such a friendly way. Was it possible she didn't know exactly what Daisy did for a living? Maybe she didn't understand about working at the saloon—no, Daisy stopped that train of thought. Nobody was that naïve.

Still, she had gone out of her way to make small talk about the buttons and Daisy had not sensed any condescension in her attitude. She had told her the truth about the baby, too. Could it be the girl was just friendly?

Iris burst into the room from behind her and bounced over to the other window. She, too, watched the women walk sullenly down the boardwalk, obviously less than chipper after their run-in with Rose. Iris giggled in a bratty way.

Wearily, Daisy looked over at her and saw that the redhead had already poured herself a glass of whiskey. It was her ritual for preparing for the night's work. "What's so funny?"

"I was just thinking, we'll have to get some rotten vegetables and practice our aim the next time they come to the store."

Daisy scowled angrily at her co-worker. "Why do you want to say things like that, Iris? Those girls haven't done anything to you?"

Iris arched her eyebrows in surprise at Daisy's sudden show of emotion then sneered. "They ain't done nothin' *for* me either."

"Oh, just go on back to your room. I don't want any company right now."

Iris flung a nervous glance to the door then backed up closer to the window. "Well, I kinda wanted to stay in here for a bit." Daisy understood. There was safety in numbers. None of them knew what mood Rose might be in when she emerged from Mr. McIntyre's office. Iris had left the door open and Daisy thought perhaps she would shut it against any unwanted guests. As she ambled towards it, however, Lily slipped in.

Quietly she shut the door behind her and looked at the other two women. "I listened for a second. I think he must've been choking' her 'cause I never heard Rose say a word."

They all shared uneasy glances and Daisy wondered what new Hell Rose would unleash on them when she recovered.

~~~

The sisters slogged down the street in silence. With all these people staring at her, intentionally jostling her, Naomi felt as if she was holding on to her emotional control by a single, fraying thread. Her sisters' silence only added to the burden. She had started out so well. She could have avoided a fight with Rose, as long as she had stayed focused on Naomi. But when she had gone after Hannah, if not for Mr. McIntyre's timely interference, there would have been a positively hellish display of temper. Naomi was sure of it. Blood, hair, fingernails and shreds of clothing would have flown. It didn't happen, but it would have. Who was the white trash now?

Sick of this town and her own uncontrollable temper, Naomi didn't think she could feel any more like a failure. Why couldn't she learn patience and wisdom? Why couldn't she walk away like Rebecca had?

Naomi glanced over at Hannah who was trudging doggedly alongside them but her face said she was as lost in thought as Naomi.

Lord, you're going to have to melt me down and start all over because I wanted to kill that woman back there. I was ready to scrap like an alley cat and not regret a second of it. Nobody talks about Hannah that way. Oh, Lord, how can you possibly use someone like me? How can I take them the light when I need a magnifying glass to find my own?

"Well, that was something," Rebecca mused, perhaps trying to fill the silence. "Rose is a rather thorny flower." She patted her sister on the back. "I thought you did well, Naomi, holding your tongue like you did."

The observation made Naomi feel worse and she snorted in disgust. "The only thing I did was get saved from myself by Mr. McIntyre, of all people. That's the closest I've come to a real fight since I was sixteen."

Rebecca grinned. "Betty Jean Campbell. You sat on her and shoved her face in the dirt." All three sisters smiled at that, but Naomi's quickly melted away.

Hannah looked slowly back over her shoulder at the saloon. "How did that woman know about the baby? I'm sure it was more than a lucky guess." Naomi rolled that around in her head, but didn't have an answer. Rebecca didn't offer a comment, either.

Hannah fiddled distractedly with an escapee from her braid, working to tuck it back in its home while she thought. "I saw something in her eyes. She's not right in the head and I think it's more than just crazy."

"I'm the crazy one," Naomi admitted in disgrace. "She lit such a fire under me I could've knocked her into next Tuesday."

Rebecca nodded emphatically. "That's exactly what she was counting on, I think. If she scared you she won, if you fought her she won. She had all the angles covered."

"Well, she didn't scare me." It was not a boast, merely a statement of fact.

Rebecca gave a frustrated sigh. "I know and that's what worries me. She *should* have scared you. I think Hannah's right. There's something evil in her eyes. You heard what Mr. McIntyre said."

Hannah huffed out a breath, disturbing the golden tendrils around her face. "Another minute of that stare and *I* would have run screaming out the door."

Abruptly, Naomi shoved her hands heavenwards. "What are we doing here?" she asked loudly enough to cause the men to stare, for different reasons this time. "We don't belong here. To call us fish out of water is an understatement of Biblical proportions!"

Rebecca shushed her, but sullenly agreed. "I know. I know. It's like a cross between a schoolyard and a battlefield here. Try to remember that we're here—"

"Here for a reason," Naomi sang with flagrant sarcasm, wondering what possible reason God could have for stripping her of her one love and her sanity.

Hannah clutched her small package of buttons to her chest and eyed her sister disapprovingly. "If He didn't think we could do it, He wouldn't have sent us. Look at that girl Daisy. What if we're the only Believers in her life who are ever willing to share with her. What if God sent us here"—she motioned to the town surrounding them—"went to all this trouble—just to help one person? Would he do that?"

Naomi rubbed her temple, feeling the stirrings of a headache. "He might," she muttered, humbled by Hannah's ever-increasing faith and compassion. "But I think there is more at stake here than just one soul." Rebecca and Hannah agreed with slow nods, looking around at the grizzled, bewhiskered, unwashed faces passing by them. As Naomi had pointed out to Rose, God had brought them here. She may not agree with the plan or the way He had done things, but that didn't change their location or circumstances.

But she was so seriously flawed how could God possibly use her? She second-guessed Him at every step and couldn't even turn the other cheek to the town's version of a schoolyard bully. She would never be a missionary and had no desire to be so.

She ached to hear John tell her she was a work in progress, to give God time, but she would never hear his voice again this side of heaven. Feeling broken and defeated by Defiance, Naomi walked the rest of the way in silence.

Chapter 17

After his run-in with Mr. McIntyre, Emilio had come back to the inn and started chopping wood like a crazed beaver. He thought perhaps if he chopped loud and fast, he could sweat out the guilt. His burden did not last too long before he heard the voices of the sisters. He couldn't tell from their tones, though, how things had gone at the store. When he stopped to wipe his forehead, he saw Naomi standing on the back stoop and a flood of relief swept across his soul.

"Senora Naomi," he breathed, thrilled to see her alive and not bleeding from any obvious places. He lodged the ax in a log. "Everything ees OK? Yes?"

She looked puzzled by his inquiry, but smiled a greeting. "Yes, everything's fine. I was wondering, Emilio, we're having two stoves delivered tomorrow. Do you think Mr. McIntyre will allow you to help us again?"

His shoulders sagged as he remembered the hurried but pointed conversation he'd had with Mr. McIntyre. Instead of rushing back here to work like he should have, he had waited at the Iron Horse to see if Rose's trip to the mercantile would turn into a blood sport.

He was hiding behind a post watching the store when Mr. McIntyre stepped outside. He gave Emilio a stern look and that was all it took to make him spill the beans. Completely aware that he was calling down Rose's wrath, he told Mr. McIntyre of her order to spy on the sisters and let her know their whereabouts.

Today his news was useless, though. Rose and the flowers had already spotted the gringa girls going into the store. Mr. McIntyre had charged toward the mercantile with the thunder of God in his eyes. Wisely, Emilio had not waited around to see the outcome.

The weight of his betrayal was too heavy and he felt compelled to confess his actions. He lowered his head as if waiting for a beating. "Did my seester give you much problems in the store?"

Naomi looked at first like she couldn't track the path of the question, then she sucked in a breath. "You had said your sister's name was Rose. I can't believe I didn't realize..."

He nodded meekly. "I'm sorry if she did anything to you. I told her to leave you alone but..." he looked heavenward, hoping the explanation for his sister's behavior floated up there somewhere. "I don't know." He shook his head. "She's just angry." Or plain evil.

"But how did you know—" Naomi stopped short.

Looking betrayed, because she had been, Naomi gazed out across the backyard, past Sampson and the mules, across the stream, to the mountains. And probably farther than that, Emilio guessed. He hoped she found a peaceful place, at least for a minute.

Coming back with compassion in her eyes, she shrugged. "We'd still like you to stay for dinner…if you will."

Hannah had draped her fabric around herself and was parading about the room like a queen as Rebecca laid a pattern and sewing items out on the bed. Naomi, who had trudged up the stairs and stopped a few steps from the top, watched them quietly over the top of the banister. She felt, and probably looked, awfully crestfallen, wondering if there was such a thing as honor or truth in Defiance. But watching her little sister whirling around in what would be a new dress with a loose, comfortable fit, cheered Naomi up considerably. Hannah's joy had always been infectious.

Smiling, Naomi dropped her elbows on the banister and rested her chin on her hands. "Well, that makes the encounter with the she-devils well worth it. You'll be beautiful and comfortable."

"Oh, and it will feeeel so much better," Hannah nearly cried with delight. "I can't wait to get a few finished."

Naomi started to offer a compliment on Rebecca's seamstress skills, but decided her sister looked too distracted. With an intent, somber look on her face, Rebecca pulled straight pins from a new box and carefully stuck them into the pin cushion on her wrist. Naomi would have been willing to bet her older sister was imagining Hannah's future here. No dress, even one tailored to fit a horse, would hide the situation forever.

Hannah stopped spinning and eyed her sisters with suspicion. "My, you both have the most serious looks on your faces."

Naomi scratched her nose thoughtfully then changed positions from resting on the banister to taking the last few steps up to their level. Leaning back on the rail, she folded her arms and fired the cannon. "Rose is Emilio's sister. At her request, he's been spying on us."

Naomi questioned how many more shocks like this her sisters could take. Eyes wide and mouths agape, it took them longer to recover every time another lightning bolt struck. Stroking her jawline with the tail of her braid, Naomi shared her thoughts out loud. "I asked him to stay for dinner anyway. It seems to me, if I had a sister like Rose...well, I think she could be pretty awful. He probably just did it because she told him to."

Rebecca took a few steps back and plopped down on the bed. "But what could he tell her? It's not like we're hiding anything."

"That's exactly why I invited him. We don't have anything to hide. At least not after the melodrama in the general store."

Hannah's face showed she was plainly troubled by something. "What if Rose is as mean to Emilio as she apparently is to everyone else? That girl Daisy told me she practices witchcraft. But she said she uses it mostly to scare people."

Rebecca raised an eyebrow at that news. "She is very theatrical. I could see where she would flaunt something like that for the effect of it, whether she believes it or not. Oh, poor Emilio," she lamented, shoulders drooping. "He probably witnesses the most unimaginable things in that saloon." Rebecca's lip trembled and she flung an almost accusatory glance at Naomi. "The poor darling. Of course you should have invited him to dinner."

Naomi was a little startled at Rebecca's emphatic reaction. "Well, it's not that I didn't think we should invi—"

"Do you suppose she beats him?" Hannah interrupted. Mindful of the items on the bed, she dropped down beside Rebecca, eyes reflecting the horror of the possibilities.

Rebecca shook her head. "It wouldn't surprise me." Suddenly she sat up, straight as a pin, as if someone had jammed a rod down her spine. "We'll just have to tell Mr. McIntyre the boy's become indispensable to us."

Hannah excitedly clutched her hands over her heart. "Yes, maybe we could hire him away. He doesn't need to work there. I'm sure we need him more than Mr. McIntyre does."

Naomi rubbed her arms and simply listened as her sisters cut her out of the conversation and eagerly devised a scheme to come to Emilio's aid. Naomi had been so sure there would not be one sole in this town worth caring about, and then they had met a little orphaned Mexican boy. His dark eyes reminded her of melted chocolate and his sad life did make her want to take him under their roof.

As Rebecca and Hannah bantered ideas back and forth on how to do just that, Naomi considered Rose and what she would think of her little brother making friends with crazy Christian Bible-toters. She suspected she wouldn't like it. Not one little cauldron-boiling bit.

~~~

Staying away from the sisters for what he thought was an acceptable number of days, McIntyre felt compelled to join Ian for a visit. He wanted to reassure them that Rose had settled down a bit, and determine whether they had recovered from the shock of their encounter with her.

McIntyre knocked on the inn's door, but when no one responded, he and Ian let themselves in. For a fleeting, heavenly moment the two turned up their noses and enjoyed the heady smell of truly good home-cooking. Biscuits. Roast. Potatoes. McIntyre's stomach growled enthusiastically.

They also listened to the sound of female chatter and giggles and the clatter of dishes as they prepared the meal.

"Aye, that's a pleasant sound." Ian grinned as a wistful contentment settled on his face. "Reminds me o' my sisters back in Sco'land."

McIntyre marveled over the fact that women still spoke to each other with such cheerfulness and kindness. He had an irksome suspicion that being around soiled doves for nearly two decades *was* making him more unsuitable for genteel company than he had imagined.

Pushing away such irrelevant thoughts, he called out to announce their arrival. "Mrs. Miller, ladies…"

The noise in the kitchen ceased abruptly and Naomi stepped out from the apartment, wiping her hands on a towel. McIntyre did not miss the lightning flash from disdain for him to cheerfulness for Ian.

She flashed a wide smile. "Mr. Donoghue." The smiled faded. "Mr. McIntyre. What can we do for you gentlemen?"

Eagerly, Ian waved his completed blueprints and walked forward, McIntyre trailing, a position which was quite unusual. "I've finished the plans, and Mr. McIntyre and I have some things we'd like to discuss with ye, if no' is a good time. If we're interruptin' din—"

"Have you eaten?" A pleasant, if not slightly cool, smile returned to her face. Neither of them had and their hesitation in responding answered her question. "Come join us and we can talk over dinner."

The two men entered the crowded little apartment and absorbed its warm smells and warmer atmosphere. McIntyre was stunned to find Emilio setting a tray of hot cornbread on the table and cocked his head to one side. "I didn't know you cooked, Emilio."

The boy nodded awkwardly then stepped away from the table waiting for something else to do. The other girls greeted the two new guests with bright smiles, but Rebecca's melted away abruptly, replaced with concern.

"Chairs, we don't have enough chairs…We can use the small flower barrel." She pointed at the barrel against the wall behind Ian. He immediately lifted it up and placed it at the table. "And there's a crate…" Hand on her hip, Rebecca looked around the room which was now a jumble of the last boxes from the wagon. She found an empty one and handed it to Emilio. They pulled the makeshift seating together and everyone sat down. McIntyre took the opposite side of the table from Naomi and Ian squeezed between him and Rebecca. Hannah and Emilio were off to McIntyre's right. The small table created a cozy, informal environment. The irony of eating a simple, wholesome meal around a piece of furniture that normally supported some pretty weighty sins wasn't lost on him.

As he pondered the vice and corruption that had no doubt occurred here, the sisters locked hands to pray. Rebecca reached to her right and took Ian's hand. Awkwardly, Emilio took Hannah's hand. Then, looking as if he would rather crawl under the table, the boy hesitantly extended his other hand to McIntyre. McIntyre found himself caught between Emilio's outstretched hand and Ian's and felt as awkward as a prostitute in church. Grinning hugely, obviously enjoying his friend's distress, Ian grabbed McIntyre's hand and motioned for him to take Emilio's.

His discomfort was not lost on a waiting Naomi. "We'd like to say the blessing." She nodded towards Emilio's hand. "I don't think he'll bite you."

Feeling foolish and all too equal with Emilio, a mere boy who slept on a cot in the back of his saloon, McIntyre grudgingly did as he was bid. Together, the group bowed their heads and waited.

Rebecca offered the blessing. "Father, thank you for being the Savior to all men and thank you for the precious blood Jesus willingly spilt on the cross. Thank you for the meal we're enjoying tonight, as well as the special fellowship with our new neighbors and friends and we just ask that You would bless this meal. In your Son's name we pray. Amen."

McIntyre released the hands a little too quickly and grabbed his napkin off the table as the food started circulating. Eager to find familiar footing in this uncomfortable situation, he jumped right into business.

"We stopped by, Mrs. Miller to discuss with you and your sisters—"

"First," Ian waved his hand over the table. "We've to thank our lovely hostesses for this enchantin' meal." He eyed Rebecca. "I canna remember the last time food smelled this good. I'll live on the beauty of the aroma, even if it tastes like sawdust." He winked at her and grinned. "Though I doubt tha'll be the case."

Trying to hold back her own grin, she passed him the mashed potatoes. "Well, we are planning on opening a restaurant. At least one of us had better be able to cook."

"We already know which one of us can't." The good-natured jab from Hannah extracted a giggle from her and Rebecca, but Naomi's face hardened.

"I made the biscuits." Clearly displeased they were discussing her lack of culinary talents, Naomi took a violent bite of cornbread. Momentarily, a look of ecstasy flooded her face. "Oh, my biscuits are good but this cornbread is straight from heaven, Emilio." She waved the piece in the air and spoke with an unlady-like mouthful. "Mr. McIntyre, we might steal him from you. He made the cornbread and I think it's the best I ever had. Surely puts my biscuits to shame."

"We've established that there are some wonderful cooks in the room." His overly loud comment laced with irritation brought the activity at the table to a standstill. He felt the urge to apologize for his brusqueness, but fought it. "Their talents, however, will go to waste if we do not tend to the business of getting this restaurant open."

Naomi swallowed her mouthful. "What's the matter, Mr. McIntyre? Afraid you might lose a few dollars if we dally over supper and actually try to *enjoy* the meal?"

McIntyre appraised Naomi, noting the shimmering golden hair that cascaded down her shoulders, unflinching wide eyes, squared shoulders and tanned skin that glowed against her starched white shirt. Sassy, opinionated, beautiful, and an absolute joy to tease. "Your Ladyship, the *only* thing I am afraid of is losing money."

Naomi's lips tightened into a thin line and her eyes narrowed, but she didn't pursue the verbal battle. Certain he was the winner of their little exchange, McIntyre cleared his throat and moved on. "Mr. Donoghue and I have finished the blueprints for both the restaurant and the hotel. We have a crew coming in tomorrow to start the renovations. Here," he pulled some papers out of his vest pocket and unfolded them, "is a project list. The second page is the estimated cost to complete it." He passed it down to Naomi.

She went straight to the back page and took in the bottom line with raised eyebrows, then scanned both pages for more information to justify his price. With disapproval evident on her face, she handed the paper to Rebecca. "Mr. McIntyre, your labor costs are entirely unreasonable. Why is everything in Defiance so high?"

"It's a matter o' supply and demand." Ian's answer sounded rushed to McIntyre, as if he was trying to avoid more fireworks. Yet, lighting a fire under Mrs. Miller was entertaining sport and he intended to continue. She was far more attractive flustered and frustrated than she was as a grieving widow.

McIntyre leaned back in his chair and laced his fingers. "Most of the men in this town want to look for gold and a lot of them find it one way or the other. The more gold comes out of the ground, the higher the prices of everything climb."

The answer apparently didn't wash with Naomi. "I purchased two stoves the other day that cost us almost twice what we would have paid in Cary. Profit is one thing, but blind greed is another."

"Greed is often in the eye of the beholder, Mrs. Miller. Defiance doesn't sit on a flat, easy plain with railroad tracks all around. We are in a difficult and remote location. That adds significantly to our freight costs. Not to mention, the men who do the carpentry work around here leave the gold fields to take on jobs for princesses such as yourself. In their minds, they're giving up a possible strike to make a day's wages. They just want their time to be well spent."

"Do these men work for you?" The tilt of her head told him she already knew the answer.

McIntyre sliced off a piece of roast, but did not take his eyes off her. "You can hire my men and I'll see to it that the job is done right, or you can piecemeal the work, putting together carpenters with an unknown amount of skill, expertise and work ethic and see what you get. Don't let your pride make you foolish, Princess."

He could see neither option appealed to her, but would she have the wisdom to let his crew do the work? McIntyre had made it clear he had an honest interest in seeing the hotel succeed. Did she believe that? He enjoyed watching her squirm under the subtle, pleading looks from Rebecca and Hannah. They begged her to choose the devil they knew as opposed to ones they didn't. Naomi nodded in reluctant compliance. McIntyre fought down a triumphant smile.

"Very well then, Mr. McIntyre." He had the distinct feeling she would say the name Lucifer with more warmth. "But what about items we can't get from Montgomery Ward, such as groceries?"

McIntyre glanced over at Emilio. He was uncomfortable discussing the details in front of the boy and sensed he was uncomfortable being there. As McIntyre was pondering a way to excuse Emilio, he practically inhaled his last bite then asked if there was anything else he could do before he left.

McIntyre waved his hand. "I think they're done with you for the evening."

Rebecca leaned forward. "We could use him back tomorrow. If it's all right."

McIntyre for some reason wasn't exactly pleased with the way the sisters were all but adopting the boy, but his usefulness to them was undeniable. He would have to trust Emilio to keep his mouth shut around Rose. He dipped his head. "That would be fine."

As Emilio stood up to depart, McIntyre snagged his sleeve. "Remember our conversation. Remind your sister if it becomes necessary." Emilio simply nodded and left.

When she heard the front door shut, Naomi followed up on that subject. "Speaking of Rose, why was she so bent on picking a fight with us the other day? We don't even know her."

"You rarely need to know someone, Mrs. Miller, to assume they are your enemy." He shrugged, knowing there was no way to explain Rose to a woman like Naomi. "Rose is territorial and she had incorrectly assumed you had crossed into her *domain,* if you will. I have since clarified her boundaries."

"Again," huffed Ian, but he clenched his jaw too late as the complaint escaped.

The girls waited for an explanation. McIntyre's first reaction was to change the subject back to the hotel, but perhaps if they knew what Rose was really like, they would be less inclined to dally with her...as Naomi had clearly thought to do. Having these girls cut up—or worse—would serve no purpose and only complicate matters.

"In the summer of last year I added a new flower to my garden." He preferred using that euphemism for such delicate company. "However, Rose got it into her head that Black-eyed Suzy was attempting to steal my affections." McIntyre reached for his water. "After a few cross words, Rose stabbed her in the face and throat."

He swallowed and in the sudden stillness, the noise was deafening.

Hannah clutched her throat. "Is she all right?"

"She did not die and I sent her back to Denver, costing me a lost investment of $700."

This time, the hush was brought on by, he knew, the insensitivity of his summation. Perhaps McIntyre had been a little too candid for the genteel company, but he was what he was and he was not here to impress these girls.

While her sisters, and even Ian, looked shocked at the thoughtlessness of his remark, Naomi merely stared at him with irritated disdain. Her eyes told him that she not only *expected* such callous comments, but that they defined the core of who and what he was—an unbelieving, money-grubbing miscreant. She had him pegged as a worthless heathen and nothing short of a miracle would elevate him to something better.

He shook off the unexpected irritation her opinion caused him and decided to find the humor in vexing her. He enjoyed seeing her fume and blush. It was a game. How far could he push her before he turned on his charm and reeled her back in? Childish, he admitted, but he suspected the conquest would be so well worth the effort.

"I apologize for the crassness of my remark, ladies, but the garden is after all, a business. It's not wise to become attached to my flowers."

Agitated, Naomi bounced her fork in her hand. "Is that why you've given them the names of plants rather than people? So you don't have to deal with their humanity…or your sinfulness?"

That ignited a real spark of annoyance. He was not going to engage in a conversation about sin. For reasons he couldn't explain, he never delved into his spirituality and certainly would not do so now. "Perhaps someday, your Ladyship, I will be inclined to listen to a sermon, but this is not that day." Their eyes warred as he thought about reminding her of her Pharisee-like arrogance. He would not let her, or anybody else, but especially her, preach to him about the way he lived his life.

Ian cleared his throat to break the tension. "Mrs. Miller, I think it goes without sayin' that McIntyre lives by a different book than ye, namely a ledger." He cast a reproving glance to his friend. "Politics and business do make strange bedfellows." He scanned the sisters' faces. "Perhaps if we just stuck to business, *hotel* business."

When no one responded, McIntyre finally took his eyes off Naomi. He was more than willing to get back to the important conversation but having her look down her nose at him like that was, well, a difficult pill to swallow. No, he wasn't a missionary feeding the homeless and adopting orphans, but she wasn't perfect either. Clearly, she was far from it. He decided he was indeed going to enjoy showing her just how human she was.

Saving all that for another day, he went back to his salvation: business. "I expect the hotel renovations will take approximately three months or so. However, if we go ahead and order the kitchen and dining room items immediately, Ian and I are in agreement that you can have the restaurant open by the end of September perhaps."

The discussion of things to do, orders that could be sent by telegraph, cost of the project, and a million little deadlines and details kept them talking until well after ten. Though the conversation was at times as strained as government negotiations with the Ute Indians, at least between himself and Naomi, business was accomplished.

There was something else going on at the table as well. McIntyre didn't miss the subtle but friendly glances between Rebecca and Ian during the evening. Or the way their conversation halted momentarily if their elbows happen to brush. His first reaction led him to wonder how such an alliance might impact the business at hand. Since there was nothing he could do about it at the moment, he opted to let it play out on its own. At least for now.

When Hannah nodded off at the table, everyone concluded it was time to end the meeting. They would pick back up in the morning. Ian warned the girls that the carpenters would arrive with the sun. Ian and McIntyre then thanked their hostesses for the meal, telling them they would let themselves out.

As the two men grabbed their hats from the counter out front, Ian shook his head in disgust. "Mac, I say this in the spirit of friendship. Ye need polishing. Ye've the manners of a goot."

"A what?"

"A goot."

McIntyre frowned, wishing his friend would learn to speak English. Ian sighed in frustration. "The farm animal—"

McIntyre yanked his hat down. "Never mind. I understand your point."

Scowling, he stepped into the cool night air and watched the busy street for a moment. His emotions were unclear, bordering as they were on irritation. Naomi was a frosty, but entertaining, handful. The bustle of Defiance reminded him, though, that he may have more to worry about than playing cat-and-mouse with Her Highness. Three beautiful, respectable women were an explosive ingredient in a town that was a powder keg anyway.

He hadn't counted on keeping randy miners *and* hostile prostitutes away from the sisters, while butting heads with Naomi in an honest attempt to help build their business. He had his own matters to manage, including a mine with over a hundred employees. Now he had to keep an eye on Ian and Rebecca, too, to make sure any relationship there developed in *his* best interest.

Frankly, manners were the least of his concerns.

~~~

Naomi dried the last plate and set it in the rack next to the sink. The pan of dishwater needed to be dumped, but it could wait till morning. She had finished cleaning the kitchen alone because she had insisted that Rebecca and Hannah retire. Wisely, they had left her alone. The events of the last few days, much less the last few weeks, weighed on her like boat anchors. She needed time alone and knew she wouldn't sleep anyway...again. The infernal beating of that out-of-tune piano every night was enough to make her scream. Now someone had added a tortuous harmonica.

Trying hard to shake off the frustration and sadness, Naomi grabbed a quilt they had packed dishes in, wrapped it around herself and headed down to her spot by the stream. Sitting down on a large piece of driftwood near the water's edge, she gazed up at the richly glittering night tapestry. She could stare at the infinite weaving of twinkling lights, shooting stars and ancient constellations for hours. In the vast grandeur of the Colorado sky she could lose herself. The beauty of it was the only thing *right* with this place.

She had come here every night since stumbling into Defiance. In her heart she wanted to pray, but the grief was still too fresh, her anger too blinding. Instead, she had just floated away into the velvety, twinkling heavens or drifted off with the gurgling sound of the stream. She felt God approved; her spirit was weary and sometimes all a parent needed to do was hold his child. Words could come later.

Tonight, however, there was no peace in the works of His hand. She was angry. She was grieving. She was disappointed in herself.

And, finally, she was ready to pray.

"I am failing you so badly, Father. My relationship with you is in shambles and this is the last place on earth you should have sent me."

Naomi sat still then for a long time considering things, seeing the faces of Dermot Guibne, those two harlots on the street, the flowers from The Iron Horse; not to mention, Rose, and Mr. McIntyre. Their ugly attitudes in her mind were representative of the whole town. "I don't like these people, God, and I don't have compassion for any of them." She was whining, but at least she was praying. "I know you want me to care, but they've all *chosen* their lives here. They choose to wallow in whiskey. They choose to debase themselves and barter in flesh. Then so be it," she fussed dismissively. "Your own word says that a man reaps what he sows."

She felt a sting in her conscience. Naomi knew with that last statement, she had overstepped her bounds in this discussion.

He didn't send her here to tell them about justice.

God was offering the gift of grace to Defiance. Who was she to decide whether the gift was delivered?

"I'm sorry. I'm sorry," she cried, hiding her face in her hands. "I need John here. He softened my rough edges. Corrected me with a gentle heart. If

John was here, he could have helped me see them as lost souls, not just enemies, not just prideful, arrogant sinners blinded by their own rebelliousness." Slowly, though, a faint light of understanding dawned in her heart with those last words. She peered through her fingers at the water shimmering in the moonlight. "That—that wasn't his job, though, was it?"

Emilio popped into her mind. She hadn't expected to find anyone in this town worthy of her compassion and now she and her sisters had practically adopted the waif. Then she thought of Daisy. Barely older than Hannah, how had she come to be here? What was her story? What had brought her to this place, this way of life?

What had turned Rose's heart to pure hate? Had she ever thought once about a god who loves her? Could Mr. McIntyre ever be made to understand the sacrifice Christ made and why? Hate, anger, self-loathing, rebellion, greed, all things that grew in this town like weeds. Yet God's redeeming love was here, too, and someone had to tell them about their hope. John wasn't here to do it for her. Rebecca and Hannah couldn't do it alone.

In her dream, God had asked her to take them the light.

"But we're so unprepared, Father. At least *I am*." She sniffled and wiped her nose with the back of her hand. "Rebecca and Hannah are miles ahead of me in their faith. They're full of compassion. I'm full of grief and anger. At the people of Defiance…At You."

She pulled the blanket tighter and thought about her losses. "I feel like I'm nothing without John. But I *know* I'm nothing without you. "

Naomi continued to stare at the stream for a time, no thoughts, no words, no more arguments. Crickets filled the silence and she waited.

Look at my cross, the Lord whispered. *You can see it now. John no longer stands between us. Look with your own eyes and your own heart and see that I gave my life even for these.*

That revelation grew in her heart and like a burning sun, overtook the darkness of her grief.

"You've broken my heart, Lord," Naomi mourned, her heart full of memories of John. As if she was lifting the weight of the world, she stood and looked up at the black sky dusted with diamonds. Eyes shining with tears, she opened her arms in surrender. "You took the one thing that mattered most to me in this world. Please help me to accept it and do what you've sent me here to do." She collapsed to her knees, sobbing. "Break me…here am I, Lord, use me," she begged, hoping God would finish this painful work in her. "Help me love You again. Help me love these people if that's what You want."

McIntyre stumbled across Naomi and quickly hid behind the branches of a small pine. Spellbound, he watched her sit and stare up at the stars, agony in her face. He knew he should go, but he couldn't pull himself away. Then she spoke. She talked and wept as if God was standing right beside her…and what she said, she was so candid, speaking her heart, holding nothing back from God. It made Him seem almost…real.

He had taken his midnight walk thinking the sound of the water would clear his head and show him how to handle the women and the town. *This* was far more than he had gambled on. He actually felt a pang of guilt, knowing she would be horrified to realize he was listening. Yet, he couldn't move, couldn't *stop* listening. He watched transfixed as she wrestled with God, spoke to Him boldly. She was intimate with Him and painfully vulnerable. There was no place in her soul that was hidden from Him.

And then, most amazingly of all, she begged him to break her…so that she could have compassion on this town of sinners and reprobates.

Dumbfounded by her prayer, he stepped back, staggered over the rocky ground and turned away. He was confused and a little alarmed by the emotions warring within him. What had he just seen? Why was his heart racing?

He rested against a boulder to find his mental footing on that foundation of serene rebellion and self-gratification. He re-visited the atrocities he had witnessed, the barbaric violence, the blood, the destruction. His life was fine, built as it was around himself and his desires. God was a nuisance, a crutch, a disinterested father.

Yet, his heart wouldn't harden. Perplexed, he discovered that he felt different somehow, but couldn't put words to it. It was deeper than words were allowed to go.

Off-balance, and angry at being so, he shook the confusion off his shoulders and decided to do what any man would do with unwanted emotions: drown them with rye whiskey and a willing woman.

Chapter 18

If August had a sound, Naomi would always associate the one of '77 with the continual whack of hammers or the melodic rhythm of hand saws. Daily, the carpenters showed up at the hotel with the sun and worked till it had set behind the mountains. Constant, but mercifully brief, meetings with Mr. McIntyre and Ian kept the inn's progress on track.

Naomi noted and appreciated that Mr. McIntyre seemed pre-occupied in her presence and a trifle less arrogant. She assumed he was busy with other projects, and didn't mind one bit that their conversations had become less of a battle. She had caught him staring at her a time or two, but in an odd way, as if she had two heads. As long as it made him keep his distance, she didn't need to know the why of it.

In rapid fire succession, telegrams went out daily, items were ordered, and the girls spent almost as much time studying the Montgomery Ward catalog as they did the Bible. Eager to stay busy, they also pitched in on the construction, hauling out debris, painting, fetching nails, whatever the crew and Ian needed. But Naomi and Rebecca saw to it that Hannah handled the lighter duties.

When they realized with surprise that the month of August had all but disappeared, more than just the hotel was dramatically transforming. Even loose-fitting dresses were unable to hide something happening at Hannah's midsection.

Naomi, worried about more trouble for her little sister, asked Hannah to cut down significantly on her trips outside the inn. The questioning looks were turning into bold, knowing stares and gossip had begun following them down the boardwalk. Even the men working on the hotel discussed her in hushed whispers and with sideways glances. In light of things, Hannah had acquiesced.

~~~

Hannah sifted flour into a bowl and thought about the way time was flying by. Daddy used to say it felt as if all he did was get up, shave in the mirror, and do it again—a knock at the back door brought her out of her reverie and she stepped into the hallway.

"I'll see who it is."

Rebecca and Naomi, sweeping up sawdust out front, straightened and held onto the brooms with death grips. Hannah, strangely confident trouble was *not* knocking, ignored their concerned looks and flung open the door. To her delight, Daisy stood on the back stoop with two large packages wrapped in brown paper.

"Oh, here let me help." Hannah took one of the cumbersome packages from Daisy. "Please, come in." She turned away, fully expecting the girl to follow. Given no choice, their guest entered and trailed Hannah into the kitchen, looking wary, like a rabbit expecting to hear baying dogs any second.

The renovation in here was nearly complete and a huge farm-style table graced the middle of the kitchen. Hannah set her package down and turned to take the other from Daisy.

"Thank you for bringing this. Is it from Mr. McIntyre?"

The girl shook her head, setting the package on the table. "Oh, no. I—I had some clothes I thought you might could use." Hannah cocked her head, unclear on her meaning. Daisy motioned towards Hannah's abdomen. "What are you, about seven months or so now? I had a bunch of clothes left over...and there's a few things in there for the baby, too."

Naomi and Rebecca peeked into the kitchen, looking confused and surprised to find Daisy. Just the same, they greeted her with enthusiasm and warm smiles.

"Look what she brought me." Hannah tapped on one package. "Clothes. Clothes for my *special* time and even some baby things."

Her sisters sucked in a simultaneous breath. Leaning on the door frame, Naomi shoved her hands into her apron. "Daisy, how kind of you. You don't know how badly Hannah needs those. Can we pay you for them?"

"Oh, no." Daisy waved her hand, stepping sideways toward the exit. "I just don't need them anymore."

Obviously, she wanted out, but Hannah hated to let her leave with just a thank you. Her sisters came to the rescue. Acting as if they only wanted to get into the kitchen and see the clothes, they slowly crowded Daisy away from the door. Rebecca placed a gentle hand on the girl's shoulder. "Daisy, won't you stay and have some coffee with us while we see what you've brought our sister?"

Hannah clutched Daisy's hand. "Oh, please stay. It'll be like Christmas. I haven't had any new clothes in, well, since Christmas, I guess."

Rebecca pulled out a chair for Daisy. "We would really love for you to stay…if you can?"

Daisy was profoundly impressed by what seemed a sincere desire for her company. It had been so long since she had been amongst friends. Not that they were, but she liked them immensely; felt drawn to them, in fact. Hannah might be expecting out of wedlock but it was plain as the nose on Daisy's face that these weren't the same kind of women as those that flowered in Mr. McIntyre's garden. She had told the other girls that when they gossiped about the sisters, but they didn't care to listen to Daisy.

Curious, and desperately lonely for the innocence of simple friendship, she agreed, with an almost imperceptible nod, to stay. The girls showered her with laughter and smiles as Naomi put on a pot of coffee.

While Hannah opened the packages and they all oohed and aaahed over the new clothes, Daisy slowly let out bits and pieces of her story. She was a Kansas girl who fell in love with a cowboy. For awhile they owned their own spread but he wasn't much of a businessman. Word of gold nuggets jumping out of the ground drew them to Colorado, from one lonely mining town to the next. Defiance, they had decided, would be the make-it or break-it town.

When Hannah draped a blue gingham jumper over herself to model, Daisy told them how she had come to work for Mr. McIntyre.

"We'd only been here a month when Dan found his first gold nugget. He was so proud and so sure he was on the edge of a huge strike." Daisy nervously fidgeted with her fingers, a bad habit she'd had since childhood. "Word got out, though, and two days later someone shot him dead on his way to the Assayer's office."

An awkward, but empathetic, silence filled the room. Compassion in her eyes, Naomi patted Daisy's hand. "I'm sorry for your loss. I know what that's like."

Daisy nodded, having heard the rumor of *her* husband's death. "Claim jumpers took our claim, burned our tent. I guess the stress of everything…" She shrugged, resigned to the way the story had turned out. "I lost the baby. After that, nothing much mattered. Mr. McIntyre gave me a roof over my head…" she looked down then, expecting the haughty glances that were coming, the quick excuses they would invent to send her out.

Instead, Hannah sat down and took Daisy's hand. "Daisy, would you tell us your real name?"

Blinking, bewildered, she whispered, "Mollie. Dan used to call me Li'l M."

Hannah shook Daisy's limp hand. "We're proud to know you, Mollie."

It was a watershed moment in Daisy's life. She felt liked and wanted and maybe even accepted here. She didn't know how that could be, but she wanted to come back, would come back, soon…if they would let her.

Naomi looked up at their new clock hanging above the new red and white cook stove. "Mollie, would you like to eat dinner with us? It's nothing special but we hear it's better than what the Kitchen is slinging out."

Daisy laughed a wonderful, clear, light-hearted laugh that still held the ring of innocence. "Emilio says he's gained five pounds eating dinner with you all…" but the mirth quickly faded. "Lily and I are working the floor this afternoon," she paused almost imperceptibly here then added, "Mr. McIntyre doesn't like it if we're even one minute late on Fridays or Saturdays." The pained looks on their faces told Daisy they understood. Daisy rose and the sisters with her. "Thank you for the coffee."

Hannah touched Daisy lightly on the elbow. "Can you come back tomorrow?" Daisy couldn't believe the hope she saw in the girl's eyes. "For lunch or dinner?

Daisy shifted nervously. "Well, I…"

"We'd love for you to join us." Rebecca took a step closer as if to emphasize her point.

"Well, maybe later…sometime."

Hannah smiled, what looked like an easy, sincere smile to Daisy. "Anytime. You're welcome here anytime." The compassion in the girl's voice warmed Daisy's lonely heart.

During her shift at work, as men pawed at her, or did worse, Daisy kept the sisters in the forefront of her mind. They knew who she was and what she did for a living and yet they had responded to her with kindness and respect. They had made her feel that if there had been a pastor's wife or school teacher in the room, she still would have been treated the same. Feeling valued again was not something she had expected—

A drunken, smelly, and barely-still-vertical miner practically fell on her as she approached the bar with her empty tray. A toothless grin filled his face and dried mud caked his beard. Fondling and grinding on her with no shame, he waved two sizable gold nuggets in her face.

"Wan' some of this, don' ya, girlie," he mumbled in her face, breathing whiskey and rotten vegetables all over her. Daisy's stomach nearly rolled over as she grimaced and pulled away. "This'd buy you s' perty dresses," he slurred heavily as his hand claimed her bottom, stopping her retreat.

Setting the tray on the counter, Daisy grit her teeth and turned her head away to seek fresh air before his reeking breath brought up her lunch. "I don't know, Jed. I think you've had too much to drink to manage a poke."

"Oh, I'll manage!" Wildly waving his one free arm, he held on to Daisy firmly with the other and started dragging her to the steps. "Just get me up these stairs, Daisy, girl, and I'll do the rest."

The men drinking nearby pointed and laughed. "Don't rob him blind, Daisy," one yelled and the others hee-hawed in drunken hysteria over the irony. Daisy was known for her honesty; she never went through her customers' trousers. She could only hope that this foul-smelling body of debauchery would pass out the moment he touched her bed. She would happily sleep on the floor to avoid a roll in the hay with him.

Rose watched them struggle up the stairs and grinned triumphantly. Ol' Jed was drunk as a bear drowning in salmon, and smelled worse, but he was obedient. Rose had encouraged him to give Daisy some company and he had swaggered his way to her. Even if he couldn't perform the task, he had made the little wretch miserable for a few minutes. That was enough revenge for Rose and she would make sure Daisy knew there was more where that came from if she visited the gringa sisters again.

As Daisy's door closed, Jed's willingness to follow orders gave Rose ideas and a cold sneer danced across her lips. The dark mirth behind it bubbled up from an evil, powerful place in her soul and she liked it.

Naomi snuffed the lantern hanging in the kitchen, waited for her eyes to adjust to the darkness then carried her last armload of Daisy's dresses towards the stairs. She stopped near the front doors to appreciate the brilliance of the moon and the contrasting black shadows. She was tempted to step outside and peek at the full moon, but there was still a considerable amount of traffic on the street.

Defiance never slept, it seemed, and the hotel was at the *slow* end of the street, farthest from the Iron Horse and the avenue that led into Tent Town. Shaking her head at the ambitious men in search of drink and companionship, she turned to climb the stairs.

A sound, a shuffle perhaps, followed by a loud whack right outside their front door caused Naomi to whirl on the stairs' landing. She stared into the gloom then caught a glimpse of a figure dashing past the windows. A woman, she knew, by the curves and the flutter of a skirt.

She waited, wondering why a woman had been on their porch. Then she knew, of course, there was only a handful of women in Defiance who would dare darken their door. Resigned to finding some form of mischief, Naomi wound her way back down the stairs, slowly opened the door and stepped outside.

Chapter 19

The note, tacked to the post and rustling in the light breeze, caught Naomi's attention immediately. She snatched it down and read the threat by moonlight.

The words "We'll get you" were scrawled across the paper in large, spidery letters.

Imagining her hands on Rose's throat, Naomi looked down the shadowy street and slowly, meticulously crumpled the note into a tight, compact little ball.

"Not if I get you first," she promised. Oh, but these girls were mightily mistaken if they thought they would run her out. It would take a heck of a lot more than a nasty, juvenile note.

A lot more.

~~~

Like red silk rolling off a cloth bolt, Rose poured herself into the lap of a handsome, dark-haired youth and bestowed a passionate, bewitching kiss on him. The boy beamed drunkenly, dreamy-eyed over the promises Rose's sparkling, cleavage-baring dress was making. The men at his table cheered and slapped him on the back. Rose had chosen young, dark and handsome Hank carefully and decided he would work to perfection. She led the hypnotized boy upstairs to her room then threw him on her bed. As he struggled with fumbling, drunken hands to undo his shirt buttons, she hiked her dress up and straddled him.

Wiggling suggestively, she stretched out over him ever so slowly and tasted the salt on his neck and throat. She heard him gasp as the curves of her flesh seared his pathetic, little brain. He ran his hands up and down her, touching her fiery flesh quickly over and over as if she were as hot as a buck stove.

Rose's cold smile and dark eyes glittered with power in the dimly lit room. Her voice, husky and bewitching, stole his will. "I need you to do something for me, Hank."

~~~

Daisy assumed that Lily and Iris did not consider themselves mischievous by nature, but by virtue of boredom. As the girls stood in the toiletry section of the mercantile, perusing bath water scents, she saw evil glee glittering in their eyes when Naomi came in to shop. Smacking her chewing gum, Lily ribbed Iris with devilish delight. They kept their heads lowered and watched as Naomi approached the counter.

Dreading the trouble coming down the pike, Daisy quietly slipped further down the wall to the bolts of cloth, distancing herself from the two troublemakers. Naomi handed Mr. Boot a list and he smoothed it out on the counter so the two could study it carefully. Watching them get lost in their conversation, Lily removed the pink wad of chewing gum from her mouth and grinned at Iris.

She held it up for her co-worker to see and the two girls had to slap their hands over their mouths to suppress their giggles. Iris nodded and nonchalantly meandered up to the candy at the counter. She pretended to study all the jars intently as if she just couldn't make up her mind which item appealed to her sweet tooth. She and Naomi exchanged tense nods but Naomi let her gaze linger.

"I got your note."

Iris frowned. "Note?"

Naomi studied the girl, looking as if she was deciding whether to believer her or not. "Someone, I assume one of you *flowers*, tacked a little love note to the front of our hotel. You can tell Rose or whoever penned it, it was a waste of time. We're not going anywhere."

As the tension between Naomi and Iris increased, Lily slithered up behind Naomi and studied that long cascade of flowing, golden hair. It wasn't braided today and she shot Iris a grin that showed she was clearly pleased with this opportunity. Deciding on the best way to handle this attack, Lily flattened the gum in her hand then slapped Naomi right in the middle of her back in a friendly, but forceful, greeting.

"Mrs. Miller, isn't it? How nice to see you again."

Naomi spun on the Negro girl like a badger ready for a fight. Lily raised her hands in mock surrender. "I'm sorry, I didn't mean to startle you." She started backing away quickly, and tugged on Iris's sleeve. "Tell your sisters we said hello. Especially the one with the bun in the oven." Collapsing into a fit of laughter, the two prostitutes ran from the store, delighted with their evil prank.

Naomi watched them leave, daggers fairly flying from her eyes. Feeling like a coward, Daisy dropped her gaze to a bar of soap. The joke the two girls had played made her sick to her stomach. Weren't their lives bad enough? Why did they have to go around spreading more misery? And apparently they'd left a note as well? Ashamed of them, and herself for not saying anything to Naomi, Daisy sneaked out of the store like a beaten dog avoiding its master.

Disgusted, Naomi tried to shake off the encounter and finish her business. It was not until a few hours later, when she wandered out back to the stoop to braid her hair and get a breath of fresh air, that she discovered the sabotage.

Rebecca stumbled across Naomi there, working in vain to peel and strip the hairs, one by one, out of the sticky mess. Her older sister grimaced at the disaster. "What is that?"

Naomi glanced up, well aware that her expression could singe the hair off Satan's tail. "If I'm not mistaken, it's chewing gum."

"How in the world...?"

"I took a little trip to the mercantile today and two of our neighborly saloon girls were in there. The black one slapped me on the back by way of a *greeting*. I suspect that's when she left me this little gift."

Shaking her head with obvious dismay, Rebecca grabbed the nest of gum and examined it more closely. The confection was matted and tangled in Naomi's locks as stubbornly as manure in a sheep's coat. "Sister, I think I'd better get my scissors."

Naomi felt the blood drain from her face. If there was one single thing over which she had ever allowed herself some vanity, it was her rich, thick golden head of hair. Oh, how John had loved to run his hands through it.

Rebecca comforted her sister with the brighter side. "I'll have to take off about four inches, but it's not a disaster. It will still be plenty long."

Naomi had worked for years at getting her hair down past her waist. Now that was to be stripped away too. Deciding, however, with angry resolution not to give those *girls* the satisfaction of the small triumph, she straightened. "Take what you have to. It's only hair."

Rebecca pulled a chair outside and Naomi dropped down on to it. She sat scowling in silence as her big sister carefully and gingerly cut her shimmering tresses.

Hair fell in heeps around their feet. "I know this is the kind of thing that makes you see red, Naomi, but before you get too mad and go claw out their eyes, I was wondering if you might consider what would prompt these girls to do this."

"Meanness? Vindictiveness? Pure evil?"

"Self-loathing?" Rebecca spoke softly and patiently. "Jealousy? Anger caused by frustration and hopelessness?"

Naomi considered that. No doubt, their lives were probably something less than pleasant.

Rebecca stroked her sister's head. "I just think that turning the other cheek is far more important than it's ever been. We're in a different place now, Naomi, and I'm not talking about geography."

"That's easy for you to say. You're not cutting spearmint chewing gum out of your hair." When Rebecca didn't respond, Naomi relented and dropped her chin. "I know, Rebecca. I know. I'll try to turn the other cheek." She pivoted in the seat and looked up at her sister, the threat on the mysterious note still fresh in her mind. "But I've only got two and they're both stinging."

~~~

McIntyre was distracted, a problem that had been growing in intensity since that night he caught Naomi praying. And the more distracted he grew, the more irritable he got. His card playing skills, however, had not been affected and he walked away tonight with easily several hundred dollars in gold dust. It had tired him, though, staring into the dull, hopeless eyes of miners and prospectors. Their lack of passion had taken the challenge out of the game. Or was the lack his?

He had even been bored with Rose last night. She had dutifully come when called, shared her passion, ignited his, but afterwards, lying with her in the dark, he could barely stand to touch her. He wondered if that was how his flowers felt after each and every customer.

He shook his head. From where was this creeping dissatisfaction with life coming? And why, when it tried to rear its ugly head, did he repeatedly wander back to that moment when he had found Naomi praying? Why did that haunt him so?

Desperate for a break, but determined to avoid the stream, he excused himself from the pointless game, tossed Brannagh the bag of gold for safekeeping, and snatched his hat off the table. Stretching, he ventured instead to the boardwalk. The chilly temperature bothered his leg and begged to make his limp more pronounced, but he wouldn't give in to his souvenir from Chicamauga. Enjoying the crisp, clean mountain air, he lit his ever-present cheroot. Seconds later, Ian joined him. The two men stood in silence, watching their breath and the cigar smoke curl and dance in the cold night.

Ian looked up at the distant mountains. "I believe winter is comin' early this year. I had planned on leaving by the end of September, but now, I'm thinkin' Defiance has become a wee bit more interestin'. Wouldn't ye say?" He quirked an eyebrow at his friend and offered the smallest hint of a smile.

McIntyre shrugged non-commitally as he watched the men and horses flow by. Saturday was always busy. Men wandered, either on foot or horseback, drunk and sober, back and forth between the Iron Horse and the tent saloons in the other part of town. Faintly, in the distance, they heard the popping sound of small caliber gunfire. Probably a Derringer going off over at the Wolf's Head.

Ian shoved his hands in his pockets and tapped his foot in time with *Buffalo Gals* floating out from the Iron Horse. "Are ye serious about cleanin' up Defiance?"

McIntyre inhaled. There was a change in the air tonight, more of a bite to it. Winter was coming. It was his favorite season, though it was extremely unforgiving in Defiance. "Yes, yes, I am. We'll never get the railroad in here if we don't."

"Then I'm thinkin' ye need to start with that marshal. Does he actually know how to do anything other than take orders from ye?"

"Well, that is why I hired him. He's one of my best employees. Wade is loyal to a fault."

"Precisely. He won't arrest anyone or enforce a law unless he checks with ye first. Defiance can't keep being this free-for-all if ye want respectability. Ye need laws and ye need a lawman who can enforce them."

Suspicious, McIntyre looked up at his friend. "When did you develop this sudden interest in making Defiance a town full of law abiding citizens?"

"When I started thinkin' maybe my travelin' days are over."

McIntyre rolled the cheroot around in his mouth. "It's the black-haired one you're fond of. What makes her so special? Other than business meetings, you've hardly talked to the woman."

Ian grinned like a schoolboy. "Aye, and I'd like to talk to her some more to see if I want to talk to her some more."

The mischievous expression on his friend's weathered face made McIntyre laugh. "I think the lot of them maybe more trouble than they're worth." He slapped Ian on the shoulder. "But it is good to see you taking an interest in something."

Before he could reply, gunfire erupted again, but much closer this time. The boom was thunderous and came from a definite location. The two men eyed each with alarm.

"That sounded like a sho'gun—" Ian observed. Before he could finish, McIntyre had tossed aside his cheroot and was running like a man on fire toward the other end of town, leaving his hat in the dust.

Chapter 20

McIntyre ran as if he was racing the devil. He bounded down the boardwalks then on to the hotel's porch. The front door was open and he could hear a commotion of some kind upstairs. Drawing his gun, he bolted up the stairs.

"Mrs. Miller, ladies, are you all right?"

He turned the corner and paused to get his bearings. The second floor was no longer one, large open space. Fifteen rooms had been roughed in and he now found himself staring down a darkened hall. Light was coming from the last doorway on the right and he could hear several frantic voices, yelling and screaming all at once.

"Mrs. Miller," he yelled again, bolting down the hallway. He leaped into the room, gun pointed at—

Hank Barrows. The young man was kneeling on the floor, hands laced behind his head, and he was peppered with bloody wounds down a good portion of the left side of his body. His shirt hung from him in shreds. Still wearing her faded, blue day dress, Naomi was holding a shotgun on him, smoke whisping from its barrel. Rebecca and Hannah, in their nightclothes, were cowering behind her. When they saw McIntyre, all of them started talking at once to him, but Naomi kept the gun trained on Hank.

"He broke in here—"

"I only meant to scare'em!"

"Started yelling crazy stuff—"

"Said he was going to rip off our clothes—"

"I wasn't gonna hurt anybody!"

"QUIET!" McIntyre yelled. The room fell silent. "Put that gun away, Mrs. Miller, before you shoot *me*. I can see the barrel shaking from here."

Slowly, Naomi lowered the gun. Hank started to lower his hands, but McIntyre waved his gun at him. "Keep them up until you tell me what happened…or you bleed to death."

The boy started shaking his head back and forth as if he couldn't stand his pain. "I swear I wasn't gonna hurt'em! Rose said she'd let me have a poke for free if I'd just scare these girls. That's all. I wasn't even gonna touch'em!"

"Then what were you doing leaning over the bed?" Rebecca's voice and eyes were wild with fear.

The sound of boots tromping up the stairs stopped her hysterics and, a moment later, Ian appeared. He assessed the situation quickly. "Are you all right, ladies?" When they nodded, he went to Hank. Helping him to his feet, he looked him over. "Ye're fortunate her aim was off. Ye're peppered up good, but you willna die. A wee touch more to the right and ye'd be without your worthless head, though."

Naomi raised her gun again. "I was trying to miss. I only wanted to scare *him*."

The marshal entered at that moment, gun drawn, and, after taking in the scene, looked to McIntyre for instruction. "Take him to the jail, Wade." Disgusted with all this unnecessary high drama, McIntyre grabbed Hank's shoulder and shoved him towards the marshal. "I'll be by shortly to have a talk with him. Get one of the flowers to come over and clean him up."

Without hesitating, the marshal grabbed the whimpering sot by the arm and led him out of the room as McIntyre holstered his gun. Clear out to the street they could hear Hank bewailing the misunderstanding. "I was only gonna scare'em. I wouldn't have hurt'em. Just scare'em; that's all. Am I dying...?"

As his voice faded, Naomi let the hammers down on her shotgun and breathed.

"Tell me what happened." The gentleness with which he'd asked the question surprised even him.

"Here, ladies..." Ian went to Rebecca and Hannah. "Why don't ye come with me? We'll have a spo' of warm tea to calm our nerves." With his hand on their backs, he gently led them out of the room.

Naomi leaned the gun in the corner and sat down on the bed. "Our rooms are almost finished. One more night and Hannah would have been in here alone." McIntyre found her dull stare disconcerting and her deadpan voice even more so. He approached the bed and leaned on a post. She looked weary both in body and spirit. He thought again of that night he had caught her praying and wondered if she was praying right now. He saw her eyes begin to glisten and she wiped the unwanted tears away angrily. He had the sudden urge to hold her, to comfort her, to feel the warmth of her head on his shoulder. The desire startled him to the point that he actually backed away a step.

"I came in from the backyard and the hotel was so quiet, but then I heard the stairs creek. They hadn't done that before, not that I'd noticed." She turned her head to look at the wall behind him. He followed her gaze to the paneling, ripped and splintered from buckshot. "I just knew something was wrong and we keep the gun behind the door. I heard a voice whispering but it wasn't Rebecca or Hannah." She shook her and frowned. "I tried to be so quiet...When I crept into the room, I saw him standing at the end of the bed...just staring at them."

Naomi looked at him then and the depth of pain and confusion he saw drew him back to the end of the bed, but no closer.

"I warned him. I tried to get him to leave." She swallowed. "What if I'd killed him? I nearly did." She wasn't asking about the legal ramifications, he knew, but the deeper meaning of taking a life. "A kind of blind fear came over me, but I was blind with rage at the same time. How can that be?"

He didn't know the answer to that, but he did know her experience wasn't unique. He remembered standing almost frozen with fear and yet firing with blind rage at whooping, screaming Indians intent on cutting his throat and dismembering his body. That strange mix of fear and fury had come over him repeatedly during the war as well.

Turning from the bloody memories, he offered encouragement. "You didn't kill him...and I dare say once word of your shotgun gets out, you won't have any more unwanted visitors."

"He said Rose put him up to it. Why does she hate us so?" Naomi's chin quivered and he heard tears in her voice. He knew, though, that she wouldn't cry in front of him. No matter what it took, she wouldn't do that in front of him. He understood the need to hide weakness and vulnerability.

"I suspect she wants you to leave. You needn't concern yourself with her now. She'll be on the morning stage. I'll see to it personally."

"I appreciate you coming by. Please let us know if we can press charges....if it even goes that far."

He detected cynicism in the comment. She didn't trust that anything would happen to the boy. Nothing had happened to Guibne. "I'll stop by the jail and tell Wade to start the proceedings. He'll be punished." He hoped the promise would reassure her.

She offered nothing more and stared down at her hands in her lap. He realized he was dismissed. Wishing for something more to say, he motioned as if tipping his hat "Until tomorrow then, Mrs. Miller."

Defiant against any emotions that might make her tolerate the man, much less *like* him, Naomi stood, straight and tall as she could manage, to watch Mr. McIntyre leave. She hoped she looked regal and collected. She wanted him to know she was strong and didn't need him to lean on…unlike Daisy or any of those other women in his employ.

Yet, in spite of herself, Naomi felt a slight kindness towards Mr. McIntyre. She assumed his gentle voice and attempted heroism were lulling her into a false sense of trust. He was a cad, a man who led women into prostitution; a dishonest, disreputable business man not worth her time. He was here now out of a need to protect his investment and nothing else. But she was so tired of fighting this town, the men, these evil women and their plots—

She waited till she heard his boots on the stairs then fell backward across the bed. She was too stunned and too tired to cry. She merely wanted to get away from this hellish place, to go somewhere people weren't constantly trying to insult, injure, or ogle them. She wanted to lie down and feel John's arms around her. Hoping her mind would stay numb, she rolled over and curled up into a tight little ball, like a child awaiting the safehaven of sleep.

Rebecca and Hannah watched Ian bustle confidently about the kitchen as he made the tea and admired the new counters and cabinets. "I'm quite pleased," he muttered as he put water on to boil. "They've done a wonderful job. This is a much more functional kitchen for a commercial venture."

Neither of the sisters replied. Suddenly aware that they were in their night things, Hannah pulled her gown closer and hunched beneath the table, trying to make herself insignificant.

Rebecca slid her hand over and clutched Hannah's. "Are you all right?"

Hannah half-nodded, half shook her head. "I don't know. I guess so. I'm not sure really what I think. I don't know if I'm more shaken by that man coming in our room or by Naomi trying to shoot him."

"She tried to miss. A scatter gun has a wide pattern."

"She pulled the trigger."

"She had the *guts* to pull the trigger. That's not an easy burden to carry. To have a temper like that must be frightening."

Hannah bit her lip, willing to ponder that point. If not for what Rebecca had said, Hannah wouldn't have thought of it in that way. And maybe because Naomi *was* willing to use a gun, whether out of courage or fury, there would be no more trouble. She prayed it was so. She was scared enough as it was. Glancing down at her ever-growing mid-section, she tried not to fear the future.

Ian set cups on the table then returned with a kettle of hot water. Rebecca assisted by putting the tea and strainers in each cup. He poured the water, returned the kettle to the stove then sat down with them. Dunking the strainer, he eyed the girls with compassion.

"Ye've been through a lo' since ye departed yer home. I think ye're holding up remarkably well. I'd be willing to bet that once words of this gets out, ye'll have no more trouble."

Hannah wasn't so sure. She had a strong suspicion that there was one woman in town who wasn't feeling too peaceable. "What about Rose? Is she going to let this go?"

"I believe Rose's time in Defiance has come to an end. Mac has no patience for troublesome wh—flowers. Rose has been a thorn in his side for some time now. I suspect he'll be pruning her from the garden forthwith."

Rebecca stirred a little honey into her tea and offered Ian a melancholy smile. "I can't believe how far we've come from Cary and I don't mean miles. That life seems a million years in the past."

"Aye, I know what ye mean. My life as a young man in Scotland is a vague memory now. Everywhere I've traveled, in fact, seems vague and shadowy. I regret not having put down roots somewhere but my wanderlust wouldna let me be." He sipped his tea and thought for a moment. "I landed in Defiance last year and thought to leave this fall..." The look on his face transformed to something deeper and softer. Hannah knew if she could see the change, so could Rebecca. "I think now I'll stay a wee bit longer. I'd like to see the hotel up and runnin'."

Rebecca paused with her tea almost at her lips. "Do you think you'll ever go back to Scotland?"

Ian shook his head. "I knew when I left I wouldna see home again. I'm more interested in lookin' forward than back. The past is done and there's no changin' it. We can best honor our dead by livin' well."

Rebecca considered his words and nodded, her eyes aglow with what looked like a new understanding.

Ian straightened up in his seat, as if he was intent on making his next point. "Movin' forward dusna mean ye love them any less. It just means *ye're* still alive." A shadow of a memory crossed his face. "I just thank God He dinna leave me to die alone with a bottle in Glasgow. After Annie died, I came close."

Rebecca's eyes widened. "You're a believer?"

"I am a man of faith, but admittedly a wayward faith. Though, somehow I feel the prodigal son is returnin' home. It's just taken me twenty-five years and seven thousand miles."

"I'm glad you found your way back." Rebecca's reply was so soft, the statement was barely above a whisper. Hannah took note of her sister's sparkling eyes aimed at Ian and the intent way he in turn studied her. Realizing that she was exhausted and no one had heard from Naomi, she stood up. It wasn't as if Rebecca and Mr. Donoghue would miss her.

Mr. McIntyre popped his head in before she could leave the table and bid everyone good night. "Ladies, I hope you are recovered from your ordeal. I'm going down to the marshal's office and will let you know how we handle this."

"Thank you," Hannah interjected, acknowledging that no one had bothered to show him or Ian any appreciation. "You came running when you heard the shots. Both of you. Thank you."

Mr. McIntyre simply nodded and disappeared out the door.

~~~

When McIntyre walked into the jail, Wade looked up from his dime novel and shrugged apologetically. "I reckon he'll live, Mr. McIntyre, but he's sleepin' it off now. Squalled like a baby all the way here, then went out like a lamp when his head hit the pillow."

Displeased that he couldn't question Hank, McIntyre strode over to the cell and looked in on the new guest, barely visible in the low light. His drunken snoring, the wet, sloppy sound of a hog rooting through thick mud, convinced McIntyre he was indeed alive.

"Lily cleaned him up some, but I told her not to worry too much about him. He ain't dyin'."

He studied the boy for a moment and decided he probably hadn't meant any harm, but McIntyre would make an example of him. It was that or face the belligerent High-and-Mighty Queen at the end of the street.

"Charge him with breaking and entering, keep him here fifteen days and fine him $150. When his pa comes into see him, tell him to find me."

That handled, he marched across the street to pack Rose. He was not looking forward to the scene she would cause. These melodramas both embarrassed and infuriated him. Tonight, however, was the end of it. It was only four or five hours to the morning stage and she was going to be on it, no ifs, ands, or buts.

He shot straight to her room and burst in unannounced. To his great annoyance, the room was empty and some of her toiletry items were missing from her dresser. He checked her closet. Nearly all of her clothes were gone. Staring at the all-but-empty clothes rod, he traced his beard thoughtfully, trying to deal with her unexpected departure.

"She's gone." Jasmine's voice was flat and devoid of any emotion. McIntyre turned to study his new Asian acquisition. Sultry and slender, he had been immediately impressed with her in Denver and paid well for her. Now, she bored him too, even in her in her exotic, traditional blue silk dress. "She said you would not lay your hands on her again."

"And?"

Jasmine shrugged, her expression inscrutable. "She was very angry and not making any sense, going in and out of Spanish. I did hear her say you better keep looking over your shoulder. That she'd be back."

McIntyre muttered a vile name for Rose and slammed the closet door. She couldn't have gone far; she had to be hiding somewhere in Tent Town. He would dispatch some men to turn the slum upside down if necessary, but he would find her and he would put her on that stage. It was obvious that she was vindictive, vengeful, and more than a little crazy. If she managed to stay in hiding in Defiance, the next time he saw her beautiful, ugly face might be his last.

Chapter 21

When no one could find Rose by sunup, McIntyre called off the search. It troubled him that she had so easily disappeared. Feeling the lack of sleep slowing his mind, he told Wade he was going to rest for a few hours but to wake him if he heard anything. At noon, Wade did just that. McIntyre was already dressed and working on a cup of coffee when the marshal came to his room.

"Gustav Jorgensen said Rose paid his brother $100 to take her over to Alta last night. You reckon she's outta your hair?"

Seeing that Alta was only seven miles on the other side of Boomerang Pass, he rather doubted it.

"For now," was all he said to the marshal. "For now."

He decided he would give Rose time to settle in and feel comfortable. In a few weeks or so, he would send someone to escort her back to Mexico. *Then* she would be out of his hair.

~~~

At a meeting at his mine office, McIntyre told Ian that Rose had slipped away. He didn't tell him he was worried about what she might do now. McIntyre did allude to the fact that Rose was the cause of most trouble in town and with her gone, things should settle down for the sisters.

Sitting on the other side of McIntyre's desk, Ian looked doubtful. "Hank's escapade might embolden other men. I think these women need watchin' over and I mean more than the marshal passing by or escortin' them down the street."

McIntyre heartily disagreed, shaking his head. He leaned back in his chair amidst squeaking leather and springs. "Mrs. Miller's run-in with Guibne showed everyone she's feisty. Now they know she's not afraid to actually pull a trigger. That's probably more than enough to get even the worst drunks in Defiance to stand-down."

"Mac, the reality of the situation is that ye dunna control every randy miner, prospector and gambler in these parts. Three women with no men around is an awfully tempting prize, gun or no gun. If ye'll not do something more, I will."

A grin leaped to McIntyre's face. He realized where this was going and decided to help his friend. "By all means, then, I think you should spend as much time as possible with them." He couldn't help but add one dash of sarcasm, though. "I for one will sleep much better at night knowing their knight in shining armor is watching over them."

Ian harumphed irritably at the comment, but didn't argue. And if pressed, McIntyre might admit to a twinge of jealousy. Just a twinge. He had been the first to rush into that room the other night but Naomi had acted as if the event was somehow his fault. There was no pleasing the woman. Given that she viewed him somewhere above pond scum but a step below snakes, he would simply have to try harder—

He heard the sparking, grinding scream of mental brakes.

Try harder? No, he thought with a curse. He wouldn't try at all. This was ridiculous. No woman was worth this amount of distraction. And how had he gone from planning to get her into bed to actually caring what she thought of him? When had that happened?

He shook his head as if to ward off this confounded confusion. "I'm going to be extremely busy with our mine, Ian." His irritable bark caused a look of surprise on his friend's face. "Feel free to take over the inn as your project. I'll come around to check the progress, but you can be there night and day if it pleases you."

~~~

Leaning over a list at the kitchen table, Rebecca and Hannah finished writing up an order for linens then stared at each other with dread in their eyes.

Hannah glanced down at her mid-section. "I'm not going to take it the telegraph office and you can't go alone."

Ian, only a few feet away supervising the pump installation, excused himself from the carpenters and offered his elbow to Rebecca. "If ye'll have me?"

Swallowing nervously, Rebecca nodded. Ian grabbed his cane from the corner and came back to her with his hand extended. She commanded the heat in her face to subside, to no avail, and lightly clutched his fingers.

Rising to her feet, she looked at Hannah, who was wearing an unabashedly smug grin on her face. "Are you sure you don't want to come with us?"

Hannah shook her head resolutely and grinned wider. "No…and you two don't need me."

Rebecca honestly didn't mind the company, but Hannah was now beyond hiding her condition. The few remarks they had heard thus far on the street were far from kind and her little sister didn't need to subject herself to any more of them. Comments about penny's falling out and using a half-dollar next time took time for the sisters to comprehend, but eventually the meanings became quite clear. If Hannah was content hiding, then perhaps that was the best way to handle things for now.

As Ian and Rebecca stepped outside, she noticed his cane with the ornately carved wolf's head on top. "It's beautiful. I think it makes you look very distinguished."

He twirled the cane around as they strolled at a comfortable, casual speed. "It is very old and belonged to my father. Alas, I fear it makes me look as ancient as Methuselah."

"Hardly. You're dapper and handsome with it." She looked away, flushed with embarrassment over the bold comment that had just leaped out of her mouth.

Ian scratched his beard and grinned at her. Cringing with embarrassment, Rebecca prayed that God would strike her dumb and stop this run away mouth of hers.

"Ms. Rebecca, how is that there is such a spread in yer ages? Are there other siblings between ye and yer sisters?"

She shook her head, resigned to the implication that she was noticeably older than her sisters. "No, Momma and Daddy had me and after several years of no more children, pretty much assumed I was it. Then, low and behold, came Naomi twelve years later. They thought she was a small miracle, but then six years after Naomi was born, Hannah surprised everyone. When Momma and Daddy passed away so close to each other, Naomi and I were at least old enough to help raise her up." *Though if we had done a better job, she might not be in this predicament right now.*

"God knows the plans he has for ye…" Ian quoted as if he had read her thoughts or at least her face. "Ye must trust in that."

"We do, every day." *Especially here.*

"If ye don't mind me asking, where is the father of Hannah's babe?" It was the first time he had mentioned the situation.

Rebecca tugged nervously on her braid. "I don't know exactly." Rebecca had taken quite a shine to Ian, but that didn't mean she should go spouting off the family secrets. Besides, she didn't want him to think poorly of Hannah. "His father was going to send him to some Ivy League school this fall. I hope they both think it was worth abandoning her and the baby for it."

"I take it the lad dinna marry her then?" His voice was gentle and lacking any accusations. When Rebecca didn't answer immediately, he cleared his throat and apologized. "I'm sorry. That's none o' me business. Hannah seems a very sweet girl—"

"And Billy Page is a fast-talkin', quick-movin' scallywag." Rebecca was immediately sorry the unexpected gush of anger had taken control of her mouth. Crossing her arms, she shook her head and sighed. "He has no idea how many hearts he's broken."

They walked in silence after that until they reached the telegraph office. Ian plucked the order from Rebecca's hand. "Allow me. It won't take a moment. Rest on the bench and enjoy these last warm rays of the sun. Winter is comin' and it comes to Defiance with a vengeance."

She thanked him and sat down. Rebecca watched the town bustle about like any busy, civilized city back east. Everyday new folks rolled in, on the stage, with mule trains, or on their own, sure they could simply pluck ten-pound nuggets from the creeks. She heard that most prospectors, after fruitless months of panning, eventually gave up seeking their own fortunes and went to work for Mr. McIntyre in his mine.

The disproportionate number of women among the men was alarming. Ian had told them there were fewer thirty women in town and that females sparked ninety percent of the fights. She felt safe with him, though, and knew he was watching over them.

Over her?

It had been so long since a man had looked at her. Even longer since she'd wanted to look back. Ian made her feel as though he could see right past her wrinkles and seasoned age to the girl she used to be. Near as she could tell, he hadn't looked twice at Naomi or Hannah.

But was she getting ahead of herself? Ian clearly favored her, but how much and in what way? Rebecca had no desire to risk a heartbreak. Maybe he favored her precisely because of her age. That she was someone safe with whom he could be friends and there wouldn't be any romantic entanglements. Besides, Rebecca wasn't so sure she was ready for anything like that. She had her silly, romantic daydreams about Ian. That would have to do for now. Illusions were safe and didn't put either of them in awkward situations.

She settled on the bench more comfortably and shut her eyes to enjoy the gentle warmth on her face. Back home, the first day of September was just as hot as the first day of July. Here, in these mountains, at this altitude, she doubted it would ever be hot enough to melt candles like Southern heat could.

The bench moved as Ian sat beside her and she opened her eyes to thank him for sending the telegraph. To her dismay, a total stranger sat beside her, grinning widely through broken teeth and a scruffy beard. Another man stood near him, just as filthy and leering with an unnerving hunger.

"You're one of those new girls, ain't ya?" The man sitting beside her looked her up and down lecherously. "We heard about you up at our camp. You must be the oldest one, but you're still mighty pretty." He slapped his friend on the leg and laughed. "That's all right. I like'em seasoned. Sometimes them young'uns don't really know how to please a man—"

"Sir," Rebecca surged to her feet. "Your conversation is rude and vulgar. Please excuse me." She thought to push past the man who was standing and slip into the telegraph office, but the man on the bench came to his feet suddenly and grabbed her arm as the other one blocked her way.

"No streetwalker talks to Texas Jack that way—"

The raised voices brought Ian out of the office and immediately to Rebecca's defense. With stunning force, he violently heaved the man holding Rebecca into his friend, nearly bowling them both down. As they fought to regain their balance, Ian pressed the end of his cane into the man's chest.

"Apologize to the lady for yer impertinence or I'll part yer skull." His warning was clear and Rebecca knew with a heart-pounding certainty it should be heeded. The fire in the stranger's eyes fairly screamed that he had other plans. He grabbed for his sidearm, but Ian laid his cane right down the middle of the man's head with a thunderous crack. As he fell, Ian swiftly stabbed the cane into the other man's gut and watched him double over and slide to his knees, clutching his midsection. Without hesitation, he smacked him on the head as well, and, in what seemed the blink of an eye, both men were lying at their feet. Rebecca gasped, stunned by the complete efficiency with which Ian had dispatched both men.

"Our business here is concluded." Gently, he took her arm. "Let's be on our way."

"I've never seen anything like that." Rebecca was reeling from the swiftness and perfect skill of his attack. Mouth agape, she looked back at the men, one still lying motionless on the ground and the other alternately grabbing his head and his mid-section and groaning. "Where did you learn to do that?"

"The streets of Edinborough."

After a few minutes, she recovered from the fright of the violent tustle and played the man's words over and over in her head. With each repeating of it, she found her spirits sinking lower and lower. Streetwalker. She had never in her life heard the word, but its meaning was perfectly clear.

Without looking at Ian, she broached the man's comment. "He called me a streetwalker." She felt the muscles in his arm tense. "Is that what we've done? Just by coming into this town, we're automatically branded as…" she couldn't even say the word. "Is that what everyone really thinks of us?"

Looking distracted and somber, he steered her down the alley between two buildings and led her down toward the stream. "Let's take a less traveled path."

The fact that he didn't answer right away disturbed Rebecca. Did the men in this town think they were in the process of building another brothel no matter what message Mr. McIntyre had tried to disperse? What did Ian think?

"Oh, this is horrible!" Mortified, Rebecca collapsed on to a boulder at the water's edge. "Does everyone think we're building a brothel? Do you?"

"No, no, no," he declared, lighting beside her. "I think nothin' of the sort. Mac has gone to great pains to let folks know that you're only opening a respectable place…but there are a lot of men in this area who don't get into town that much." He rubbed his neck as if the stress was getting the better of him. "Men will think what they want to think. Ye'll just have to prove them wrong…and that might take some time."

Rebecca was stunned. She realized they had all been living in this fairy tale world, thinking that if they didn't look or act like prostitutes, eventually they would convince the men of the truth. She thought of the many trips she and her sisters had made to the bank, general store and telegraph office and cringed. The whispers and the stares, the soft laughter that followed them down the boardwalk, even when the marshal was with them. Did everyone think this was a huge joke and when the inn was open, they would rush the doors seeking *entertainment* rather than a simple meal?

Gently, Ian took Rebecca's hand. She slowly raised her face to look at him. Serene, hazel eyes calmed her soul. She had the strangest certainty that he wanted to kiss her. "If I might offer a suggestion…" For a moment, he was lost for words but she waited expectantly while she tried to slow her galloping heart. "Perhaps if ye were seen in the company of a respectable man more often…" Her brow furrowed, unsure of his meaning. He muttered a mild oath under his breath and sighed. "What I'm tryin' to say, very badly, is that I'd like permission to call on ye, if ye've a mind to be courted by an old goot like meself."

Her eyes saucered in surprise, but after a moment, a smile was born. "The thought of having you around more is not an unpleasant one," she answered as honestly as she could.

His face fell. "But…"

"But it's been a very, very long time since I—well, I'm not a teenager anymore, Ian. The idea of courting is…"

"A bit fast for ye?"

Terrifying, she wanted to say, but didn't. Instead, she nodded, thankful that excuse kept her from having to discuss her wrinkles and other insecurities. Her age was the real reason she shied away from Ian. Rebecca was thirty-eight. She wasn't young and desirable anymore. Even at fifty, he was still handsome and distinguished looking. Could he really want a relationship with a woman who was at the point in life of trading beauty for wisdom? Rebecca felt so weathered and dull compared to her sisters, how could he see past them to her?

"Then may I have permission to call on ye as a friend…a dear friend."

Plain or not, she couldn't help herself and squeezed his hand, marveling over how warm and right it felt in hers. "Yes, a very dear friend." Taking a risk, she admitted, "I'd like that more than you can imagine."

~~~

Naomi stared at the chicken coop and fumed. Rebecca had overseen the men who brought the cages in here and as a result, everything was perfect for her Amazonian sister to reach, but at least a foot too high for Naomi. Gathering eggs was now her least favorite chore as it usually resulted in a pricked elbow from jagged chicken wire or an unpleasant stain on the front of her apron. She tried not to think about their coop back home. John had built her a perfect hen house: neat, prim, tidy and at an easy height to steal the eggs. He had delighted in building something that pleased her so...

Eager to save that memory for a later time, she looked around the little lean-to. Perhaps there was something she could stand on? She saw a few rusty tools, some nails spilled in the dirt and a pine stump about two feet tall and a foot or so around. It would be wobbly, Naomi knew, but perhaps she could steady herself long enough...

She set her basket atop the chicken cages and wiggled the surprisingly heavy stump over in front of them. She eyed it warily and pushed on it. The ground was uneven and it wiggled around some, but Naomi was confident of her balance. Hiking up her skirt, she stepped gingerly on the stump. Slowly, she stood up as much as the low roof would allow. So far, so good.

She reached for the basket and the motion threatened to topple her stand, but she managed to stay on top by freezing in place. Hoping she had her balance back, she reached again for the basket and opened the first cage.

From his position on the back porch, McIntyre watched Naomi set up the makeshift stool and smiled with mischievous delight. He could see disaster right around the corner and decided to help it along. Though he had vowed to avoid her, the potential for a little fun at Her Highness's expense was simply too tempting.

Quiet as an Indian, he stole behind her as she ever-so-slowly reached under the reticent hen and retrieved an egg. Oblivious to his presence, she moved to drop the egg in her basket. The change in direction caused the stump to wobble. Naomi froze, the egg still in her hand.

A breathless moment passed as she waited to make sure things were under control. Her balance regained, she let out a breath and placed the egg in her basket.

McIntyre moved a step closer. "Good morning, Mrs. Miller." Naomi squeaked in fear at the unusually loud greeting, the stump wobbled, her feet went out from under her and she fell right into his arms...as planned, though he'd been forced to moved a little quicker than he'd anticipated to catch this falling angel.

Feigning shock, he rolled his eyes. "Really, Mrs. Miller. Must you throw yourself at me? It is rather embarrassing."

Practically growling, she fought to get away from him, but he held fast for just a breath. He saw the fury percolating in her eyes, but he didn't miss the flash of something else, either. Enjoying the feel of her pressed against him, he pulled her closer and grinned like the devil.

Fuming, and blushing, she punched him in the shoulder. "Put me down this instant!"

Surprised by the ferocity behind the fist, he knew better than to press his luck. Her Highness had one whale of a punch. Unceremoniously, he released her. Naomi had to claw at his lapel to keep from falling flat on her rear end. Gaining her feet, she angrily pushed away from him, brushed a stray hair from her face and checked to see if she still had an egg in her basket.

Things in their proper places, she drew back and delivered another stunning blow to McIntyre's left bicep. "What's the matter with you? I could have broken my neck."

Mustering his pride, he resisted the urge to rub his thumping muscle. Instead, he pretended exaggerated emotional distress. He clutched his vest over his heart as if she had stabbed him with a real weapon. "You have wounded me, M'lady. Have you no gratitude for the peasant who saved you?"

"Saved me? You nearly killed me!"

He leaned in, pressing, he knew, too close for comfort. "If I wanted you dead..."

Naomi huffed and moved back. "Then what *do* you want? I'm busy."

McIntyre straightened up and shrugged in a casual way. "To check on things." She did not need to know he had surveyed the hotel on his way out here. Construction had progressed quite well and he was pleased. Getting his arms around her had been a bonus. Recently widowed or not, her vehement reaction, including those glowing cheeks, spoke volumes about her vulnerability to him. Perhaps the two of them mixed like oil and water, but somewhere in the recipe there was also a little nitroglycerin. His ego was stroked and he'd left her with something to think about. That would have to do for now. "Well, I believe my work here is done."

Naomi sucked in a breath and her shocked face drained of its color. She took another step back, bumping into the chicken cage. McIntyre was alarmed at her sudden pastiness. "Mrs. Miller, are you all right?"

"My husband used to say that very same thing when he would tease me. How..." She swallowed and shook her head, looking terribly rattled by his words.

"I do apologize, Mrs. Miller, if I caused you any pain."

"No." She pulled herself together, admirably well, he thought, considering how shaken she looked. "No, you didn't. It just caught me off guard."

The fun of a few moments ago obscured by this curtain of grief, McIntyre thought it best to take his leave. His simple teasing had been meant to act as a diversion, pleasant or not. Instead, it had launched her straight back to thinking of her husband, someone, in truth, he would prefer she forget. Feeling a little chagrined at the backfire, he touched the brim of his hat. "Then I will bid you good day." He glanced at the stump. "Do try to be careful, won't you?"

With a quick nod, he left her and headed down toward the back trail. McIntyre did not currently feel like dealing with the bustle of the street, and the sound of the river always settled him. He rubbed his arm as he walked. He could still feel the sting of her punch, but he could also feel her gathered up against him. She was a boney package compared to the buxom Rose, and yet he had liked holding her. Strange, she was nothing like any of the women he'd ever been attracted to. Surely the fireworks were more about lust and conquest and a bored man's desire for variety...than, say, something more noble? He shivered at the thought. Deciding that avoiding Naomi *was* actually the safest course here until he figured out these strange feelings, he pushed her to the back of his mind.

McIntyre suspected, however, the stubborn little wench wouldn't stay there.

Naomi leaned her head against a knotty cedar pole holding up the lean-to and let a few tears fall. Her meeting with Mr. McIntyre had been emotionally tumultuous, to say the least. She thought about the last time John had said those words to her, in the back yard of their home. And now, to hear them uttered fifteen hundred miles away by a scoundrel in the truest sense of the word was beyond comprehension.

She was disgusted by the whole scene, by his hypnotic, penetrating brown eyes, maddening, devilish grin and shocking boldness. He had purposely held her far longer than necessary, affording her ample opportunity to feel the sinewy, muscular strength of his lean frame. How could he treat her like that, a grieving widow? Had he no shame? She straightened up and wiped her eyes. She had too much to make her cry to ad him to the list. Gathering her wits about her, she stepped back up on the stump and wished Mr. McIntyre would obligingly step off the edge of the earth.

Chapter 22

Hugging herself to ward off the chilly hint of approaching fall, Hannah stood waiting on the front porch of the hotel for Rebecca and Naomi. Even with what had happened to Rebecca and Ian a few weeks ago, the sisters had decided they wouldn't be prisoners in the hotel. Or at least, that worked for the two of them. Extremely self-conscious about her pregnancy, Hannah opted to stay close to home until the baby was born. Agreeing with her concerns, they held resolute to their independence and shuttled off to the mercantile.

But the continual stares of the men passing by drove Hannah to the bench where she could sit and attempt to hide her stomach. Nestled in the corner of the bench, feeling shrouded by the lengthening evening shadows, she wondered what the men thought when they looked at her these days.

When she and her sisters had first come to Defiance, they had given her the once-over rudely but appreciatively. Now, they saw her stomach first, devised evil assumptions then tossed her a knowing look. A look that made her feel naked and degraded.

That was the truth of a baby: it announced something about you to the world. In Hannah's case, the something wasn't very nice. She knew she was forgiven but there were certainly days when that was harder to remember than others. It was also becoming harder and harder to remember Billy's face. Oh, she could still hear his voice, feel the touch of his hands, even taste his heart-melting kisses, but the mischievous blue eyes and dashing smile were fading from her memory.

You'd think I could remember forever the man who gave me a child. The fact that she couldn't made her feel cheap and foolish.

Condemnation trying to swamp her, Hannah looked up with relief when she heard her sisters. She saw Naomi rolling a wheelbarrow down the side of the street, loaded with several large sheaves of hay, four colossal pumpkins and at least half a dozen ears of red and black Indian corn. Her sister weaved and dipped drunkenly with the heavy load as she tried frantically, laughably, to keep from spilling the whole thing. Rebecca was no help as her arms were full of two smaller pumpkins and more corn. Any attempt at trying to stabilize the wheelbarrow resulted in her frantically juggling her own load.

The two women were laughing and squealing, hysterical over the mock melodrama of the teetering cargo. Hannah couldn't remember how long it had been since they'd all shared some good, rich, side-splitting humor; even passers-by on the street grinned at the comical picture of the two girls trying to control the precarious cargo. The comedy of the situation was infectious and Hannah's own heart took flight.

Not about to be left out, she hurried down the steps to meet her sisters. "Look at those pumpkins," she sang joyfully. "They're so bright, they look like they're on fire."

"Here, quick," Rebecca extended her load to Hannah. "Take these and I'll help Naomi."

As Rebecca tried to pass her freight off, Hannah's rotund abdomen got in the way. The pumpkins and corn cascaded to the ground in a blur of fall colors as the two futilely scrambled to catch them. Naomi dropped the wheelbarrow and the sisters collapsed into laughing hysterics. They were off to the side of the traffic but probably wouldn't have cared if they had been in the middle of the road. Hannah held her stomach against the pain that racked her sides and purely heehawed till tears poured down her cheeks. Maybe it wasn't all *that* funny, but it felt so good to let go.

Seconds later a shadow fell across them. The laughter began to fizzle out grudgingly as the girls realized a man on horseback had ridden up and was watching the fun. Shielding their eyes against the setting sun, they struggled to douse their giggles.

Hannah took in the tall figure of a clean-shaven man, forty or so, dressed in a tan suit and light jacket with a derby atop his head. With exacting aim, he spit tobacco juice squarely at her feet. "You Hannah Frink?"

That and his solemn voice sobered them like a lightning bolt. Naomi straightened up, her body language issuing a defiant warning. "Who she is is none of your business."

The man smiled but Hannah saw only darkness in his eyes. "'Fraid you're wrong."

Dismissing them, he quickly surveyed the town, spotted what he was looking for and trotted off in the direction of the Iron Horse. Speechless, the sisters watched him go.

Chapter 23

Watching the stranger disappear into the traffic, Naomi spoke to her sisters over her shoulder. "Rebecca, you and Hannah get these things on to the front porch. I'm going to see what I can find out about him."

She did not wait for a reply. Keeping low and moving quickly, Naomi darted down the street, ignoring the men who tipped their hats in mock politeness. She dared anybody to stop her now as she focused on finding out who this man was, but she stopped short when she saw him pull up in front of the marshal's office.

The man dismounted, tied his horse and marched inside. Naomi hid behind a post and debated her next move. Before she formed a plan, he and Marshal Hayes emerged together and crossed the street to the Iron Horse.

Naomi knew there was no way she could eavesdrop on the conversation from the street. She could either wait and address the man when he left the Iron Horse or she could barge in and demand an explanation.

Tapping her foot in agitation, Naomi debated the situation for several minutes. Would it be a complete scandal if she waltzed in there right now? Would the flowers try to pick a fight with her? Would her entrance into the saloon be telegraphed all over the valley, giving credence to the rumor that their hotel was merely a brothel?

She looked around at the human traffic and weighed the curious stares aimed at her as she clung, hiding, to the pole. At the moment, did she care what these people thought?

Naomi stomped down the boardwalk and barged through the saloon's swinging doors.

Slowly her eyes adjusted to the deep shadows caused by the smoke, setting sun and low lights. Practically announcing her presence with a trumpet by standing silhouetted in the door, she moved deeper into the saloon. Through the smokey haze, she could see the Iron Horse was about half-full and the man she wanted was at the bar. As she took a step to move into the crowd, Mr. McIntyre came from nowhere, hooked her waist and swung her around like they were square dancing. Before Naomi realized what was happening, she was back out on the boardwalk with Mr. McIntyre's arm around her.

Angrily shoving him off her—something that was becoming a habit it seemed—she stepped back and attempted to stare him down. "What do you think you're doing? There's a man in there I need to see."

"I don't care if Jesus Christ himself is in there, Mrs. Miller," his eyes blazed with fury, "The last place you need to be seen is my saloon. Blast you, woman, use your head."

Naomi blinked, surprised by his anger. "That man," she pointed at the saloon. "He was asking about Hannah. I have to find out who he is."

"My bartender says he is a Pinkerton from San Francisco. Pender Beckwith. He's seen him many times."

Naomi was stunned, but only for a second. She quickly surmised there was only one person who would have sent a Pinkerton to find Hannah.

Mr. McIntyre encircled Naomi again, pulling her away from the front door and down the walk several feet. Strangely discomfited by his nearness, she quickly stepped away. It bothered her greatly that each time he put an arm around her it became a little less detestable.

"Now, I have to ask, Mrs. Miller, what is a Pinkerton doing in Defiance looking for Hannah, of all people?"

"Frank Page," she muttered in disgust, taking a seat on the nearby bench. "That no-good, greedy tyrant..." She trailed off, certain her face betrayed her anger.

After a moment, Mr. McIntyre joined her. "Does this have anything to do with the father of Hannah's baby?"

"The grandfather," she spat. "He owns everything in Cary. He runs everything in Cary." She cut Mr. McIntyre a side-ways glance. "Much like you. He, however, has big plans for his son. Oh, yes, indeed, Billy's going to be a NC senator in a few years, as soon as he's done with college. Then after that, Frank plans to run him for president." Incredible. "His ambition knows no bounds. He made it clear that Hannah's blood wasn't blue enough for her to be the wife of a senator or a president. He whisked Billy out of town and wouldn't allow him to return until the situation was resolved."

"And by resolved, I assume you mean he ran you and your family out?"

"Not exactly," Naomi huffed indignantly. "He bought our farms and John, Rebecca and I agreed not to contact Billy. We refused to make that same promise for Hannah. She decided on her own to leave but didn't explicitly promise anything. I guess Frank figures he needs to keep up with her whereabouts."

Mr. McIntyre nodded. "Yes, I can see where it would be embarrassing for Hannah to show up in a few years declaring that the junior senator from North Carolina is the father of her child. The scandal would ruin the boy's career."

"He doesn't have enough sense to know that Hannah would never do that." Naomi leaned forward and rested her head in her hands. "Now I suppose we'll have to put up with detectives checking on us every so often."

"If I was Frank, I would want regular reports."

You would, Naomi thought. "Great minds think alike," she confirmed, her voice rich with sarcasm.

Mr. McIntyre harumphed and rose to his feet. "This is probably the first of semi-annual reports the Pinkertons will send back. Neither Ian, Wade nor I will tell this man anything, but the rest of the town will talk...freely. I can't stop that."

Shaking her head wearily, Naomi stood as well. "If there's any chance that he's here on Billy's behalf, and I highly doubt that, I'd appreciate you letting us know. Otherwise, I don't care what he finds out." She shrugged, at a loss for a plan of action. "I don't know anything to do other than just go on with our lives."

Chapter 24

Fall didn't creep into the Rockies, Hannah decided, it erupted almost overnight. The Aspens suddenly blazed orange and yellow, splashing the surrounding mountains with pockets of fire. The air went from warm and flirting with humidity to drier and colder, all at once. The change in seasons made her all too aware of her rapidly expanding middle. Though she had of course noted the rounding of her stomach, without mirrors for a daily view she wasn't able to gauge the true impact of her new profile—until she caught sight of her shadow one morning in the backyard. The alien silhouette stopped her in her tracks.

Is that my shadow? she wondered in awe. With six more weeks to go, this baby was going to be huge. *I'll be as big as Sampson by the time he's born!*

Hannah pulled her skirt in beneath her stomach to accentuate the shape. She turned this way and that, stretched and leaned back. Suddenly, a stabbing pain struck deep at her mid-section and she doubled over with a loud, "Oooow!"

As if by magic, Rebecca was suddenly at her side, leading Hannah over to the porch. "Here, sit down." Gingerly, she helped Hannah settle down on the back steps. "What happened? Are you all right? Has this happened before?"

Hannah laughed at her sister's concern. "It's fine. The baby just kicked me. Hard."

Rebecca seemed to accept the answer and dropped down beside her sister. The two sat in silence for a time, studying the distant peaks and considering things. Finally, Rebecca looked at Hannah. "Are you scared?"

On the surface, it was a ridiculous question, but Hannah somberly shook her head. "Only a little. Every time the baby moves, unless he kicks the daylights out of me, I think that he's such a miracle. I feel so humbled that God would let something so good and beautiful come out of such a horrible mistake."

She hugged her perfectly round potbelly, anxious to meet her child, and let her mind wander home to Cary. "I wonder where Billy is. I wonder if he misses me. I wonder if he'll ever meet his baby." She looked back at Rebecca and spoke with regret in her voice. "But I'm beginning to forget what he looks like. He's the father of my child. How can I do that?"

A rhetorical question, she didn't really expect an answer. Instead, squaring her shoulders, Hannah moved her focus beyond her mistake and tried to think of the bigger picture. "But I know without a doubt that everything has happened for a reason. It's been a hard row to hoe, especially here just trying to walk down the street, but I'm doing all right. I'm closer to God than I've ever been in my whole life and I've seen what He can do with me if I let Him. In all honesty, I'd give Billy up for that."

"Better is one day in your courts than thousands elsewhere," Rebecca quoted softly.

"Exactly." Hannah bobbed her head emphatically. "I never knew what that meant, never bothered to consider it, until these last few months. When I think about the transformation that Mr. Whicker went through, the way he looked…" Hannah smiled. "This is exactly where I want to be. I'm in the palm of his hand. I don't know if I'll ever see Billy again, but if I don't, then I just hope I can accept God's plan for me." She glanced down. "For us."

Considering Hannah's statement, Rebecca laced her fingers and twirled her thumbs. "I don't think Naomi is quite there yet."

"No, she's still wrestling with God. She hasn't accepted that we're here by design. And she still goes down to the stream every night when she thinks we're asleep. But I do think *something* is changing in her heart. She's less angry. I think that means she's dealing with her grief."

"I thought I saw some changes, too, but after that episode with Hank, I don't know. She seems so…" Rebecca shook her head. "Disappointed in herself. The fact that she was able to pull the trigger on that gun haunts her. I think she thinks God won't use her if she's too…"

"Hot-headed? Willful? Self-reliant?" Naomi volunteered from behind them. "Or perhaps brash and immature are the words you're looking for?"

Rebecca flinched. "I'm sorry. We shouldn't talk about you as if we're dissecting a bug."

"No, it's all right." Naomi waved away her sister's guilt and took a seat between them. She had her Bible and stared at it for a moment, then set it down behind her. "You're just trying to understand me. And so am I. Ever since John died, I've had some heated conversations with God. It's hard to let go of the only thing you've ever wanted in your whole life."

"You mean John?" Rebecca asked delicately.

Naomi looked her sister in the eye. "I had the wrong person on the throne. I loved John more than God." She sighed deeply, as if the admission was painful and Hannah saw her chin quivering. "Accepting that scared me, but it freed me, too. Freed me to *start over* searching for the only relationship that really matters. Trying to let go of John and trading my dreams for God's has been the hardest thing He's ever asked of me—" Her voice broke as she dropped her head into her hands. When she spoke again, Hannah could hear the tears and the frustration. "Why did He have to work things this way, though? This place is horrible. The people are cruel and stupid. But I'm trying, I'm trying so hard to care about them and not hate them."

Hannah laid her hand gently on Naomi's back. "Maybe you just have to go one person at a time. Starting with Emilio…"

Rebecca pulled her long, black braid around and fiddled thoughtfully with the end of it. "Considering the way you've been tested, Naomi, I think you've done well." Her voice was soft and re-assuring. "You didn't let John's death incapacitate you and you've tried to turn the other cheek. You let the gum incident go."

"And then a few days later I nearly shot a man in our room"

"Well, it was a very stressful situation. He's all right now and I would bet he'll never bother us again. Like Hannah said, maybe for you the best way to deal with Defiance is one person at a time."

Naomi clearly gave the suggestion intent consideration for a minute. Finally, she screwed up a look of courage on her face and produced her Bible. "I know that I'm being stubborn. I've asked Him to help me care about these people…"

Movement down by the stream stole Hannah's attention. She half-heard Naomi's voice trail off as she and her sisters watched someone ambling slowly along down by the water. They sat silently as Daisy—no, it was Mollie now—picked her way thoughtfully along the bank, head down, her shawl pulled tightly around her.

"She hasn't seen us yet," Rebecca noted.

"I'll go invite her up." Hannah worked to get to her feet, with a shove from Naomi. She waddled down to the water, hailed her friend, and the two drew near.

"It's good to see you, Mollie." And Hannah truly was glad. "Do you have time to come eat some lunch with us? We were going to do a quick

Bible study outside then make sandwiches for the men and us." Hannah could see a deep loneliness in Daisy's eyes. "Please?"

Daisy looked at Hannah's dress, the blue gingham jumper. "I see the clothes are fitting?"

Hannah nodded but kept what she hoped were puppy-dog eyes trained on her friend. Buckling, Daisy nodded. Gleefully, Hannah hooked her arm through Daisy's and walked her friend up to her sisters.

"Hello, Mollie," Rebecca greeted.

Naomi nodded at the girl. "Nice to see you again."

Daisy dipped her chin in return and smiled self-consciously at them.

Hannah squeezed her friend's arm with warm invitation. "I told Mollie we were going to do a quick study then go inside and get lunch ready for everyone. She's agreed to stay and help."

"But I want to stay in the kitchen," Daisy told them quickly. "I don't want any of the men to see me."

"Well, for our study why don't we go sit by the fire pit?" Naomi suggested as she stood up. "There are more seats."

The group moved and as they settled down on the makeshift log seats, Hannah prayed for a scripture that might speak to Daisy. Instead, questions came to mind.

"Mollie, how long did you say you've worked for Mr. McIntyre?"

"A year and a half. Originally I thought I would stay for a year, long enough to save up stagecoach money to go home to Kansas."

The answer seemed to beg for follow-up so Hannah didn't feel too intrusive with another. "If you don't mind me asking, then why are you still there?"

Hannah saw Daisy suck in an almost imperceptible breath as she stared in to the cold, blackened remnants of a fire. "After awhile this life," the light died in her eyes, "it makes you feel so dirty and worthless. Your spirit dies. You feel like you'll never be able to forget what you've done so why try. I couldn't go home now and face my mother." She looked up then. "I just couldn't. She'd never understand how I can do what I do." Daisy shook her head. "She'd never forgive me."

At first, Hannah was taken aback by Daisy's honesty, but obviously the girl felt comfortable enough to open up. Perhaps it was because Hannah had been so forthright about her baby. Maybe here in this circle, she knew she wasn't judged.

"I felt the same way at first," Hannah offered, re-living the memory of bitterly scornful comments from her closest *friends*. "After I, you know, was *with* Billy, I carried that sin around like a load of bricks. I felt so filthy. I couldn't tell anybody. And I couldn't talk to God about it because I just knew He hated me. I was so isolated from everyone that mattered to me." Daisy leaned forward, listening intently.

"Then when I found out about the baby," Hannah rolled her eyes, remembering that sick feeling of fear and shame. "I knew everything I'd done was going to come out. The people I loved most in the world were going to hate me. I was sure God had turned his back on me, disappointed in one of His children who claimed to know Him. I'd shamed Him, I'd shamed my family. Then Billy left." She marveled over how the admission still hurt. "He just rode off without a look back." Hannah chuckled bitterly and realized she harbored more resentment toward Billy than she'd allowed herself to consider.

"To say I was heartbroken doesn't begin to express my grief." She shared a look with Daisy that she hoped communicated all her fear and shame. "I can't tell you how miserable I was, Mollie. How much of a failure I thought I was." Hannah shook her head, remembering how desperately disgusted with herself she had been at that point in time.

Daisy's face was rapt with attention. "You seem so content now. What happened? What did you do? What happened to change your mind?"

Hannah took the Bible from Naomi and held it up for Daisy to see. "This. This is God's love letter to us, Mollie. And I needed desperately to know that He still loved me. So I started reading it as if my life depended on it. I think it did. Let me tell you one of the first things I saw." With a silent prayer, Hannah opened the Bible to John 3:16 and began reading, "For God so loved the world that He gave His only begotten son, that whosoever believeth in Him should not perish but have everlasting life." Then Hannah emphasized the last sentence. "For God did not send His son into the world to condemn the world, but to *save* the world through Him.

"I saw for the first time right there, Mollie, God's desire to show us mercy. I kept thinking, 'God didn't send His son to condemn me. So how can I find my way back to Him? How can I make this mess right?'"

Daisy picked up a stick and poked distractedly at the dead coals. "What did you do?" She sounded like someone who wanted very specific directions and Hannah tried to oblige.

"I saw myself through God's eyes." She turned to Luke 15. "I read this: Then Jesus told them this parable: Suppose one of you has a hundred sheep and loses one of them. Does he not leave the ninety-nine in the open country and go after the lost sheep until he finds it? And when he finds it, he *joyfully* puts it on his shoulders and goes home. Then he calls his friends and neighbors together and says, 'Rejoice with me. I have found my lost sheep.' I tell you that in the same way there will be *more rejoicing in heaven over one sinner who repents* than over ninety-nine righteous persons who do not need to repent."

She looked up at Daisy. "I was that lost sheep and my Father put me on His shoulders and carried me home." Tears unexpectedly slipped down Hannah's cheeks as she swallowed a knot in her throat. "He rejoiced over my repentance. I *matter* to him; he cares what happens to me. There are so many other places in this book, Mollie, that tell us how much God loves us and how willing he is to forgive us when we sin. It says that His mercies are new every day. I still hang on to a little shame, but it's not like it was and it's only me, not God."

"Senoras," Emilio called from the stoop, jerking the girls out of this special moment. "Another freight wagon is here. I theenk these one has all the beds." That meant they had to leave. Rebecca and Naomi stood with regret in their eyes, but Hannah didn't rise. She sat, wiping her eyes with her apron.

"You two take your time." Naomi glanced over at Rebecca. "We'll take care of the wagon."

Daisy was thankful for the interruption. Hannah's words had frightened her. They seemed to push her against a wall, issuing a challenge for her to accept or deny her beliefs about herself. Was she worthy to be loved, to be forgiven? It was too big and complicated to ponder here right now in front of these other women.

She realized Hannah was looking at her, waiting for an answer to a question she had not heard. "I'm sorry…"

"Do you mind helping with lunch? I can use extra hands since Rebecca and Naomi need to check the freight." She dabbed at her eyes and smiled. "I'll try to quit being a cry baby."

Daisy laughed with more bitterness than she meant to share. "When I was pregnant, I cried all the time…" *And I cried for two months straight when Dan died…then nothing could make me cry.* She forced a happier smile. "Yes, I would like to stay and help."

With Rebecca and Naomi occupied out front, Daisy was eager to ask Hannah a million questions about this idea of God's forgiveness. Ian and another man were in the kitchen, though, finishing up the serving window. Keeping thoughts and questions hidden in her heart, she quietly went to work helping prepare lunch.

McIntyre noticed the two large freight wagons rumbling past and knew they were headed to the hotel. He grabbed his hat and followed after them. The first delivery a few weeks ago had brought most of the items for the kitchen. He was anxious to see if this would finish it out so they could project an opening date for the restaurant.

As he walked, he enjoyed the cool of the air and the few aspen leaves that blew across his path. Fall in Georgia had been his favorite time of year as a child. The heat would break to something tolerable and slaves would harvest the crops. His mother would decorate their home with pumpkins and Indian corn all around, creating an innocent, festive air.

Fall also had heralded the start of a new school year and the excitement of going off to the various private schools he had attended. An enterprising lad always, school had been the opportunity to hone his entrepreneurial skills. He chuckled at the thought, remembering business ventures with everything from shoe polish to cigars. In college he had upped the ante to include whisky, gambling and, right before the war, women.

Now, years later, he was the self-appointed king of a booming mining town. Ian's urging to set up a real town government and duly deputized marshal were valid suggestions if Defiance was to go to the next step of metropolitan growth. In the last ten years, McIntyre had seen mining towns spring up overnight, develop an economy based on nothing but gold or silver and when the ore played out, the town also *died* overnight.

He did not want that to happen to Defiance. It was his responsibility to move the town forward, not just manage an ever-increasing population. With proper planning, this could be a mining town with stable alternate economies based on lumber, farming and ranching. Since the arrival of Naomi and her sisters, he had actually entertained the thought that brothels and liquor might not be the cornerstone of his future.

McIntyre considered that mental change of direction as he watched Rebecca and Naomi take the bill of lading from a wagon driver. It was interesting to him how he had been pondering growth for Defiance anyway. Yet, in spite of himself, something about that feisty little princess made him want see his plans yield fruit sooner rather than later. He despised admitting that.

As she took every opportunity to look down her nose at him, he had begun feeling that his accomplishments in Defiance were meaningless. Why her opinion mattered, he couldn't say. He had tried, again, to avoid her since that afternoon she had tumbled into his arms. He liked the feel of her a little too much. The line between lust and something more dangerous was blurred and fuzzy when he was around her. Yet, here he was walking towards her again.

Worse, as he mulled over plans and dreams for Defiance, he found himself wanting to run them by her, to *share* them with her. He didn't just want her to faint with passion—though that would be nice—it wasn't enough. He wanted her to acknowledge that *he* had built this town and had noble plans for it.

In short, McIntyre realized with a jolt, he wanted her to admire him.

She, however, regarded him as a predator and stayed wary around him. She never let her guard down, never said anything that could be construed as friendly; she was always cold and distant. Yet, if McIntyre knew one thing, he knew women. His instincts told him there was something between the two of them but she fought it like the plague…Was she riddled with guilt over being attracted to someone else after so recently being widowed…or did she honestly dislike him? McIntyre found that scenario unlikely, but Naomi Miller vexed him greatly, and he approached her and her sister with the intent to study her a bit more.

"Mrs. Castleberry, Mrs. Miller." He touched his hat in greeting. They both smiled at him pleasantly enough, but he noticed *her* smile faded faster and she went back to the bill of lading more quickly than Rebecca. "What treasures have arrived today?"

Rebecca waived the bill of lading at the wagon. "Well, it looks as if we've got everything to finish off the kitchen, and some tables for the dining room. If we can get some chairs, which may be in the second wagon," she looked over at Naomi for agreement, "and start getting groceries and staples stocked, I think we can open the restaurant by the end of this month."

"Have you given your establishment a name yet? There is a fine sign painter in town. You need to get your moniker up there."

"Yes," Naomi gushed unexpectedly. "We decided to call it The Trinity Inn."

"That has a far more sophisticated ring to it than The Elbow Inn," he quipped and Naomi almost laughed.

A puzzled look from Rebecca prompted McIntyre to explain. "I had originally thought to call it that because the hotel sits where the road bends to follow the river. It doesn't quite have the sophistication of *The Trinity Inn.*"

"Oh," she nodded, but looked as if she didn't quite get the joke. "Well, lunch should be coming right along. We'll get some men to unload all this then break. Would you like to join us?"

Before he could reply, Naomi excused herself. "I'm going to chop some wood since Emilio is helping with the carpentry work." She nodded a good-bye to McIntyre and squeezed Rebecca's arm. "I'll be out back if you need me."

McIntyre had to control the urge to offer one of his men for the task. Instead, he saw another opportunity. He nodded good-bye to Naomi then turned back to Rebecca.

"I would have thought the beds would be arriving by now, too," he puzzled.

"That's what Emilio initially thought these were. But tables are good too." As she spoke, he noticed the new feminine touches to the front of the hotel. He saw pots with bunches of Columbine planted in them, a few rocking chairs waiting invitingly, but he was moved unexpectedly by the bundled sheaves of hay, pumpkins, and Indian corn set out as seasonal decorations.

"Where in the world did you get those?"

She followed his gaze and smiled. "We mentioned to Mr. Boot that we'd love to have some pumpkins and Indian corn. Three days later, voila!"

He shook off an unexpected sense of melancholy and shoved his hands into his pockets. "It is...inviting."

McIntyre let himself in to the hotel and quickly surveyed the new entrance. A false wall had been built separating the small hotel lobby from the dining area. A large open serving window and two swinging doors had been cut into the wall separating the kitchen from the eating area. A good cleaning to remove the stray lumber and sawdust, add some tables and chairs, and this restaurant was just about ready for customers.

Pleased with the progress, he pushed through the bat wings into the kitchen and was astonished to see Daisy deftly assisting Hannah with lunch. He didn't mind her helping so much as her presence here would cast doubts on the ladies' reputations: guilt by association, as it were. Ian had already dealt with a misunderstanding recently; when the workers saw her here, it would only lead to others.

"Daisy." He spoke her name carefully, trying to sound as unruffled as possible. She glanced up from a tray of unbaked biscuits then practically leaped to attention. "I thought it was your day to clean the saloon."

"No, it's Jasmine's day."

"Well," he thought quickly, trying not to sound harsh, "I would also like you to do an inventory for me this afternoon. Could you manage that?"

Looking disappointed, Hannah spoke up. "Does she have time to help me finish? We're trying to get lunch ready for twelve men, and Mr. Donoghue and you, if you're joining us."

Ian, who had been leaning over the new pump tightening a bolt, straightened and gave McIntyre a hard look. "Very well, be quick about it." The girls nodded and went back to their chores. McIntyre nodded at his friend and slipped out of the kitchen, headed for the back door.

But not fast enough. Ian caught him just as he reached for the doorknob and addressed him with an angry whisper. "Why are ye makin' her leave? It would do the girl well to make decent friends. Are ye afraid of losin' her as an employee?"

"Afraid?" McIntyre couldn't believe his friend thought that. "After rescuing Rebecca, I'm surprised you have to ask about my reasons. If Daisy is seen hanging about here, then every man in Defiance will think he was right about these women. They'll think this hotel is nothing but a front for a high-priced social club."

Ian pointed his finger at McIntyre as if to argue, but slowly dropped his hand. His weathered face showing disapproval, he turned and strode slowly toward the front of the hotel.

~~~

Not long after Ian departed, the other man working on the sink left to retrieve a tool from his wagon, freeing Daisy and Hannah to chat. Daisy couldn't wait to ask at least one question. She knew she didn't have much time before she had to head on back to the Iron Horse.

She sat at the table sawing off thin slices of ham with distracted skill. "Hannah, can a person sin so much that God will never forgive them?"

"No." Hannah sounded resolute as she peeled eggs on the opposite side of the table. "The Bible says that nothing can separate us from His love." She paused, as if trying to remember something. "For I am convinced that neither death nor life, neither angels nor demons, neither the present nor the future, nor any powers, neither height nor depth, nor anything else in all creation will be able to separate us from the love of God that is in Christ Jesus our Lord. Romans 8:38 and 39."

Daisy liked that passage, but wasn't sure it addressed her question. She had a lot of sin under her belt. "But, Hannah, you can love someone without forgiving them."

"No, I don't think that's true." Hannah stopped what she was doing to look at Daisy. "Not if you really love them and they ask. Take me for example. If Billy Page walked through that door right now and told me he was sorry that he ran off and left me to go through this all alone, I would forgive him. How could I keep loving him, but hold the sin over his head?"

"Because God loves us, he'll never stop offering forgiveness and since His word says nothing can separate us from His love, I guess that means he'll never stop offering forgiveness." Hannah laughed, hoping Daisy saw the humor in the circular reasoning. "In other words, there is no escape clause for God. He loves us and wants to forgive us. Period. It's not complicated."

Daisy doubted that. Everything in life, her life, had been exceptionally complicated.

"For me," Hannah added sounding sad, "It's been much harder to forgive myself. My mistake was like a pebble dropped in a pond. The ripple effect has impacted everyone I love."

Daisy saw the pain in her friend's eyes, but didn't know how to help. The awkward moment prompted her to change the subject. "As soon as I finish slicing this, I'd better go." The thought formed a knot in her stomach.

"All right," Hannah bobbed her head. "But when you leave, take my Bible with you." She gestured toward the book sitting at the end of the table. "You've got questions, and your answers are in there. When you come back, we'll talk about them."

Daisy didn't have much time to read, but she sure was curious. She eyed the black, leather-covered book sitting over there waiting for her and nodded.

~~~

McIntyre watched Naomi for a minute from the stoop, hands in his pockets, hat tilted back on his head. He was quite impressed by her skill with an ax. She split several pieces of wood, each with one single, unnerving swing.

Musing over this little princess who seemed tougher than most men he knew, McIntyre sauntered down from the stoop. "Remind me not to make you angry."

Naomi stopped the ax in mid-swing and scowled. "Too late…What do you want?"

"A kind word. A civil tone."

She held his gaze for only a moment, then sagged and let the ax rest on her arm. She shook her head and sighed. "I'm sorry. You are a true scoundrel, but just because I don't like you is no reason to be so rude."

"And I do so want to be friends."

Frowning deeply at his sarcasm, she went back to her work. She wasn't going to get off that easy, he thought, as he ambled down the steps. "The importance of the work you're doing cannot be underestimated. If you don't stock up enough firewood for the winter, you'll be burning all this new furniture for warmth by January."

"That's why I'm out here." She carefully balanced a log on the chopping stump. "We're trying to keep someone on this chore sun up to sun down."

"Well, I've come to assist."

Her eyebrows shot up and she looked at his perfectly manicured hands. "With those?"

He approached her, stepping in too close because he knew it bothered her, and took the ax. "I can chop wood. If you recall, I was one of the first white men in this valley when the closest town was over four hundred miles away."

"I'm sure you can chop wood." Naomi backed away and crossed her arms. "But judging by those pretty hands, I'd say it's been awhile."

With everything he had seen and done, how could she think him such worthless Fancy Dan? Determined to split the log with one swipe of the ax, he took hold of the handle and hoped, almost prayed, for a perfect split. Naomi moved away another step and tapped her foot. Her body language challenged him to fail. Focusing, he raised the ax over his head and slammed it into the log. It split cleanly and fell to either side of the block. McIntyre breathed a mental sigh of relief.

Naomi pursed her lips then relaxed. "All right, I'll accept your help graciously and do the stacking." She started loading her left arm. "Just quit whenever your hands get sore."

McIntyre bristled at the comment. He wouldn't give her the satisfaction. He would work until his hands bled or *she* quit. Naomi went to work stacking the firewood lying about on the ground. They worked in silence for awhile and eventually fell into a rhythm. After fifteen minutes or so, McIntyre was wiping sweat from his brow and had draped his coat, vest, and hat over the corral fence. Ian popped out of the hotel, looked as if he started to ask something then apparently lost his train of thought.

"Did you need something, Ian?" McIntyre was not amused by his friend's bemused expression.

The Scotsman chuckled. "No, I think not."

Not long after, Hannah came out to announce lunch. Both McIntyre and Naomi were red-faced and sweaty and said they would be right there. However, when Naomi kept stacking, McIntyre kept chopping, despite the fact that, yes, his hands were beginning to form blisters.

Hannah re-appeared moments later with two tall pewter mugs of cold water. "Straight from our kitchen sink," she announced, mentioning the new convenience with great enthusiasm. McIntyre and Naomi exchanged tentative glances, but when she acquiesced and reached for the drink, he set the ax down and took the other. "I'll bring you something to eat...so why don't you both sit down before you fall down?"

Naomi walked away and took a seat on a log near their fire pit. McIntyre followed directly. She looked up at the mountains and he could tell she admired them. "I don't care for Defiance *at all*, but I love these mountains." She took a long sip of water then rested the mug on her knee. The longer she stared at the distant range, the more her body relaxed. "Long about midnight, the biggest moon I've ever seen sits right on top of that peak over there. It's amazing."

"Yes, I know. I take a walk along the stream almost every night. The sky is beautiful here, but the full moon is breath-taking."

"A nightly walk?" She looked at him as if he'd suddenly changed into another species. "You have time for such trivial pursuits as admiring God's handiwork?"

McIntyre clucked his tongue. "There you go again, talking down to your subjects with such arrogance. It is unbecoming, even for a princess." A confused, perhaps even hurt looked passed quickly over Naomi's face. She didn't apologize but he could see she was a tad humbled. Good enough. "A walk helps me clear my mind." She nodded as if that was an acceptable explanation. He took a swig of the cold water and let the crispness of it cool his throat. "It gets hot here, but nothing like the South. Do you miss Carolina?"

She glanced over at him, this time with guarded suspicion in her eyes.

He held out his hands. "I'm just trying to make friendly conversation."

Naomi drummed her fingers on the mug then shook her head ever so slightly. "No, the truth is, I don't miss it a bit. You'd think I would." She bit her lip, looking puzzled over her lack of sentimentality. "The fact is I never felt particularly attached to the country, just my family. Land is land...except for here." She cast her eyes back out to the distant sentinels ringing the valley.

He drained his cup and rolled it restlessly between his hands. "Do you mind telling me about your husband?" The question clearly caught her off guard. "I'm just curious what kind of man was able to live with a wolverine like you." He had hoped to lighten the mood with his sarcasm, but he could see the question instead took her racing down memory lane.

"How do you describe the person who completes you? He was everything I'm not. Strong and kind, loving, funny, romantic." She glanced down at the ground and the expression on her face softened to one of complete joy and peace.

Naomi looked like someone strolling contentedly through an album of cherished memories. McIntyre was amazed at the transformation that came over her, the countenance of serenity, the warm glow of love. It fascinated him.

What must a man do to touch a woman's heart like that? he wondered.

"He was so solid in his faith…And everything was black-and-white to John. There were no shades of gray."

"It sounds to me as if you had more in common than you think." From his perspective, he would have described her using the same words, with, perhaps, the exception of romantic. He couldn't speak to that.

"No," she shook her head. "He was far more mature. He rarely flew off the handle…unlike me. He called me his little wild cat because of my temper and my mouth."

"Ah, well, I have seen those demonstrated. I'd say you're equally proficient with both."

The look of peace left her, replaced by one of deep regret. "I know, I know. Unlike my sisters, I haven't achieved that meek and quiet spirit yet."

"Surely you don't see that as a failure?"

"I realize that I'm too confrontational and too quick with my tongue. Not ideal attributes for a Christian woman."

"The West, and especially Defiance, is not an ideal setting." He straightened up to ad emphasis to his point. "If every woman who came out here was as compassionate as Hannah or as kind as Rebecca, they wouldn't last five minutes. This land requires grit and perseverance and independence. Frankly, what you see as your greatest weakness, I see as your greatest strength. Forgive me for the pun, but it is women like you who will defy the challenges of this land and settle the West."

Naomi blinked. For the first time in her life someone saw her strong spirit not as a flaw to be corrected but as a mark of beauty. For twenty-six years she had been struggling to hold in check every urge to ever speak her mind, stand up to someone or address an injustice. Even John had tried to temper her spirit. Was it even remotely possible that she was the way God wanted her? Not perfect of course, but more in need of wisdom than temperance? She had never entertained the possibility.

"Don't misunderstand," he hurried on, apparently perplexed at her expression. "I still think you could learn a thing or two from charm school..." His rakish grin reappeared. "But the West needs women like you."

The emotional wall that Naomi used to keep Mr. McIntyre at a safe distance crumbled a bit at that moment. He wasn't a person with whom she would ever associate, much less call a friend, but he was the first who had ever suggested there might be something good in her spirited ways. In spite of everything she knew about him, she looked at him with different eyes now. Could he be more than a manipulative, callous scallywag after all? Did his thoughts run deeper than money and how to get more of it?

In a hesitant attempt to offer a very small olive branch, she asked him a personal question. "How did you come by your limp? Is it a war wound?"

He patted his right thigh. "General Braxton Bragg made sure no one, Confederate troops or Yankees, left Chickamauga without a souvenir."

How odd, she knew that battle. "Chickamauga?"

"In the mountains of Tennessee. The terrain was so rough and rocky, it was more like mayhem than a battlefield." Naomi watched his eyes cloud over as the battle came back to him. "A small group of Yankees surprised my company by popping up out of a ravine." He cocked his head as if remembering something. "I took a bullet in the leg, and it was a boy from North Carolina who dragged me to safety."

Mr. McIntyre began spinning his mug around his finger as he stared into space. She wondered if he was hearing again the blast of cannons and the crack of rifles. "Took a piece of led in the neck for his trouble. A wonder it didn't kill him."

"My husband was at Chickamauga. He was injured as well."

"A lot of good men died during that battle. On both sides. Your husband and I were fortunate." He stopped the mug and his eyes glittered with a strange intensity. "What regiment was your husband in?"

"The 26th." She paused. Goosebumps rose on her skin. "Why?"

"If you'll excuse me, Mrs. Miller." Mr. McIntyre surged to his feet as if his pants had caught fire. "I really must be going."

"But wait," Naomi pleaded, following close on his heels. "What is it?"

He stopped, took a breath and seemed to regain his composure. Casually he handed her the mug and gathered his clothes and hat from the corral fence. "It's nothing. I remembered I have an appointment this afternoon." Shoving his hat on his head, he smiled at her. "I do have other interests, if you recall. I apologize for the abruptness of my departure, but I really must go."

She touched his arm, halting his exit. "Why do I feel like you're keeping something from me? And please don't lie."

He relaxed his shoulders. "It's the battle. Chickamauga is something I've tried to forget."

She debated the truth of the answer and after a moment pulled her hand away. What choice did she have but to accept it? Without saying anything further, he strode off toward the stream, taking the back way to wherever he was going.

Chapter 25

Once McIntyre rounded the bend in the trail and knew he was out of Naomi's sight, he picked up his pace significantly. Skirting aspens and out buildings, he practically jogged back to the Iron Horse. His mind burning with the impossibility, he cut through the back of the saloon, skimming the edge of the lunch crowd, and shot straight up the stairs to his room.

Once inside, McIntyre tossed his clothes on his bed and snatched open his closet door. A few minutes of digging and diving through boxes, suitcases and shoes and he emerged with his Confederate-issue haversack. Taking no time to reminisce over the bullet hole in the worn, leather flap, he summarily dumped the bag's contents on his bed. Dirt, dust, and a small dead bug tumbled out along with a rusty razor, wooden comb, a bone-handled toothbrush and a stack of letters tied with a yellowed piece of cotton twine.

McIntyre saw the letters and froze. He reached for them then withdrew his hand, clenching it into a fist. It simply couldn't be the same John Miller. And certainly he had remembered the name incorrectly. Perhaps it was Naomi Franks or French.

Reaching again for the stack, he recalled waking up in the field hospital in September '63, on his nineteenth birthday. The nauseating smell of blood and sweat assaulted him, squeezed his guts. He and the other boy lay side-by-side on cots in the makeshift infirmary. McIntyre raised his head and saw his right pant leg was glistening with blood. The gauze pad on his fellow soldier's neck was dark red, saturated with blood as well.

"I'm sorry that happened," McIntyre whispered as an almost-unbearable throbbing shot up and down his leg.

The boy shrugged weakly and touched the pad at his neck. His voice was weak and raspy. "Now I know why you wanted us to bring up the rear." He smiled at his joke and took in his surroundings. "You get me here?"

McIntyre let his head down and tried to block out the pain. "Barely." And that was the truth of it. He had taken a bullet trying to save this giant of a man. It was a miracle they weren't both lying in a pile of bodies outside.

The boy swallowed. "Thanks."

The surgeon, a grizzled old man in a grotesquely blood-spattered white coat approached McIntyre and lifted the flap of his torn pant leg. "You can wait." He moved to the boy and carefully lifted the gauze away from his neck. Blood gushed over his fingers and his eyes widened slightly. "You first." The doctor hollered over his shoulder, "Get this man ready for surgery now."

A weary voice from somewhere at the doorway of the tent grunted. "We need at least ten minutes to clean up."

"You've got five." The surgeon replaced the bandage and moved on to the next row of cots.

McIntyre hoped that meant his wound wasn't serious, but the boy he had risked his life to save was evidently still in peril.

He thought it foolish to introduce himself under these circumstances but also unacceptable not to. "I'm Charles McIntyre."

The boy focused blank hazel eyes on him. He was a large, strapping lad, sturdy like an ox and as blonde as corn silk. He looked invincible and had been nearly impossible to drag to the rear.

"I'm John Miller. You wouldn't happen to have a pencil and some paper on you?"

McIntyre raised himself up on his elbows and looked around his cot and down his body, trying to ignore the shredded, bloody pant leg and its painful drumbeat. "My haversack..." Low and behold, it was still hanging from his body. Gingerly, every movement making his leg pound worse, he pulled the sack over his head and laid it on his lap. Taking a breath, he braced for the pain and pushed himself up to a sitting position.

Sweat popped out on his brow and his leg throbbed thunderously as he fished through the sack. He found the paper easily enough, three wrinkled sheets with torn edges, and eventually the stubby pencil with a dull point. Lying back down, he passed them over to John.

Propping himself up on his left elbow, John held the paper with that hand and wrote with his right. McIntyre saw blood leaking in rivulets out from under John's glistening bandage as he composed. The boy scribbled with determination for an interminably long time, then carefully folded the one-page note and addressed the outside. With shaking hands, he passed it, and the supplies, to McIntyre. All his strength poured into the letter, he lay back exhausted.

"If I don't come back in here, will you get that to her?"

McIntyre glanced at the letter's addressee then shoved the items back into his sack. "Surely. But you'll be fine." He hoped he sounded convincing. "It'll take more than one Yankee ball to fell a tree like you."

John sniggered softly. "I reckon." With that, he closed his eyes and drifted off to sleep. Almost immediately two soldiers arrived and lifted him onto a stretcher. McIntyre watched them take the boy out of the tent. Curious, he retrieved the letter from his sack and again read the name. A sweetheart back in this town of Cary? McIntyre hoped he wouldn't have to mail it to her.

A day later, both men lay recovering from their wounds and the letter fell forgotten to the bottom of his sack. He never thought to ask John if he wanted it back; John never asked for its return. McIntyre wondered later if he even remembered writing it as he had lost a fair amount of blood.

The letter stayed for several months at the bottom of the sack until he tied it neatly into the stack of letters from his mother and a few female acquaintances. For no logical reason, he had never felt comfortable discarding it or reading it. He simply carried it then buried it with his other Civil War souvenirs in the back of his closet. He hadn't looked at any of the items in at least a dozen years.

Now, as he went through the letters one by one, he discovered that he didn't remember any of the females who had written him. His heart reacted slightly to seeing his mother's elegant handwriting, and then the letter from the soldier stared up at him. He caught his breath and sat down on the bed.

After all this time, the paper had yellowed, was brittle and wrinkled, and the pencil had faded some, but the name was inarguably legible.

The letter was, indeed, addressed to Ms. Naomi Frink of Cary, North Carolina.

McIntyre's heart dropped to his stomach. Could it actually be her? He sought to deny it and played the evidence over in his mind, one fact at a time. The soldier's name was John Miller. Naomi's husband was named John Miller. Rebecca was a widow, according to Ian. Hannah, the only sister not married, went by the maiden name of Frink. That would make Naomi's maiden name Frink.

She had said her husband was in the North Carolina 26th Infantry. McIntyre's regiment and the 26th from North Carolina had been called on together to flank the Yankees. In their conversations during recovery, John had told him he was from Cary and his sweetheart was a sassy fireball.

If that alone didn't describe Naomi Miller, then his name was Abraham Lincoln.

McIntyre closed his eyes and pressed his fingers to his forehead. The facts were undeniable. He was stunned by this incomprehensible coincidence. Of all the cities, towns and villages between here and the South, the wife of the man whose life he had saved shows up in Defiance.

He was dumbfounded.

Flummoxed, he threw the letter down on the bed as if he expected it to erupt in to flames, and paced the room. With each step he grew calmer and more confident. Coincidence. That's all, merely a strange, even eerie, coincidence.

Like that time he ran into Lockwood Watkins, his friend from VMI, on the streets of New Orleans. That was an amazing fluke. What were the odds that two men who had known each other three years earlier would be on Bourbon Street at the same time on a winter's evening?

Ridiculous chance. That's all. Sometimes it happened that way. It didn't necessarily mean anything earth-shattering. It didn't mean that fate had intervened in Naomi's life or his and brought them together for some profound, life-altering manipulation of their destinies. It wasn't as if lightning had struck him out of a clear blue sky.

But judging by the way things had been going lately, that was probably next.

~~~

Daisy woke, knowing it was close to noon. She lay in her bed, a gray melancholy washing over her...again. For so long she had been numb to the smell of cigar smoke, whiskey and sweat that permeated her sheets. The last few weeks, however, it greeted her every morning like a slap in the face. Clawing her way out of bed to face another day was becoming harder and harder. She'd had moments lately in which the smell of unwashed men, their nasty hands on her body, their drunken groping had made her want to run screaming into the street...or just put a gun to her head and end it.

Why can't I deal with it anymore? she wondered, unable to discern why the feeling of hopelessness had crept back into her life. She preferred being numb. She supposed she could handle it like the other girls—most of them drank at least half a bottle of whiskey daily. Iris said it smoothed over the rough days.

Daisy rolled over and her eyes fell on the night stand beside the bed. The Bible Hannah had given her sat in the drawer…untouched. She hadn't been back to visit her, mostly because of Mr. McIntyre, but also because she felt she should at least browse the book before returning it to her friend.

Looking for something other than whiskey to smooth over the rough, she slid open the drawer and reached inside.

Chapter 26

"All right, a little to the left," Naomi called as Charles Cody and his brother Dalton straightened then hammered the last nails into the new sign. "The Trinity Inn" hung high over the entrance of their new business, announcing itself in bright gold and red letters. Beneath that, but smaller, the sign read, "Serving the Bread of Life and Offering Rest for the Weary." She felt an unexpected sense of pride that she and her sisters had been able to accomplish the task of opening their own business.

Pushing his hat back on his head, Mr. McIntyre studied the sign as he approached the sisters and Ian gathered in the street. "Clever. Elaborate but still tasteful. Do you think you'll be ready for tomorrow?"

Naomi pulled her shawl closer and raised her chin with confidence. "I think everything is in place for us to open and start serving supper."

"We hope to add lunch by November," Rebecca shared cautiously. "We'll just see how things go."

Though traffic was slow, Ian kept a watchful eye on an approaching wagon as he shared his thoughts on the future. "A lot of the prospectors are leavin' before the snows come, but I'd bet most of the miners who stay will prefer spendin' their evenings eating with ye ladies than in their cold tents and one-room cabins."

Mr. McIntyre shoved his hands into his pockets and hunched his shoulders against the fall chill. "We're counting on it, and I don't think it will take much to get Martha and her Kitchen to close down for the winter."

Hannah's face registered clear disgust. "I would be pleased if she'd just start selling better food."

Ian put his arms out and gently ushered the sisters a step forward, giving the wagon room to pass. The movement pushed Naomi closer to Mr. McIntyre, but she didn't back away, though she couldn't exactly say why. Instead, she looked to him with a question. "Mr. McIntyre, how much does the town change in the winter? Will many people leave?"

"The stagecoach drops down to one trip a week around the middle of October, less frequently than that depending on the snow. Same for the freight wagons. When the snow is deep, supplies come in by mule, if they can make it. Like Ian said, most of the prospector's leave, but my men stay because we run the mine 24/7. There is definitely a change in the pace of the town, but it keeps moving."

She almost liked the sound of it, a slower pace, less noise. "I'm sure your restaurant will stay busy, though you would have trouble filling rooms in the winter. Next year will be different. Ian and I have plans to build industries in this town that will not be seasonal. Your inn will eventually be busy year-round. Especially once we get the railroad."

"It will be interesting to see all that unfold," Rebecca mused. "So, we will see you gentlemen this evening?" Her eyes unmistakably lingered on Ian.

"Seven sharp," Ian replied. "We're eager to be yer first customers."

"Or guinea pigs," Hannah joked.

As the laughter and banter went back and forth, Naomi suddenly felt someone's eyes boring into her. She turned and looked down the street, convinced she would spot someone watching them, but saw only the normal, busy jostling of Defiance at midday. Disturbed, she continued to study the traffic, the sidewalks, the windows on the second floors. No one seemed to be paying them any attention...*strange*, she thought. *I could have sworn—*

"Is anything wrong?" Mr. McIntyre disengaged from the conversation and followed her stare down the street.

"No," she murmured, knowing the denial sounded weak. "Do you ever have that feeling that someone is watching you? The Pinkerton man left a week ago." She rubbed her arms, shaking off the feeling. "Silly. I guess I'm just nervous about all this responsibility."

"Probably." Mr. McIntyre tilted his head, and continued to study the street. To Naomi, he didn't look or sound convinced, especially when he repeated himself. "Probably."

~~~

Before going down to help with dinner, Naomi sat on her bed and took a moment to be still. She looked around her Spartan room, unable at this instant to imagine its potential. All the rooms smelled like fresh pine, which was charming, but they lacked trim, wainscots, painting, decorations and draperies. They were coming along, though.

She and her sisters had headed west with few personal possessions, so there were no pictures or homey needlepoint on the walls, no furniture yet, except for beds, and they were still living out of trunks. The only splash of color came from the quilts on their beds. Yet, it was all right. She had finally come to peace at least with their location, if not the plan for bringing them here.

She picked up the wedding photo of her and John that sat on a box beside her bed. Naomi would have given almost anything for a different ending to that part of her life, but God was easing the pain. The first night alone in this new bed had been a sleepless one, but strangely, she had revisited Mr. McIntyre's comments about her personal strengths and that had helped distract her mind from the empty side of the bed. Not seeing herself as such a failure had given Naomi the hope that God could use her in this wild, isolated place for a good purpose. That would at least give some meaning to John's death.

And she was trying hard to see the residents of Defiance as lost souls, not merely rebellious miscreants. Emilio and Daisy had gone a long way in softening her heart.

She tried daily to follow Rebecca's advice: ask what could make these people so wild and unholy. Like the flowers in the brothel, many of them were no doubt sad, lonely, lost, frustrated and hopeless. Were they mean? Without a doubt. Did they follow the wicked leanings of their hearts? Surely. Did God still love them? Absolutely. Were things changing?

That last question perplexed Naomi. Were they?

Hannah had blossomed in her faith to a level Naomi would never have expected. They had all reached out to Daisy, and Hannah had even given her a Bible. Emilio was their unofficially adopted brother. Rebecca had a light in her eyes no one had seen in years. Naomi herself felt a little more pliable in God's hands. Admittedly, her heart was softer.

Why, she could even spare a ray of kindness for Mr. McIntyre. She knew he was keeping something from her, but even in that that she had found the patience to let things unfold in God's timing.

Yes, things *were* changing. Not at the speed of a racehorse, but at God's speed. That was as it should be.

As Ian and Mr. McIntyre arrived, Naomi was lighting the last candle on the table. She couldn't help but appraise her guests, freshly bathed and smelling of lilac water, clothes pressed and boots shined. Naomi was surprised at herself for noticing the way Mr. McIntyre's still-wet black hair curled lazily over his white collar and the smoothness of his freshly-shaven face and neatly trimmed beard.

"My, my, gentleman. I am dutifully impressed. You both look very handsome." The statement was innocent enough, but Naomi couldn't help feeling that she had somehow crossed a line. Friendly was fine with Ian, but such a familiarity with Mr. McIntyre bothered her. Perhaps because that was an intimate level of friendship she told herself she had no desire to reach.

"Thank you," Ian replied, motioning Mr. McIntyre to the table. "This isn't just any other night."

Mr. McIntyre agreed, dropping his hat on a nearby table. "It is an auspicious occasion." Both men took an instant to survey the room. Naomi could see they were impressed.

Red-checked table cloths covered each table, along with simple centerpieces of pine branches and holly berries. In the center, a white candle glowed invitingly. Though there were lamps on the walls and one large light hanging over the center of the room, they were all turned low. Several candles burned on the hearth, as well. The setting was simple but elegant in its own rustic way.

Mr. McIntyre pulled his chair out. "You have all done a wonderful job, but it is a little too refined for Defiance."

Naomi shook the match to extinguish it. "I know, but tomorrow night the lights will be turned up all the way and we'll be filled to rafters with less-than-elegant customers." Or, at least, they all hoped.

Rebecca pushed her way through the batwings and Hannah came to the serving window at the sound of the voices.

"Good evening, gentlemen." Rebecca nodded to them and smiled at her sister. "Naomi, we're ready if you're ready."

"I am."

Hannah passed the first tray out with a pitcher of tea and glasses. As Rebecca and Naomi served, Ian noticed their appearance.

"Will these be yer uniforms then?"

Naomi and Rebecca stepped back from the table to model their outfits. They had sewn simple black skirts matched with white shirts and covered with white aprons. Hannah wore a loose black dress covered with a white pinafore, which she twirled in as she brought the last item from the kitchen.

She glanced at Rebecca then Ian. Giggling, she set the tray on the table. "We'll all wear our hair braided when we open, of course, but for tonight we wanted to get out the curling iron."

Ian and Mr. McIntyre looked as if they didn't get the joke, but smiled indulgently at Hannah. Thankfully, Naomi thought, her little sister refrained from explaining to the men that the curled hair had been Rebecca's idea, a suggestion totally out of character for her. Naomi and Hannah had gone along with the plan out of sheer amazement.

Now, their hair streamed down in spiraling, glistening rivers of gold and chocolate tresses. Naomi acknowledged that a blind man would have been able to see the light in Ian's eyes when he looked at Rebecca. At peace with that, Naomi hid a smile in her heart.

McIntyre noted the way the candlelight turned Naomi's hair the color of spun gold and had to make a conscious effort to keep his eyes on Ian, Rebecca, anyone but her. He couldn't help himself, though, watching her move, the grace and confidence with which she poured coffee, the way the tailored shirt clung to alluring curves. The light dancing in her eyes reflected the soul of a strong, passionate, fiercely courageous woman. He found the picture bewitching.

The food flowed quickly and smoothly and reached the table hot. Before long, they were all seated and enjoying a mouth-watering meal. The conversation was as appealing as the food, and McIntyre enjoyed the way talk of the future came naturally and with optimism. Even from Naomi.

Now that they had a good cook stove, the sisters told him vegetable canning was underway as well. Not to mention, the backyard had been transformed into a small farm, with chicken coops and a cow and, next spring, a garden. The cow had come when Naomi had offered Sampson as trade, probably one of the most difficult things she had done on this journey, McIntyre surmised. But a milk cow was worth two Sampsons. And so they were fairly settled in their new home and ready to open their doors to the public…pending approval of the meal by himself and Ian.

Based on the empty plates and the apple pie which had practically been inhaled, McIntyre was fairly certain the girls knew they had passed muster.

Ian wiped his mouth and laid his napkin on an empty plate. "If the meals come out tha' wonderfully every night, I will be a regular customer."

"I share your sentiments," McIntyre drawled, leaning back casually in his chair and crossing his legs. "I believe you ladies have found your true calling."

True calling? Naomi had to admit she had enjoyed getting the restaurant up and running. It was a nice feeling to be enjoying the fruits of their labor with friends—though she couldn't really call Mr. McIntyre a friend, exactly. She was harboring less animosity towards him, though, since their day of chopping wood together.

Not only because of his insightful comments regarding her feisty streak, but she had seen the ax he used. The handle was smeared with blood. He had chopped wood until his hands bled, *while* his hands bled, in fact. She didn't know why he'd done it, but his perseverance had impressed her. Under the silk shirts and callous demeanor, she considered that he might be more than an egotistical, immoral, self-absorbed corrupter of women. Now, if she just knew what he was hiding from her...

The night waned and Naomi thought Hannah looked pretty done-in. When her little sister yawned, Rebecca quickly offered to do the clean up. The sisters started to protest, but when Ian proposed his assistance, everyone took the hint.

"Well," Mr. McIntyre pushed back from the table and stood. "I have a few things to check on. Ladies, I can't remember when I've had a more agreeable meal." His eyes seemed to linger on Naomi, but she passed it off as her imagination. He looked quickly at Ian and nodded. "I'll see you in the morning?"

"Aye. The plans are finished; I'll have them with me."

Grabbing his hat, Mr. McIntyre nodded a farewell, but his eyes did not fall again on Naomi.

"I guess we'll hit the hay, too," Naomi hinted, dropping a hand on Hannah's shoulder. "Let's leave the grown-ups to talk." Rising, she pulled the chair out for her little sister and helped her up. "Thank you for coming tonight, Ian."

"Yes, we hope you enjoyed it." Unable to hold in her giggles, Hannah added, "Don't stay up too late, children."

Embarrassed, Rebecca threw a napkin at her. "Get yourself to bed, little sister."

As McIntyre trekked back to the saloon, he mulled over the relaxed atmosphere at the table. In fact, he thought he noticed a definite change in Naomi's attitude towards him. She actually laughed once at a joke of his, instead of favoring him with a sarcastic comment. She did not engage him in conversation as much as the others, but there was a difference in her manner. If not for that damnable letter tucked away in his room, he might actually feel encouraged—

Abruptly coming from the shadows, Marshal Hayes bounded up on the boardwalk and fell into step beside his boss. When Wade didn't speak immediately, McIntyre knew he had something he didn't want to share.

"What is it, Wade?"

"There's a fella in the saloon I knew when I worked over in Alta. I figured I'd ask him if he'd seen Rose lately…"

"And…" McIntyre prompted irritably when Wade wasn't quick with the information.

"Well, Rose had a tent there and one of her customers came in and caught her doing some of her Mayan witchcraft mess." He blew a cold breath into the air, clearly disturbed by what he had to say next. "She stabbed him in the eyes, Mr. McIntyre. Then hit him with him somethin', maybe his gun, but she knocked him clean unconscious."

Struggling to spit out the last part of the story, he stopped McIntyre and leaned into him. Looking around to make sure no one was paying them any attention, he added the last piece of information in a desperately hushed voice. "Then she carved three crosses on his chest."

Three crosses?

"Whatcha reckon that means?"

The news troubled McIntyre deeply. "Where is Rose now?"

The marshal rubbed his neck nervously, obviously preferring not to deliver this news. "That's the other thing I came to tell ya. She's gone again."

McIntyre glanced down the street in the direction of the inn. He wasn't sure if he should be more worried about himself or the sisters. Were the crosses a message? Was Rose somewhere in town? Was she content to cut up strangers in Alta or did she have her sights set on a victim here in Defiance? Since Rose had left, McIntyre had taken to wearing his sidearm on a more regular basis, though, tonight he was without. He realized he needed to stay armed, and Naomi and her sisters needed to be warned.

"Watch the town tonight, especially the inn. Split the shift with Charlie Ford and his brother. Tomorrow, I want you and some men to do a house-to-house search for Rose. Find out if she's here. Turn this town inside-out and back again. Five hundred dollars to the man who finds her."

~~~

As the sound of Hannah's and Naomi's footsteps and whispering voices faded, Ian turned his chair so he could look at Rebecca more squarely. Rubbing his beard, he studied her in the candlelight. Rebecca tried not to squirm, but his eyes drilled into her. Before she could ask why the scrutiny, he cleared his throat.

"I've high hopes for yer restaurant. It'll be no time at all and ye'll be needin' to hire more help."

The suggestion brought Rebecca round to a question she'd meant to ask him a hundred times. An issue had come to the sisters' attention, but the time had not seemed right to address it. However, the days were passing so quickly now, there was no more time to wait. "Ian, I've heard rumors of mid-wives in Tent Town, but is there a good doctor in Defiance? I haven't seen an office or heard anyone mention him…"

"Aye, there is a doctor, of sorts. A mine that employs over two hundred men must have one. His office is down near the mine entrance, just outside o' town."

"Why do you call him a doctor *of sorts*?"

"The truth is, when he's sober, he's a fine physician."

"Sober?" Rebecca felt a sinking feeling hit her gut. "You mean he's a drunk?"

"Aye, like a lo' of the men in this town, they're here because they're not fit for decent society. Dr. Cook, I believe, has a checkered past. That dusna mean he canna deliver a baby, though."

Rebecca was very unhappy with this news. She wanted the best care possible for Hannah, especially if anything went wrong. "I assume he's our only choice."

Ian thought for a moment. "Well, on occasion I have heard that Mary Two-Horse, a Ute medicine woman, can be availed upon for such needs. I believe a few of the girls from the Iron Horse have required her assistance in, uh, well, ending a pregnancy."

"Abortion?" Rebecca's stomach rolled. "Our choices are midwives with who-knows-what level of skill, a drunken doctor or a baby-killer."

Ian leaned over and took her hand to offer some comfort. "Hannah is young, strong, and healthy. There's no reason at all to assume the worst." Rebecca knew her eyes revealed her fear. "God dinna bring her all this way to just let the child die, either of them."

Considering what they had been through thus far, Rebecca wasn't so sure, but she appreciated his effort at comfort. In fact, for a moment, she let herself get lost in those steely gray eyes that touched her soul. The powerful force that attraction can be pulled them closer. Rebecca's rational mind flew right out the window as she wondered if he might draw her even closer for a kiss. How long had it been since a man's lips had touched hers…?

When he was close enough for her to feel his breath, he whispered, "Perhaps we'd best get to the dishes."

She blinked and pulled away, her cheeks burning. "Yes, yes, absolutely." Rebecca jumped up. Rattled and more than a little embarrassed, she started clearing the table with jittery hands. Ian stood and assisted in a calm, measured manner as Rebecca's heart galloped like a wild mustang's. Still, she didn't miss the slight smile playing around the corners of his mouth.

Chapter 27

Opening day for the restaurant came with an explosion of small crises, wrong deliveries, shortages, overcooked food, and a packed house. Anticipating the crowd, and their possible lack of manners, McIntyre and Ian came by to lend visible moral support and crowd control if necessary. Before long, the Scotsman was in the kitchen with an apron wrapped around his waist frying steaks. McIntyre instructed the marshal to stay till closing and maintain a high profile with his badge. That, he felt, was all the contribution he cared to make.

Leaving before someone tied an apron on him, he spent the evening tending to business at the Iron Horse. He had hoped to speak with Naomi about Rose, but it was obvious from the whirling dervish she and her sisters were in opening night, it would have to wait a day or so. With men scheduled to patrol the town and keep an eye on the inn, he was cautiously optimistic that things were in hand.

Naomi realized that the presence of Ian and Mr. McIntyre, and then the marshal, a proxy for Mr. McIntyre, clearly sent the message patrons were to behave as gentlemanly as possible. It helped that the house rules were posted outside next to the front door. Marshal Hayes unceremoniously turned away anyone who was obviously inebriated or in desperate need of a bath, per Mr. McIntyre's explicit directions.

Many of the customers were bold and somewhat foul-mouthed the first several nights, testing the rules as it were, but Naomi dealt with them on a professional and polite basis. Every once in awhile she would slip into the kitchen, bite down on a spoon and scream, but other than that she was proud of her refusal to spar with the patrons. A few were foolish enough to attempt some groping of their waitress, and the marshal summarily evicted them. Unable to get Naomi to spark to any of their comments, and unwilling to lose their place at the table, the men eventually slacked off to enjoy their meals and look at the pretty girls who could cook a mean steak.

~~~

McIntyre waited until the following Sunday afternoon to share his warning about Rose with Naomi. Aware that the sisters had a custom of holding an informal church service in the morning, he dropped by shortly after noon. He found the girls, along with Ian and Emilio, sitting in the dining room gathered around a Bible. He felt like the odd man out, again, and despised this feeling of not being the one in control.

"I am sorry for the intrusion," he apologized awkwardly, setting his hat on a table, "but I was wondering if I might have a word with you, Mrs. Miller."

He sent Ian a knowing glance and the man nodded. Taking his cue to provide McIntyre and Naomi some privacy, Ian suggested the group finish up in the kitchen.

Rebecca, looking puzzled but apparently willing to go along, offered up an excuse to leave the room. "We need to watch that roast anyway. It should be ready in a few minutes. Mr. McIntyre, you're invited to join us if you care for pork roast."

His mouth fairly watered at the invitation. "It smells too wonderful to pass up."

When the room was clear, he sat down opposite Naomi and dove in with small talk first. "Your first several days have gone well, I heard."

"Yes. Rebecca and Hannah have turned out to be quite good chefs and managers. I wonder every day what I'm good for."

"Wade says you're very skilled at keeping the customers in line."

"It's hard work, though. I mean the cooking. Especially on Hannah. She's tiring more easily now. We expect the baby to come sometime around October 23rd or so. We need to get her off her feet more."

This was the first time Naomi had broached the subject with him since that day the Pinkerton had arrived in town. He appreciated her willingness to share a confidence. "Have you had Dr. Cook come down and check on her?"

Naomi hiked her shoulder up and rotated it, as if the question caused her tension. "Well, I wanted to ask you about him. Ian said he has a checkered past and he drinks to excess."

Ian? Yet he was still "Mr. McIntyre."

"Yes on both counts but he's a fine doctor. I'll have him come down, cold sober, and check on Hannah. When it's close to her time, I'll keep him sober."

"That will have to do, then," she huffed, apparently resigned to the situation as it was. "We should have had him come check on her sooner but we were hesitant about his credentials. Whatever you can do to keep him sober would of course be greatly appreciated. Like everything else, though, Hannah's health is in God's hands."

"So, what did you need to see me about?"

"I want you to be suspicious of anything or anyone that doesn't seem right."

Concern clouded her face. "Why? What's the matter?"

"Rose attacked a man a few weeks ago in Alta. She stabbed him in the eyes and carved three crosses on his chest." Saying it aloud like that to a woman, he almost flinched from the violent image. "Does that mean anything to you?"

Her brows knit together as she thought. "Jesus was crucified with two thieves..." She shrugged. "There are three of us...I don't know. Do you think it was a message?"

"The only thing that I'm sure of is Hell hath no fury like a woman scorned. Rose was different from the day you came into town. When I," he paused searching for the right words to describe his relationship with Rose, "*Re-affirmed* the details of our working relationship, she didn't take it very well. I think it made her resentful...dangerous."

"Re-affirmed?"

"Rose and I were," McIntyre tugged on his collar, chafing at sharing this information with Naomi. "Well, *intimate* for a number of months and it gave her certain ideas that she had a claim, so to speak, on some of my affairs. She was harboring under a gross misconception."

"Oooh," Naomi dragged out a long, slow nod. "That explains a lot of things; Rose was *jealous*, not just *territorial* as you put it. She saw us as a threat."

"Rose is also violent and very patient." He drummed his fingers on the table, sorry he'd ever met the woman. "I've seen a lot of wh—excuse me—prostitutes with nasty attitudes. They so often come from horrific backgrounds, as did Rose. But she was more steely than the average girl. The fact is, I knew she would be trouble, but I wasn't exactly thinking with my head..." Naomi didn't flinch under the details, but nodded rather stoically.

"And I was arrogant enough to think I could control her. Now I can't even find her."

Naomi laced and unlaced her fingers nervously, revealing her concern. "What do you think we should do?"

"Keep the doors locked at night. Watch the customers carefully. I could be wrong, but I'd bet she's not working alone. Stay together, and I would urge you to have those late-night prayer sessions in the hotel instead of down by the stream."

Naomi froze. "How did you know I go down there to pray?"

McIntyre felt an icy wind of disaster blow over him. Stuttering, he recovered quickly. "I, well, you mentioned you take walks. I—I just assumed that meant you prayed." He ended the answer sounding more confident than he felt, but she let out a breath, apparently satisfied with the explanation.

"I know you know how to shoot a shotgun," he continued, anxiously turning them back to the matter at hand. "Do you know how to use a pistol? Do you even have one?"

"I have my husband's revolver. I suppose I can manage it if I have to."

"Keep it close."

"Does Ian know?"

"Yes, I told him almost immediately, but asked him not to say anything until I could talk to you. You need to decide what to tell your sisters. In the meantime, I have stepped up patrols of the town and have my men watching the inn closely."

"Thank you." A quizzical look crossed her face and she leaned forward. "Why don't you join us for lunch? I'm going to tell Hannah and Rebecca. You can add anything you like."

There was more than a civil tone in her voice and almost a soft look in her eyes. McIntyre wondered if perhaps he'd finally paid his penance for all the perceived wrongs he'd done.

"Another minute of smelling that roast and I would have invited myself."

Chapter 28

Rebecca watched from the doorway as Hannah stared at the calendar pinned to her bedroom wall. The blur of motion and work at the inn made the publication an inconsequential scrap of paper to everyone but her little sister. Hannah had drawn an X through each day as it ended, but October 25 was circled with a question mark drawn in the center. It was only a guess, give or take two weeks, the doctor had said. Another exhausting day of cooking behind her, Hannah carefully drew an X through October 15.

One more down, Rebecca thought. *How many more to go?*

Sizing up her little sister's weary appearance, she knew what she had to say was the right thing. Though they had been letting her sleep as late as she needed, it wasn't enough.

"Naomi and I have been talking. You've got to get more rest. You can help us prep for dinner in the afternoons if you'd like, but we want you to take the evenings off."

Hannah rubbed her back and glanced down at her feet which had been swelling uncomfortably over the last few weeks. With enough energy left for some humor, she squared her shoulders and saluted. "Aye, aye captain."

Rebecca smiled but it faded quickly when her hand went to her pocket and she felt the note. One more thing for Hannah to worry over. But she had a right to know...

"Listen," Rebecca sighed, pulling the folded square of paper from her pocket. "There is something else." She held it out for her sister and Hannah started to reach for it. "It's Billy's address at Harvard." The explanation froze Hannah's hand in mid-air. "According to Ian, Mr. McIntyre went to great effort and expense to get this information out of the Pinkerton man. I thought that was rather decent of him."

Hannah dropped her hand and turned away. Rebecca flinched and pressed the note to her chest. "He is the father and I suppose that gives him some rights."

"Being a father is about more than bloodlines." Hannah's voice wasn't cold, exactly, but Rebecca didn't miss the edge it carried, either.

"It's up to you, little sister. Whatever you decide, Naomi and I will stand behind you. You didn't promise Frank Page anything."

When Hannah didn't respond, Rebecca set the note on the bed. It looked small and inconsequential against the background of loudly colored quilting squares. Strange how it was anything but.

"I think I've come too far to travel back down that road." Hannah turned and Rebecca saw a quiet strength in her sister's young eyes. "My son is the only Page that matters to me now."

~~~

Clutching a coat and a small, neatly wrapped package, Daisy raised her hand to knock on the hotel's back door. With a fair amount of cooking noises and chatter coming from the kitchen, she realized no one would hear her and slowly pushed open the door. Stepping inside, she peered meekly into the kitchen. She watched for a bit as Rebecca, Ian and Emilio tended to the business of cooking with efficiency and organization. Ian pulled orders off the rack in the window and hung them over the stove. Rebecca and Emilio quickly discussed the orders then flew into motion. The three hustled and bustled about the kitchen like well trained soldiers, cutting meat, flipping steaks, stirring pots of steaming vegetables. As Rebecca pulled a tray of biscuits out of the oven and turned to set them on the table, she caught sight of Daisy.

"I—I brought these for Hannah," the girl stammered, quickly thrusting out her arms as if to pass off the gifts.

"Oh, thank you," Rebecca gushed, "Why don't you give them to her in person? I know Hannah would *love* to have some company. Really she would."

"I need more steaks." Ian came to the table and slid a cutting board loaded with a slab of meat closer to him. "Good evenin', Daisy." He yanked the knife from the shank of beef and raised it into the air for a violent blow.

"Here, I'll do that." Rebecca took the knife from him. "Why don't you finish with those in the pan. Emilio, we're going to need more potatoes."

The boy withdrew the spoon from the stew he had been stirring and disappeared around the corner, headed to the store room. Daisy realized she was just in the way and stepped out in the hallway. To get upstairs she had to skirt the edge of the dining room which was full of customers and she wasn't supposed to be here. What if someone told Mr. McIntyre?

She decided she wanted to see Hannah badly enough to risk another stern talking-to by her employer. Head down and turned away from the guests, she clung to the wall and darted up the stairs to the second floor. Apparently no one saw her or paid any attention, and she strode quietly down the hall to Hannah's room. At least there was light coming from underneath one door only, so she assumed it was hers. Daisy knocked timidly and waited for Hannah to let her in.

"Come in," the girl chirped, opening the door.

Hannah acted tickled to see her, and not just because she was bearing more gifts. Entering the room with Hannah, Daisy handed over a new wool coat and a box of chocolates.

The sight of the candy almost put Hannah in a faint, Daisy noted with amusement.

"Where did you get these? I love chocolate!"

Daisy waved the question away, preferring to avoid the details. "A friend brings me things some times. The coat is huge on me, but I thought you could use it to tuck the baby in when you need to go somewhere."

Shocking Daisy, Hannah reached out and hugged her with bubbling enthusiasm. "Thank you so much, Mollie. You are such a special blessing."

Daisy hugged her back, tentatively at first, then with more confidence. It felt good to have a friend.

"How is the restaurant doing?" she questioned, pulling away. "The men sure have been talking about it down at the Iron Horse."

"Really?" Curiosity lit a glow in Hannah's eyes. "What do they say?" She took the coat and candy to her bed and gratefully plopped down on the mattress.

Daisy quickly weeded out the crass comments, especially about Hannah being with child. She had taken it upon herself to spread the rumor that Hannah had been abandoned by her husband. That was something men in a mining town could understand, since many of them had left home and hearth due to an infection of Gold Fever. Starting to believe that their newest citizens were exactly what they appeared to be, the men were finding things to respect about the sisters.

"It's funny, but they don't talk about the food as much as they do you and your sisters. I think a lot of the men are actually glad that maybe the town might be settling down some now." She realized then that many of the comments lumped her in with the bad elements in town, but shared them anyway. "One man said that when a few respectable girls come into town, a church and schools won't be far behind.

"I overheard Matt Wilson tell Nate Ledford that even if the food tasted like cow dung he'd come just to sit and watch you pour his tea. Isn't that funny?"

Hanna laughed and shook her head. "It's almost like they *want* a chance to act civilized."

"Defiance is out of hand because of a few really bad folks and just to stay alive, you have to be mean, too. Or at least pretend to be. I know for a fact, though, that not everyone in this town is a gun-totin, whiskey-drinkin' whoremonger. Take Mr. Donoghue for example. Why, I don't think he's ever visited the garden, not once. I've never even seen him have more than a few drinks.

"And there are some other men in town who have their wives with them and they keep to themselves. The worst group is among the prospectors. They're just drifters, going from gold camp to gold camp. They're the ones who start most of the trouble."

Hannah patted the bed. "Forgive my manners. Please, have a seat. Tell me, what about the men who work in the mine? Are they a rough lot? I've tried so hard to say behind closed doors, I feel like a hermit."

"Well, the miners aren't so bad, really," Daisy sat down on the bed, almost at the opposite end. For her, it was a comfortable space. "Most of them aren't boys any more. They've tried their hand at prospecting and would rather just have a regular paycheck. A ton of them send money back home to mothers and wives and, since Mr. McIntyre won't tolerate drunk or sloppy workers, they pretty much mind their P's and Q's."

The conversation dragged then and Daisy thought Hannah looked preoccupied. Finally, her new friend asked about the Bible. "So, have you had a chance to do any reading."

The sudden change of direction opened the door for Daisy to in turn ask a question that had burned in her heart since hearing those scriptures out in the backyard. "Some. A little. It's hard for me, though." She leaned forward and asked with sincerity, "Is it wrong to have a Bible in a saloon?"

Hannah thought about the question then shook her head. "I wouldn't think so. Jesus said it's not the healthy who need a doctor but the sick. And he was accused of being a wine-bibber because he ate so often with known sinners. But they came to hear him speak. They wanted to be near him because he didn't judge them."

Hannah took a deep breath and smiled warmly at Daisy. "Look, Mollie, I've never been around prostitutes. I can't imagine what your life is like. But you said it makes you feel dirty and worthless. *That* I do know something about. And I know Jesus didn't die so I could stay trapped in those feelings." Daisy's heart started racing again. The fire in Hannah's eyes captivated her soul; she found her passion was contagious.

"God loves us just the way we are but he refuses to leave us that way. Think about giving Him your heart, Mollie. If you can accept that He forgives you, I promise He'll change your life.

"You'll feel clean again. He'll restore your dignity and make a way for you to get out of that life, but may be best of all, He'll refresh your spirit."

Hannah scooted over and clutched Daisy's hands. "He is so willing to forgive you. In fact, His word says, if we confess our sins, He is faithful and just and will forgive us our sins and *purify* us from all unrighteousness."

Daisy bit her lip as her eyes teared up. Hannah believed so ardently in Jesus, she made it hard to turn away from Him. "I don't mean to push you, Mollie, and I know you probably have lots of questions. It's just that, sometimes, I feel like you're the reason we're here." Daisy looked away, unwilling to comprehend what she meant. "In my wildest dreams, I would have never thought things would turn out like this. But I'm glad we're here…and I'm glad I've gotten to know you."

Daisy blinked back tears and thought about the life she was living. "Are there any women like me in the Bible?" Was there, she wanted to know, a black-and-white example of what Jesus would say to someone like her?

"Yes. And he loved them dearly."

Hannah had a pencil and several sheets of paper sitting on the trunk next to her bed. She took a sheet and the pencil and started writing, using her great, round abdomen for a desk. She quickly scribbled something down and handed the paper over to Daisy. "Once you've read these, will you come back and tell me what you think?"

Hand trembling, Daisy carefully took the paper and nodded.

When Daisy returned to the saloon that night, she tucked the sheet of paper away in her night stand with the Bible and started dressing for work. With the fastening of each button in her worn, low-cut dress, her spirits sank deeper and deeper. By the time she went downstairs, she had the mood of a woman dressed for an execution. The lewd laughter, the choking smoke, the stench of unwashed bodies and the bawdy music assaulted her like physical blows with each step down the staircase. A group of prospectors departing the next day for warmer climates had invaded the Iron Horse. For one more Friday night in Defiance, they brought hell to earth...at least for her. The shame and guilt of it left her unable to even look at the Bible for days.

Chapter 29

The end of October was feeling fickle and decided one morning to drop an unexpected autumn snow on Defiance. A pure, undefiled blanket of white draped itself gently over the town, hiding its sins. Naomi stood on the porch, amazed at the deceptive beauty of it…and the silence. For an hour or so at dawn, Defiance laid still and quiet as if everyone had agreed not to disturb the picturesque scene.

As she embraced the quiet, Hannah screamed from upstairs. The fear and pain in her little sister's voice jolted Naomi out of her reverie. Heart in her throat, she raced to Hannah's room, fearing unimaginable tragedy. Instead, she found Rebecca calmly helping an ash-white Hannah back to bed.

"The baby's coming." Rebecca sounded calm as she pulled the covers over Hannah. "She said she's been having contractions since around midnight, but they're only a few minutes apart now and more intense."

Naomi swallowed the fear that tried to tighten her throat. "What should we do?" Just then another contraction hit Hannah. A deep groan escaped as her face contorted into a grim mask of pain. She writhed in the bed but Rebecca held onto her hand and whispered comforting words in a soothing voice.

"I should get the doctor." *Oh, God, please let him be sober,* Naomi prayed.

"Yes, but let's pray first."

Hannah nodded emphatically at Rebecca's suggestion as the pain faded away.

Naomi practically ran to the bed and knelt on the floor. She caressed her little sister's forehead then took her hand and Rebecca's. "Everything is going to be just fine…" Naomi wasn't sure who she was trying to convince, but felt strongly the words needed to be repeated. "Just fine."

Unclear on how to contact the doctor, which now struck her as a painfully stupid lack of preparation, Naomi was forced to go to the saloon. She stopped in the middle of the dark, silent room and simply shouted for Mr. McIntyre. She didn't know which room was his and she had no desire to go upstairs knocking on doors at this hour. If her yelling woke the entire building, so be it. He came out of the first room at the top of the stairs, tugging on a robe and looking astonished to find her standing in his saloon. Other doors opened and flowers, Naomi assumed, peered down as well.

"The doctor. We need the doctor. Hannah's baby is coming."

Despite the groggy look in his eyes, Mr. McIntyre didn't hesitate in responding. "I'll dress and fetch him immediately."

By early afternoon, Hannah delivered a healthy, seven-pound baby boy who shared an uncanny resemblance to his father. She had known all along he would be a boy just as she had known all along his name would be William Aaron Page. The Page part, of course, was legally debatable, but no one in Defiance would ever have cause to argue it.

Cuddling her little fat, pink cherub, Hannah wondered where Billy was right at that moment. Did he ever think of her? If he could see his newborn son, she had no doubt he would fall in love with the round face, blue eyes and perfect little hands. He was adorable and beautiful, and Hannah's heart overflowed into her eyes. She couldn't recall ever having cried out of sheer joy. Overcome with peace and gratitude, she kissed her precious angel on the forehead and mused over how amazingly good God had been to her.

A gentle knock on her door brought her out of her tender daydreaming. She quickly dried her face with her one free hand and smoothed her hair. "Come in."

Awkwardly, hesitantly, Emilio peered around the door. A true sense of deep friendship washed over her at the sight of him. "Emilio, I'm so glad to see you. Please come in."

Softly, he shut the door and wandered over to the bed. Hands behind his back, he leaned over to take a peek at the new arrival. Hannah moved the blanket out of the way for a better view and Emilio's face lit up.

"Aah, hees so beautiful."

Hannah grinned, as much from pride as enjoyment of Emilio's company. She thought of him now as a brother and couldn't imagine life without him. She would always be eternally grateful that God had let their paths cross in this far away town.

The boy straightened up and shook his head. In a matter-of-fact voice he murmured, "The father. I theenk he ees an idiot."

~~~

Naomi acknowledged with pride that Hannah was an excellent, capable mother. Within days, she was back in the kitchen, along with a crib that that had been a gift from her sisters, ordered from Montgomery Ward. Little Billy seemed comforted by the sounds of sizzling meat and boiling soup, and he slept contentedly in the warm kitchen. Naomi and Rebecca had prayed specifically that Hannah's first baby would be healthy, happy and easy-going and God had answered that prayer to the letter.

A gregarious infant, he loved for anyone to hold him but was especially fascinated by Ian's deep voice and beard. When his uncontrollable little hands happened upon the fuzzy hair, he pulled and tugged with surprising determination. Or perhaps it was the absurd facial expressions "Uncle" Ian made that the baby liked so much.

The first time Naomi had heard Ian refer to himself as "Uncle", she'd gaped at Rebecca who merely shrugged over her pile of peeled potatoes, just as surprised as she. Ian appeared not to have noticed the way he'd attached the word to himself. Naomi rather liked it. She looked him up and down as he cradled the baby, and decided that he might make an acceptable brother-in-law after all. Now, if Rebecca would give the man a little encouragement.

~~~

The restaurant was closed on Thanksgiving Day, a decision the girls had made with great difficulty. They wanted, however, a time to truly thank God for the fact they were still together and that Hannah's baby was just perfect. They insisted that Emilio join them and Ian arrived with a stunning gift of fancy candies. Hannah had invited Daisy by way of Emilio, but she had politely turned down the offer.

As Naomi set the table and listened to the easy conversation coming from the kitchen, she pondered the strange mix of people who would sit around this table today...and those who wouldn't. She missed John terribly, sometimes more than others, but Defiance had forced her to cope with the loss. He was gone and he wasn't coming back. It still hurt, but she tried to occupy her heart with the things she could control: taking care of Hannah, opening the restaurant, making a life here.

She had toyed with the idea of inviting Mr. McIntyre for Thanksgiving, but shied away from it in the end, puzzled she'd even thought of him. This was a gathering of friends and loved ones, she argued, setting an apple pie on the table. Not meeting her definition of either, Mr. McIntyre was something of a round peg in a square hole. She didn't know what to do with him.

The thought brought her to a halt. Why did she have to do anything at all with him? He was an acquaintance and one didn't necessarily invite acquaintances for Thanksgiving supper.

Convinced she was satisfied with that reasoning, Naomi headed back to the kitchen for more food.

~~~

Thanksgiving Day for Daisy was quiet. She knew the saloon would be slow until evening. Bored, she looked out her window at the falling snow and questioned what to do with her free time. Of course, the answer nagged at her, but she was almost afraid of what she might find if she read the stories of those Bible women. Had Jesus chastised them for living this way? Had he challenged them to do anything, sweep streets, sew clothes, beg even, before settling for this lifestyle? Or had he so touched their hearts with his forgiveness that the women had up-ended their lives to follow him, casting off everything they had become to start over fresh and changed?

She stared at the nightstand. How many customers had she been with since her last visit to Hannah? A dozen? More? She didn't want to face God with the stench of sin on her, but she didn't want to face her friend not having read those stories. And she wanted to see Hannah, to see the baby, maybe hold him...

Sighing nervously, she walked over to the nightstand. The piece of paper Hannah had given her sat on top of the book. She looked at the first scripture written on it then flipped her way over to John 8. She sat down and began to read a story that spoke to her as if she had been there herself.

She saw the woman, thrown like a filthy little pawn into the midst of the arrogant, puffed-up men. Daisy wondered if the woman's heart had beat at a breakneck pace as the men accused her, badgered Jesus and urged him to allow them to stone her. In her humiliation had she wanted to crawl into a cave or had she stared defiantly at those vipers? She wondered what Jesus wrote in the sand as he knelt down, trying to ignore their complaints. Then she saw the most miraculous thing of all: he had focused on *their* sins, not those of the woman.

"So when they continued asking him, he lifted up himself, and said unto them, He that is without sin among you, let him first cast a stone at her. And again he stooped down, and wrote on the ground. And they which heard it, being convicted by their own conscience, went out one by one, beginning at the eldest, even unto the last: and Jesus was left alone, and the woman standing in the midst. When Jesus had lifted up himself, and saw none but the woman, he said unto her, Woman, where are those thine accusers? hath no man condemned thee? She said, No man, Lord. And Jesus said unto her, Neither do I condemn thee: go and sin no more."

Daisy read the last sentence at least ten times. *Neither do I condemn thee. Go and sin no more.* It kept running through her head as she stared down at the words. He had forgiven that woman so easily; in fact, he had been more interested in making a point to the hypocrites who had paraded her out to him. He had spoken to the woman with kindness but firmness.

It amazed Daisy. This glimpse at Christ's heart toward a loose woman intrigued her; made her hunger to know more. Eagerly, she flipped to Luke 7 and read the story of a prostitute who had slipped in to the Pharisees' home without a word and began humbly ministering to Jesus. She felt this woman's tears and broken heart as she desperately and with reverence washed her Lord's feet.

What did Jesus see when he looked at her? Her desperate desire to find forgiveness, to know that someone cared about her? She wasn't welcome in this home, but had come anyway, to offer up this simple act of love. Had she come expecting him to forgive her sins, or did she so love this savior that to serve him was all that mattered?

Daisy imagined he had touched her cheek lovingly when he announced, "Wherefore I say unto thee, Her sins, which are many, are forgiven; for she loved much: but to whom little is forgiven, the same loveth little. And he said unto her, Thy sins are forgiven. And he said to the woman, thy faith has saved thee; go in peace."

Her sins, which are many, are forgiven.
Thy faith hath saved thee; go in peace.

If he could forgive her—could he, would he forgive the flower known as Daisy? Did he know that her real name was Mollie Stewart?

Crying, she held the Bible to her chest and slipped to her knees to find out.

Chapter 30

The sisters had taken Emilio completely under their wings after clearing it with Mr. McIntyre, and moved the boy into the small room beneath the stairs, behind the hotel's new registration desk. Because of his proximity to the front, he was the first to hear the desperate knocking in the middle of the night. Afraid of who might be standing on the other side at this late hour, he lit a lamp and called out to the sisters.

"Senoras, Senoras! There ees someone at the door!"

Immediately jumping out of bed, Naomi threw on her robe and grabbed the shotgun. She raced down the stairs, followed by Rebecca. Hannah stopped at the landing, obviously unwilling to go too far away from little Billy.

A female voice called from the other side of the door. "It's me, Lily. Please come quick. Daisy's been—"

Naomi jerked the door half way open. When she saw the girl was alone, she opened it wider, and let her come in along with a whirl of snowflakes. The Negro girl from the garden wasn't even wearing a coat, but was, instead, running about in a very revealing dress. Rubbing the chill and snow from her dark arms, she frantically blurted out a jumble of details.

"Woah, woah, woah," Naomi bellowed, grabbing her shoulder. "Calm down. Now *what* about Daisy?"

The girl breathed and tried again. "She's hurt real bad. A customer knocked her around her when she wouldn't go along. She asked if Hannah would come."

Hannah laced her fingers over her stomach, as if quelling butterflies.

"Get dressed, Hannah." Naomi looked over her shoulder and read concern in her sister's eyes. "Little Billy will be all right for awhile."

"You go with her, Hannah." Rebecca walked back to the stairs. "I'll tend to Billy."

Naomi grabbed a coat from the rack beside the door and hung it on Lilly. "We'll be right along. Tell Daisy we're coming."

The two women exchanged understanding glances then Lilly sprinted out the door.

Mr. McIntyre greeted Hannah and Naomi as they climbed the stairs in the closed saloon.

Naomi stopped one step below him. She felt a dangerous fury coming to a boil because whatever trouble was on the other side of that door was his fault. "Have you called the doctor?"

"She insisted on seeing Hannah first." She hoped her expression showed that she did not approve of that answer. He tried to explain. "She seemed rather emphatic about it."

Gently, Hannah pushed past them both and went to the door. Opening it slowly, she looked back at Naomi and motioned for her to follow. They found Daisy lying on the bed asleep while Jasmine, an Asian flower, dabbed delicately at a bloodied and bruised cheekbone. Both sisters gasped when they saw Daisy's face, almost unrecognizable from the swelling, discoloration and drying blood.

Jasmine immediately passed the bowl of water and hand towel to Hannah, her beautiful face inscrutable and cold. "She's been waiting for you."

Naomi grabbed Jasmine's arm as the girl attempted to slip past her. "Can you get us some witch hazel, liniment, and a steak?" It wasn't really a request.

Without meeting Naomi's gaze, the girl nodded and added dryly, "I think you will need bandages also. Her ribs are broken."

Naomi watched her leave then drew in a breath. Hannah had already sat down next to Daisy and was tending to the cut on her cheek. Daisy's left eye was red, black and blue, and completely swollen shut. Her top lip, smeared with blood, was puffed up to twice its normal size. A trail of dried blood trickled from one nostril in her slightly askew nose and there were bruises on her throat that clearly matched the placement of fingers. As Hannah dabbed at the blood, unbridled tears ran down her face.

Naomi wanted to cry too, and scream, and beat the ever-loving daylights out of the monster who had done this. Reining in her anger for the moment, she touched Hannah on the shoulder. "I need to pull the blanket back. That girl said she's got some broken ribs. I need to check and see if there are any other injuries."

Hannah nodded and moved enough to allow the blanket to come down. Slowly, trying not to wake Daisy, Naomi pulled the cover back and saw that they had stripped the girl. The abuse her body had taken from the customer was obvious. Her ribs were turning all shades of blue, bruises were discoloring her thighs; her knees and elbows were scratched and bloodied, and her right hand was wrapped in a cold, damp towel resting on her chest. Naomi covered her back up, but left the hand on top of the blanket. Carefully, she pulled the towel away and saw that three of Daisy's fingers were bent in grotesque angles. Not broken, necessarily, but badly dislocated.

Hannah regarded her sister with grief-stricken eyes. "We're going to have to get the doctor."

Daisy moaned as Hannah dabbed at a cut along her jaw. "It's all right, Mollie. We're here now. Everything's going to be fine."

Her one good eye fluttered open and she tried to smile when she saw her friend. She attempted to talk, but Hannah shushed her. "Don't say anything. Just be quiet—"

Daisy rolled her head weakly from side to side and tried again to talk. Her voice was raspy at first but she persisted. Finally, hoarsely, she whispered, "Go and sin no more." She closed her eye and swallowed hard against the pain. "My sins are forgiven." Then she smiled as big as she could. "He told me so."

Naomi and Hannah cleaned Daisy up as much as they could, then assisted when the doctor arrived. The girls smelled whisky on his breath, but he seemed sober enough. An elderly gentleman with a short shock of tousled, gray hair and thick, silver glasses, he handled Daisy like a china doll as he wrapped her ribs. Perhaps he was a slave to liquor, but he was extremely compassionate with his patients. He had been kind and reassuring with Hannah during her labor and now treated Daisy as if she was a princess. Lifting the girl and moving her caused her extreme pain but he dealt with her gingerly, speaking low and soothingly.

Naomi appreciated his bedside manner, especially when he got to the last task at hand. They had cleaned Daisy's wounds, placed a steak over her eye, bandaged her ribs…now he had to relocate her fingers.

"Now, Daisy," he rubbed her arm gently, "this is going to hurt like the devil, but when it's over, it's over. The pain will stop almost instantly, unlike those ribs of yours." He grasped her index finger and looked at her. She closed her eye and nodded.

He had to perform the procedure three times and each time Daisy cried out, writhing in pain. Hannah sat on the other side of the bed, holding her free hand and whispering calm words. When the last finger was done, Dr. Cook gave her a teaspoon of laudanum and packed up his bag. He stepped away from the bed and brought Naomi with him.

"I think she'll be all right, despite the fact that she looks as if she was run over by a freight wagon. She's mostly just going to be very sore." He handed her the bottle of laudanum. "Give her a teaspoon of this every four to six hours for two days. Start slacking off after that."

Naomi took the bottle and clutched it to her heart. "When can we move her?"

His eyebrows shot up. "Move her? To where?"

"To our hotel. She's leaving this place and never coming back."

He thought for a moment, scratching his chin. "Well, it's not far, but those ribs of hers are going to make her wish she were dead. I suppose, though, you could move her tomorrow sometime. Give her a dose of that," he pointed at the medicine, "wait for it to take effect then do it...*carefully*. Use a stretcher."

He gave Daisy one last, sad look. "This is the worst I've seen in awhile. It's enough to take the steam out of a man."

Naomi shut the door behind him thinking angrily, *I'd like to do just that.* The man who did this was a vile monster, but what kind of a man opened a business that traded in the flesh of women as if they were horses—no, worse—mere toys for a man's amusement? It was sick and disgusting. It was the height of selfishness and arrogance. She wanted to throw him into the sea with a millstone tied around his neck. Naomi felt a painful new level of loathing for Mr. McIntyre, though she didn't exactly understand why it should grieve her so to feel this way about him.

Daisy slept quietly now and Hannah fidgeted as she stared uncertainly at her sister. "I need to go, Naomi. I've been gone too long."

Lost in her own, angry thoughts, it took a moment for Hanna's voice to intrude. "What? Oh, I'm sorry. Yes, yes, of course you must go. Send Rebecca down when it's light."

Hannah patted her friend's hand one more time then started for the door. Something stopped her, though. Gazing over her shoulder at her sister she warned, "Hate and anger just give Satan a foothold in our lives, Naomi.

I know you're angry; I'm angry, but we can't hate the people responsible for this."

Naomi's lips thinned into a hard, angry line and she offered no reply. Nothing she could say at this moment would sound very Christian.

When Naomi didn't reply, Hannah opened the door only to find Mr. McIntyre about to knock. "I was just coming to check on the patient."

"Certainly." Hannah stepped aside for him. "I'll see you in awhile, Naomi. Mr. McIntyre." With that, she slipped out the door. Naomi stepped closer to the bed to avoid being near Mr. McIntyre and reported on Daisy's condition with her back to him. "Dr. Cook says she'll recover. Cuts and bruises. Broken ribs."

She shook her head, so angry she wasn't sure she could stop the tears. Her chin quivered as she fought for control. Swallowing, she turned on Mr. McIntyre.

McIntyre saw right away that where a possible friendship might have blossomed, now there was only ashes. Her eyes hid nothing of her heart. She blamed him for Daisy's injuries and, he supposed, in a roundabout way, it was his fault.

"Where's the man who did this to her?"

"In the jail."

"What will he be charged with?"

He sensed no answer would be the right one, but he told the truth nonetheless. "Assault and battery. He'll get thirty days in jail and a $75 fine."

"And you? Will he compensate you for lost revenue?"

The arrogant, angry look in her eyes affected him, though he couldn't say just how. He had almost seen a spark of happiness in her eyes lately when she looked at him; not now. The passion he saw burning there at the moment was not the kind he ever wanted to see again. She hated him, even loathed him. It left him speechless—the heat of it, the disappointment of it.

"What kind of a man are you? How can you live with yourself? These women are human beings, not horses to hook up to a freight wagon. In fact, you probably treat your horses better." Shuffling sounds behind him drew her eyes to the hallway. He knew his flowers had gathered in the shadows to listen-in.

Naomi raised her chin. "We're moving Mollie out of here tomorrow. She has a room at our hotel as long as she wants it." She shifted her attention to the audience in the hallway. "*None* of you has to live like this." Her voice was choked with anger, but she was pleading as well. "You are beautiful, valuable children of God and He loves you. He sees your spirit and your dignity. He sees your strength and your will to survive. You are daughters of the King and He doesn't want you living in this filth. Mollie discovered that, which is why she said 'no more.'"

McIntyre heard Iris's cynical cackle. "Yea, and look where that got her."

"Heaven," Naomi fired back. "And eternity with the King. Until then, a home with us." Out of the corner of his eye, he watched the shadowy, inscrutable figures shift under the weight of Naomi's pleading gaze. She moved to the door and spoke in a softer, kinder voice. "We have room for you. Any time you want to leave this place, this life. Knock on our door."

A strange, tense silence hung in the air; no one breathed, no one moved. Finished, Naomi stepped back and gestured toward the door. "Mr. McIntyre, please..." He studied her for a moment, searching for even the most ghostly hint of compassion towards him. There was only a chill in her eyes, so brutal it burned him and his heart was inexplicably heavy.

He walked toward the door and stopped just before the threshold. Without looking at her, he straightened a bit, like a man willing to accept his fate, and whispered a painful confession. "I am what I am, Mrs. Miller...but for the first time in my life, I'm sorry for it."

"Then choose a better life."

He wondered if he had imagined the slightly desperate sound in her voice. It didn't matter. He had made such choices long ago. Eyes focused on the darkness, he left the room.

Chapter 31

McIntyre read over the mining report but couldn't take in the staggering numbers. His vein of quartz was making him and Ian wealthy beyond imagination, yet that wasn't the reason the numbers wouldn't sink in. He kept seeing Daisy's bloodied and battered face...and that frigid look in Naomi's eyes.

He noticed the burst of cold air that accompanied his front door opening, but didn't look up. Ian paused at the door and cleared his throat to get McIntyre's attention.

"Good afternoon, Mac." Peeling off his coat, the Scotsman hung it on the hook just inside the entrance and slid into a seat in front of the desk. "How is the mining business today?"

McIntyre tried to pretend he had actually read the report he'd been staring at for the last ten minutes. "A sixty-foot thick vein of quartz that stretches from here to Animas Forks, partner. I would say we'll be in business for quite some time to come."

Ian crossed his legs and nodded.

"How is Daisy?" McIntyre shuffled the papers non-chalantly. "Is she settled?"

"Aye, and I believe I've seen improvements in her just today. Gettin' out of that hole you call a saloon was the best thing that could've happened to her. I'm only sorry I never said anything to ye about her...or any of them for that matter."

McIntyre leaned back in his chair. "Have you come to preach to me, Ian? I warn you, I've had enough chastising for one day."

To his frustration, Ian chuckled. "I heard. I went back to the saloon to pick up a few more of Daisy's belongings and your *flowers* told me what Naomi said to ye. Burnt your ears, dinna she, lad?" McIntyre clenched and unclenched his fists but kept silent. "Dunna look at me like that. If ye want Defiance to be a respectable town, if you want to be a respectable businessman, nay," Ian pointed his index finger at him for emphasis, "if ye want to be a respectable *man*, then ye should shut down yer garden, if not the whole saloon."

McIntyre drummed his fingers on his desk. He had gambled, sold whiskey and run prostitutes since before the war. It was a setup with which he was comfortable. If the mine shut down, if the price of timber dropped, if cattle bottomed out, he could always sell whiskey and women. No, it wasn't a pretty way to make a living but it had always kept him up in style. Usually, the girls were manageable, unlike Rose, and the violence was minor, unlike Daisy's beating. "I guess I'm just not ready to be that respectable yet."

Casually, Ian settled more comfortably in his chair and put his feet up on McIntyre's desk. "The winters in Defiance are long and cold. Now me, I am enjoyin' the company of fine, sweet sisters such as they are. Their inn is filled with laughter and warmth, the scent of baking bread and roast meat. The fact that they've taken in misfits such as meself and Emilio and now Daisy, well, we're like one odd but happy family.

"At fifty years of age, I saw nothin' in my future but roamin' aimlessly across this country, wrestling with God everyday and slowly killing meself with whiskey and boredom. Now I have new plans for my twilight years and I'm as excited about them as a child on Christmas morn. Bein' respectable, in my humble opinion, is quite underappreciated."

"You plan to marry that girl, then? Rebecca?"

"I've become very fond of all of them, but especially Rebecca. If she willna marry me then I'll just have to stay on as a cook."

"You never talked much about your faith before they showed up. What changed?"

Ian chewed on the question for a minute. "We're in the middle of nowhere and three beautiful, decent, God-fearin' women fall into our laps, no pun intended. If ye dunna see the hand of God in that, mon, you're blind, stubborn and stupid. Their comin' here was no accident and as far I'm concerned, they've saved my life. Ye'd do well yerself to give the Lord a word of thanks."

It was McIntyre's turn to chuckle. "I'll thank Him when I'm convinced they're a blessing and not a curse. Given a choice, I think they'd run me out of town on a rail for being such an unrepentant sinner."

A devilishly delighted grin illuminated Ian's face. "Well, you know what they say: if you canna beat'em, join'em."

Long after Ian departed, McIntyre was still rolling the idea of Divine Intervention around and around in his head. Had the Almighty literally manipulated things so these women would wind up in this gritty hell-hole at this precise time? Had he saved John Miller's life all those years ago just so the man could bring his wife to within spitting distance of Defiance before conveniently dying? Why? To what end? Did God really care so much he would engineer a grand plan for one remote town...one selfish man?

As if answering the questions, McIntyre heard his mother's voice from long ago reading a familiar scripture.

For the Son of man is come to seek and to save that which was lost.

~~~

Daisy didn't know if she could be any happier. Defiance had dragged her to the bottom of a deep, murky well, but because of Jesus, she had burst forth from the depths and was drinking from the fountain of living water! She lay in bed recovering from her wounds and had moments when she wanted to run and shout praises to God, her heart was so full of gratitude. She blessed the name of Jesus and thanked him every day for her release from captivity. She might wind up on the street tomorrow, but she knew she'd never have to go back to *that* life.

As she pondered the blessings of finding Jesus, Naomi entered carrying her breakfast.

"Good morning, Mollie."

As she set the tray on her lap, Daisy clutched the woman's hand and looked her in the eye. "If you hadn't come here, most likely no one would have ever told me about Jesus and I think I would have died in that saloon."

"I'm so sorry you lost your man along the way, but I pray that someday you'll think it was worth it...that *I* was worth it."

Naomi smiled and sat down on the bed. "You know, Hannah asked me months ago if God would have sent us here on behalf of one person. Initially, I told her no, but now, after seeing you freed from that life," she nodded contentedly, "I think it has been worth it."

"Oh, but there will be more!" Daisy squeezed Naomi's arm with fervor. "If God can pour out this much mercy on me, think what He can do in this town."

Chapter 32

Naomi moved her bedroom curtain aside and gazed out upon the delicate flakes floating to the ground. In the weeks before Christmas, Defiance had seemed perpetually engulfed by a gray sky and chaotic, white flurries. And when the sky wasn't merely flirting with the idea of snow, snow fell in great, fluffy, overwhelming quantities. The odd little family at the Trinity Inn hadn't minded the weather; in fact they reveled in it and the Christmas spirit. Together they had decorated the hotel from one end to the other with garlands made of pine boughs, popcorn and red gingham bows. Candles sat in every window, burned at every table amidst more pine boughs and holly berries.

The girls went about their chores humming Christmas carols, Ian sang Jingle Bells to little Billy at least once a day while bouncing him on his knee, and they all had quietly tucked Christmas packages for each other in the corner where the Christmas tree would go. It was going to be a fine Christmas, Naomi thought. Different, poignant, but filled with cheer, warmth and love. What more could Christmas be?

If it wasn't for a nagging sense of loss related to Mr. McIntyre, she would actually be happy today. She felt completely justified in her anger towards him, but she was also a little disappointed in the loss of his friendship—not that they were friends...not that she wanted to be friends. She couldn't really explain what she thought she'd lost. Frustrated by these nonsensical thoughts about a man she barely knew, she dropped the curtain and turned away.

A commotion in the backyard below drew her again to the window and she watched as Daisy, Hannah and Emilio spilled out into the snow. Within seconds the snowballs were flying and the girls had teamed up on the boy.

Naomi shifted for a better view and pondered Daisy. After a few weeks of rest and short, stiff walks around the inn, the girl had begged them to let her join in and be useful. She had taken it easy at first, folding napkins and washing the silverware, but it wasn't long before the bruises had faded and her strength had returned. Daisy boldly credited the renewed energy she felt to the desire to live a new life full of Jesus. Her face was always aglow with a smile, and there was a weak, but noticeable, spring in her step.

Watching her now, gingerly tossing snowballs, Naomi knew that she had meant what she'd said: Daisy was worth it. There was an abundance of heartbreak in Defiance, but even here there was also the joy of the Lord. She smiled at the battle scene below and decided Emilio could use some assistance.

~~~

Emilio carried a basket of freshly cut pine boughs into the dining room and presented them to Daisy, who was busy prepping tables for the evening meal. "Thees will be enough, si?"

Daisy looked at the basket filled to overflowing and giggled, realizing he must have stripped the valley to get that many. "That should be more than enough, unless we don't want to leave room for the plates." Missing the joke, he nodded and set the basket on the floor.

Daisy proceeded to the next table and snapped a red-checked tablecloth into the air. She watched it float down and settle effortlessly on the table. It felt good to work…good, clean, honest work. She glanced over at Emilio, pleased that he had gotten out, too…and without the bruises to show for his time served.

"Are you well?" His question came quickly, as if he was nervous. "Ees everything healed now?"

Daisy shrugged. "Mostly. My ribs are sore. I think I overdid it in our snowball fight yesterday."

"The other girls, they ask me when they see me. They always want to know about you."

That impressed Daisy. So often just existing at the garden was such a cat fight; looking out for yourself, vying for business, fighting over who got to take a night off, much less tending to the horrible customers. She sure didn't miss it. But as she straightened the cloth and smoothed out a wrinkle, she wondered about the flowers. She hadn't had a chance to tell them about the new man in her life.

Daisy felt as if she had changed so much since leaving the Iron Horse. She truly did feel like Jesus had handed her the deed to a new life, an eternal life. And it was wonderful. This new life gave her a totally fresh perspective on the other girls. Though Lily and Iris never spoke of it, they were just as miserable as she had been. Daisy clearly remembered the weariness and hopelessness in their eyes and how they acted it out with aggression and anger. Thank God, not her anymore. The truth had set her free and she would happily tell them of her changed life if they would listen.

"Emilio, would you take a note down to the flowers?" She had a crazy idea, but one to which she was sure the sisters would agree.

~~~

Rebecca stared at shelves filled with mason jars of green beans, cucumbers, squash...what had she come in here for?

She had tried to lose herself in restaurant business and the holiday spirit, but was admittedly becoming more and more distracted by something. Like a flighty little teenager, her mind wandered off to thoughts of Ian at the drop of a hat.

They had taken to closing down the kitchen together at night and finishing the evening with a cup of coffee. It was her favorite time of the day, as his presence had grown on her. She loved the way he had fallen so seamlessly into their midst, tied on an apron, and joined them in the kitchen as if he had been destined to this...to them. She looked forward to standing beside him at the stove, flipping and frying and joshing frivolously over whatever funny things had happened that day. When he tended to little Billy like a natural father, her heart melted. Lately, the touch of his hand in the small of her back or the brush of his shoulder as they stood side-by-side cooking was like a streak of liquid heat in her blood. Oh, yes, he had definitely grown on her.

Yet, there was a fly of doubt buzzing 'round Rebecca's head.

Snatching three jars of green beans off the shelf, she trudged into the kitchen and stumbled on Daisy starting preparations for cornbread. The girl looked up and greeted her warmly. "Are you ready for Christmas, Rebecca?"

Rebecca slowly set the jars on the table one by one and shook her head. "No, I've still got a few gifts to finish up."

Daisy nodded, cracking an egg. "Me, too, but they're coming along."

Rebecca watched her continue working on the bread but said nothing else. Scooping the cornmeal into the bowl, Daisy replaced the lid on the bin and wiped her hands on her apron. "You're staring. Is there something on your mind, Rebecca?" Rebecca set her last jar on the table but didn't answer. "I think I can guess what's got your tongue. Is it Mr. Donoghue?"

Rebecca wrung her hands nervously and nodded. "Yes, but I don't know how to…"

"Just ask."

Clearing her throat, Rebecca took her advice. "Have you—or any of the other flowers—not that you're a flower any more—but, I was wondering if you could tell me if he ever visited the garden."

This was a question Rebecca had dreaded asking, attempting to talk herself out of it repeatedly. The answer didn't really matter. He was widowed, alone. Female companionship, especially on a long, cold night…well, it was understandable if he had been there. Not right, but understandable.

"Mr. Donoghue is one of the few men in this town who does not, to my knowledge, consort with sportin' gals." Daisy smiled understandingly. "I thought he always sort of looked at us with more pity than lust. Least ways, that was my opinion.

"He would come in, have a few drinks, play a few hands of cards and then just sit and chat with Mr. McIntyre. I'm not aware that he ever went upstairs for that." She raised a shoulder. "I suspect he drinks more when he's in his cabin, but Defiance can drive a person to that. It's just loneliness."

Rebecca breathed easier. The question was out and it had been answered in such a way as to leave all her hope intact. He was a good man; she had known it all along…and maybe not such a lonely one anymore.

"He's a fine man, Rebecca. I've heard Mr. McIntyre say he should run for mayor, maybe even governor of the territory, because he can't be bought. There aren't many like that."

"Thank you." Rebecca grinned and she knew it was a foolish, schoolgirl grin. "Thank you so much."

~~~

On Christmas Day, as they had opened presents, then prepared and sat down to a feast fit for a king, Naomi was disturbed by the direction her mind kept wandering. She was puzzled by how seamlessly her brain went from thinking about John and remembering last Christmas to what Mr. McIntyre might be doing with this most special of days. Since none of the flowers had accepted Daisy's invitation to join them, she wondered if they were keeping him company? Were they exchanging gifts of some sort? What exactly did saloon girls do with a day off? Would he do anything special for them?

Irritated at how her brain repeatedly jumped to the wrong track, she purposely looked around the table, taking in the smiling faces and warm laughter. Last year, Pastor Barton and Ruby had eaten with them and friends had come and gone all day long, bringing gifts and Christmas cheer. This year, apparently, there would be no visitors, but there was at least plenty of cheer.

She couldn't help but wonder if her argument to *not* invite Mr. McIntyre for Christmas had been a mistake. Not wishing to make her or Daisy ill-at-ease, everyone had acquiesced, though Ian had said he would visit him for a spell. Besides, if the flowers did come, having Mr. McIntyre here would make it an awkward Christmas.

Confused and waffling between anger and compassion, Naomi was haunted by his last statement to her. He had said he was sorry for the kind of man he was. If he had been invited, would he have come? And if he had, would the flowers have also joined them? Had he kept them from coming or were they just too uncomfortable to celebrate Christmas with the sisters?

Lost in her jumbled thoughts, Naomi let out a long sigh and Daisy, sitting closest to her, misread the sound. "They still might show. I told them anytime around—"

At exactly that moment, the front door opened slowly and Lily, Iris, and Jasmine filed tentatively in to the lobby.

Chapter 33

Daisy couldn't believe the flowers from the Iron Horse had come for Christmas dinner. For an instant, everyone at the table was too stunned to react then together they jumped to their feet like a fire brigade and all but ran to the women. They greeted them at the door with handshakes and a flurry of "Thank you for coming," "It's so nice to see you," and "Merry Christmas." Daisy gave them all hugs, evoking shocked looks from the flowers.

Then Ian, ever the gentleman, offered to take their coats. Apprehensive glances fluttered among Lily, Iris and Jasmine. Reluctantly, Lily slowly removed her cape and handed it to him. She was wearing a low-cut plum dress, a bit tattered and faded, but Daisy knew it was the best—and most modest—in her collection.

Seeing her embarrassment, Naomi responded a little too eagerly. "That's a lovely dress."

Lily didn't thank her for the compliment; she merely nodded. That broke the tension at least and Iris and Jasmine then slid out of their coats, handing them to Ian. Their dresses were no more modest but the judgment of their fashion choices had been removed.

"Rebecca…" Naomi pulled her sister away from the group. "Why don't you and I bus the table to make room for our guests?"

Rebecca called over her shoulder to the flowers, "We'll be ready in just a moment."

With their departure, the conversation lagged a bit in the lobby as the girls took in their surroundings. Daisy garnered especially long, studious looks. She stood there, beaming at them, feeling as though she could walk on air. Fresh-faced and wearing a buttoned-up-to-her chin red plaid dress courtesy of Hannah, she knew she bore very little resemblance to the battered and bruised girl they had seen carried from the saloon. Nor was she the frail, quiet, tortured soul Rose used to verbally abuse for sheer amusement.

Daisy had been re-born and knew her hope shined in her eyes.

"You look, um…" Lily struggled for the right word, but settled weakly for, "well. Very well."

"I am *restored*," Daisy gushed, delighted that they had come.

A baby's hungry cry from upstairs interrupted her and Hannah apologized. "Oh, I'm sorry, there's my little one and he's hungry. Please excuse me. We'll be down as soon as we can." She looked the girls over and smiled warmly. "We really are glad that you're here." She left the group and dashed up the stairs.

Ian excused himself as well. "Let me see what I can do help clear the table. Pardon me, ladies."

When he was out of earshot, Iris stepped closer to Daisy. "Why do you want us here? We haven't been nice to you or them."

"We invited you because we all want you to see how different your lives can be. You're not trapped in the Iron Horse. I'll help you. They'll help you."

Lily looked highly skeptical of that statement. "Why would they care about us?"

Daisy knew the question was easy to answer with her heart, but more difficult to nail down with words. "Will you come and eat with us? Enjoy the day then I'll try to answer that."

She seated the flowers at the table, Ian pulling chairs out for each of them as if they were eating at Delmonico's in New York. Rebecca and Naomi re-heated the food and served everything as warm and fresh as possible. They waited on the girls hand and foot, anticipating their needs and treating them like royalty.

Once settled, the sisters joined them, delicately inquiring about their histories, asking how long each girl had been in Defiance, where their hometowns were, did they have family somewhere. Gradually, the conversation warmed, thawing the icy atmosphere. When Hannah rejoined them with little Billy, there were plenty of maternal oohs and aaahs, and Iris even asked if she could hold him. The baby, dressed in a festive red velvet suit like a little elf, liked her immediately. Smiling and cooing innocently, he delighted in running his hands through those inviting strands of red curls. Iris held him close, talking sweetly and indulgently.

Daisy watched the interaction between flower and baby and was amazed at this tender side of the feisty redhead. Iris studied the baby's face longingly, stroked his cheek, softly blew air in his face and watched the startled but curious reaction. After a moment, the peaceful look on the prostitute's face changed to a more melancholy one. "Did Rose guess right? Is this boy a bas—illegitimate?"

The question froze the polite atmosphere like an arctic wind, stopping jaws in mid-bite.

"Left me high and dry," Hannah half-joked, her humor not quite masking the pain. "Promised me the moon, then took off like a shot when I gave him the news." There was no bitterness in her voice, just the sound of acceptance.

"That's just like a man." Lily stabbed her turkey a little too hard and her fork clinked on her plate. "Do most of their thinkin' with everything but their brains."

"Now ladies," Ian held up his hands, surrendering to their superior numbers, "in defense of my fellow twits, I must point out that we're no' all like that."

"Most of you are, though," Jasmine argued in her stoic, Asian way. "I will agree you are the most gentlemanly gentleman I have ever met, but you, Mr. Donoghue, are the exception. Generally speaking, men are the same brand the world over."

"Aye, that may be true, but not one hundred percent of the time. Nothin' says ye must choose the rule. Instead, find the exception. Raise yer sights."

Daisy knew the unspoken thought that went through the flowers' minds was that based on their profession, they could not expect better. She begged to differ. "You asked me why we care about you. I'll tell you. We know a man who loves us for our souls, not our bodies. He is a king and we are his daughters. As daughters of the king, He wants better for us. Living the way I was living, the way you're still living, it breaks His heart.

"When I read how willing he was to forgive me and then what he did to prove how much he loved me, it changed everything: The way I saw myself, the way I saw the future, the way I wanted to live every day.

"I'll never go back to any place like the Iron Horse Saloon. I have the faith to know I don't have to."

~~~

While his flowers were receiving a delicate sprinkling of the gospel, McIntyre passed the holiday engaged in business. Defiance was going to change. For better or worse, it was going to change. To that end, he had spent the day in his room writing several letters and telegrams to friends and acquaintances. There was too much gold, too much timber, too much grass, too much opportunity for a man in search of a vision to not see the potential in Defiance.

This had been his plan all along, yet now there was an added sense of urgency to his goal. As he composed, he chose not to analyze the reasons for the feeling that the stakes had become more personal. He stood to make a lot of money, yes, but he had come to appreciate the legacy of it. He wanted to build Defiance into a sophisticated, successful municipality and have his name remembered with respect and dignity.

Of course, this business plan meant the women and the whiskey had to go. It would be a leap of faith. What if he failed and Defiance turned out to be nothing but another dirty, seedy, mining eyesore? Or worse, a ghost town?

It didn't matter. He had a gift. He could lose everything today, start over tomorrow and be rich again in less than a year.

While Ian becomes the beloved patriarch of three beautiful, loving, tight-knit sisters, he thought sourly.

Frustrated, he poured himself a shot of brandy and went to his window. The snow was still coming down and Defiance looked like a Courier and Ives Christmas card. He could see the inn at the end of town, the windows casting a warm, amber glow on the empty street. Taking a sip, he wondered what they were doing in there. Were all his flowers going to come back dressed in white with halos floating above their heads? Perhaps he should convert the saloon into a church and keep the flowers just to pass the collection plate.

The thought made him smile wryly, but the truth was, shutting it down would show the Denver and Rio Grande he was serious about taking the town in a new direction. It would make her Highness happy as well. Not that he cared. Besides, he doubted anything would get him back into her good graces. That was most likely moral high ground he would never see.

More light spilled on to the street and he saw his girls walk out of the inn and head up the boardwalk. They walked slowly, somberly, not as if they were unhappy, but more like they were lost in thought. He could see they were carrying items, gifts perhaps.

Gifts? Well, the little missionaries had thought of everything.

To his surprise, when the girls entered the saloon, they came straight to his room and delivered leftovers to him. "From the sisters." Lily held a lunch pail out to him. In her other arm, she clutched a small package.

He took the bucket and Iris and Jasmine set theirs down on his desk. They hesitated, as if they wanted to say something, but apparently couldn't find their voice or nerves. After an awkward moment, they nodded to him and left.

As Iris shut the door, she wished him a Merry Christmas.

Chapter 34

Iris had barely finished changing into a negligee when she heard a knock on her door. She quickly tied her robe closed, out of habit, not modesty, and yelled, "It's open."

Lily and Jasmine sauntered in, dressed in their delicates as well, and took up positions lolling on the furniture. Settling in a corner chair, Lily absently filed her fingernails as Jasmine draped herself on the settee like a Siamese cat. Well aware that none of them felt like spending Christmas night alone with their thoughts, Iris poured them each a shot of whiskey then reclined on her fancy brass bed; one Mr. McIntyre had shipped in special from San Francisco.

Iris stared at her unwrapped gift resting at the end of the bed. "That was nice of them to give us those sachets. They sure smell sweet."

"I'll tell you what smelled sweet…" Lily sounded awed as she absently inspected her index fingernail. "That hotel. It smelled like my Mama's house back in Ohio, all filled up with the scent of cinnamon and nutmeg and a Christmas tree."

"I know, the Christmas tree was wonderful." Iris smiled, recalling the beauty of it and the homey, warm smells in the hotel. Together, they brought back scores of memories of a good home before things had gone bad. Before she had followed a ramblin' man down the Mississippi to adventure—or ruin. Depended on how one looked at her life, she supposed. In an attempt to burn out the memory, she threw back her drink.

"The Chinese don't celebrate Christmas." Jasmine stretched languidly and reached for the pillow at her feet. "I thought it was nice, though. Pleasant. We Asians pour so much formal ceremony into everything." She tucked the cushion behind her head and settled more comfortably on the couch.

"Daisy sure looked different." Lily turned the conversation to what they really wanted to discuss. The other girls nodded in complete agreement. "Makes you wonder…" she trailed off.

Iris had been *wondering* all afternoon, since Daisy hugged them. Was it that easy to walk away from this life? Was Jesus all they really needed? Would He make all their problems go away? "Oh, well, she never really belonged here anyway."

"None of us do," Lily replied somberly.

After considering that in silence, Iris shrugged. "Then why are we still here?"

"Because we have no place else to go."

Jasmine's pragmatic answers could be downright annoying, Iris decided. And perhaps, wrong. She wondered if she had enough fire left within her to hope. "Maybe we do."

"Do you think they meant it?" Lily curled her legs up into the chair and stared at the untouched whiskey sitting on the small table next to her. "That we could stay there until..."

"Until what?" Jasmine looked at them as if they were starry-eyed children to be pitied. "We learn to cook or sew? Pick up some new skill? Open a Chinese laundry?"

"It would be a start." Iris leaned forward and rested her arms on the brass rail at the end of her bed. "If we worked in a hotel or a kitchen, it would be a way to distance ourselves from what we're doing now."

"And just what do you think Mr. McIntyre would do?" Jasmine seemed to love playing the spoiler. "Smile and wave as we walk out the door?"

"Frankly, I don't think he'd notice." Lily got up to examine Iris' sachet. "He aint' been the same since the belles rolled into town." She took the item from Iris' hand and studied the fine, delicate tatting work, sniffed the sweet scents stuffed inside it. "Somethins' caught in his craw about'em."

"I think it is the middle one—Naomi," Jasmine ventured, sounding confident with her guess. "From what I gather, she sort of looks down her nose at him and I don't think Mr. McIntyre likes it."

Iris cocked her head to one side and considered that. "Maybe 'cause he likes her."

"I don't know, could be I guess." Lily raised a shoulder. "He sure put tracks up Rose's backside for messin' with'em. And he has seemed sort of bored with things here lately. Be just like a man to go sniffin' after a woman who wouldn't give him the time of day...but she didn't act like that towards us and she must know we were the ones who put the gum in her hair."

Iris squirmed under the memory, half-way wishing she could take back the childish act. "She did treat us well. It was the first purely sociable meal I've had in years. They never once treated us like sportin' gals."

"Maybe Daisy, uh—" Lily scowled at her mistake, "I mean, Mollie. Maybe Mollie is right about how we see ourselves. She kept tellin' us that Jesus sees us as daughters of the king. Maybe we count for more than we think. Maybe we do matter to someone."

Iris sat up, intrigued by the thought. "Just because folks say our kind is trash doesn't mean it's so. There are a lot of losers in Defiance, who says we have to be part of 'em?"

Lily and Iris looked at each other, and Iris thought she saw a spark of something hopeful in the black girl's eyes.

"If God thinks we're beautiful," Lily pondered, "maybe we are?"

McIntyre took a step away from the door, deciding he had heard enough. He wasn't sure what he had learned, exactly, other than perhaps the seeds of discontent and hope had been planted in the remaining flowers' hearts. He wouldn't be surprised if tomorrow Naomi showed up at his door holding a staff and yelling, "Let my people go!" He almost chuckled at the image but didn't because it was entirely possible.

Yearning for something to fill an unexpected sense of loneliness—even emptiness—plaguing him, he decided a walk down the snowy street might lift his mood.

Change was coming to Defiance, he could feel it. In the Christmas dusk, he sensed it.

She had asked him to choose a better life.

Kicking at snow as he ambled down the boardwalk, he wondered what it would take to change that look in her eyes to something better...to say, love? If he cleaned up the town, if he cleaned up his own life, would that melt the ice in her heart?

Did God know? Did He care about a two-bit hustler on this side of hell? He hated that the answers to these questions mattered. But matter, they did...

Chapter 35

During the first week of February, a mule train managed to make it up from Animas City, the first in nearly five weeks. Along with needed supplies, there was an abundance of mail. The marshal delivered a good handful to McIntyre at his office at the mine then sat down to update him on Rose.

"I asked Harley and Buddy if they'd heard anything down in Animas City. It sounds like Rose might have settled for the winter in Ouray. There've been a couple of mean catfights over there that sound like her style."

Ouray wasn't all that far away, less than forty miles. Rose was waiting for something, circling the town like a bird of prey. McIntyre sensed it with a great certainty.

Absently shuffling through the mail as he spoke, he told the marshal, "Pay a gold piece to any man that reports when she leav—" He stopped abruptly, staring at a postcard he had come within a hair of discarding.

The front was a sketch of the Rocky Mountains with a cowgirl shooting off a pistol. On the back someone had drawn three crosses, but that was all. No salutation, no signature. Just the crosses. The card was postmarked Denver, October 21. The missing signature notwithstanding, he was certain the post card was from Rose.

Disturbed, McIntyre handed it over to the marshal for his review. "You see what you can do to confirm whether Rose is in Ouray or not. This postmark doesn't convince me. I doubt she's in Denver, if she was ever there in the first place."

Wade looked at the drawings then the postmark. "You thinkin' she could've had somebody mail it for her?"

"How it was mailed is of less concern to me than why. She's trying to tell me something with these crosses and I don't know what it is." He looked intently at Wade then, his soul dark with conviction. "She's coming back to Defiance and when she does, we need to be a step ahead of her."

~~~

The men from the mule train were the first official guests of the Trinity Inn. It had taken them eight days to make the 50-mile trek up from Animas City. Averaging only about seven and-a-half miles a day in good weather but deep snow, the effort had sucked the life out of them. The six men were bone-tired, cold and hungry. Though the hotel was weeks away from opening, there was not a chance the sisters would have turned them away.

As Hannah checked them in at the hotel desk, little Billy wiggling on her hip, Naomi marveled over the human peculiarity of perseverance. Life in Defiance was hard, the weather unforgiving and the people lawless. But this place proved a person's mettle. Everyone from gritty, weathered mountain men to gentle, petite mothers like Hannah discovered an inner strength folks back in Cary would never know. Naomi was astonished to realize she felt a little pride over the hardy souls surviving here, herself included.

And without Mr. McIntyre, the town might not have been settled at all. Perhaps he was the hardiest soul of all. He had certainly proven one thing: he did not need the sisters or their food. The man hadn't set foot in the place since Naomi had raked him over the coals. Her suggestion that he look for a better life had apparently fallen on deaf ears. Apparently, Mr. McIntyre didn't need or want her friendship.

Fine. She could live with that. He was, according to Ian, working on something important and that was filling his days.

Fine.

She didn't need his irreverent talk or sarcastic titles of royalty bestowed upon her. She didn't need to hear "your ladyship," or "your highness." Naomi was just fine without him.

~~~

Hannah cooed and snuggled little Billy as she slowly descended the stairs that evening. She was making the turn on the landing when Lily, Jasmine and Iris sauntered in for dinner. Dressed in feathers and finery, this was the first time since Christmas that the flowers had come by.

"Ladies, what a pleasant surprise."

Iris shrugged her coat off and grinned at Hannah and the blessing in her arms. "We're here to celebrate, Miss Hannah."

The flowers nodded in agreement as they removed their cloaks and hung them on the tree as well. Readjusting Billy to her other hip, Hannah motioned toward the dining area. "Well then, let me give you our finest table." She gazed at the three girls and saw right away there was something different about their countenance. "I can't wait to hear your news…if you'll be sharing it."

Heads high, shoulders squared, the girls giggled and sniggered and followed Hannah over to a table. The men at the surrounding tables, including those from the mule train, stopped in mid-bite, holding forks in the air as the girls strolled on by.

Naomi and Daisy acknowledged the flowers with obvious delight as they delivered food to the waiting, stunned customers.

"I'll be right with you girls," Naomi told them, setting down food for the gentlemen from the mule train.

Hannah stopped at the table closest to the kitchen and leaned toward the group. "Do you girls mind if I join you for dinner? I need to feed Billy."

"Oh, do you mind if I do it?" Iris reached for the boy. "I haven't fed a baby in years."

Hannah saw the quick flash of sadness in the girl's face and wondered about Iris' past. "Of course. I would appreciate the break."

Finally, after several minutes of watching these surprising patrons settle in, moon over the baby, and order their food, one man sitting nearby attempted to investigate. Wiping catsup out of his beard, he leaned back in his chair and surveyed the unusual party. "What's the occasion, girls? Are you settin' up shop here at the inn?"

"Can we get better rates than at the Iron Horse?" another asked laughing.

"The beds are softer here anyway," a man from the mule train chimed in, drawing a furious stare from Naomi.

"And all this time those belles have been slappin' our hands if we reached for the bread too fast." The first man cut his eyes over to Daisy. "I guess Defiance must've brought'em round to our way of thinkin'."

Naomi, approaching the table with a tray of glasses and a pitcher of tea, opened her mouth to set the record straight, but Iris beat her to it. "For your information, Harley Cramer, you dirty, worthless, walking clump of cow dung, we're celebratin' quittin' the business all together. Mr. McIntyre's closin' the saloon."

Harley dropped his jaw and his fork, as did most of the men, and Naomi looked like she almost dropped the tray she was carrying.

"You're joking," Hannah squeaked in shock. "I can hardly believe it."

Hands a little unsteady, Naomi placed the glasses and tea on the flowers' table. "What brought all this about?"

Hannah was struck by the expression on her sister's face. She couldn't decide if Naomi looked surprised, pleased, suspicious, concerned or triumphant. Hannah was simply thrilled. Iris, still holding Billy, took a swig of tea before explaining, "He said he is moving past selling whiskey and women. He wants to be *respectable*."

"And," Jasmine stuck her nose in the air in mock snobbery, "he's making rich women of us." Abruptly, she lowered her voice so only Hannah and Naomi and the other girls at the table could hear. "He's giving us one thousand dollars to start over with."

"He's going to give Daisy a thousand dollars, too," Iris added softly, sliding a spoonful of creamed corn into Little Billy's gaping mouth. "It's almost like he's turned over a new leaf. I wouldn't have believed if it hadn't happened to me."

Hannah's eyes sparkled with tears. "Does Mollie know?"

"Nope." Lily shook her head from side to side, looking pleased with their secret. "We wanted to surprise her."

Hannah looked up at Naomi and grinned. She wanted to say something, but there were just no words to express her joy over God's great compassion. And to think he had used her and her sisters in some small way to bring these things about.

Naomi grinned, too. "Mollie's not your server, but I'll switch with her. Congratulations, girls."

Lily quickly dragged up a chair from the adjacent table just in time to catch Daisy as she collapsed into it.

One *thousand* dollars? Daisy blinked and said it out loud. "One thousand dollars?"

Every woman at the table shushed her vehemently. "We do not think we should announce that part to everyone in town," Jasmine scolded.

Little Billy began to fuss and Hannah took him from Iris, thanking her for feeding him. "He's so good for you, but he usually acts bored at supper with everyone else." She sat back down and bounced him gently on her knee, trying to work a burp out of the child. "Do you have plans, any of you? Do you know where you want to go?"

Dreamy expressions settled on the flowers' faces. "We are going to stay until the first stage," Jasmine explained, "but just to serve and run the games. Then I am going to go to San Francisco. I think I will buy a house and a business of some sort. I might even buy stock in the railroad."

Impressed nods greeted her apparently well-thought out plans.

"I used to could sew when I was about twelve or thereabouts," Iris volunteered. "I'd like to pick that up again and maybe open a nice, proper dress shop, somewhere in Texas. It's a big state; I think I could reinvent myself there."

"I just want to go home." Lily plopped her elbows on the table and rested her chin in her hands. "My momma had a farm just outside Dayton. I haven't written her in years, I don't even know if she's still alive. But that's where I'm gonna start."

Daisy had never heard such longing in anyone's voice and she nodded, feeling that pain, that emptiness. "Me too. I want to see my momma even if she doesn't want to see me. I just want to know she's all right."

Hannah clutched Daisy's hand. "Well, you've all been given a second chance, praise God. I pray you'll use it wisely and be abundantly blessed."

~~~

For days after the news of the saloon closing, Naomi wrestled with why she couldn't get Mr. McIntyre out of her head. Guilt-ridden, she acknowledged that with each passing day she was thinking less and less about John and more and more about the saloon owner. The confession flustered her and she angrily tossed a pillow to the head of the bed she was making.

He was the last man on earth she should give any thought to. Besides, it had been almost *three* months since she'd seen him. A person had to work pretty hard to avoid another person in a town this size. Clearly, he was done with the sisters...with her. She snatched the coverlet tight and smacked at a rebellious wrinkle. Huffing with frustration, she whipped a rag from her apron as if she was unsheathing a sword and attacked the dust on the posts.

"Naomi, what is wrong with you?" Rebecca's voice from the doorway startled her. "You're not cleaning, you're doing battle."

Naomi froze, suddenly aware she *had* been working with a vengeance. Embarrassed, she laughed nervously and shook her head. "I just have some things on my mind."

The sympathetic look in Rebecca's eyes urged her to share these crazy, confused thoughts. Overwhelmed, Naomi gave in to the need to talk to someone and hung her head. "After Mollie was beaten up, I had some harsh words with Mr. McIntyre, Rebecca. I blamed him completely for the incident. Now he's gone and shut down the saloon. Why would he do that?" Her shoulders slumped, misery and confusion weighing her down. "I've said awful things and acted so coldly toward him."

She looked up then, ashamed of herself. "He spent Christmas alone and he shouldn't have. No one should be alone on Christmas."

She twisted her head from side to side in frustration. "I don't know, Rebecca, I'm all jumbled up inside. I wrestle with why I don't think of John as much anymore. But Mr. McIntyre—it seems I think of him too much."

Rebecca folded her arms slowly, evaluating things. "You have always been so hard on yourself, Naomi. You think you haven't grieved long enough for John; that's part of this, isn't it? I think you think if you have any compassion for Mr. McIntyre that you're somehow betraying John and that's just not true."

Leaning on the door frame, Rebecca offered a cold, hard analysis. "There are two separate issues here. Time is passing and you are healing. I can tell you from experience that you never forget the love you had for a husband...but focus on the love and not the absence. Life goes on.

"As for Mr. McIntyre, he's a very likable fellow in spite of his misguided morals. I think you feel badly about the way you've treated him because you want to like him, too and you know it's not Christian to treat him this way. You've shown him a lot of anger but very little grace."

Chaffing under Rebecca's sharp, but honest, scrutiny, Naomi rubbed her neck and sat down on the bed. Why were she and Mr. McIntyre as compatible as oil and water? Naomi wondered if she was afraid of making friends with him because it stepped on the relationship she'd had with John. Or was Rebecca right and she just thought she was too good to share the love of God with such an accomplished sinner? Was it all of the above or was there something else here entirely? Did it matter? Was it too late to rebuild the bridge she'd burnt?

"Look, Naomi," Rebecca moved to sit beside her on the bed, "God loves Mr. McIntyre just like he loves the rest of us. Showing him some compassion, some kindness doesn't make you unfaithful to John." Rebecca draped her arm over Naomi's shoulders. "And it doesn't mean you approve of Mr. McIntyre's lifestyle. I don't really know what is at the root of your animosity towards him, but if it's guilt, ask his forgiveness and start over. If it's guilt over betraying John, let it go. If it's your pride, remember that all have sinned and come short of the glory of God.

"He is lost and I think he is hurting, but I also think God is moving in his life; otherwise he wouldn't be shutting down the saloon. Come along side the Lord, Naomi. Don't hinder his work." She hugged her sister for encouragement then squeezed her shoulder affectionately. "Pray about it, about him."

After Rebecca left, Naomi sat on the bed a long while pondering Rebecca's sage advice and wondering just why it was that she had such turmoil in her heart. She knelt right there beside the bed and prayed for clarity. By and by what came through was that she did owe Mr. McIntyre an apology. Oh, she had to wrestle with God over that. After all, she argued, it was Mr. McIntyre who employed the prostitutes like Daisy, supplied the liquor to the customers, and then paraded the girls in front of them. But it was also true that Daisy and her customer had made their own choices.

As a sinner, Mr. McIntyre was just as in need of seeing the extended hand of Jesus as the flowers or anyone else in this town. Salvation, the Lord reminded her, was not about justice or giving a man what he deserved. It was about the grace of God. She had availed herself of that grace many times. Why was Mr. McIntyre less worthy?

He wasn't, she acknowledged. And she determined to apologize at the earliest opportunity, though her stomach felt queasy at the thought. Seeking forgiveness had never been Naomi's strength and she doubted he would be gracious.

But there was still something between her and God. Left unspoken but there and hiding, like a rock sitting at the bottom of a dark pond. Finally, in a painful moment of surrender, she dredged it up.

It was her wayward heart.

God, please guard my heart from this man. I am...drawn to him and it grieves me. How can I have even the slightest feelings for him when my husband has been gone so short a time? Not him. Especially not him. Oh, Lord, she begged, *especially not him...*

I know that Satan is just using him somehow to divert my attention from you. I'm grieving and I'm lonely, that's all.

Naomi grabbed on to the idea as if it were a lifeline. *Satan is just toying with my heart because I am vulnerable.* That's it; she was sure of it. The idea, accepted as fact, helped her regain some focus.

Mr. McIntyre is a lost soul in need of salvation, just like Daisy, just like anyone in this town who doesn't know you. Use me to reach him, Lord, but help me keep my heart out of it.

Much to Naomi's dismay, the Holy Spirit reminded her of a scripture: *If I speak in the tongues of men and of angels, but have not love, I am only a resounding gong or a clanging cymbal.*

The scripture was clear; guarding her heart would prevent God from using her. It was all or nothing.

Father, your word says you are a husband to the husbandless. Please help me keep my eyes, and my heart, focused on you and I'll do the best I can to show Mr. McIntyre Jesus in me. Just don't let me fall…please don't let me fall.

Sunday morning, the cobbled-together little family gathered for their makeshift church service, something more akin to a Bible study, really. Naomi stood at the serving counter and poured cups full of coffee as Ian and Emilio pulled chairs together near the dining room's fireplace. Hannah gingerly tucked a sleeping baby into his crib, picked up a cup of the fragrant coffee and took a seat next to her boy. Lately, Ian had been playing a more active part in leading the discussion and they were all impressed at his knowledge of the scriptures. The more they studied, though, the more they agreed on how much of a blessing a true pastor and church family would be.

Naomi settled in between her sisters and laid her Bible in her lap. As Ian opened his mouth to lead them in prayer, the front door squeaked slowly open and the flowers furtively drifted in like lost snowflakes. Truly overjoyed to see them, Naomi had to force what felt like a huge grin from her face so as not to embarrass their guests.

By way of explanation to the pleasantly shocked little congregation, Lily told them, "Ever since you got here, things have started changing for us. Rose is gone. Dais—er, Mollie's got Jesus." She and Iris and Jasmine crept closer, clutching their coats. "We're rich women now with a future in front of us. Even Mr. McIntyre is different." She shrugged in surrender. "We started thinking maybe there could be something to your Jesus stories."

"Besides," Iris kicked in lightheartedly, "Dais—er, Mollie has been buggin' the stuffin' out of us to come one Sunday."

Laughing, and caught somewhere between shock and awe, the group stood. Daisy picked up her Bible and walked over to her friends. "I read something this morning and it made me think of you. From Psalms," she flipped to Psalm 126 and read with joy in her voice:

"Our mouths were filled with laughter, our tongues with songs of joy. Then it was said among the nations, "The Lord has done great things for them." She smiled up at her friends. "Great things, indeed."

Chapter 36

Naomi tossed a log onto the fire, shoved it further in with the poker then sat down to absorb some of the heat. She had been warned repeatedly about the winters in Defiance, but the cold only bothered her when she stopped to think about it. Compared to everything they had been through thus far, the mean temperatures were only an annoyance, one that would not get the better of her. There were too many other things to occupy her mind.

Laughter from the kitchen drew her attention and she re-examined the stunning fact that they had just shared a church service with four former prostitutes. Prostitutes who were now helping fix Sunday dinner. If she and her sisters had stayed in Cary, in their nice comfortable little world, none of this would have happened. Naomi found it mind-boggling and quite humbling what God could do if you let Him. That was the trick, though, you had to let Him.

Like now, for example. She could sit here, watching the pine burn down to coals, or she could put one foot in front of the other and follow God down to see Mr. McIntyre.

Naomi trekked quickly down the empty boardwalk, feeling a little bit nervous and a little bit nauseas. She wasn't actually sure if the Iron Horse itself was closed yet, but she assumed it was not open for business on Sundays. She needed to see Mr. McIntyre and offer her apology, but the gap between thinking about a thing and actually doing it was like stepping off a cliff. There was a moment of no return and she was in the middle of it.

One foot in front of the other, she told herself.

The "closed" sign was hanging in the door. Tentatively, she tried the knob. It turned freely and she entered the saloon. The quiet was tomb-like and astonishing, like that morning she had come to find the doctor. She listened for a moment and heard the rustle of paper coming from Mr. McIntyre's office. Taking a deep breath, she approached his door. It was cracked and she could see his right shoulder moving as if he was writing.

Gently, she wrapped on the door then slowly pushed it open. When he saw her, he jumped to his feet obviously out of shock as much as etiquette. "Mrs. Miller, what a pleasant surprise. To what do I owe the honor?"

She fidgeted nervously and didn't answer right away. She noticed he was dressed simply, wearing only a white silk shirt and brown pants, no fancy vest today, no perfectly tailored jacket, nor had he shaved. He was the most casual looking she'd seen yet. Admittedly, she found him more appealing, more real, this way.

"May I take your coat?"

"No, no, thank you," she muttered, looking around the office.

Mr. McIntyre cocked his head to one side, a perplexed expression on his face. "Is everything all right? You seem rather nervous?"

Rather wasn't the word for it. His perplexed stare making her chafe, she darted glances at him. "We just finished with church. Lily, Jasmine and Iris came. It was nice."

"Yes, they told me they were going today." He motioned to the chair beside her as he sat down again. She did sit but on the edge of the chair so she could sprint for the door if the need arose.

"The last time I saw you, I was very angry and I blamed you for what happened to Mollie."

"To some extent I was to blame."

"But not completely, yet I chose to make you the target of my anger more than any of the other parties. I saw Mollie too much as an innocent victim and she wasn't. The man who did that to her I've hardly given any thought."

She shifted in her seat, changing her tack. "Look, it's the hardest thing in the world for me to apologize to someone. I suppose I'm not good at admitting when I'm wrong." She met his gaze then. "I've let anger keep me from reaching out to you as a Christian should. I'm sorry for that."

When he didn't offer a comment, she tried to explain further. "You should be just as welcome at our table as Mollie or the flowers or anyone else in this town. I just find it more difficult to deal with you than the others for some reason."

His eyebrows rose and he leaned slightly forward. "Why do you think that is?" He sounded honestly baffled by her statement.

Naomi could feel the water getting deep here and tried to stay close to the shore. His dark brown eyes bored into her and she looked away, fidgeting absently with her thumbnail. "I suppose it's mostly that my husband hasn't been gone long and I, I don't know, you're so different from him. You're so full of bravado and selfishness and he was such a good man—"

"And it's unfair that he's dead and I'm alive."

"No, that's not what I meant." Her retort was curt and she breathed to find her focus again. "I think I just need to care about you the way you are and—"

"Care about me," he mocked with a single raised brow.

"In a *Christian* way. You're not making this any easier."

"I'm not sure what *this* is?"

"I guess I just wanted to tell you that I'm sorry I'm so hard on you," she fumed, the pitch of her voice rising. "It just frustrates me to see the way you treat people and the way you're squandering your life away in this place. You're a born leader, you're smart, you're tough, you're handsome but you don't care about anyone but yourself."

A crooked smile worked its way across his mouth as he seemed to hang on every word she uttered. "I think I heard a few back-handed compliments in there somewhere."

Embarrassed, she stood up with a sigh and he stood with her. Well, this had gone exactly as she knew it would. The man didn't know how to be gracious. Still, she had to say her piece.

"If you were staying away because of the things I've said," she looked all around the room, anywhere but at him, "then don't, please. I told you once that we felt God led us here. I fear that when it comes to you I've been a poor witness." Finally, she did look at him again. Wetting her lips, she finished. "I'd like to start over. It's not up to me to pick and choose who I deign to share the gospel with. It shouldn't be like that. We should treat everyone the same, no matter how arrogant they are, and let God do the rest…And why are you looking at me that way?"

The more she had rattled on, the wider his smile had grown.

"Do you feel better? Have you eased your conscience?"

Naomi's spine stiffened. "I don't understand."

"Your coming here today. You've confessed your sin of arrogance at not wanting to associate with a degenerate reprobate such as myself. But you're just going through the motions. Like taking food to a sick man or visiting a lonely shut-in. It is the right thing to do but your heart is not in it. You don't really have any compassion for me. Or forgiveness."

"I didn't hear you ask for it," she shot back, feeling as if she was being chastised by a teacher.

"I shouldn't have to, not if you truly understand the god you say you represent. Are you familiar with the scripture that says, *'If I speak in the tongues of men and of angels, but have not love I am only a resounding gong or a clanging cymbal'?"* Naomi felt her stomach roll and her cheeks, which had been growing hotter by the minute, turned cold. He *would* know that one scripture.

Apparently her answer showed on her face. "I'll take that as a yes," he deadpanned. "You can forgive prostitutes, your little sisters' moment of indiscretion, even God for taking your husband, but you can't find it in your heart to forgive me."

"Because you sin with such pride and boldness." She sliced the air with her hands to emphasize her point. "You know exactly what you're doing. I've never seen a man use people with such calculated deliberation."

"And that makes me less worthy of forgiveness?"

After staring back at him defiantly for several seconds, she finally softened a bit, out of pure fatigue. "Back home, it was so much easier. Go to church on Sundays, say 'Amen' in the right places, and then have company for Sunday supper. It was easy being a believer when we didn't have to put our faith to the test every single day…here it's a challenge every second to live what we believe. I feel like all I do is make mistakes." Her shoulders sagged with the admission.

Slowly, Mr. McIntyre walked around his desk and stood before her, pushing through all her personal barriers to stand too close. He raised his hands as if to touch her, but dropped them to his sides. Naomi had the irrational desire to run but her feet wouldn't move. His eyes seemed to pin her to the spot.

"I'm closing the saloon. I retired the flowers." He stepped even closer and his nearness made her feel astonishingly light-headed. "Ian and I are setting up a town government. I've invited investors to come look the area over for opportunities in mining, timber and ranching."

Fighting the sensation that she was drowning, Naomi managed an unsteady step backward. Gently, he grasped her hand and while he didn't draw her forward, she knew he wouldn't let her retreat further. "I truly am endeavoring to make an honest living….to be a better man."

She tried to swallow the white-hot fear that had risen in her throat, tried to pull her hand away but her muscles wouldn't obey. Her heart was beating so fast, she was sure the pounding was audible.

"I haven't waited for a girl since I was fifteen. And then I only waited a week before I kissed her." Naomi's eyes widened in terror at the mention of a kiss. "Because of you I find myself revisiting assumptions I've made about my life, God...women. You have had an undeniable influence on Defiance." He caressed her hand gently with his thumb. "On me.

"I know your husband hasn't been gone even a year. I know that you and I seem to get along about as well as Lee and Sherman...But I was wondering," he lowered his voice and asked carefully, "if it's all an act. Is there the smallest possibility that you're just afraid of me because you might actually...love me?"

Naomi was sure her heart had stopped. Everything else had. Her blood. Her brain. Time. All she could see were those mesmerizing brown eyes; all she could feel was the warmth of his hand covering hers.

But like Krakatoa, the reality of who he was, the kind of man he was, the memory of her husband, it all blew up in her face. "No," she croaked, awed by how difficult it was to move away from him. Pure panic filled her veins. "No." The word came almost as a whimper, and she pulled her hand away.

Shaking her head, she stepped back, unable to express anything other than a denial of his feelings...and hers. "I can't," and like a panicked rabbit, she bolted. She turned and ran from the saloon as if her life depended on getting out of there.

Only, the moment the door slammed shut behind her and the snow was crunching beneath her feet, she knew she had lied to him.

Not so bewitched that he had lost all his pride, McIntyre stood stock still and watched her run. The urge to chase after her, spin her around and take her in his arms had been maddeningly strong, but he had resisted. She had rejected him outright, but the battle he had witnessed behind her eyes gave him the audacity to hope. He reasoned that if it had been easy for her to say no, she wouldn't have bolted and he was oddly encouraged.

McIntyre questioned, though, how much more time this was going to take. He wasn't exactly used to being a monk and having such pure thoughts about a woman, such *honorable* thoughts. This was all strikingly new territory for him. He ran his hand through his hair and sighed deeply. *Time*, he thought. *Just give her more time.*

Chapter 37

Naomi raced back to the hotel, but then stood on the porch for a full five minutes trying to regain control of her emotions. She couldn't go in there with her cheeks blazing and her breath heaving. They would think she'd seen a ghost.

If only she could. The ghost of her dead husband, the memory of him, wasn't enough to keep her from losing her heart to a man who—well, it just made no sense, she fumed. How could she possibly love him! A man who wouldn't give God the time of day if the Almighty walked right up and asked for it.

Oh, Lord, she cried out. *Please help me resist this foolish attraction. It makes no sense. No good can come of it. It's you and only you I want—*

"Naomi, what are you doing out here?" Hannah peeked through the cracked door. Naomi quickly turned her face away, wiped off the rebellious tears and tried to calm her racing heart. Her lack of a response, though, did not dissuade her little sister. Naomi heard the front door shut and Hannah persisted in her probing. "Talk to me. Maybe I can help."

Actually, Hannah was the last person Naomi wanted to confide in about man troubles. She was too young to understand her guilt and Naomi hadn't ever had kind words for Billy. Now here she was attracted to basically the same kind of man. That was justice for you.

"I'd really rather not talk about it just yet, Hannah."

Hannah mulled that over for a minute then asked a shocking question. "Is it something to do with Mr. McIntyre?" The way Naomi's head snapped around answered that question. "I noticed you disappeared after supper today. Did you go see him?"

Naomi nodded weakly. "I went to apologize for being so unforgiving of him." She shook her head in astonishment. "It just didn't turn out the way I thought it would."

"I've known there was something between you two that day I saw you choppin' wood. I didn't know what that something was, but it was there."

Miserable and getting cold, Naomi flopped down on a bench and hugged herself for warmth. "It's like he's quicksand or something. The harder I try to get away from him, the deeper I sink."

Hannah sat down beside her. "What happened?"

"He, he held my hand." Naomi swallowed her. She would have sworn she could still feel the heat there. "Then he asked if I was in love with him."

Hannah's eyes saucered. "Good gravy, I guess that did take you by surprise. Although..." She faded off, piquing Naomi's curiosity.

"What?"

"I've heard things, especially from Mollie. In retrospect, I guess a definite pattern developed but no one was looking for it." She shook her head, as if trying to re-group her thoughts. "Not long after we got here, he ended his relationship with Rose. He didn't fill the gap by visiting any of the other flowers either. In fact, they said he seemed to tire rather suddenly of the whole saloon business. He became more distracted and far less interested in them or what happened at the Iron Horse.

"I know I'm young, Naomi, but if a man turns his world upside down for a woman, surely that means he loves her."

"He's not a believer, Hannah," Naomi whispered mournfully. "How can I even consider him? Never mind the fact that I'm riddled with guilt for even thinking of another man." Naomi hung her head in despair. "I loved John with every breath I took. He was the best thing that ever happened to me in this life."

Hannah lowered her voice and framed her next question with tenderness. "Have you considered the possibility that he was the *second* best thing?"

"You mean after God." Naomi nodded, acknowledging the correction.

"No. I mean that you still have your whole life ahead of you. If Mr. McIntyre was to become a Christian, he could be an amazing man. And the two of you are so much alike."

"We're nothing alike."

"*Says you*," quipped Hannah. She snuggled up to her sister for warmth. "*I* let a man lead me astray instead of me leading him to the Lord—"

"You were young and immature in your faith."

"Exactly. And you're not. Especially after everything you've been through. If you were the tool God would use to lead Mr. McIntyre to Christ, would you surrender your heart?"

"That's not a fair question. I don't have to love him like that to lead him to the Lord."

"What if that *was* the sacrifice God required? You're holding back from God and holding back from Mr. McIntyre. You're making God qualify what he can and can't have of you. If Abraham didn't hold back his son, can you hold back your heart?"

Naomi searched Hannah's face for clarity. "What are you telling me to do? Pursue a relationship with a man who is not a believer?"

"I don't think God brought you fifteen hundred miles so you could run from him."

Exasperation fogged Naomi's weary brain. She pressed the space between her eyes, warding off a headache.

"Well, for what it's worth, Naomi, I'll tell you what I think," Hannah burrowed in even closer to her sister for warmth. "I think that God *is* going to use you to reach Mr. McIntyre. I think that Mr. McIntyre has the words 'Naomi's Destiny' stamped across his forehead. If you'd get over your guilt and fear, you'd see it. I can't explain why God didn't give you a socially respectable time to morn. Having all the answers isn't my job."

"No, apparently just having some of them is," Naomi replied with an amused sarcasm. "I hope you marry a pastor, Hannah. That way the pulpit will be in good hands when he's out of town."

~~~

McIntyre tore a biscuit in half and perused a month-old copy of the Rocky Mountain News. At his desk in the saloon, he was enjoying the quiet, if not the semi-cold ham and eggs, when Ian strolled in. The elder gentleman tossed his hat aside and sat down opposite his friend. Without looking up from his newspaper, McIntyre commented blandly, "I believe you're putting on weight, Ian."

Grinning, Ian patted his small but arguably increasing belly. "Family life agrees with me." McIntyre wasn't in the mood for his friend's annoyingly sunshiney attitude today. The Scotsman had become downright exuberant since those women had hit town. "Naomi told me she came by a few weeks ago and invited ye back in to our fold. Said she was sorry for treatin' ye so cruelly. It's no' an easy thing for her to apologize, especially to a man like ye."

McIntyre slapped the newspaper, frustrated over what he wasn't exactly sure. "Just what does that mean? Why is it that your little family can accept unwed mothers, prostitutes and orphans but it is such a tall order to associate with me? Am I not worthy of God's compassion?"

Ian's eyes widened in response to the outburst. "It's no' that any of us think you're less than worthy, my friend." He softened his voice to a conciliatory tone. "And I apologize if I've played a part in givin' ye that impression. Unlike the others, though, ye've built an empire in defiance of God, if ye'll pardon the pun. By givin' yer life to God, ye stand to lose, and gain, the most. That makes ye harder to approach."

McIntyre mulled that over. "Just because I'd like to be included in your little circle doesn't mean that I'm suddenly going to start preaching salvation and feeding the poor."

"Aye, that's exactly what I'm sayin'." Ian moved to the edge of his seat. "Ye're the most resistant because ye don't think ye need Him. Lily, Iris and Jasmine—little Chinese Jasmine who is completely unfamiliar with the concept of a Christian god—will come to know the Lord before ye do."

While McIntyre considered that, Ian asked, "Tell me this, why now? Ye've wanted all along to make Defiance a better place to live but ye've dragged yer feet. What's put the fire in ye to get the wheels turnin' now?"

"Her." There. He had said it. Saying it aloud didn't make him feel any better but he hoped his friend might have something encouraging to say that would lessen the blow of her rejection. "I want to be a respectable man because I know that's the only way a woman like her would ever consider a man like me. Before, I wanted to build the town up into something so it could serve my interests. Now, I want Defiance to be something I give a part of myself to. She's the reason."

"The changes yer makin' are fine, noble ones, but they willna be enough for her. There's always goin' to be a man between ye."

"Yes, I know the husband. But with time—"

"No' the husband" Ian shook his head and gave McIntyre a look to be heeded. "Jesus Christ. From what I've learned about these girls, and Naomi in particular, they were close to Him before coming to Defiance, but now they're more dedicated than ever. Until ye at least try to understand her relationship with God, she'll keep her heart away from ye."

McIntyre laced his fingers together and rested his chin on his hands. "Why should that be an issue? If she came to know me—"

"She has the conviction of her faith, mon. She knows the scriptures. A believer is no' to be wed to an unbeliever. It could corrupt or weaken her faith. To find your way to her heart, I suspect ye'll find the path goes through God first."

As if he was suddenly in a hurry, Ian stood. "Put that in yer pipe and smoke it. And join us for dinner tomorrow night. We've not seen much of ye lately." As he turned to leave, however, he apparently felt impressed to offer one final thought. "Ye know, ye may think ye've made all these changes and are pursuing this path of yer own volition. I'm inclined to think, though, tha' the Lord has directed your steps. Ye don't need to believe in Him for Him to believe in ye."

Chapter 38

March first stunned everyone in Defiance by dawning like a fireball. The weather did a complete, but welcome, turnabout from the snow and ice of February. The sun burned away clouds and the temperature rocketed into the forty's, melting ice and snow in a fury of rivulets. The vast, empty blue sky shocked Naomi with its brilliance as she stepped outside to sweep the front porch. She was tempted to believe spring was just around the corner, but knew not to bet on it.

Soon the false spring would be a real one and wagon trains would trudge into Defiance with more regularity than the sporadic mule trains. In fact, she had just heard from a customer that the first stagecoach would attempt to make the Defiance and Silverton route by the first week in April. With its arrival, Lily, Jasmine and Iris would be saying good-bye to Defiance. She prayed the good-bye would be figurative as well as literal.

Working hard to sweep the stubborn snow and mud off the steps, Naomi guessed Daisy would go soon as well. She had told the sisters she was satisfied to stay here through the summer since they were paying her now. Naomi doubted, however, that she would make it that long. The pull to see her family was something she mentioned on a daily basis.

Naomi wondered about her own desire to see Mr. McIntyre. Straight out, undeniably, all guilt aside, she missed him. Oh, it was not an easy thing to admit, but the truth stared at her as boldly as her reflection in the mirror. She wanted to see him, talk to him, fuss with him. She missed his arrogance and the way he called her Princess.

She had apologized for her own arrogance, invited him to start coming around again...and then rejected him by running from his office like a frightened, petulant child. No wonder he hadn't shown his face at the inn.

Her humiliation driving her to desperation, Naomi had discussed things with Ian. As she'd hoped, he had gone to see Mr. McIntyre and urged him to come to dinner. Would he, though? Had her reaction put an insurmountable wall between them? What if he did show up for dinner? What then—

Naomi's thoughts were snatched away by the unmistakable sensation of someone watching her. Standing up straight with the broom in a choke hold, she looked first up the street, then across it, then to the few buildings past the hotel. Goosebumps rose on her skin as she scanned the windows, the faces in the crowds, the men riding through on horseback and in wagons. No one met her gaze. Still, she was being watched and would have bet her life on the certainty of the feeling. Exactly like that other day back in the fall...

Realizing that she was doing exactly what the watcher wanted, she went back to sweeping, but looked up often. Almost audibly, the Holy Spirit whispered, *pray now*. So strong was the feeling that Naomi again stopped the broom and murmured, "Lord, in the name of Jesus I just ask your protection on our home, my loved ones and our friends." With each word of the prayer it was almost as if she could feel a dark, malevolent presence reluctantly slinking away. "In Your Son's holy name I pray. Amen..."

Naomi looked around the street again, but the feeling was gone. The incident chilled her to the bone. She thought of Mr. McIntyre telling her to keep her gun close, but over the months she had let herself be lulled into a false sense of security.

Uneasy, she took one last swipe at the porch then marched back inside.

Shaking off the incident, Naomi followed voices to the kitchen and found Daisy and Hannah prepping food for dinner that night. Little Billy was sitting on the floor on a blanket, pillows tucked all around him.

"Well, look at you," Naomi squealed, dropping to her knees in front of him. "What a big boy sitting up all by yourself!" Unable to resist his smiles and coos, she picked him up and hugged him, then peppered him with kisses. He was a pleasant distraction from the eerie chill she had just experienced on the front porch. "Aunt Naomi sure loves her little man. Come on, let's check on Mama."

Rising to her feet, she danced and swayed with the babe over to the table where Hannah was slicing potatoes. "Have you seen Ian?" Naomi wanted to get his thoughts on this feeling of being watched by someone.

Hannah shook her head. "Not in the last little bit."

"I heard him say he had to go see Mr. McIntyre," Daisy offered as she slid sliced carrots into a pot of boiling water. "Rebecca showed him a letter or a postcard that seemed to upset him."

Naomi didn't like the sound of that. "Where is Rebecca?"

Hannah rolled her eyes innocently. "In her room, mooning over Ian—oh, I mean, writing some letters."

Daisy chuckled. "She writes a lot these days."

"Yes." Naomi nodded, but her mind was troubled. Absently shoving little Billy into his mother's arms, garnering a perplexed look from Hannah, she headed upstairs.

Rebecca was sitting at her desk, a half-written letter in front of her, but obviously her mind had wandered. Naomi found her staring blankly at the page, pen poised to write but frozen in mid-air.

"Did we get some mail that upset Ian?"

Rebecca answered the question hesitantly. "Well, we got a postcard and he was with me when I picked it up. It did seem to disturb him, but he said he didn't want to explain why just yet."

"What did it say?"

"Here," she rifled through the mess of letters and statements on her desk and produced the card. "It's addressed to you but Ian said I should wait before I gave it to you. He wanted to talk to Mr. McIntyre first. He wouldn't tell me why." She handed her sister the card. "Perhaps I shouldn't have kept it from you, but Ian was emphatic. What's going on? Why would someone send you a postcard with nothing on it but three crosses?"

Naomi stared at the crudely drawn crosses and felt an evil chill creep over her. It was certainly no coincidence that Rose had cut three crosses into a man's chest. She had told her sisters about Rose attacking a man, but not what she had carved. The omission had been a mistake.

"That man that Rose stabbed in the eyes…she also carved three crosses on his chest."

Fear darted across Rebecca's face. "Are you in danger?"

Naomi was far less worried about herself than the others, especially little Billy. "I think it would be wise to be vigilant…and I think we should gather for prayer tonight after closing."

~~~

Mr. McIntyre came for dinner near closing time when the restaurant was down to a handful of quiet customers. Naomi was bussing a table when she looked up and saw him settling at a corner table. She had been praying about him since their *talk,* and Hannah had given her a lot to think about as well. The way her heart leaped when she saw him confirmed for Naomi it was time to step off this cliff. She prayed for wisdom, then left the tray on the table and approached him.

"It's good to see you, Mr. McIntyre." She clasped her hands in front of her, trying to look humble and repentant.

"Is it?" He leaned back in his chair and shared a smug look with her. "Are you sure you wouldn't rather run out the back door?"

He had a right to be sarcastic after her panicked departure last time. Knowing he was protecting a bruised ego, she straightened her shoulders and eyed him defiantly.

"I'm through running."

Mr. McIntyre blinked, clearly caught off-guard by the remark, and Naomi had to force down a smile. Before he could toss back a witty response, she promised, "I'll let Ian know you're here."

Ian took a rare break from the kitchen to sit down and eat with his friend. He joined McIntyre, warmly slapping him on the back. "It's good to see ye, lad." Before he even had his napkin in his lap, Naomi delivered the meals to the table. She smiled at both of them, but held McIntyre's gaze the longest. Both men noticed, but neither understood it. When she was gone, Ian scratched his head, clearly puzzled. "I've this feelin' the two of ye have turned a corner somehow. It does my spirit good."

"Something has changed." The game change was unexpected, and almost alarming. Suddenly McIntyre felt a little like a rabbit under a hawk's stare.

He and Ian ate the food while it was hot and enjoyed the lofty discussion of building the future Defiance. Eventually, however, McIntyre pulled the postcard from his breast pocket. "Have you told her about mine?"

"Nay, I wasn't sure what purpose it would serve."

McIntyre had thought to tell Naomi so she wouldn't think Rose was after only her and her sisters. Her vendetta seemed to be aimed at all of them. But perhaps Ian was right. If there wasn't a compelling reason to tell her—

"Did you get one, too?" Naomi spied the card it as she approached their table. She took it from McIntyre and studied the drawing. The art and the postal stamp were virtually the same. "Do you think it's from Rose?"

"Yes. She means to make a point with it, but I've not been able to understand her meaning. Be watchful," he told her with more concern in his voice than he had meant to share.

Her brow creased, she handed it back. "We're going to have prayer tonight when the restaurant closes. If you could stay, I'd like to talk to you afterwards."

"I'll either stay or come back." He was curious about her invitation but not enough to sit through a prayer meeting.

She nodded. "Can I get you gentlemen anything else?"

They were fine. Perfect, in fact, McIntyre thought, pleased that at least there was *something* happening in this strange relationship.

After the restaurant closed, and the cleaning was finished, the sisters, Daisy, Emilio and Ian gathered in a tight circle in the kitchen. Mr. McIntyre had made his excuses, but said he would return. In a way, Naomi was relieved. His absence left her free to focus on the spiritual battle she felt they were entering. As they reached for each others' hands, Naomi looked into the eyes of her family.

"When Rose left Defiance, I was initially under the impression she had gone for good. I didn't tell all of you, however, that she has apparently stayed in the San Juan range, in nearby towns. I also didn't tell you that the man she stabbed and blinded in Alta, she also carved three crosses on his chest." Puzzled and frightened looks made their way around the circle, though Ian only looked somber. Emilio's jaw tightened with the announcement.

"The other day I received a postcard with three crosses drawn on it. Nothing else. No note. No signature. I learned this evening that Mr. McIntyre also received a similar postcard a little over a week ago. He's convinced these postcards are from Rose. I think he also believes she's coming back to Defiance with the intention of harming us in some way."

Emilio's eyes widened with horror as she spoke. "I'm sorry," he whispered, dropping his head. "I'm so sorry. I knew she would come back. I should've killed her when I had the chance."

Hannah and Daisy, flanking the boy, sought to comfort him. Daisy squeezed his hand and Hannah shook her head in disagreement. "No, no."

Hannah put her arm around him. "You couldn't have known a thing like that, Emilio. None of this is your fault."

Clutching Naomi's hand with her left and Ian's with her right, Rebecca raised their hands. "We're going to pray, Emilio. Our God is more powerful than the darkness that has your sister in bondage. She's not going to hurt anyone here."

"She's not going to hurt *anyone* we care about," Naomi added, thinking of someone who wasn't in the room, but needed these prayers just the same. They bowed their heads and Naomi, ever ready for a fight, lifted up the first battle cry.

"Father, we know that you are King of Kings and Lord of Lords. We know that your word says that we battle not with flesh and blood, but principalities and powers of the air. You have given us power and authority over the enemies of your kingdom and we claim, in the name of Jesus, that no one here will be harmed by Rose. We put on the full armor of God, Lord, so that we may stand against evil."

Her voice grew stronger with the power and anointing of the Holy Spirit. "In the name of Jesus, we bind the demons who would come against this family and remind you that you have no power here. We lift up our shield of faith and extinguish the flaming arrows of the enemy. In the name of Jesus, in the name of Jesus, you will not prevail against the children of the Most High God!"

From across the street, hidden deep in the shadows, Rose had watched the hotel for at least an hour. With each breath, as it swirled in the chilly night air, her hatred grew exponentially. When she saw McIntyre walk down the street and enter into that awful place of light, her head nearly exploded with fury, but the voices bid her wait. And so she settled deeper into the darkness, pulling her cloak closer, listening to the sound of melting snow all around her.

The voices would tell her when the time was right. They promised her the children of the Holy One would die tonight and the Most High God would stand by silently as their blood ran. She need only be patient. Warmed by her hatred, she waited.

Feeling totally out of place at the thought of extemporaneous prayer and spiritual warfare, McIntyre had made his departure with the promise to return in an hour or so. A gentle, no, *peaceful* look in Naomi's eyes had brought him peace as well. He didn't know what she wanted to talk about, but he was eager to hear it. Of course, for all he knew, she may be preparing to tell him she was going to a convent.

Stepping out into the cold, a sudden feeling of unease wrapped its tentacles around him. Pretending to shake it off, he pulled his coat tighter and headed back to the saloon, thinking a drink might make the time pass a little faster…and ward off this sudden apprehension.

He had to tell her about the letter. The conviction came upon him strong and sudden. He dreaded it and knew whatever kind words she might have for him, they would dissipate like smoke with this news. Handing a woman a letter from her dead husband would certainly have to cause a reexamination of whatever future plans she was making. McIntyre was resigned, however, and could only let the chips fall where they may.

Rose watched McIntyre intently then listened to his steps fade. She could not see the Iron Horse from her hiding place but knew that within seconds he would be inside. She was eager to cross the street and anxiously caressed the Colt .45 in her hand.

She smiled as the dining room went dim. Minutes passed slowly and lights flickered out one by one on the second floor as she assumed the sisters and their guests turned in for the night. Rose hugged the gun to her chest as she thought of the gringas, smugly content that they were warm and safe against the beast lurking outside.

If Ian and the black-haired girl followed their pattern, they would be in the kitchen for awhile yet. Rose would sneak upstairs, find the wiry one and shoot her first, then the young girl and the baby, and then whoever else came across her path.

Now, the voices whispered abruptly. *Now*.

Rose moved, started to slither out of her darkness, when she heard the hollow footsteps of boots. She drew back and saw McIntyre strolling his way back to the hotel. Cursing, she waited. He went to the hotel door, paused then quietly slipped inside.

Blood pumping, heart pounding, the voices screamed at Rose to go. Peering out of the darkness again, she hurried across the street. Slogging through the deep spring mud, she stepped up onto the porch and stole a look through a window. She saw McIntyre gazing patiently over the batwing doors into the kitchen, hands clasped behind his back. What was he looking at?

The voices egged her on. Now was the time, they told her. *Now!* Obediently, she cocked the six-shooter in her hand.

McIntyre stood quietly, mesmerized by the divine authority in the voices and the expressions of strength in their faces. It was a power he recognized instantly as holy and pure and all-mighty. Something was happening here, something with life and death implications. He felt as if he had entered into the middle of a battle and the weapons of warfare were flying all around him.

"Hello, Mac," Rose whispered in his ear. The cold steel of a gun barrel pressed into the back of his head and he cursed himself for not having heard the door. "Let's go see your friends."

He raised his hands and they took a step forward, but Rose suddenly put her hand on his shoulder stopping him. She listened intently to the prayers coming out of the kitchen in commanding tones.

For a moment, her resolve seem to waiver. "What are they doing in there?"

McIntyre smiled grimly. "Praying."

And he offered up his own, hoping desperately God would hear the prayer of a lowly sinner. Her anger back, Rose shoved him forward, ramming the barrel painfully into his skull. The two burst through the bat wing doors. The prayers died in astonishment when the group realized McIntyre was not alone. Their circle opened up into a crescent so they could face Rose, Naomi moving to one end, Ian to the other. Rose propelled McIntyre towards Ian with a nudge from the gun barrel.

Naomi felt her body turn to glass, as if one move would shatter her. Rose had managed to trap them all together. She couldn't believe the horror of it. Shock threatened to seize up the wheels in her mind.

Rose waved her gun at Mr. McIntyre. "Slowly, my love, take your gun out…" Fury written on his face, he stood beside Ian and eased his revolver out of its holster. He held it up by two fingers awaiting further instructions. "Very good. Put it on the ground and kick it over to me."

He hesitated then did as she asked. Only, it slid across the floor stopping an equal distance between her and Naomi.

Her eyes quickly followed the gun's path then traveled on up to Naomi. "Did you get my postcard, little gringa?"

Before Naomi could answer, Rose spotted Emilio. She flamed with outrage. "Are you still here with these witches? I should shoot you first."

"No," Hannah cried, putting an arm protectively in front of the boy.

A wicked smile burned across Rose's face. "Maybe I should shoot *you* first and let him watch you die."

"Rose," Mr. McIntyre barked, drawing her attention. "What do you want?"

Rose looked taken aback, as if she couldn't believe the stupidity of the question. "I want you to die. I might have let you live if you hadn't come back here tonight, but that was your choice." She shrugged. "So be it."

"Rose, there are eight of us." Naomi spoke, but white-hot fear practically choked her. She thought of the gun pointed at her sisters and little Billy asleep and helpless upstairs. "There's no way you can kill us all."

"She's right." Mr. McIntyre pointed at the gun in Rose's hand. "Pull that trigger and the rest of us will take you down."

"Not before I take a few of you with me." She waved the gun over them, back and forth, meeting their eyes, tormenting them. "Little Daisy, did you make friends? Too bad they'll be the last ones you ever have.

"I am sorry that you're here, Mr. Donoghue. I always liked you. You were kind, all the time, kind."

"Why are ye doin this, Rose?" Naomi heard desperation creep into Ian's voice. "These girls have done nothin' to ye."

"They changed everything!" Rose screamed in rage, making the group jump. "Everything! I had everything just the way I wanted it." She growled through clenched teeth. "It was finally perfect. Money, power, this town. I had it all just the way I wanted it here and Mac was so good to me." Her face changed, softened. She looked at Mr. McIntyre, then Naomi and her face transformed back to showing the darkness within her. "They told me you gringas would come, but that my power was stronger than your god. Now look where we are. You're about to die and I will have Defiance."

"Rose, it's me you want." Attempting to bargain, Mr. McIntyre took a step forward. "Leave the others alone. Defiance is yours. The saloon, the mine, everything. Just step in take over."

She waved the gun, forcing him back in line. "Oh, that's what I will do. I had hoped to have you by my side, darling, but it appears that will not be the case."

Naomi felt a vicious fear gnawing at her as Rose eyed them each one by one. A tear rolled down Hannah's cheek and Naomi knew she was thinking of her angel upstairs. Emilio, ever-so-carefully, reached out and squeezed her little sister's hand. Rebecca glanced across the half circle at Ian and he winked bravely at her. She smiled in a pained way. Daisy looked the bravest of all, eyes closed, lips moving, she was praying fervently and Naomi drew strength from the silent words.

Finally, she looked at Mr. McIntyre who was waiting to meet her gaze. Time stopped and Naomi would have sworn she felt God rest His hand on her shoulder in that very moment. Divine power formed a bond between them, establishing a trust, cementing a plan. She understood the unmistakable message in his eyes when he glanced at the gun on the floor. She felt the peace of this plan in her soul. Mr. McIntyre gave her an almost imperceptible nod and it spoke more loudly than words…he would take the greatest risk of all.

In her mind, the room went absolutely silent. Under the amber glow of the kitchen lamp, she saw Mr. McIntyre lunge for the gun in Rose's hand and Naomi simultaneously dove for the gun on the floor. Before Naomi's body hit the wood, Rose squeezed the trigger. Naomi heard the shot, heard her sisters scream. She wrapped her fingers around the ivory handle of the Colt and in one lightning-swift move, raised the gun and fired. Rose shrieked in rage and pain as the gun jumped out of her hand. It flew over their heads, landed on the kitchen table and skittered across it as Mr. McIntyre collapsed to the floor, clutching his chest.

Like hungry lions, Ian and Emilio leaped on Rose as Naomi scrambled over to Mr. McIntyre and gathered him into her arms. She could hear the two men scuffling with Rose as the woman cursed and raged vilely against heaven.

Naomi gently rolled him over and saw the spreading stain in Mr. McIntyre's shirt. Stunned, she looked up at Rebecca.

"I'll get the doctor!" Her sister spun, already sprinting for the door.

Naomi cradled Mr. McIntyre in her lap and started praying softly, though she couldn't help thinking of the last time she'd held John. *Not him, too, Lord. Surely not him too.*

Hannah and Daisy knelt beside Mr. McIntyre, laid their hands on him and began praying in soft whispers. From behind them Naomi heard a sharp smack and Rose's tirade ended abruptly.

One of Naomi's tears fell on his cheek and his eyes fluttered open. He looked into her face and smiled weakly.

"I knew…I knew you'd get the gun. I…prayed." His voice was barely a whisper and he struggled to speak, grimacing in pain with each breath. He swallowed and tried to smile. "I…I told you…the West needs women…like you."

Caressing his cheek, tracing the thin line of that painfully perfect beard, she chuckled sadly. "That was only the second time in my whole life that I ever touched a revolver. You have no idea how miraculous a shot that was."

Flinching, he covered her hand with his and murmured weakly, "Made a believer…out of me."

No more beautiful words were ever spoken as far as Naomi could remember in her entire life. Overcome with joy and relief and the freedom to love, she leaned down and kissed him softly. "Don't you dare die on me," she commanded gently, falling into those unfathomable, brown eyes.

Letting his eyes close, he shook his head weakly side to side. "If I do, the letter…my pocket…" His voice was growing faint and Naomi couldn't understand his disjointed sentence.

"What? What letter?"

"Was going to tell you…"

Chapter 39

Naomi sat and waited for Mr. McIntyre for three days. He'd lost quite a bit of blood before the doctor was able to stop the bleeding then he'd had to operate to retrieve the bullet. A hair more to the left and the bullet would have hit a lung. Mr. McIntyre survived the exquisitely dangerous operation only to have infection attack. They had all gathered and prayed over him daily; Naomi had wiped his brow, changed his bandage and whispered desperate prayers. She couldn't believe God might take him, too, but he looked so pale, so ghostly, she thought he might slip away any second.

Naomi was with him when he awoke and watched him take in the unfamiliar surroundings of her room with a vexed expression. His eyes widened even more when he saw her and comprehension dawned on his face.

He tried to rise from his pillow and winced from pain. He eased back, touching the bandage across his chest. "Rose? Where is she?" His throat was dry and it came out as little more than a rasp.

"In jail." Beyond that simple answer she wasn't sure what she was going to say when he remembered something else.

He considered Rose for a second, then his eyes widened again. He looked at her astounded. "You kissed me." Then his expression fell. "...or did I imagine that?" Naomi cheek's burned and that made her feel ridiculous. It also made it impossible to lie. He grinned with as much satisfaction as he could muster in his weakened state. His coal black beard against his pale skin did nothing to make the smile less devilish. "I never kissed a woman with whom I wasn't on a first-name basis."

"I never kissed a man I didn't marry," she shot back.

Mr. McIntyre cleared his throat nervously and tried to pull himself up in the bed. She fluffed the pillow behind him and quickly sat back down again, all too aware of the fact that he was naked from the waist up. Naomi had touched his chest and face often while he was unconscious, marveling over how different he was from John. Yet, Mr. McIntyre was just as strong, in a lean, more lithesome way, and she wanted to feel his arms around her again. Now that he was awake and staring at her, though, such thoughts set her butterflies to fluttering. Naomi loved John, but now she could admit she loved this man, too. If only he'd given her that letter sooner...

Mr. McIntyre laid his left hand over the bandage on his chest and gathered in a deep breath. "You can take it back—the kiss—and whatever was behind it. If there was anything behind it."

Hiding a smile, she poured him a glass of water from the pitcher next to his bed and held it out for him. "You think I go around just kissing whatever wounded man falls into my lap?" He didn't answer, but instead held her gaze. He took the glass from her and their fingers touched. They both felt the weight of this moment.

"I've never known a woman like you."

"I've never known a man like you." She moved to the bed. "Tell me, what happened that night. Between you and God. I have to know. You said you were a believer and I took it to mean that you..."

He nodded. "We...came to an understanding." He took a sip of the water then handed it back to her. "I realized I would die to save you and in that moment, I understood what He did for us...and why." He shook his head, clearly bewildered by it all. "Love is an astonishing thing. It can drive a man to amazingly selfless acts." Relieved, Naomi set the water down and took hold of his hand with both of hers.

"It seems you've made a habit of saving my family."

Mr. McIntyre frowned as if he had no clue about her reference. Shocked, Naomi realized he had not read John's letter. "You had my husband's letter to me for twelve years and you never read it?"

"It wasn't addressed to me."

"Even after you realized the letter was for me, you still didn't read it?"

"I could well imagine what his last words were to his sweetheart. I didn't need to read it."

Mr. McIntyre's level of respect for a fellow soldier moved her. This man held so much promise; if only she had seen it sooner.

Based on where things now stood, Naomi felt it was appropriate to share the letter and she pulled it from her pocket. "I'd like to read it to you now." She unfolded it and glanced over the faint, slightly messy handwriting. She missed John so, but this letter was like a sign clearly pointing the way to the future.

"My dearest Naomi," she read softly, "This Civil War has claimed my body and heaven now claims my soul, but you will always possess my heart.

"I thank God for the precious little time we had together, but I urge you to go on with your life. Remember me kindly, but do not pine for me, my love. I pray you will embrace the future unflinchingly. Live the rest of your life with joy and laughter and keep your eyes lifted up to heaven.

"A man named Charles McIntyre risked his life today to save mine," she glanced up quickly then to let him know she remembered his lie, "apparently to no avail. I asked him to pass this along to you should the situation warrant. His selflessness was determined and heroic, no matter the end result. He has my eternal gratitude and I didn't want him left an unsung hero."

From the corner of her eye, Naomi could see the color returning to Mr. McIntyre's cheeks and his expression was deeply somber.

"Never forget me, Naomi, but live looking forward. I love you with all my heart, my angel, and will see you in heaven. Eternally yours, John."

Naomi carefully re-folded the letter and slipped it back into her apron. Then she looked up at Mr. McIntyre. "When I think of all the things that had to happen, that God allowed and then used to bring us to this moment, I am left speechless...and humbled." She swallowed, pushing forward with her confession. "I am so sorry for the time I wasted, working to hold you at bay." This time, her apology was real and came from deep within her heart. "Can you forgive me for being so proud and self-righteous? You are a far better man than I gave you credit for."

Mr. McIntyre held his breath and pushed himself up straighter in the bed. Then, leaning forward so that Naomi's world was filled with nothing but his gentle gaze, he drawled casually, "I agree that God went to a lot of trouble to bring you to me. I wouldn't want to disappoint Him by throwing you back, your Ladyship." They both grinned and Naomi saw the mischievous twinkle dancing in his eyes. "Embrace your future, Naomi."

Biting her lip, she whispered humbly, "Yes, Charles." Amazed at how his name sounded like a prayer on her lips, she said it again. "Charles."

He stroked her cheek and searched her eyes. "I want you with me always, Naomi. Always."

"Always," she breathed, her heart galloping in her chest as he drew closer.

Their breath mingled and their lips touched. Her mind did not race back to John for comparison. Instead, it flew forward and she saw the promise of an unmapped, unforeseeable future designed by God—one without any arguments from her. As Charles pulled her into a long-awaited embrace and literally stole her breath, she knew God's plans were far better than anything she could create for herself.

Made in the USA